WITCHBLADE

PUBLISHED BY

TOP COW PRODUCTIONS, INC.

LOS ANGELES

IMAGE COMICS, INC.

Robert Kirkman — Chief Operating Officer
Erik Larsen — Chief Financial Officer
Todd McFarlane — President
Marc Silvestri — Chief Executive Officer
Jim Valentino — Vice President
Eric Stephenson — Publisher / Chief Creative Officer
Corey Hart — Director of Sales
Jeff Boison — Director of Publishing Planning & Book Trade Sales
Chris Ross — Director of Digital Sales
Jeff Stang — Director of Specialty Sales
Kat Salazar — Director of PR & Marketing
Drew Gill — Art Director
Heather Doornink — Production Director
Nicole Lapalme — Controller

IMAGECOMICS.COM

For Top Cow Productions, Inc.
For Top Cow Productions, Inc.
Marc Silvestri - CEO
Matt Hawkins - President & COO
Elena Salcedo - Vice President of Operations
Vincent Valentine - Lead Production Artist
Henry Barajas - Director of Operations
Dylan Gray - Marketing Director

To find the comic
shop nearest you, call:
1-888-COMICBOOK

Want more info? Check out:
www.topcow.com
for news & exclusive Top Cow merchandise!

WITCHBLADE

CAITLIN KITTREDGE
WRITER

ROBERTA INGRANATA
ARTIST

BRYAN VALENZA
COLORIST

TROY PETERI
LETTERER

ERIC STEPHENSON
EDITOR

ROBERTA INGRANATA & BRYAN VALENZA
COVER

CHAPTER **SEVEN**

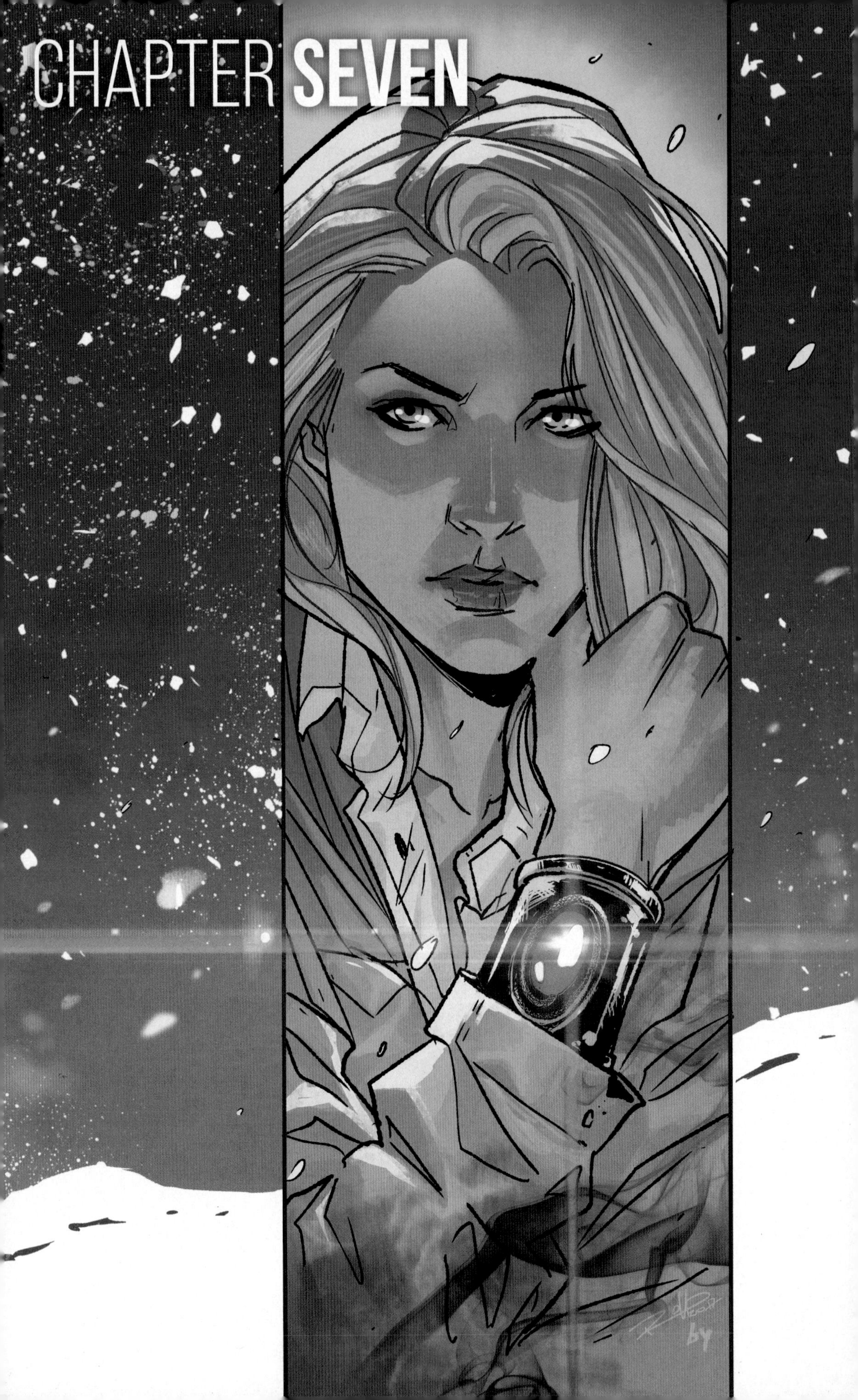

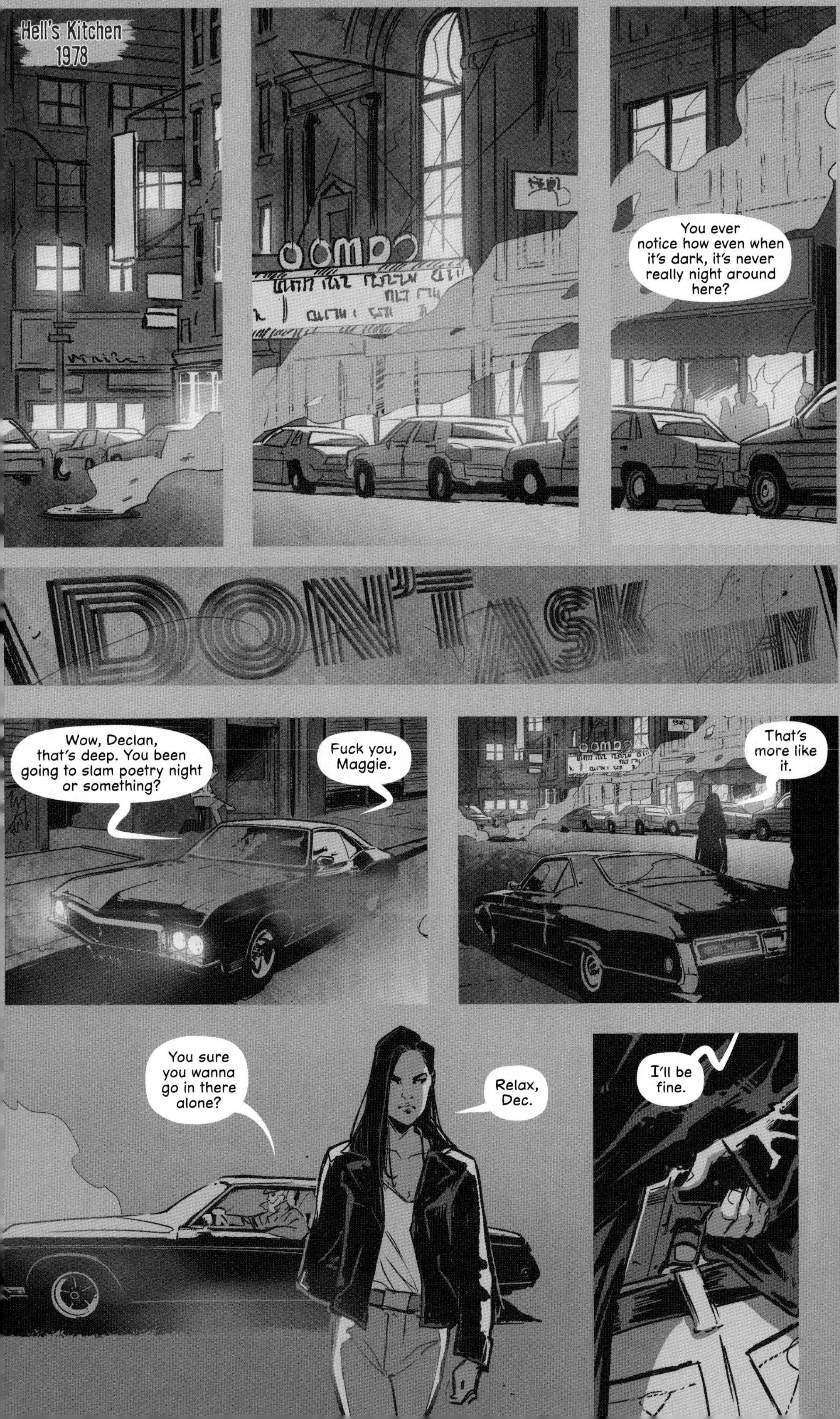
Hell's Kitchen
1978
You ever notice how even when it's dark, it's never really night around here?
DON'T ASK
Wow, Declan, that's deep. You been going to slam poetry night or something?
Fuck you, Maggie.
That's more like it.
You sure you wanna go in there alone?
Relax, Dec.
I'll be fine.

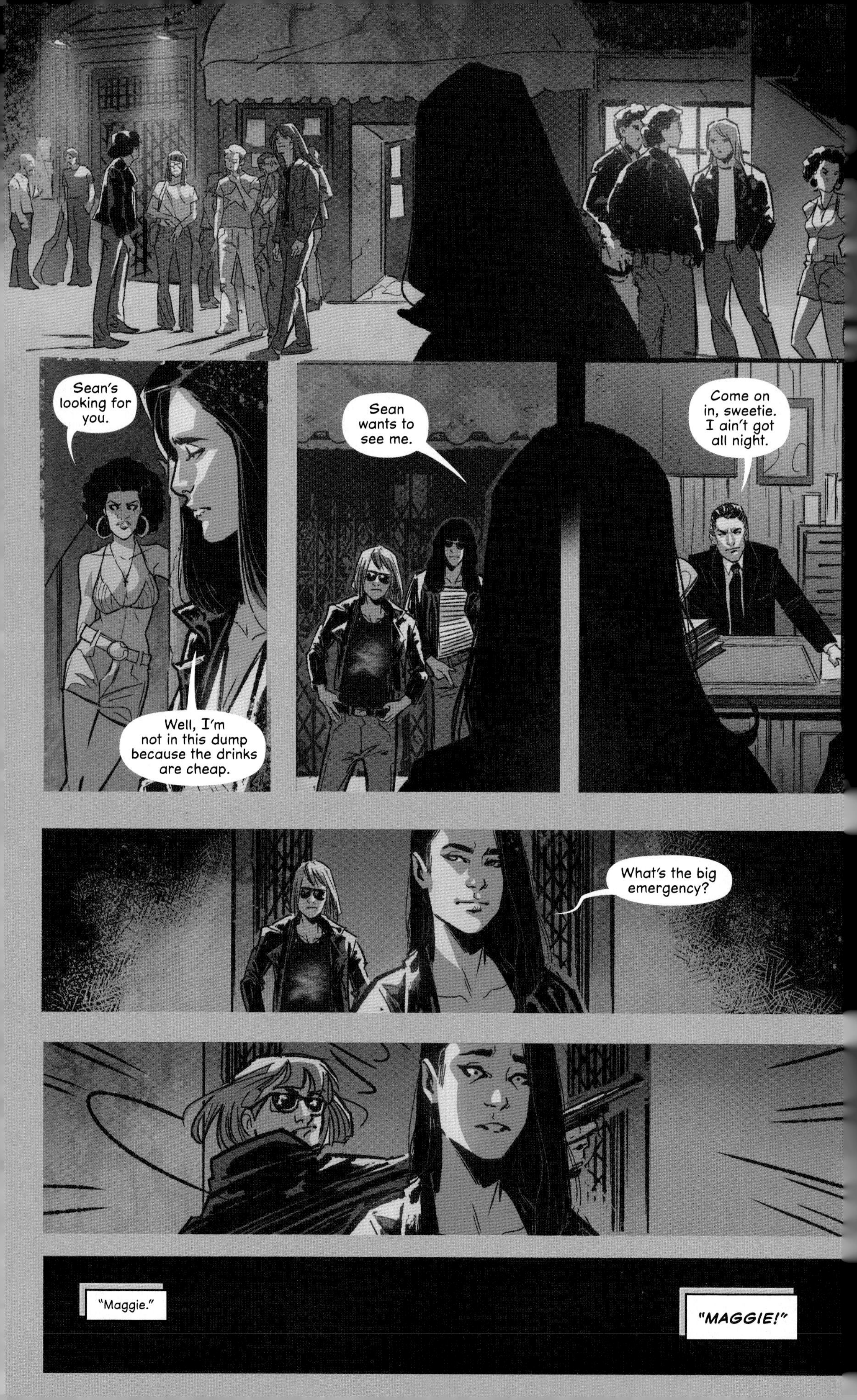
Sean's looking for you.
Well, I'm not in this dump because the drinks are cheap.
Sean wants to see me.
Come on in, sweetie. I ain't got all night.
What's the big emergency?
"Maggie."
"MAGGIE!"

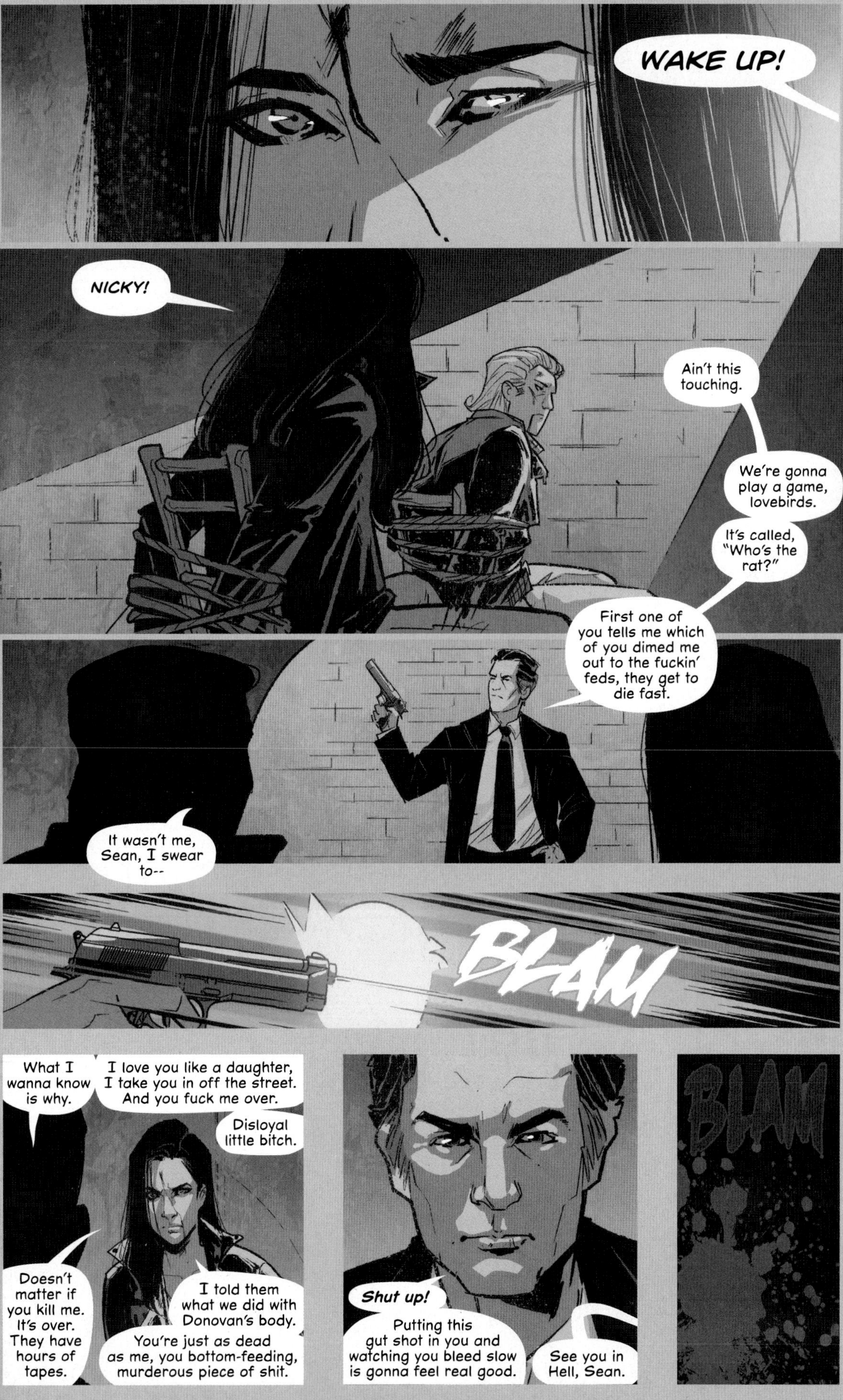
WAKE UP!
NICKY!
Ain't this touching.
We're gonna play a game, lovebirds.
It's called, "Who's the rat?"
First one of you tells me which of you dimed me out to the fuckin' feds, they get to die fast.
It wasn't me, Sean, I swear to--
BLAM
What I wanna know is why.
I love you like a daughter, I take you in off the street. And you fuck me over.
Disloyal little bitch.
Doesn't matter if you kill me. It's over. They have hours of tapes.
I told them what we did with Donovan's body.
You're just as dead as me, you bottom-feeding, murderous piece of shit.
Shut up!
Putting this gut shot in you and watching you bleed slow is gonna feel real good.
See you in Hell, Sean.
BLAM

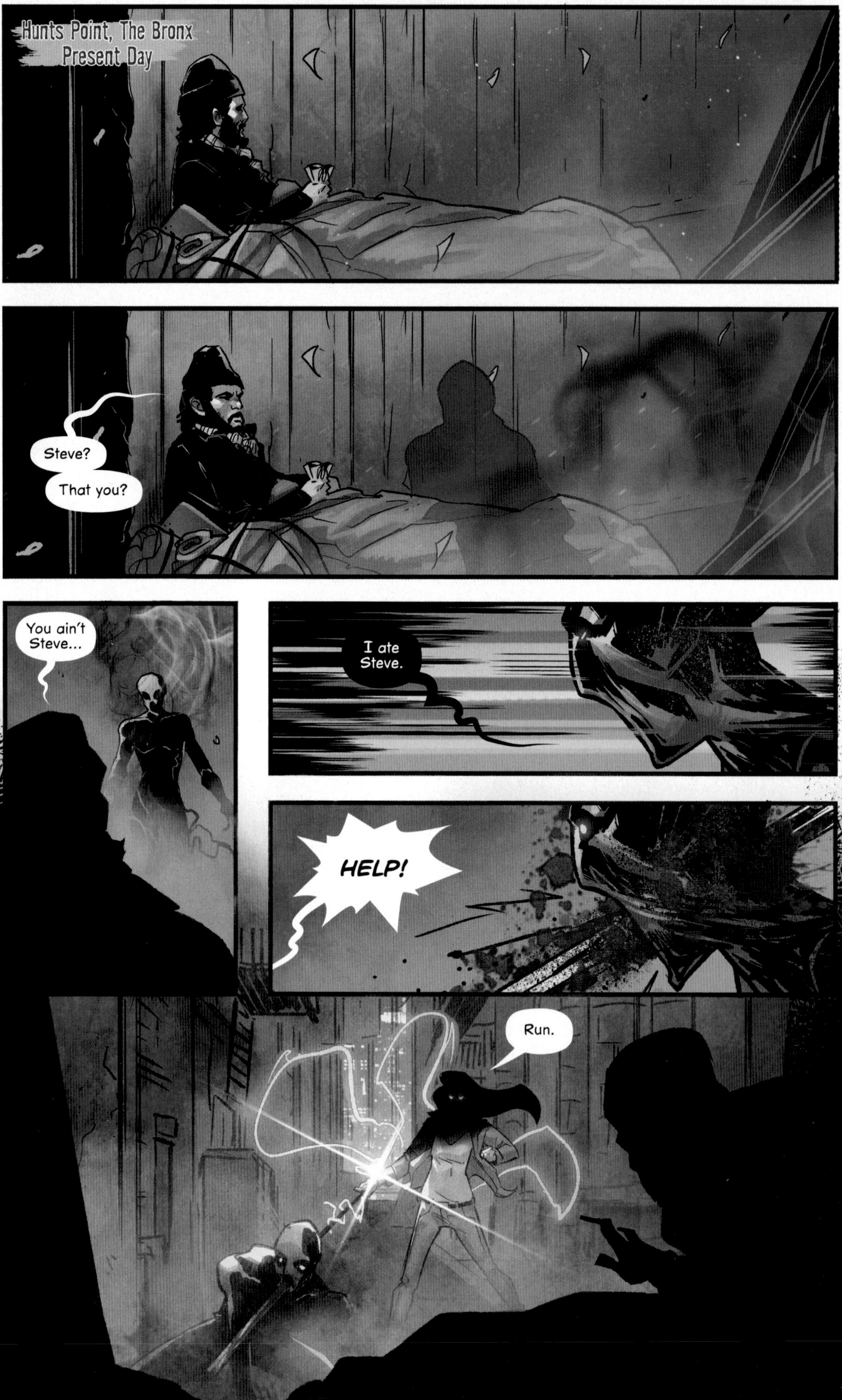
Hunts Point, The Bronx
Present Day
Steve?
That you?
You ain't
Steve...
I ate
Steve.
HELP!
Run.

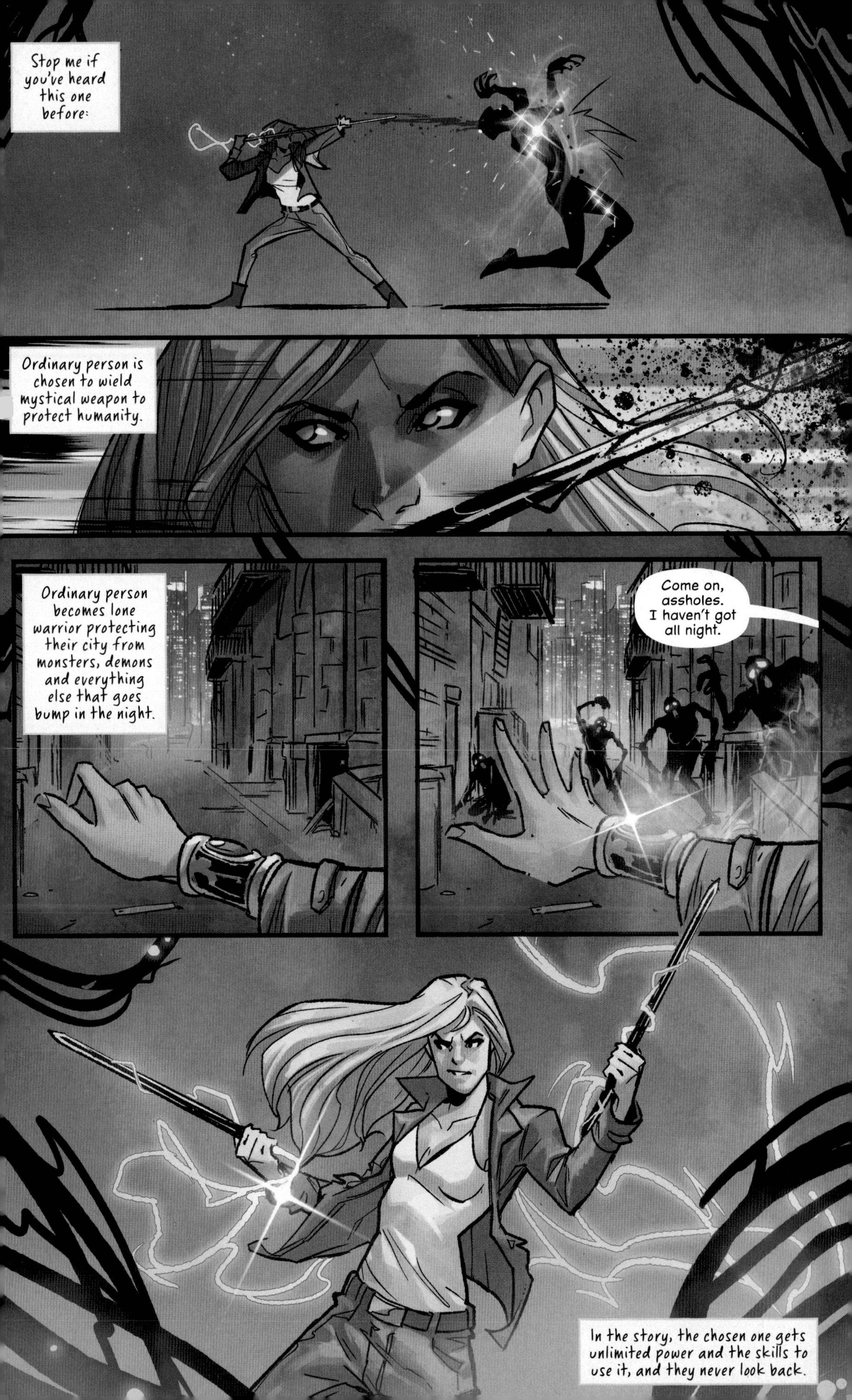
Stop me if you've heard this one before:
Ordinary person is chosen to wield mystical weapon to protect humanity.
Ordinary person becomes lone warrior protecting their city from monsters, demons and everything else that goes bump in the night.
Come on, assholes. I haven't got all night.
In the story, the chosen one gets unlimited power and the skills to use it, and they never look back.

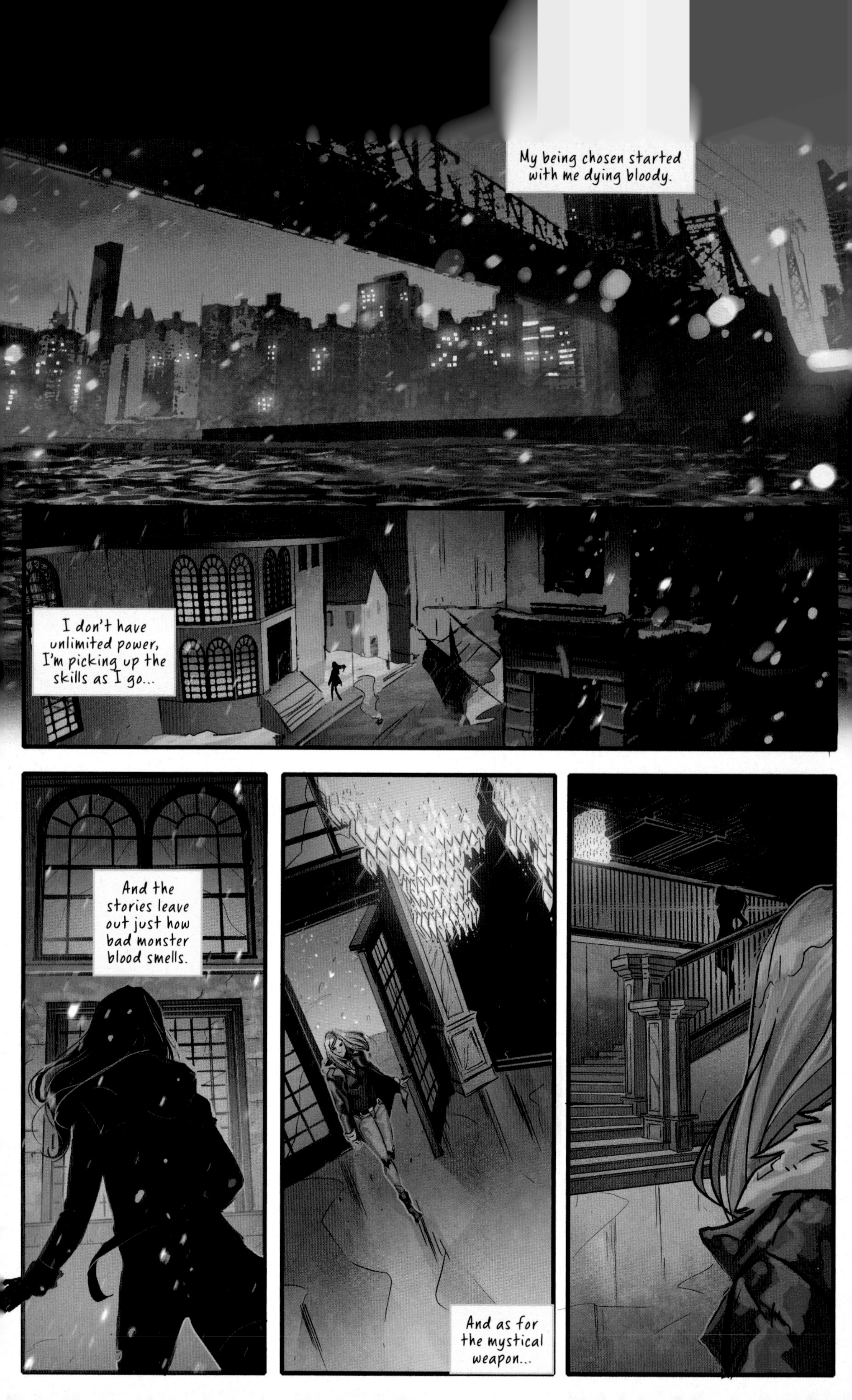
My being chosen started with me dying bloody.
I don't have unlimited power, I'm picking up the skills as I go...
And the stories leave out just how bad monster blood smells.
And as for the mystical weapon...

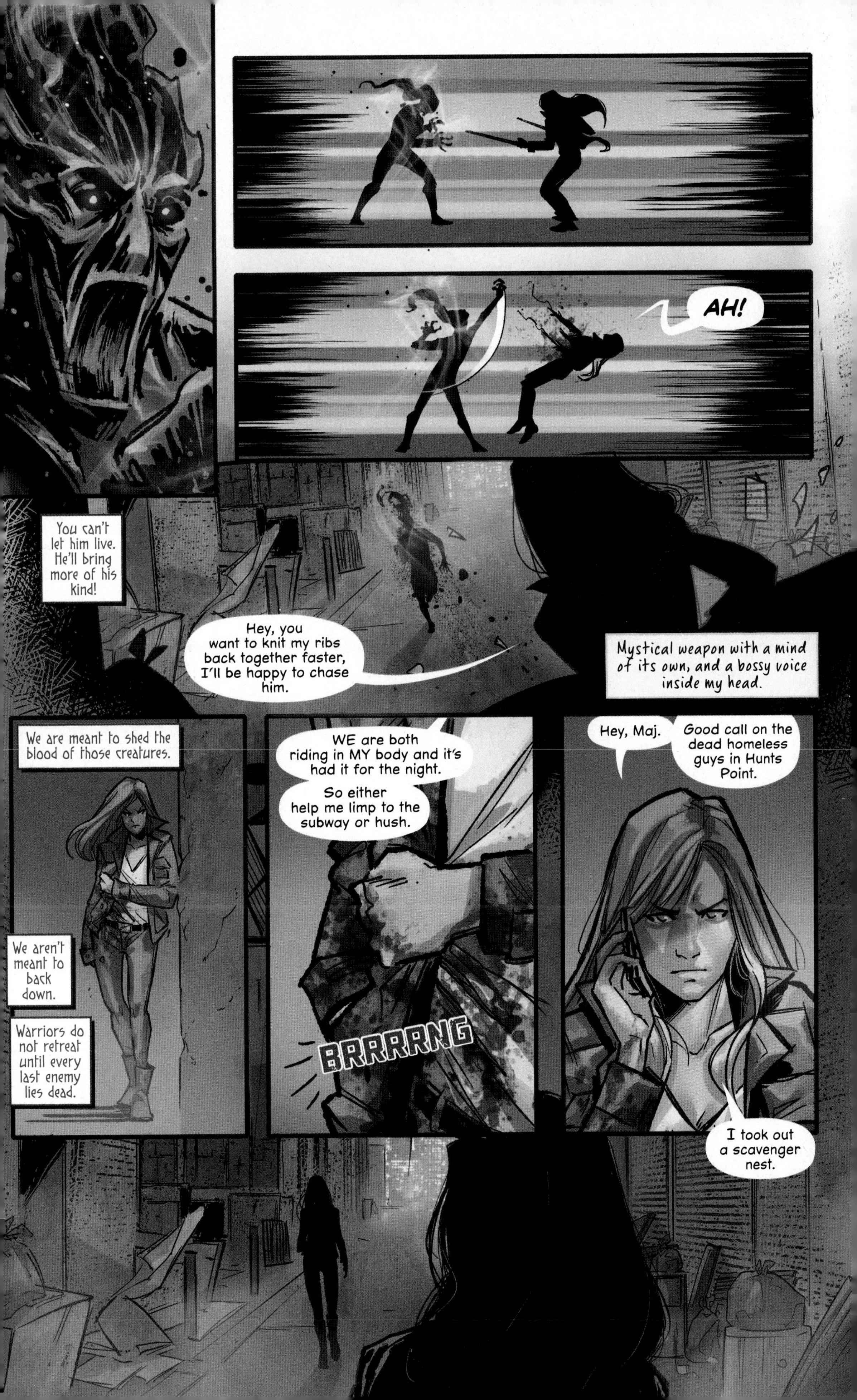
AH!
You can't let him live. He'll bring more of his kind!
Hey, you want to knit my ribs back together faster, I'll be happy to chase him.
Mystical weapon with a mind of its own, and a bossy voice inside my head.
We are meant to shed the blood of those creatures.
We aren't meant to back down.
Warriors do not retreat until every last enemy lies dead.
WE are both riding in MY body and it's had it for the night.
So either help me limp to the subway or hush.
BRRRRNG
Hey, Maj.
Good call on the dead homeless guys in Hunts Point.
I took out a scavenger nest.

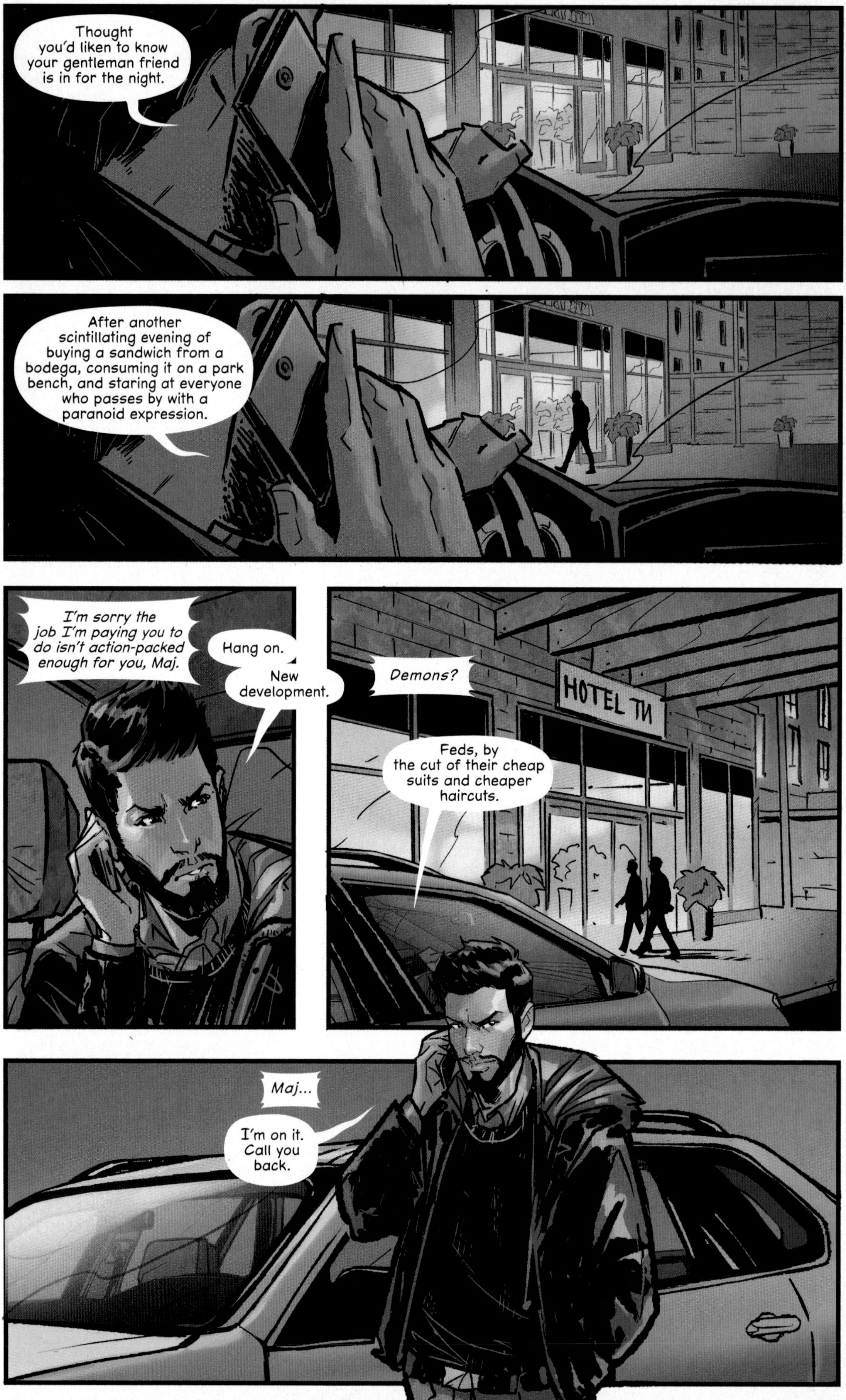
Thought you'd liken to know your gentleman friend is in for the night.
After another scintillating evening of buying a sandwich from a bodega, consuming it on a park bench, and staring at everyone who passes by with a paranoid expression.
I'm sorry the job I'm paying you to do isn't action-packed enough for you, Maj.
Hang on.
New development.
Demons?
HOTEL TU
Feds, by the cut of their cheap suits and cheaper haircuts.
Maj...
I'm on it. Call you back.

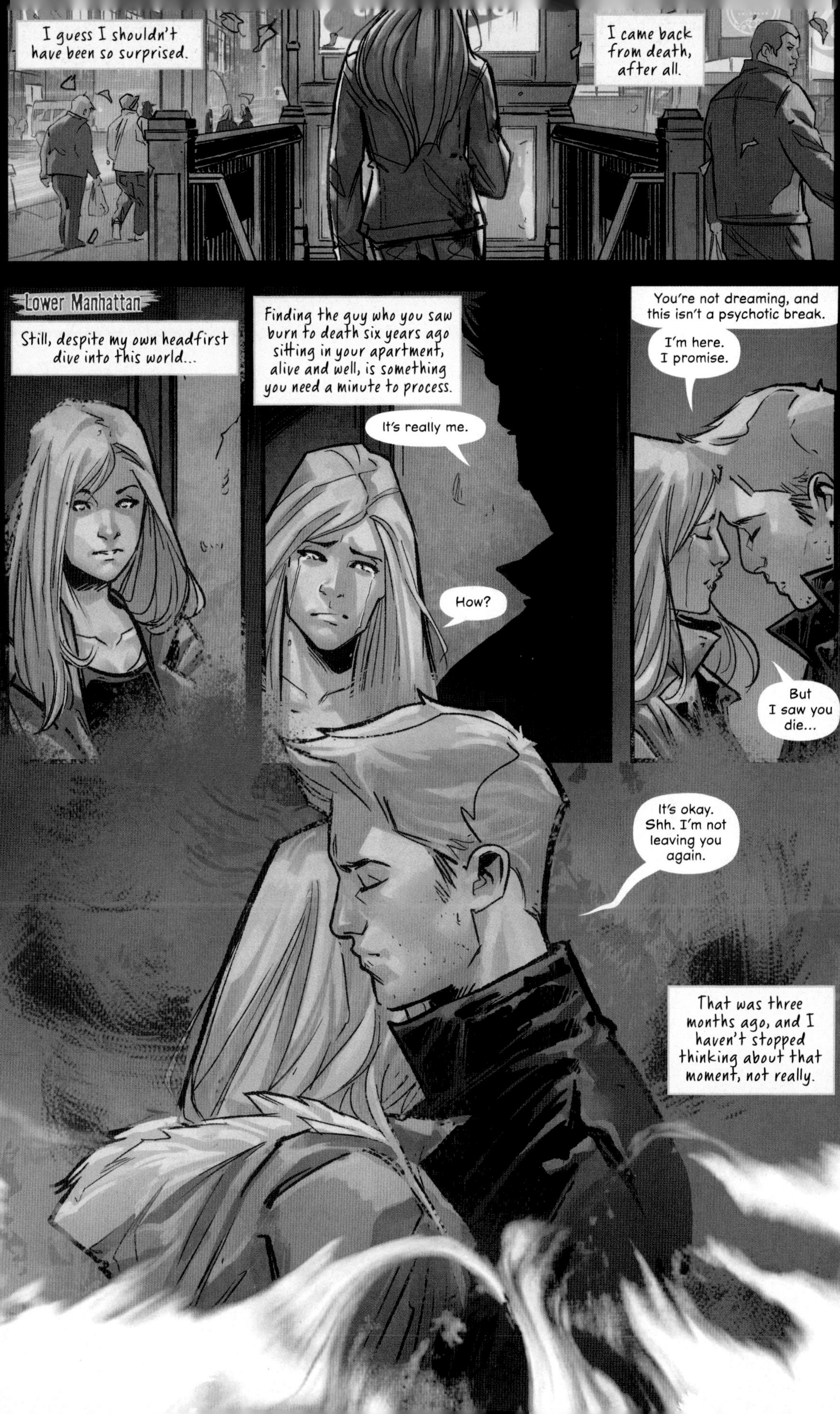
I guess I shouldn't have been so surprised.
I came back from death, after all.
Lower Manhattan
Still, despite my own headfirst dive into this world...
Finding the guy who you saw burn to death six years ago sitting in your apartment, alive and well, is something you need a minute to process.
It's really me.
How?
You're not dreaming, and this isn't a psychotic break.
I'm here. I promise.
But I saw you die...
It's okay. Shh. I'm not leaving you again.
That was three months ago, and I haven't stopped thinking about that moment, not really.

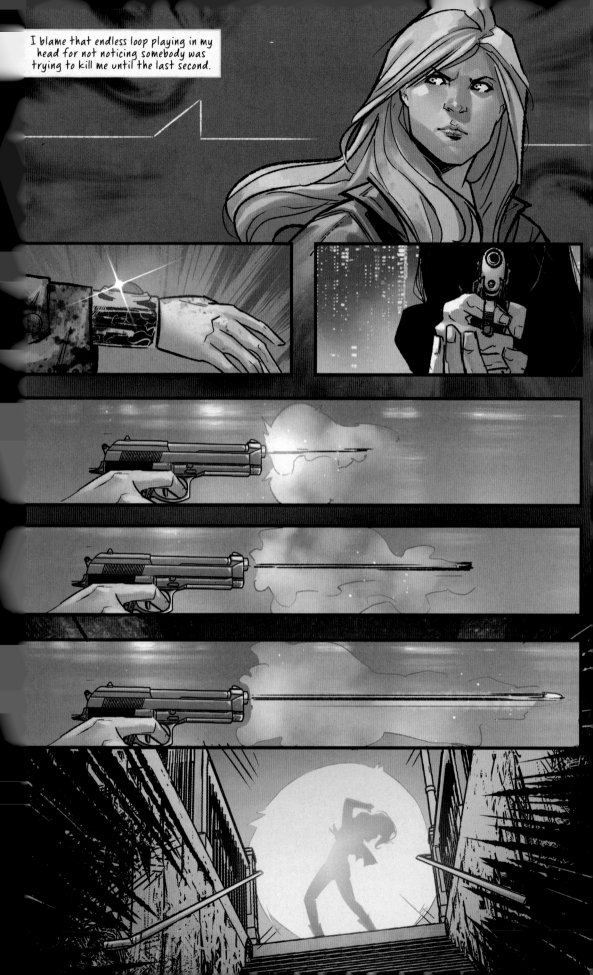

I blame that endless loop playing in my head for not noticing somebody was trying to kill me until the last second.

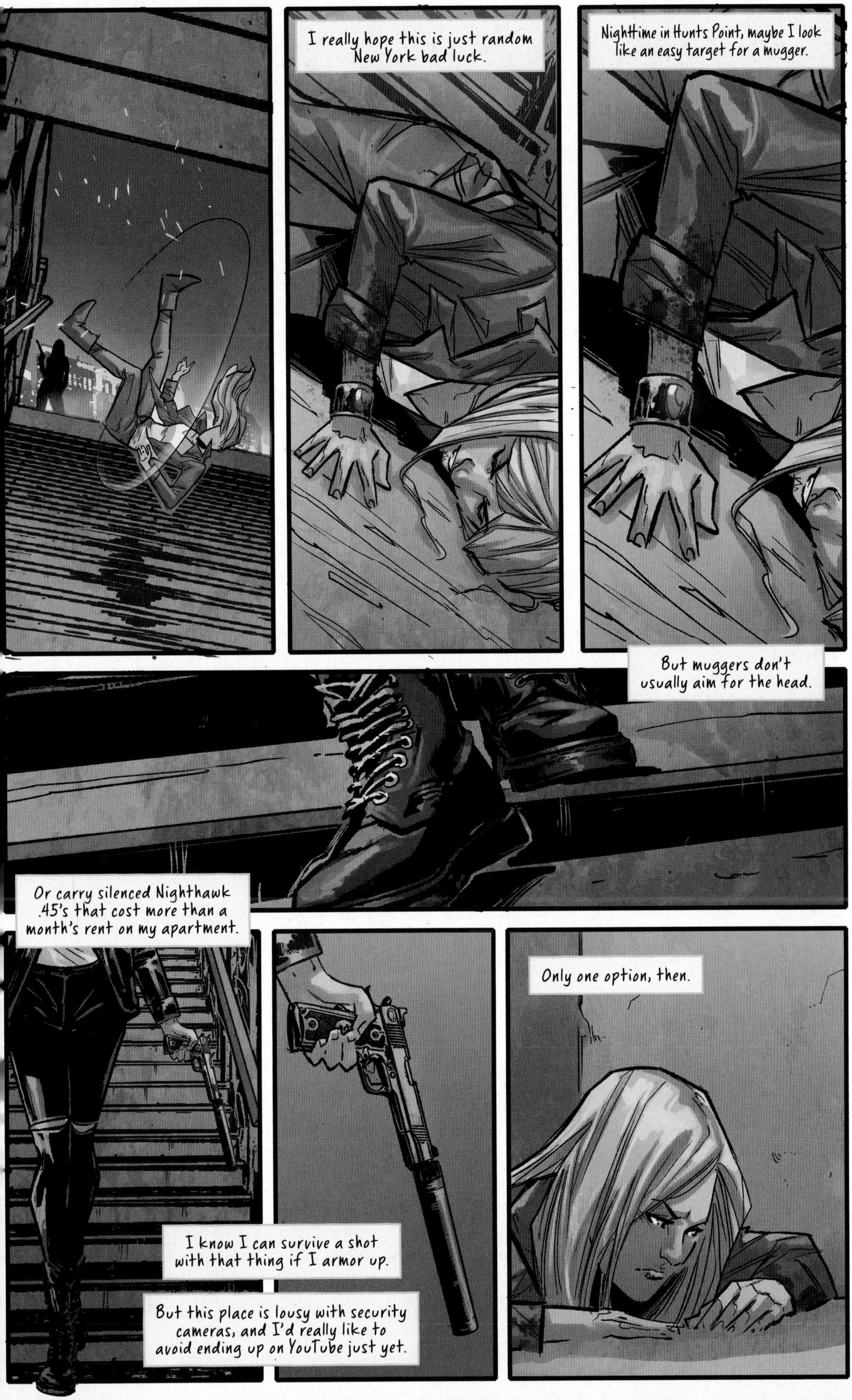
I really hope this is just random New York bad luck.
Nighttime in Hunts Point, maybe I look like an easy target for a mugger.
But muggers don't usually aim for the head.
Or carry silenced Nighthawk .45's that cost more than a month's rent on my apartment.
I know I can survive a shot with that thing if I armor up.
But this place is lousy with security cameras, and I'd really like to avoid ending up on YouTube just yet.
Only one option, then.

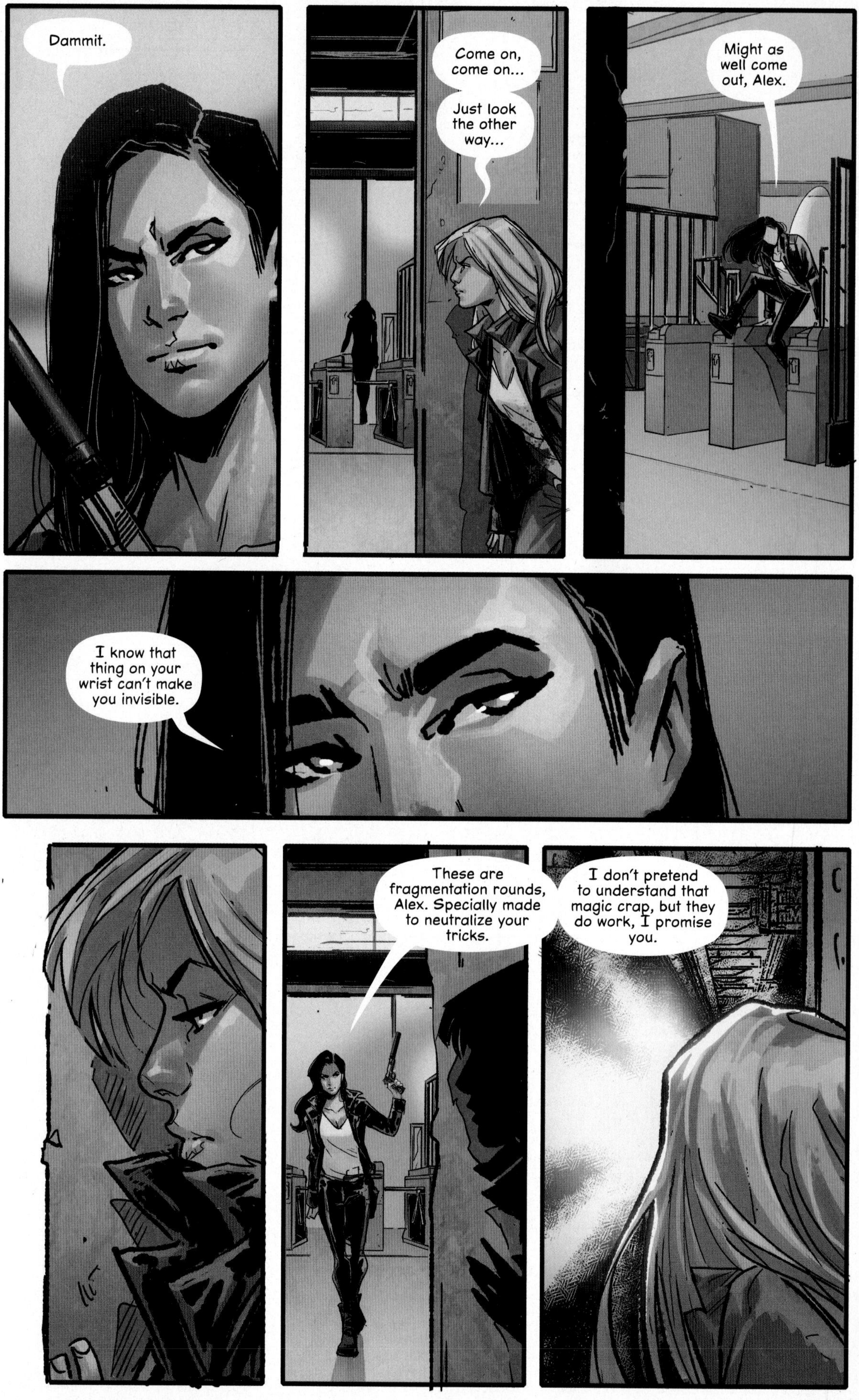
Dammit.
Come on, come on...
Just look the other way...
Might as well come out, Alex.
I know that thing on your wrist can't make you invisible.
These are fragmentation rounds, Alex. Specially made to neutralize your tricks.
I don't pretend to understand that magic crap, but they do work, I promise you.

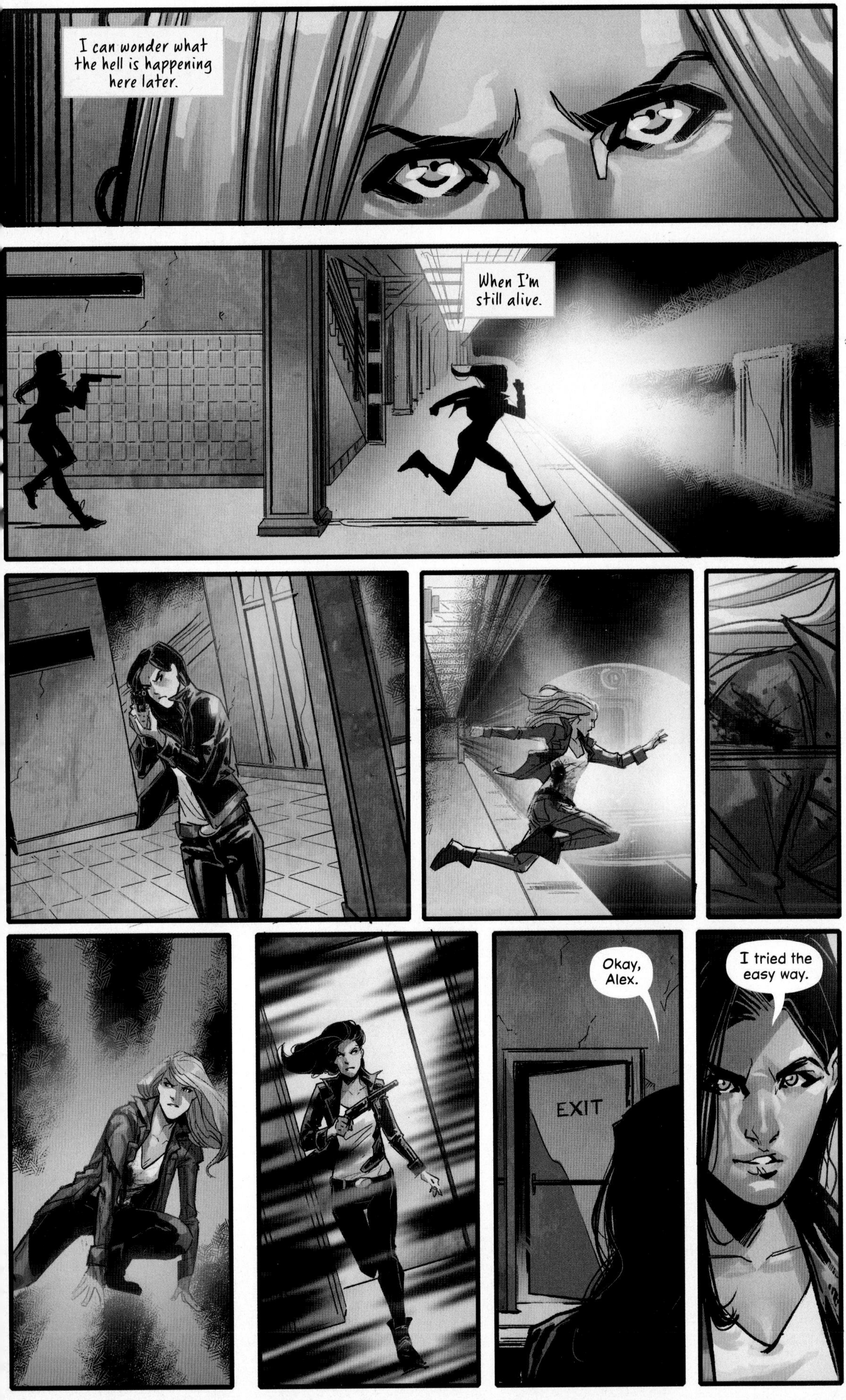
I can wonder what the hell is happening here later.
When I'm still alive.
EXIT
Okay, Alex.
I tried the easy way.

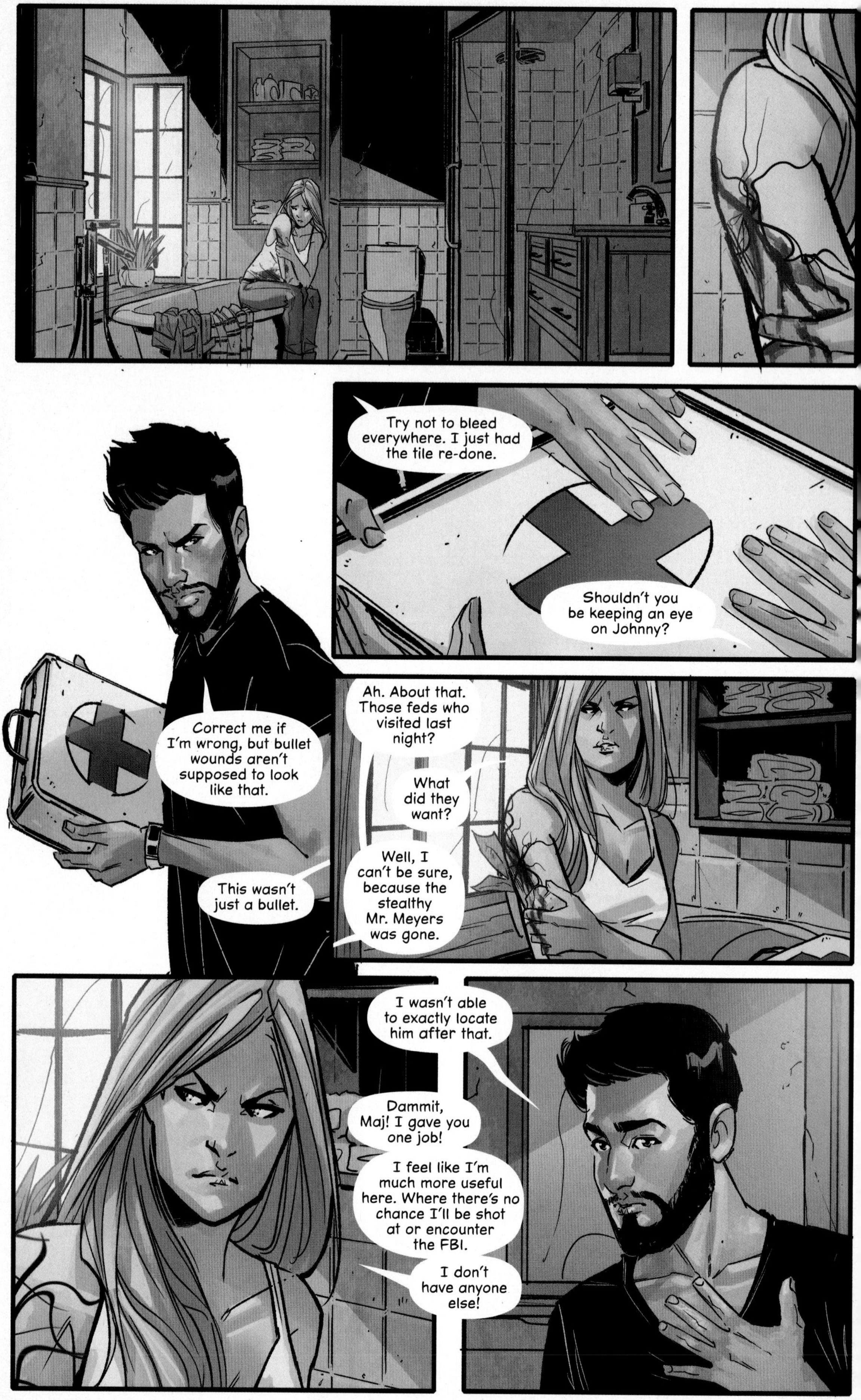
Try not to bleed everywhere. I just had the tile re-done.
Shouldn't you be keeping an eye on Johnny?
Correct me if I'm wrong, but bullet wounds aren't supposed to look like that.
This wasn't just a bullet.
Ah. About that. Those feds who visited last night?
What did they want?
Well, I can't be sure, because the stealthy Mr. Meyers was gone.
I wasn't able to exactly locate him after that.
Dammit, Maj! I gave you one job!
I feel like I'm much more useful here. Where there's no chance I'll be shot at or encounter the FBI.
I don't have anyone else!

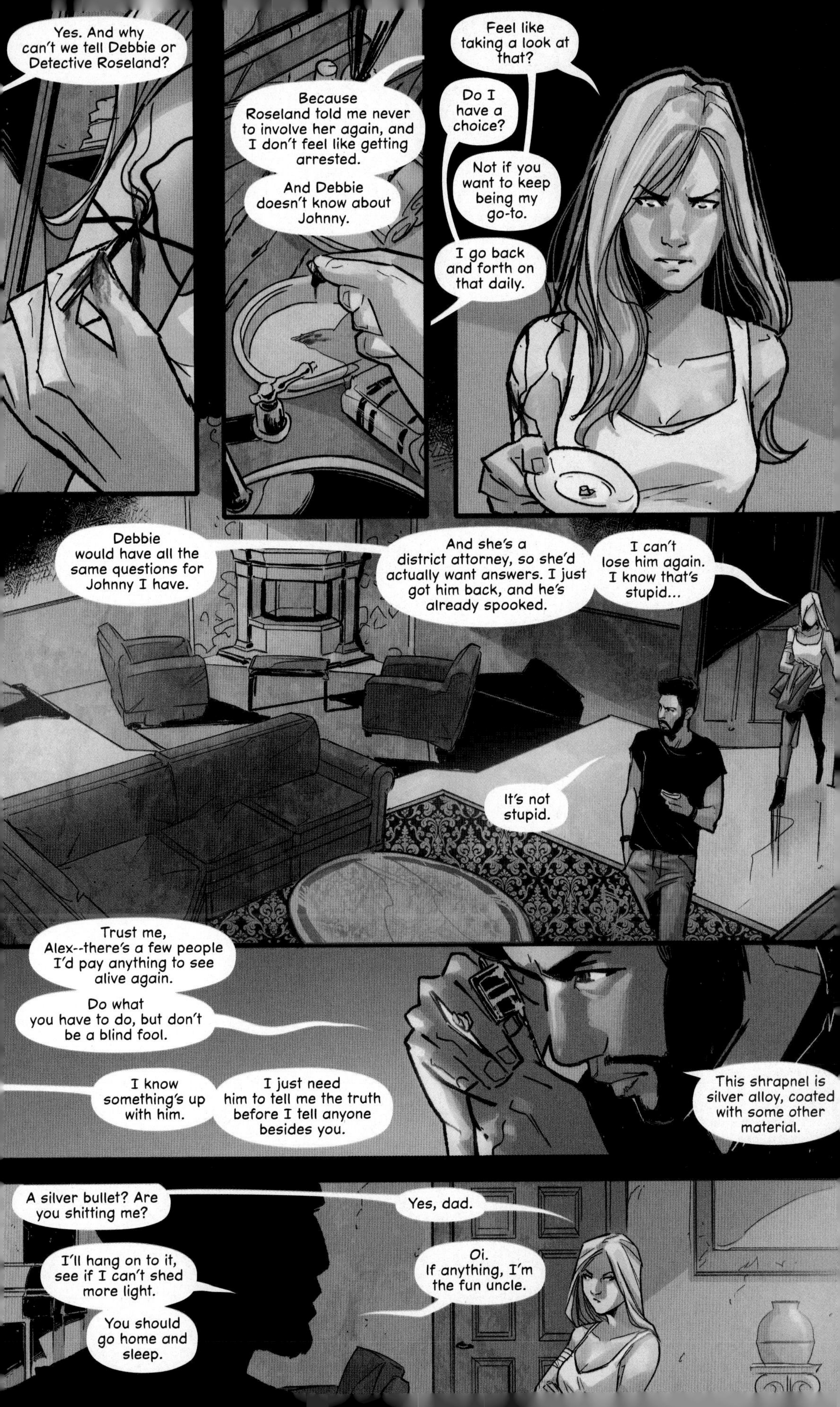
Yes. And why can't we tell Debbie or Detective Roseland?
Because Roseland told me never to involve her again, and I don't feel like getting arrested.
And Debbie doesn't know about Johnny.
Feel like taking a look at that?
Do I have a choice?
Not if you want to keep being my go-to.
I go back and forth on that daily.
Debbie would have all the same questions for Johnny I have.
And she's a district attorney, so she'd actually want answers. I just got him back, and he's already spooked.
I can't lose him again. I know that's stupid...
It's not stupid.
Trust me, Alex--there's a few people I'd pay anything to see alive again.
Do what you have to do, but don't be a blind fool.
I know something's up with him.
I just need him to tell me the truth before I tell anyone besides you.
This shrapnel is silver alloy, coated with some other material.
A silver bullet? Are you shitting me?
Yes, dad.
Oi. If anything, I'm the fun uncle.
I'll hang on to it, see if I can't shed more light.
You should go home and sleep.

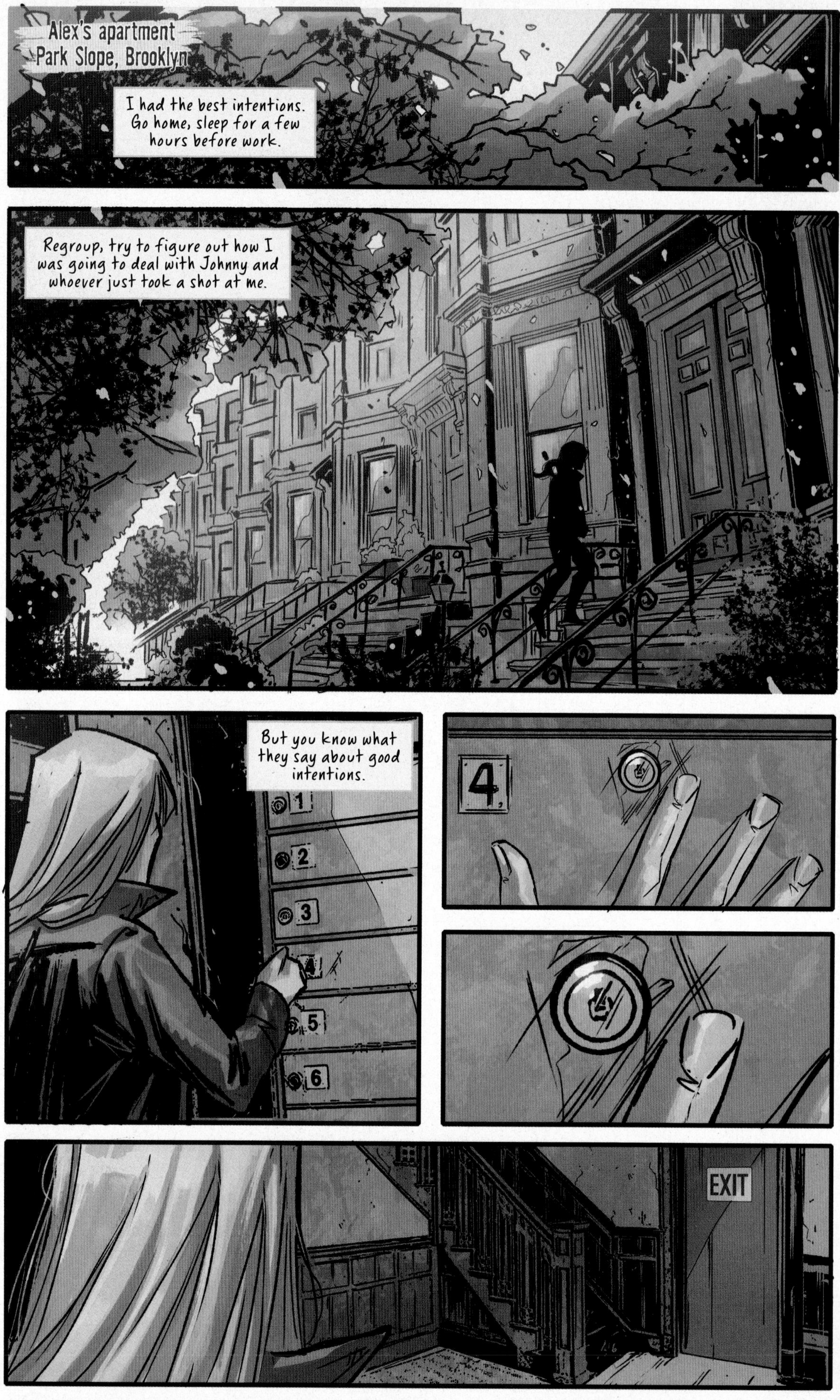
Alex's apartment
Park Slope, Brooklyn
I had the best intentions. Go home, sleep for a few hours before work.
Regroup, try to figure out how I was going to deal with Johnny and whoever just took a shot at me.
But you know what they say about good intentions.
1
2
3
4
5
6
4
EXIT

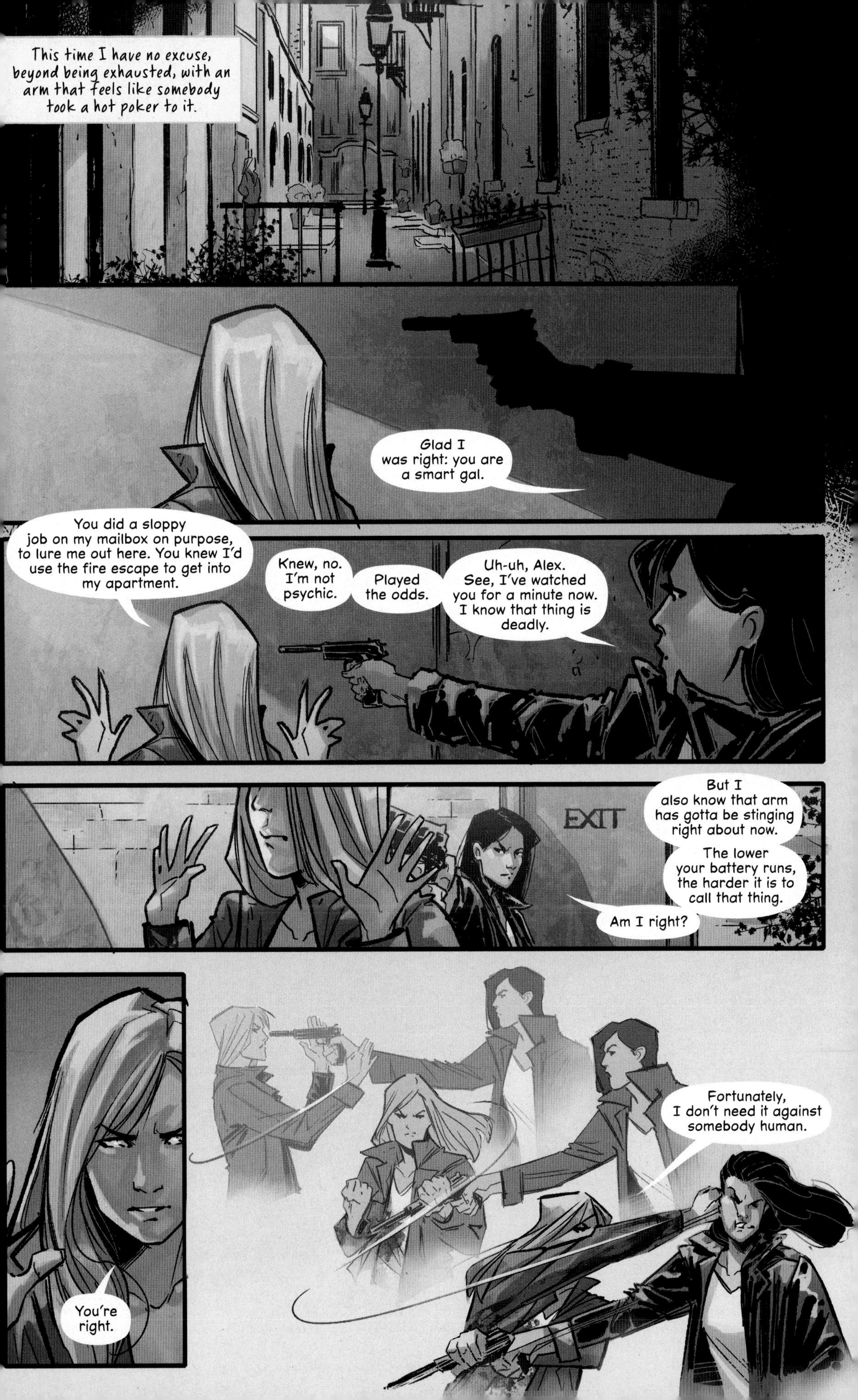
This time I have no excuse, beyond being exhausted, with an arm that feels like somebody took a hot poker to it.
Glad I was right: you are a smart gal.
You did a sloppy job on my mailbox on purpose, to lure me out here. You knew I'd use the fire escape to get into my apartment.
Knew, no. I'm not psychic.
Played the odds.
Uh-uh, Alex. See, I've watched you for a minute now. I know that thing is deadly.
EXIT
But I also know that arm has gotta be stinging right about now.
The lower your battery runs, the harder it is to call that thing.
Am I right?
You're right.
Fortunately, I don't need it against somebody human.

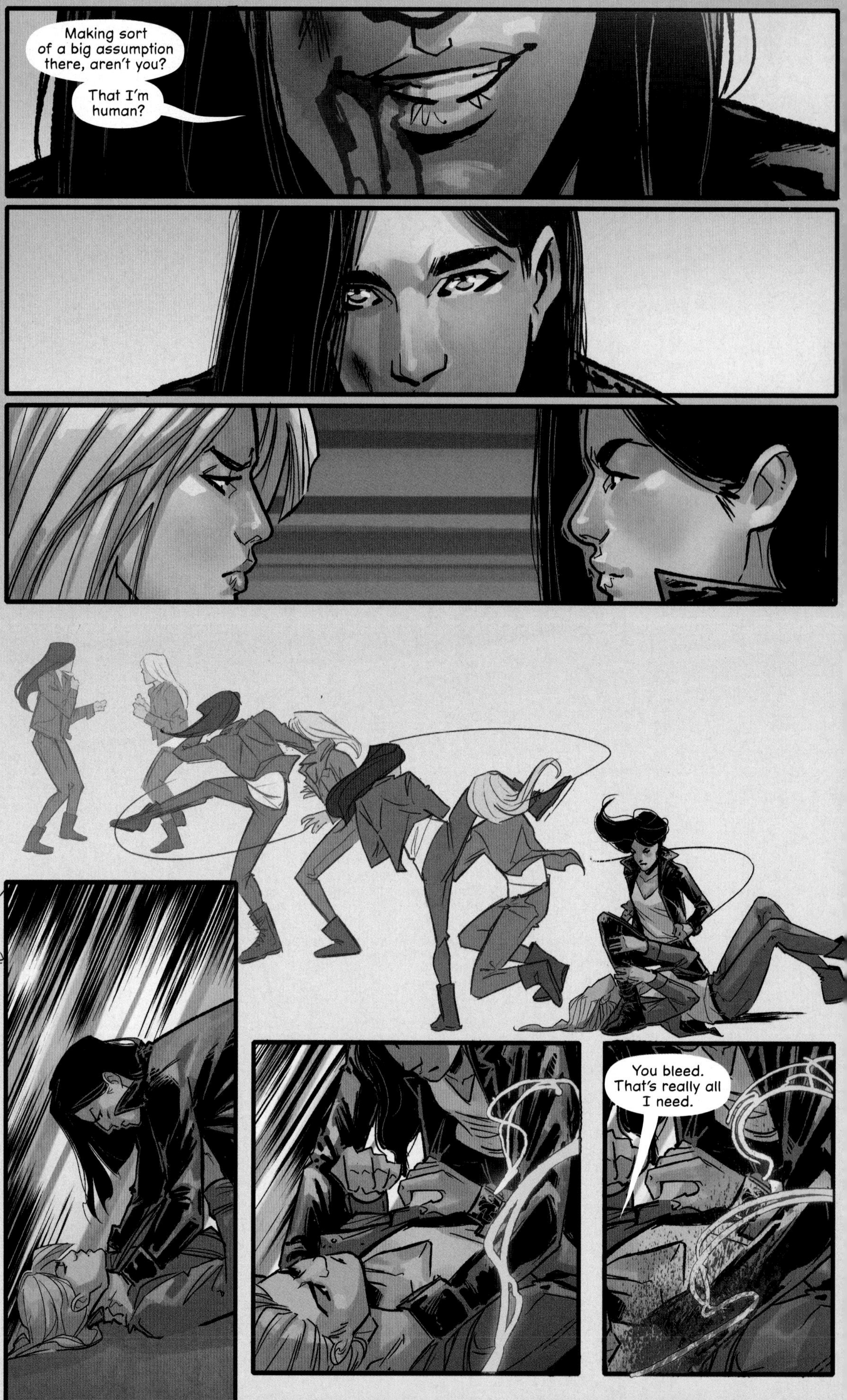
Making sort of a big assumption there, aren't you?
That I'm human?
You bleed. That's really all I need.

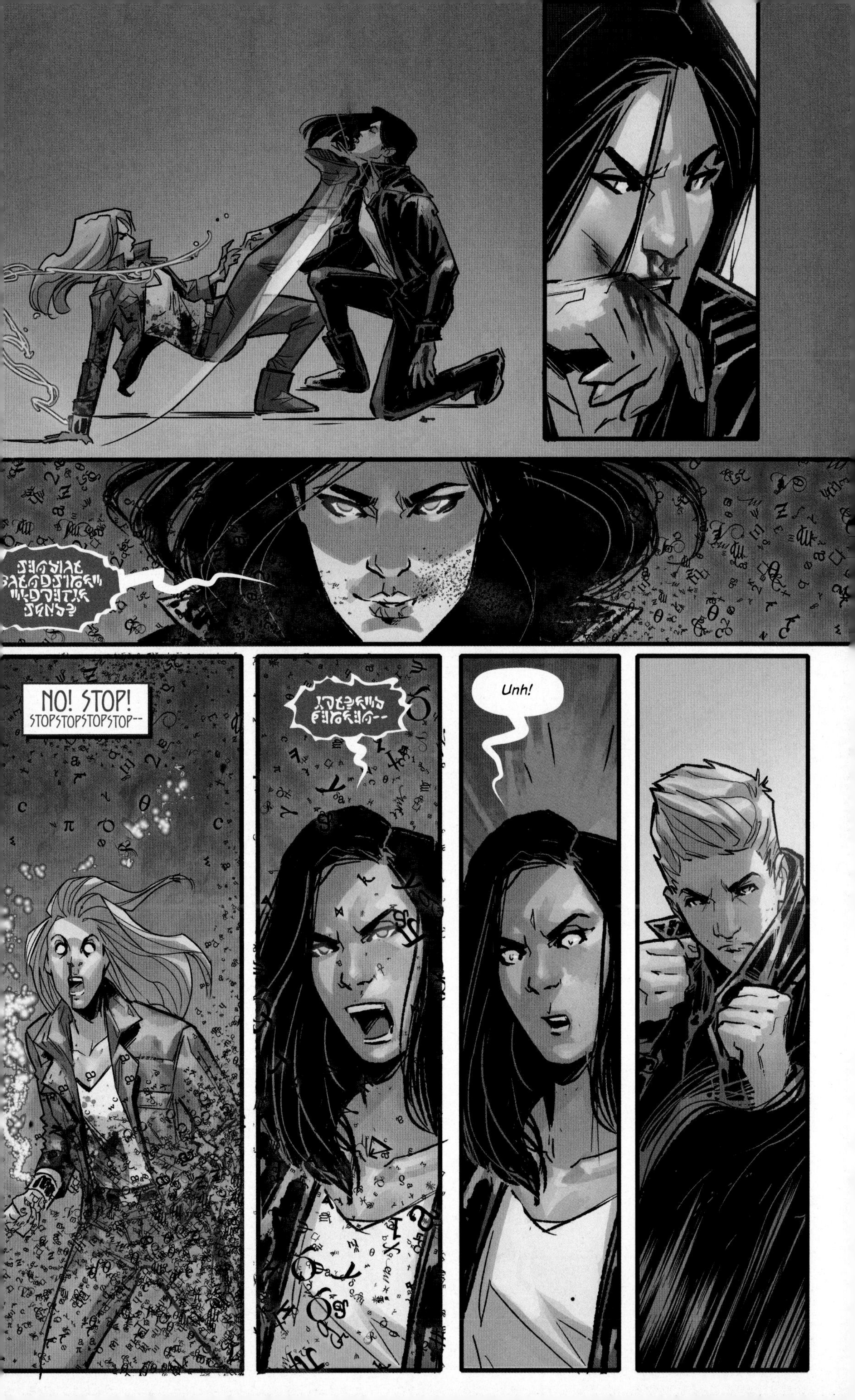
NO! STOP!
STOPSTOPSTOPSTOP--
Unh!

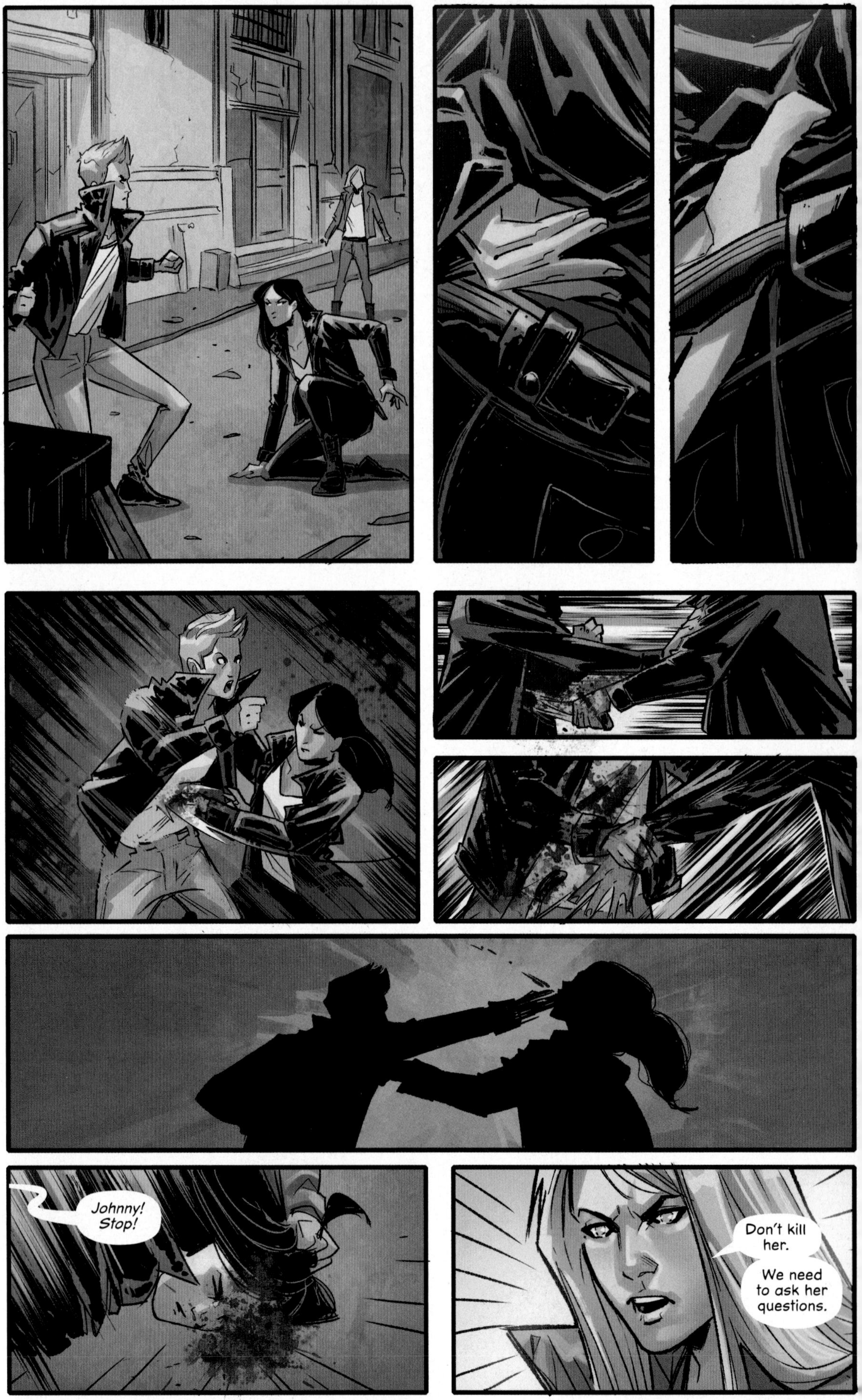
Johnny! Stop!
Don't kill her.
We need to ask her questions.

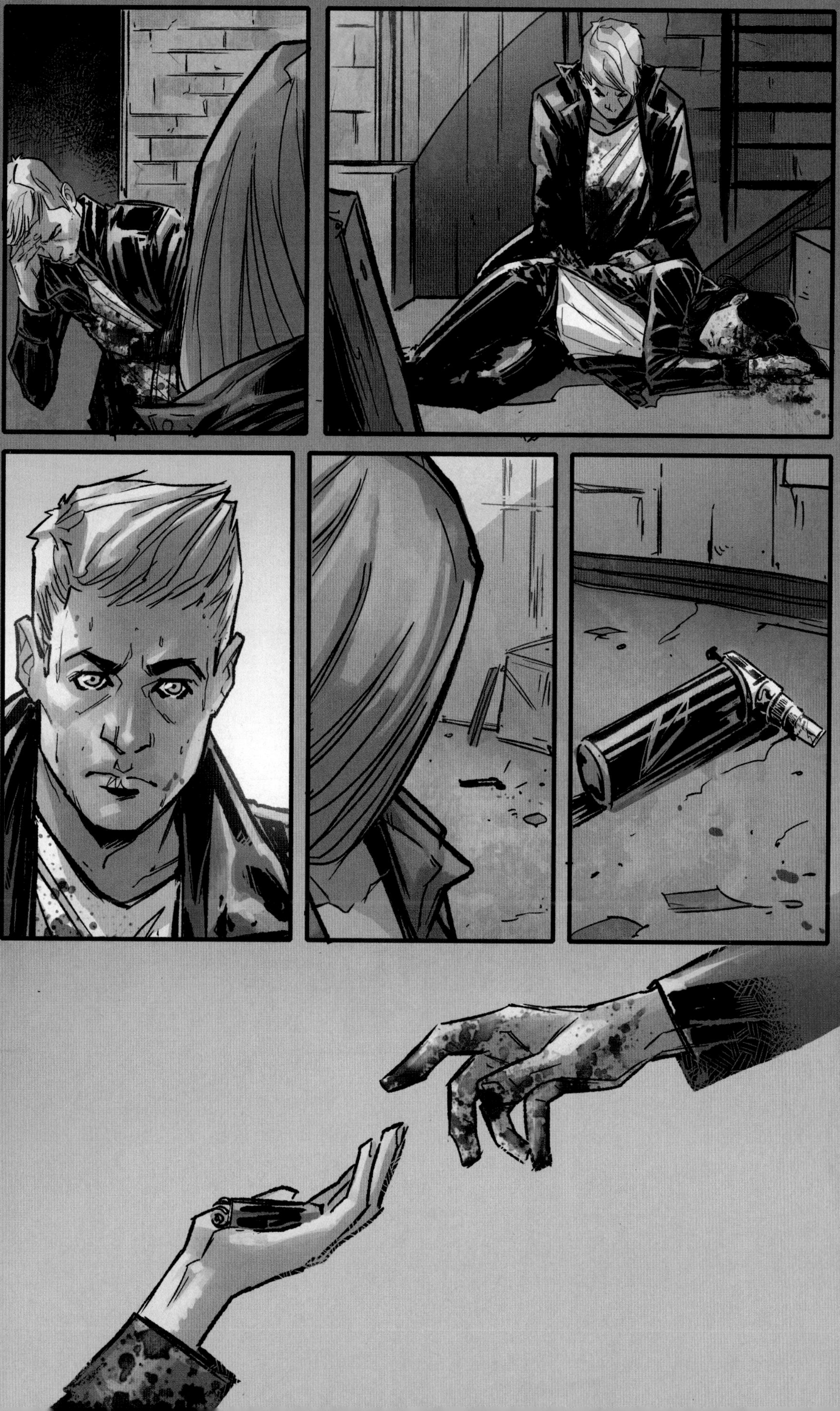

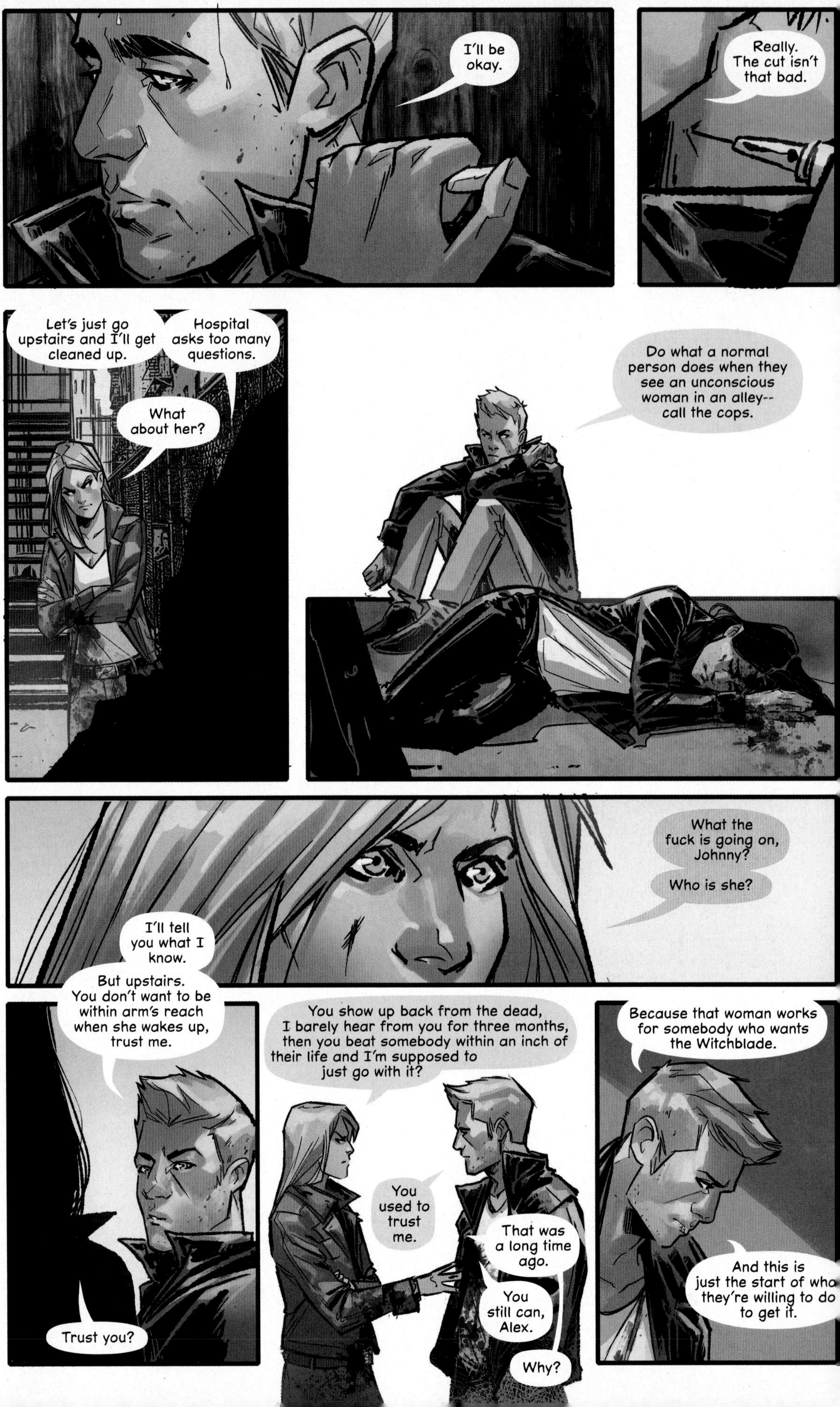

I'll be okay.
Really. The cut isn't that bad.
Let's just go upstairs and I'll get cleaned up.
Hospital asks too many questions.
What about her?
Do what a normal person does when they see an unconscious woman in an alley-- call the cops.
What the fuck is going on, Johnny?
Who is she?
I'll tell you what I know.
But upstairs. You don't want to be within arm's reach when she wakes up, trust me.
Trust you?
You show up back from the dead, I barely hear from you for three months, then you beat somebody within an inch of their life and I'm supposed to just go with it?
You used to trust me.
That was a long time ago.
You still can, Alex.
Why?
Because that woman works for somebody who wants the Witchblade.
And this is just the start of what they're willing to do to get it.

CHAPTER **EIGHT**

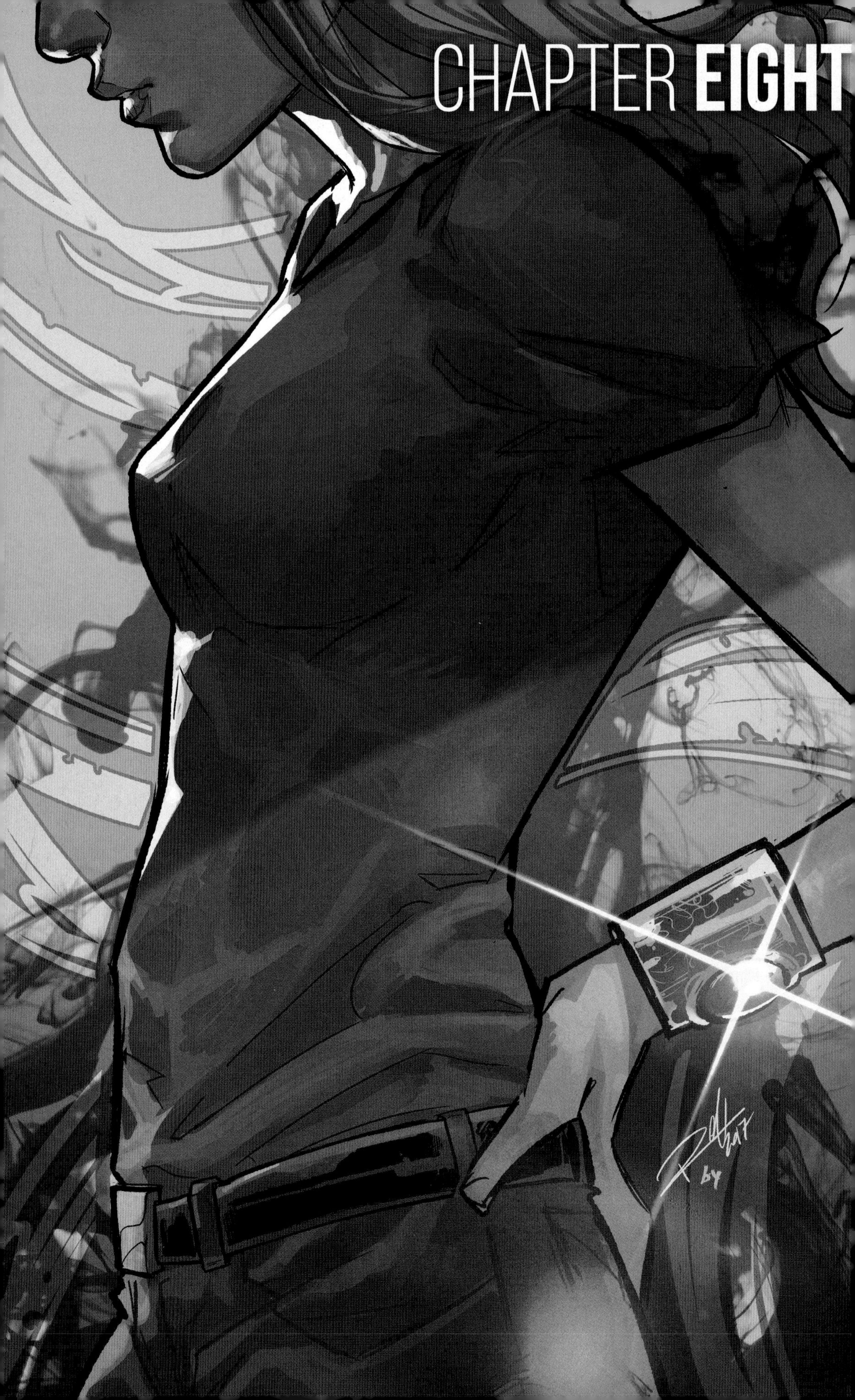

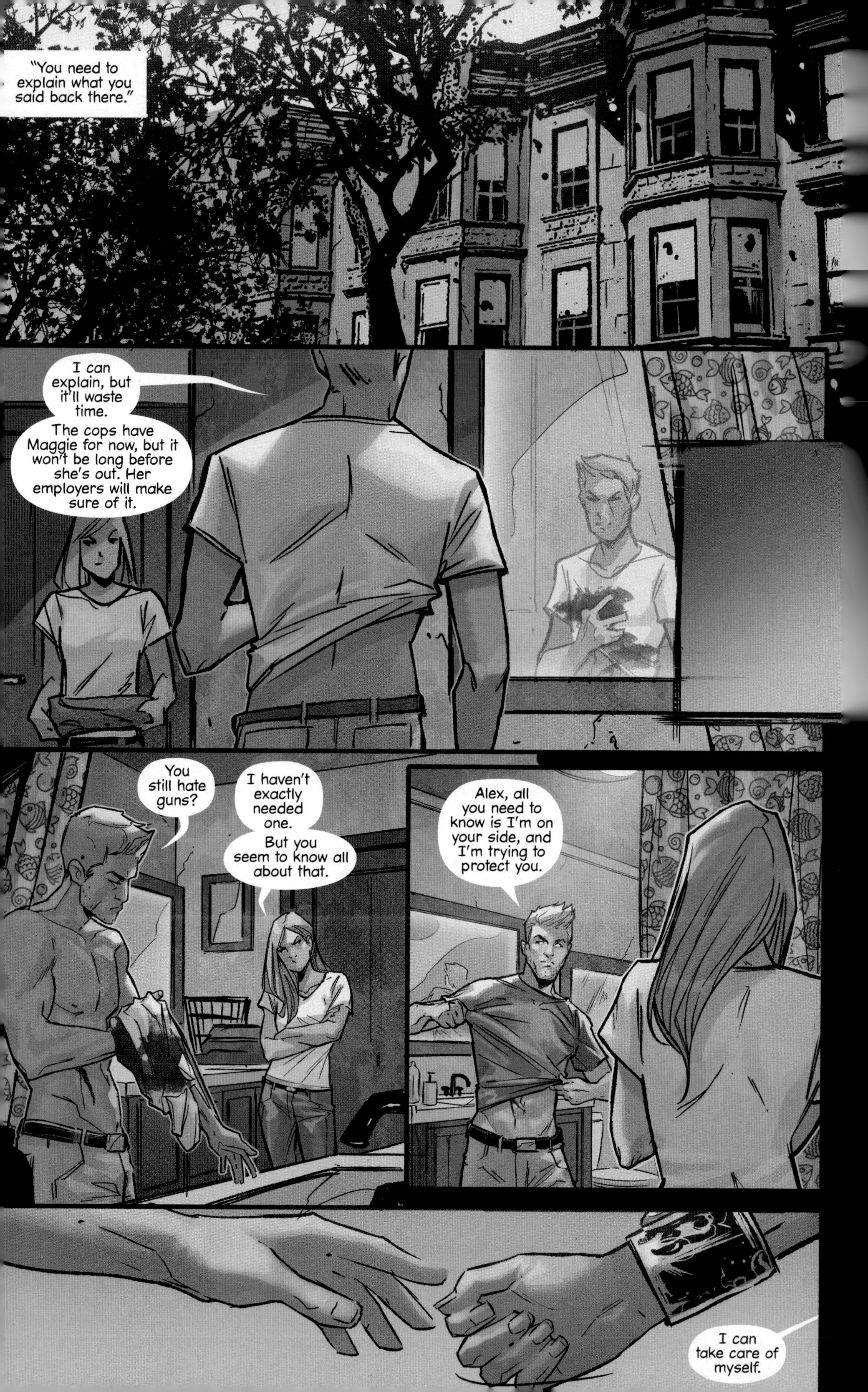
"You need to explain what you said back there."
I can explain, but it'll waste time.
The cops have Maggie for now, but it won't be long before she's out. Her employers will make sure of it.
You still hate guns?
I haven't exactly needed one.
But you seem to know all about that.
Alex, all you need to know is I'm on your side, and I'm trying to protect you.
I can take care of myself.

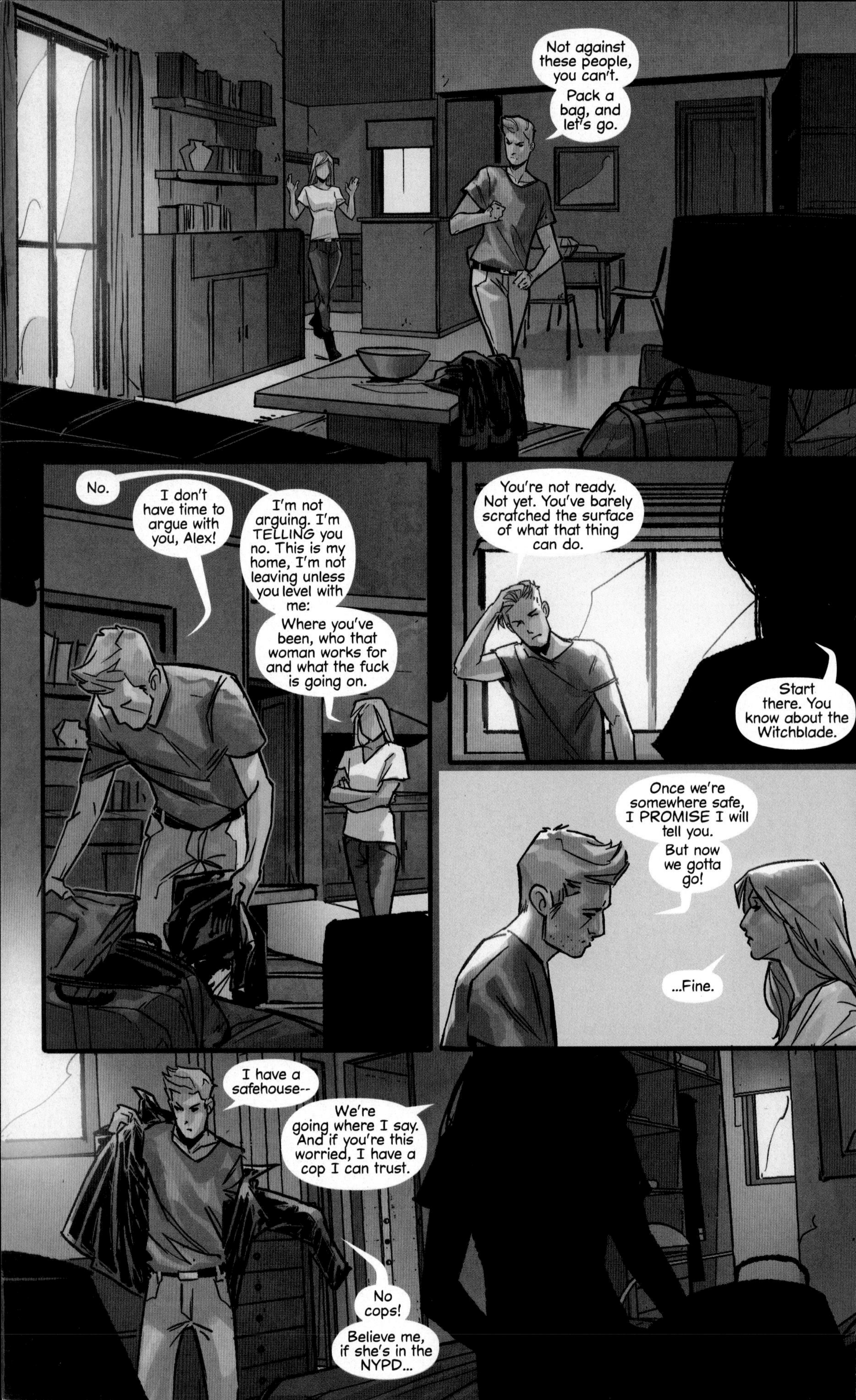
Not against these people, you can't.
Pack a bag, and let's go.
No.
I don't have time to argue with you, Alex!
I'm not arguing. I'm TELLING you no. This is my home, I'm not leaving unless you level with me:
Where you've been, who that woman works for and what the fuck is going on.
You're not ready. Not yet. You've barely scratched the surface of what that thing can do.
Start there. You know about the Witchblade.
Once we're somewhere safe, I PROMISE I will tell you.
But now we gotta go!
...Fine.
I have a safehouse--
We're going where I say. And if you're this worried, I have a cop I can trust.
No cops!
Believe me, if she's in the NYPD...

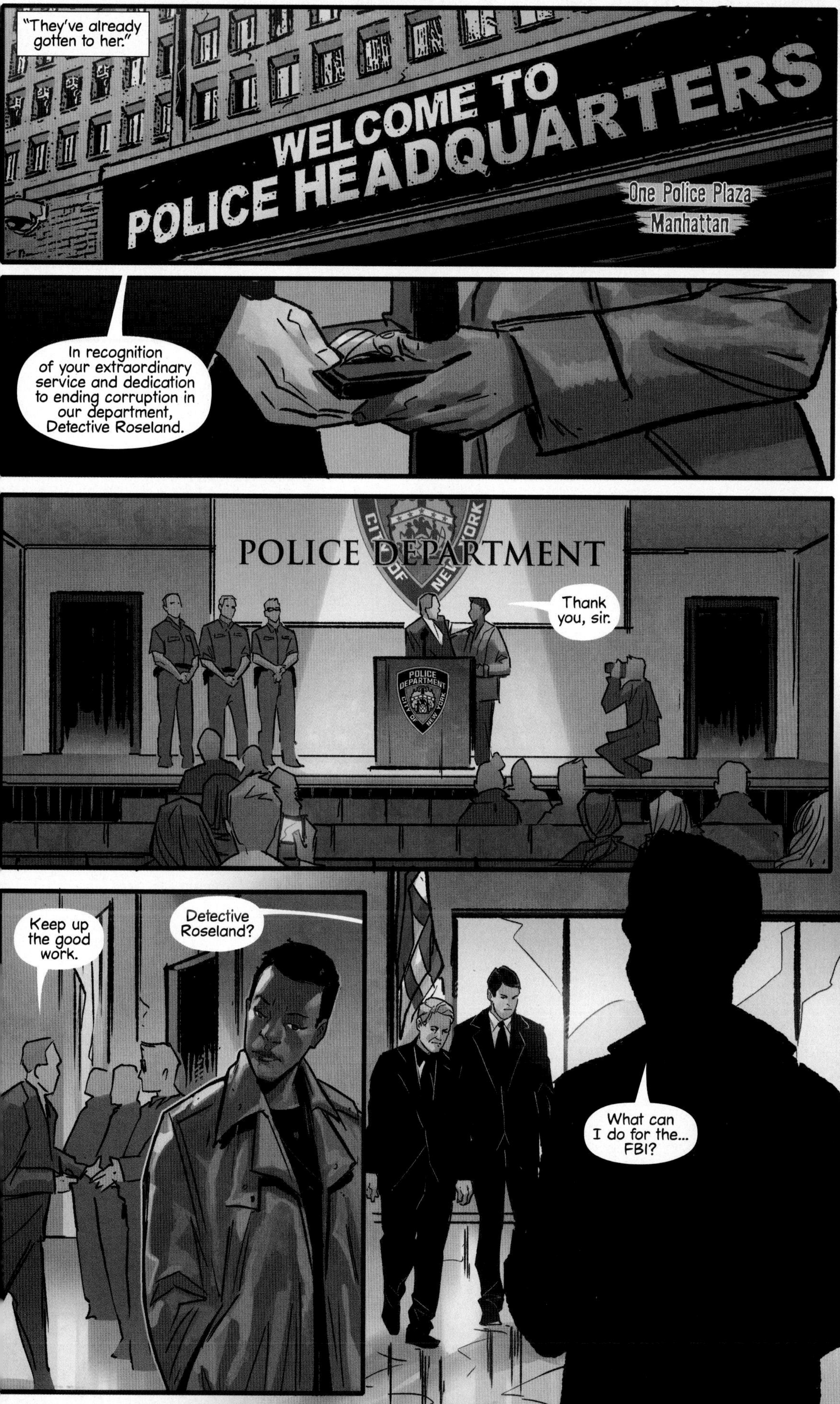
"They've already gotten to her."
WELCOME TO POLICE HEADQUARTERS
One Police Plaza
Manhattan
In recognition of your extraordinary service and dedication to ending corruption in our department, Detective Roseland.
POLICE DEPARTMENT
Thank you, sir.
Keep up the good work.
Detective Roseland?
What can I do for the... FBI?

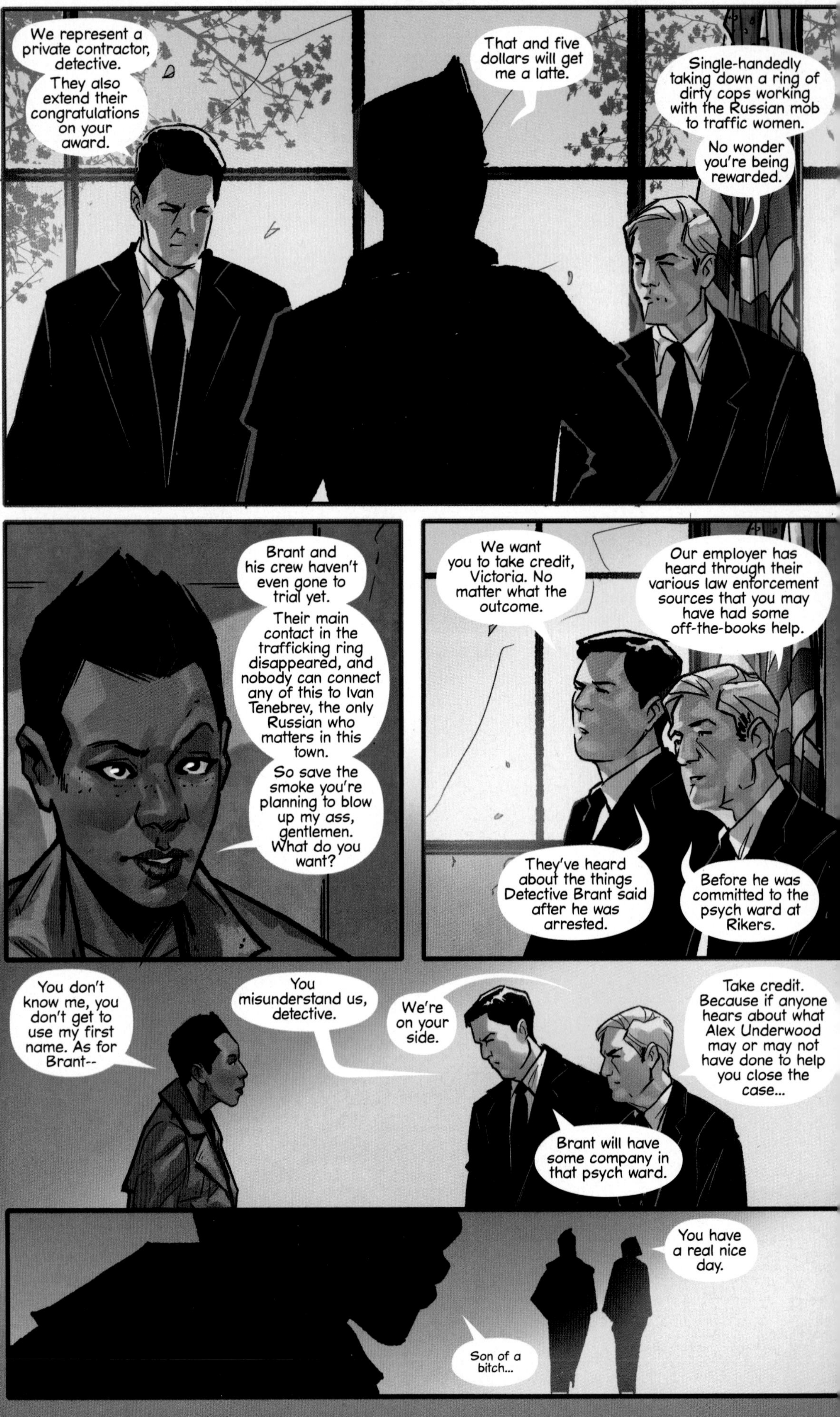
We represent a private contractor, detective.
They also extend their congratulations on your award.
That and five dollars will get me a latte.
Single-handedly taking down a ring of dirty cops working with the Russian mob to traffic women.
No wonder you're being rewarded.
Brant and his crew haven't even gone to trial yet.
Their main contact in the trafficking ring disappeared, and nobody can connect any of this to Ivan Tenebrev, the only Russian who matters in this town.
So save the smoke you're planning to blow up my ass, gentlemen. What do you want?
We want you to take credit, Victoria. No matter what the outcome.
Our employer has heard through their various law enforcement sources that you may have had some off-the-books help.
They've heard about the things Detective Brant said after he was arrested.
Before he was committed to the psych ward at Rikers.
You don't know me, you don't get to use my first name. As for Brant--
You misunderstand us, detective.
We're on your side.
Take credit. Because if anyone hears about what Alex Underwood may or may not have done to help you close the case...
Brant will have some company in that psych ward.
You have a real nice day.
Son of a bitch...

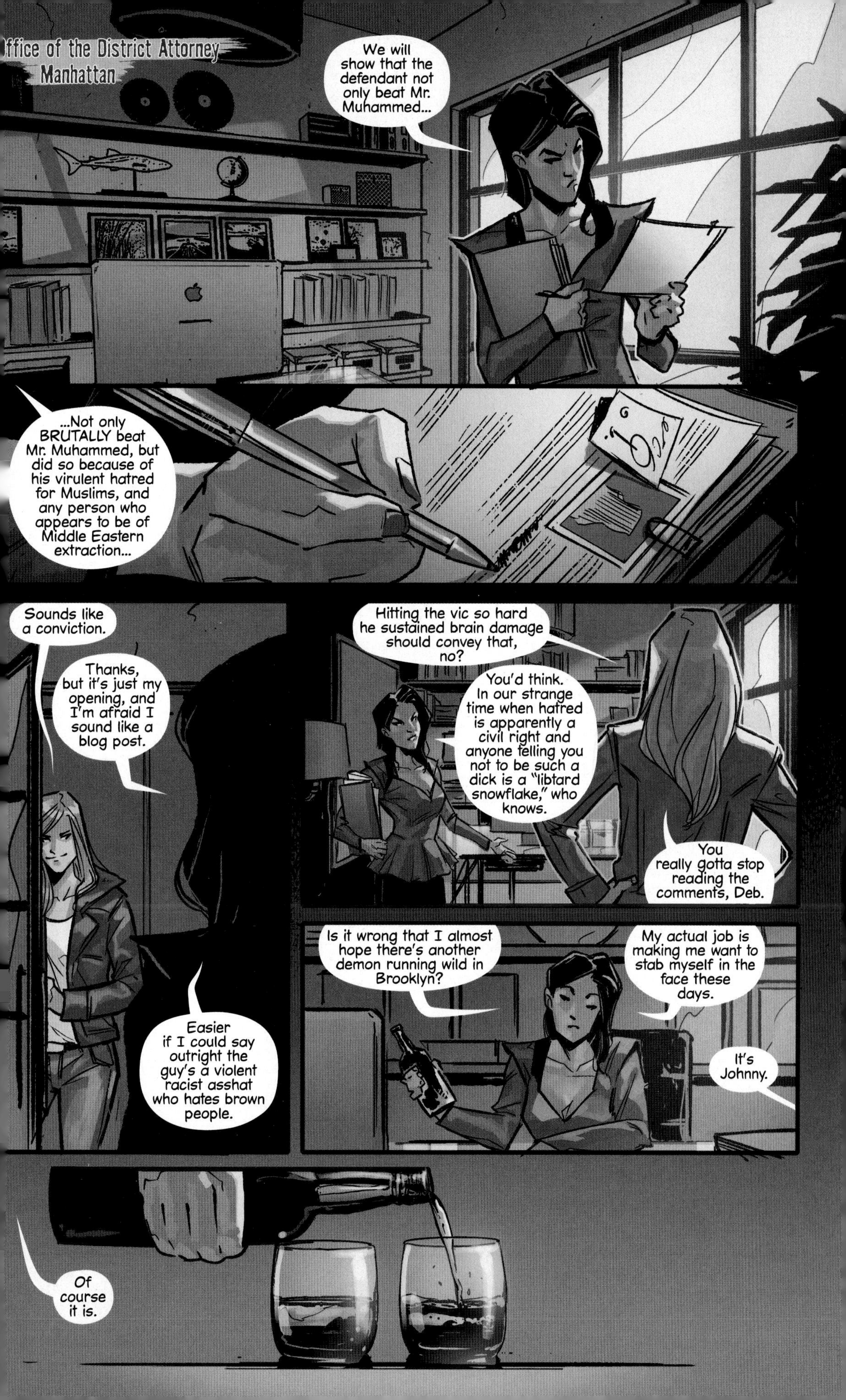
Office of the District Attorney Manhattan
We will show that the defendant not only beat Mr. Muhammed...
...Not only BRUTALLY beat Mr. Muhammed, but did so because of his virulent hatred for Muslims, and any person who appears to be of Middle Eastern extraction...
Sounds like a conviction.
Thanks, but it's just my opening, and I'm afraid I sound like a blog post.
Easier if I could say outright the guy's a violent racist asshat who hates brown people.
Hitting the vic so hard he sustained brain damage should convey that, no?
You'd think. In our strange time when hatred is apparently a civil right and anyone telling you not to be such a dick is a "libtard snowflake," who knows.
You really gotta stop reading the comments, Deb.
Is it wrong that I almost hope there's another demon running wild in Brooklyn?
My actual job is making me want to stab myself in the face these days.
It's Johnny.
Of course it is.

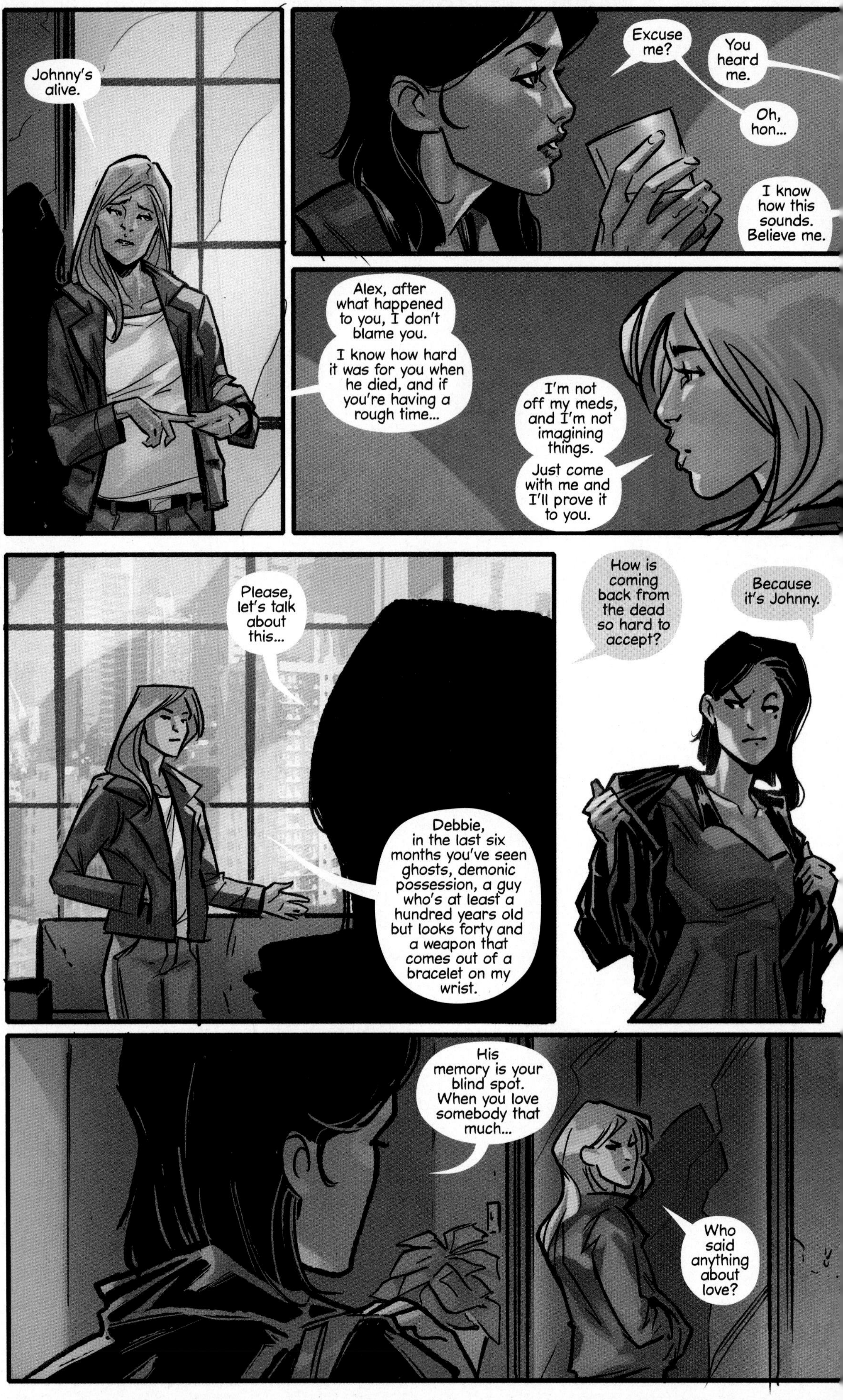
Johnny's alive.
Excuse me?
You heard me.
Oh, hon...
I know how this sounds. Believe me.
Alex, after what happened to you, I don't blame you.
I know how hard it was for you when he died, and if you're having a rough time...
I'm not off my meds, and I'm not imagining things.
Just come with me and I'll prove it to you.
Please, let's talk about this...
Debbie, in the last six months you've seen ghosts, demonic possession, a guy who's at least a hundred years old but looks forty and a weapon that comes out of a bracelet on my wrist.
How is coming back from the dead so hard to accept?
Because it's Johnny.
His memory is your blind spot. When you love somebody that much...
Who said anything about love?

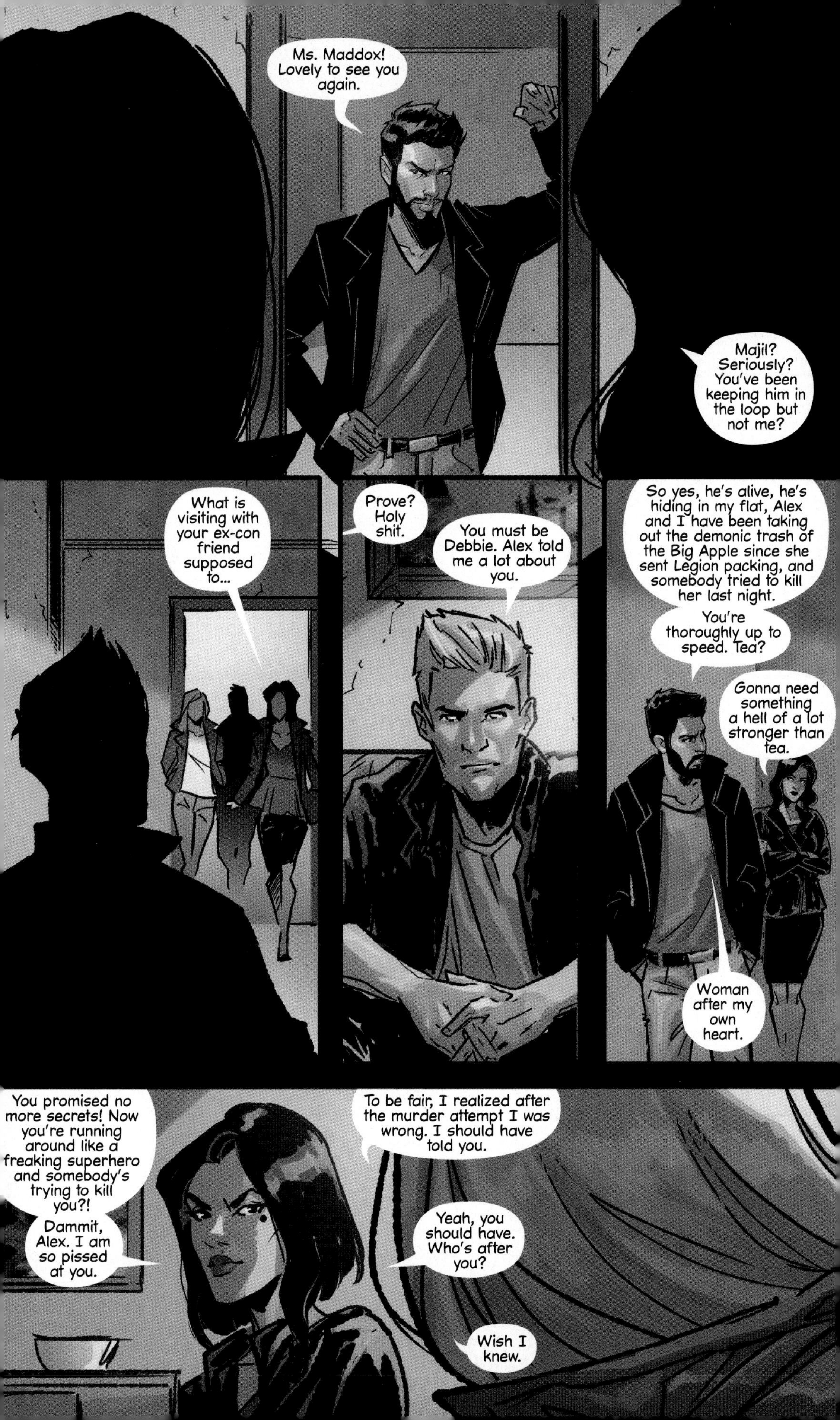
Ms. Maddox! Lovely to see you again.
Majil? Seriously? You've been keeping him in the loop but not me?
What is visiting with your ex-con friend supposed to...
Prove? Holy shit.
You must be Debbie. Alex told me a lot about you.
So yes, he's alive, he's hiding in my flat, Alex and I have been taking out the demonic trash of the Big Apple since she sent Legion packing, and somebody tried to kill her last night.
You're thoroughly up to speed. Tea?
Gonna need something a hell of a lot stronger than tea.
Woman after my own heart.
You promised no more secrets! Now you're running around like a freaking superhero and somebody's trying to kill you?!
Dammit, Alex. I am so pissed at you.
To be fair, I realized after the murder attempt I was wrong. I should have told you.
Yeah, you should have. Who's after you?
Wish I knew.

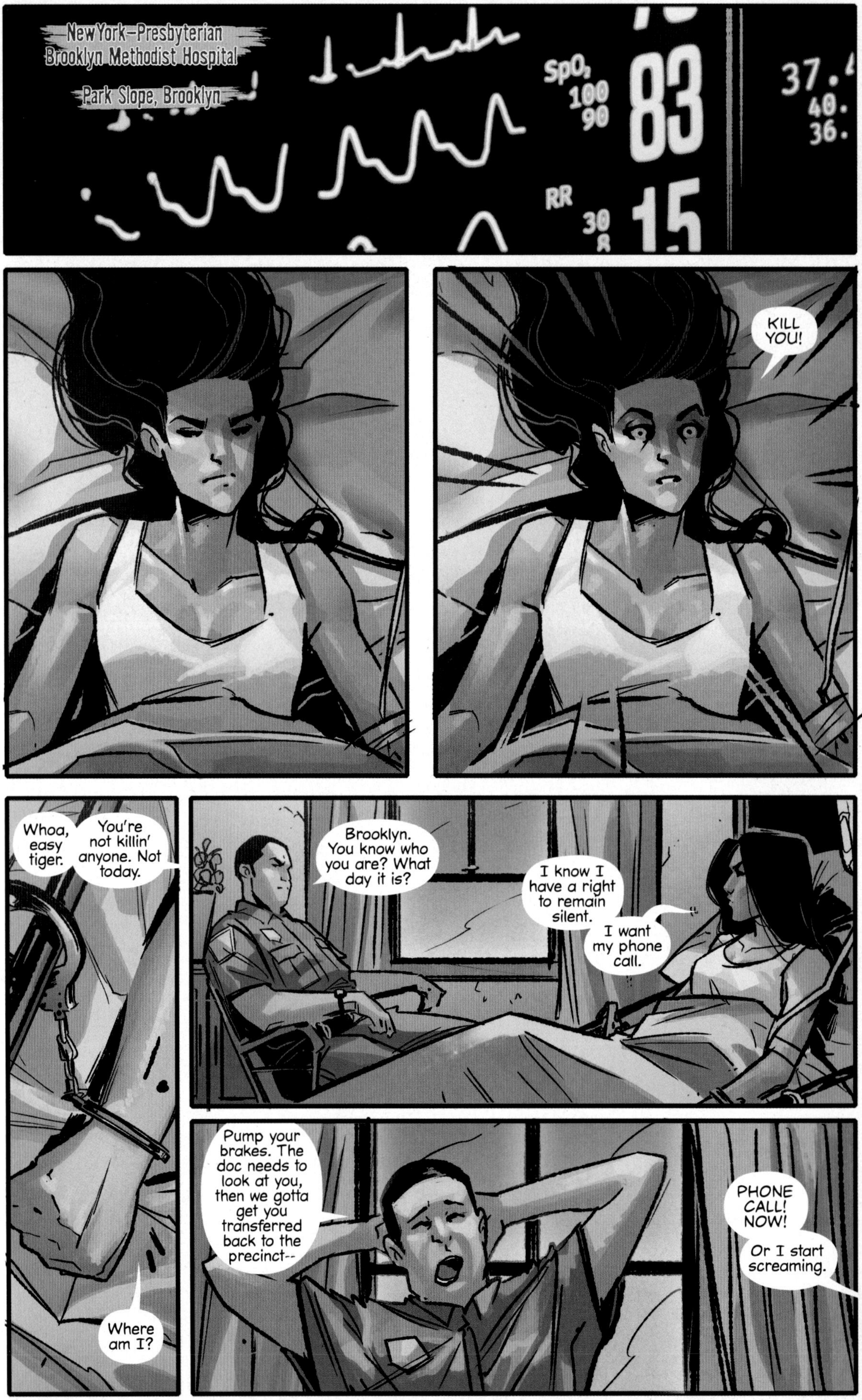
NewYork-Presbyterian Brooklyn Methodist Hospital
Park Slope, Brooklyn
SpO2
100
90
83
37.
40.
36.
RR
30
8
15
KILL YOU!
Whoa, easy tiger.
You're not killin' anyone. Not today.
Where am I?
Brooklyn. You know who you are? What day it is?
I know I have a right to remain silent.
I want my phone call.
Pump your brakes. The doc needs to look at you, then we gotta get you transferred back to the precinct--
PHONE CALL! NOW!
Or I start screaming.

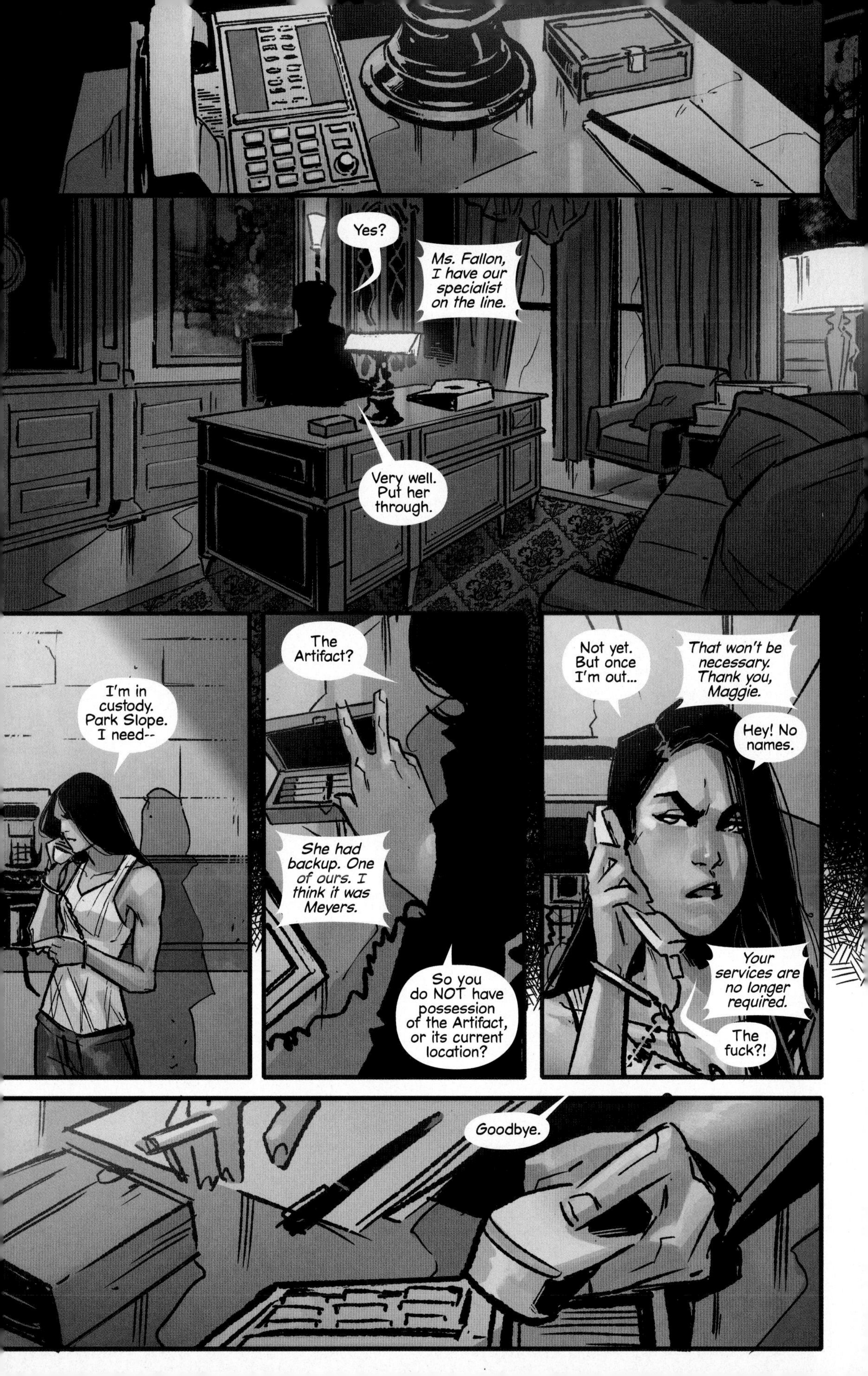
Yes?
Ms. Fallon, I have our specialist on the line.
Very well. Put her through.
I'm in custody. Park Slope. I need--
The Artifact?
She had backup. One of ours. I think it was Meyers.
So you do NOT have possession of the Artifact, or its current location?
Not yet. But once I'm out...
That won't be necessary. Thank you, Maggie.
Hey! No names.
Your services are no longer required.
The fuck?!
Goodbye.

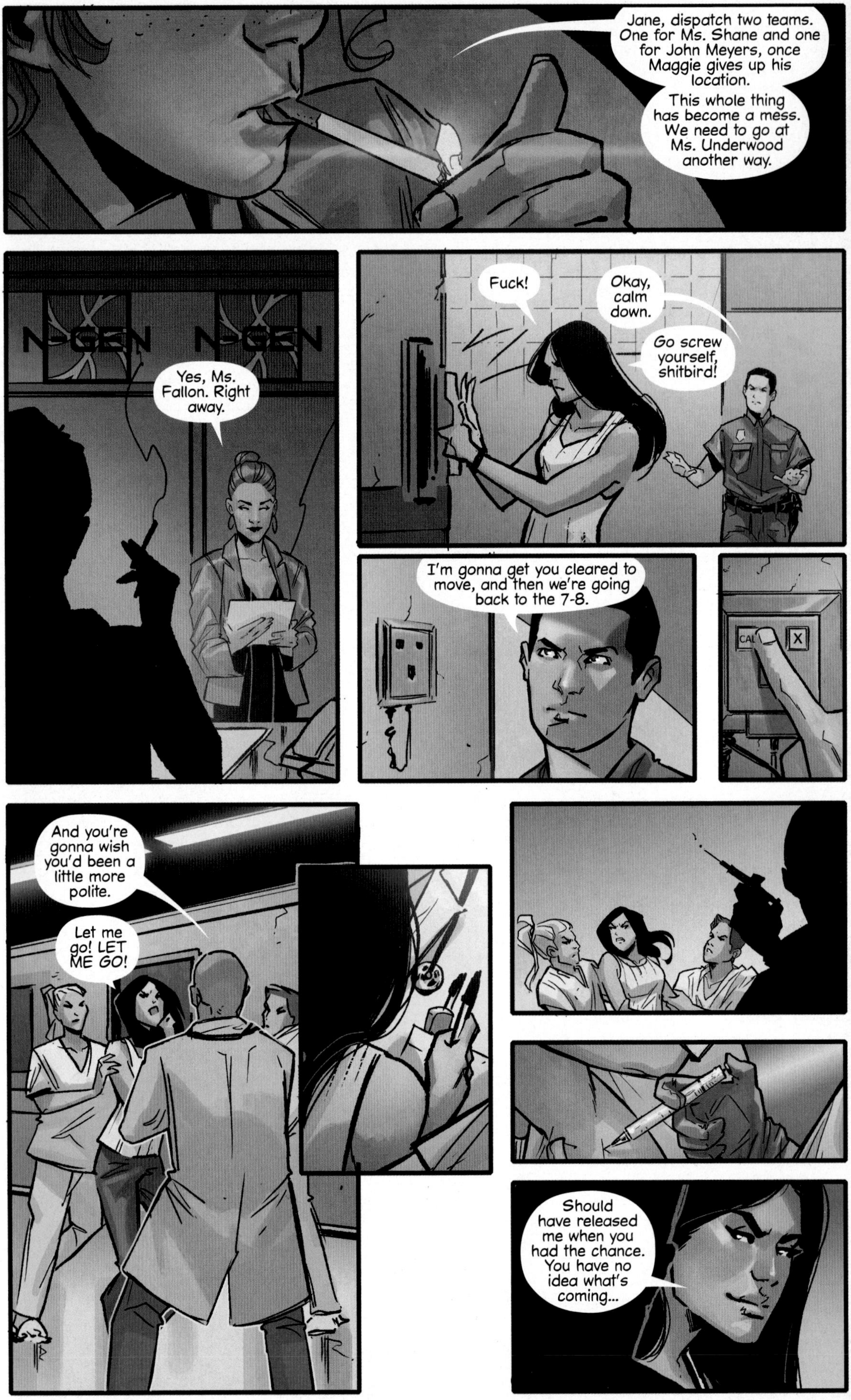
Jane, dispatch two teams. One for Ms. Shane and one for John Meyers, once Maggie gives up his location.
This whole thing has become a mess. We need to go at Ms. Underwood another way.
N-GEN
N-GEN
Yes, Ms. Fallon. Right away.
Fuck!
Okay, calm down.
Go screw yourself, shitbird!
I'm gonna get you cleared to move, and then we're going back to the 7-8.
X
And you're gonna wish you'd been a little more polite.
Let me go! LET ME GO!
Should have released me when you had the chance. You have no idea what's coming...

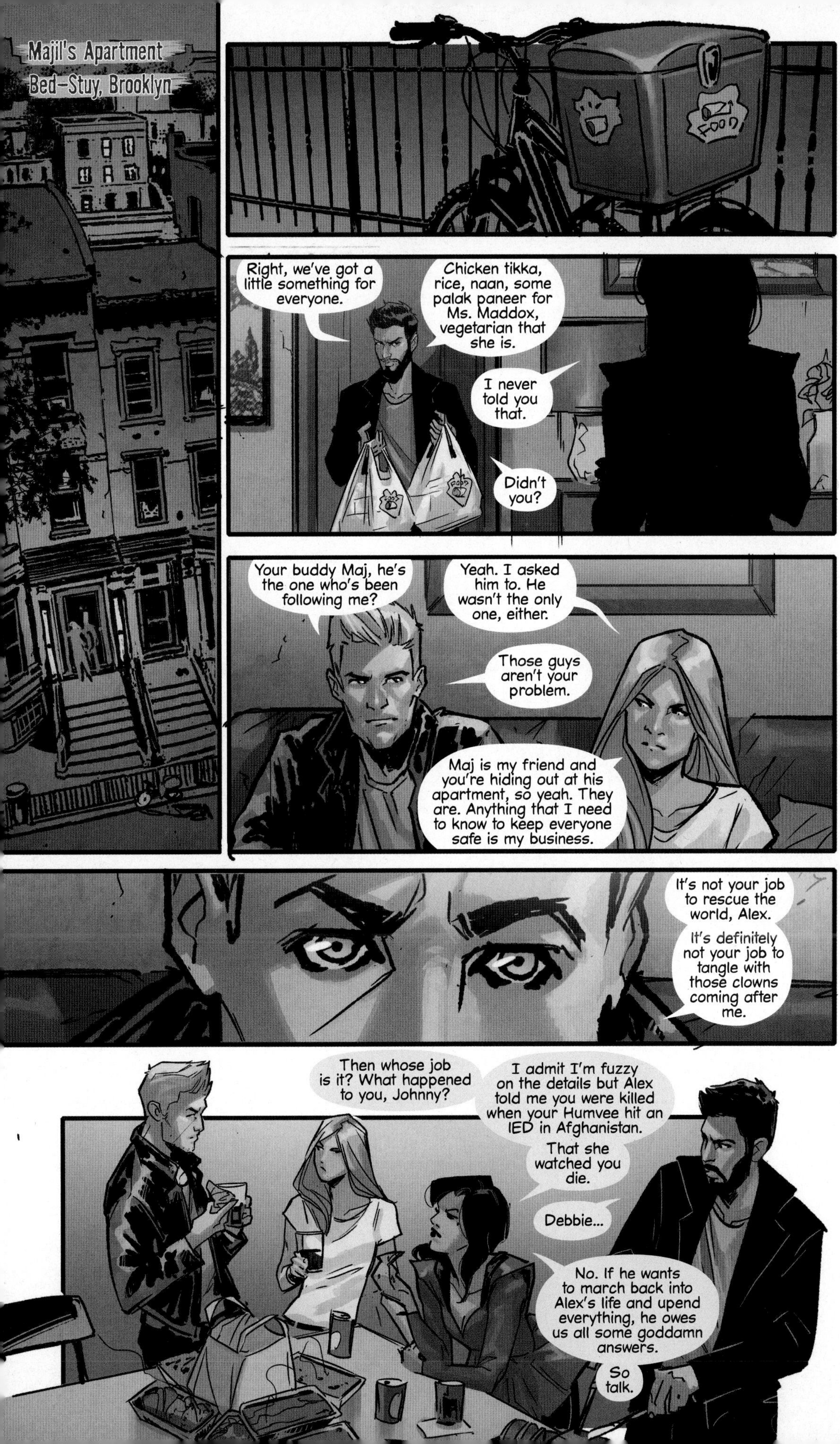
Majil's Apartment
Bed-Stuy, Brooklyn
FOOD
Right, we've got a little something for everyone.
Chicken tikka, rice, naan, some palak paneer for Ms. Maddox, vegetarian that she is.
I never told you that.
Didn't you?
Your buddy Maj, he's the one who's been following me?
Yeah. I asked him to. He wasn't the only one, either.
Those guys aren't your problem.
Maj is my friend and you're hiding out at his apartment, so yeah. They are. Anything that I need to know to keep everyone safe is my business.
It's not your job to rescue the world, Alex.
It's definitely not your job to tangle with those clowns coming after me.
Then whose job is it? What happened to you, Johnny?
I admit I'm fuzzy on the details but Alex told me you were killed when your Humvee hit an IED in Afghanistan.
That she watched you die.
Debbie...
No. If he wants to march back into Alex's life and upend everything, he owes us all some goddamn answers.
So talk.

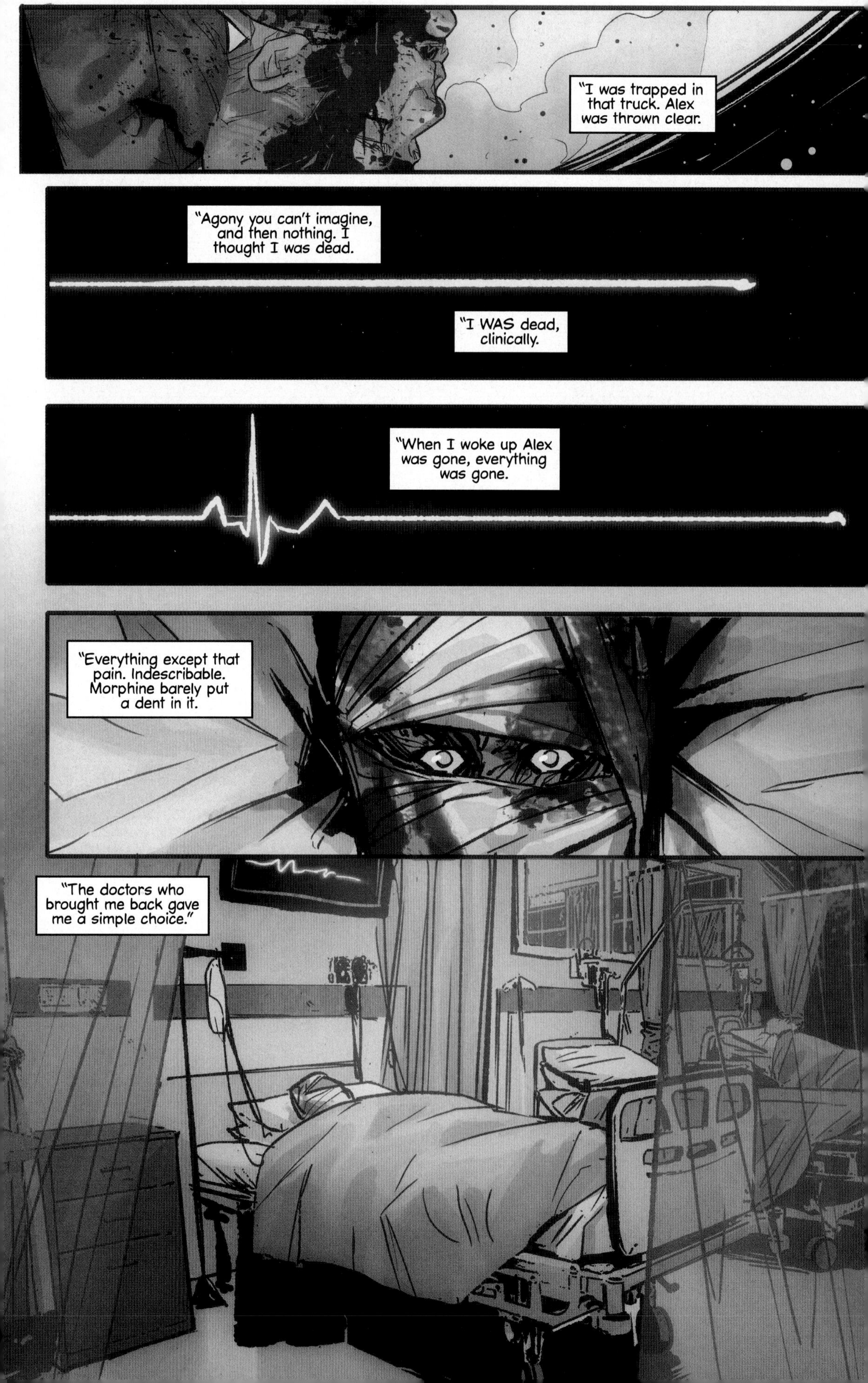
"I was trapped in that truck. Alex was thrown clear.
"Agony you can't imagine, and then nothing. I thought I was dead.
"I WAS dead, clinically.
"When I woke up Alex was gone, everything was gone.
"Everything except that pain. Indescribable. Morphine barely put a dent in it.
"The doctors who brought me back gave me a simple choice."

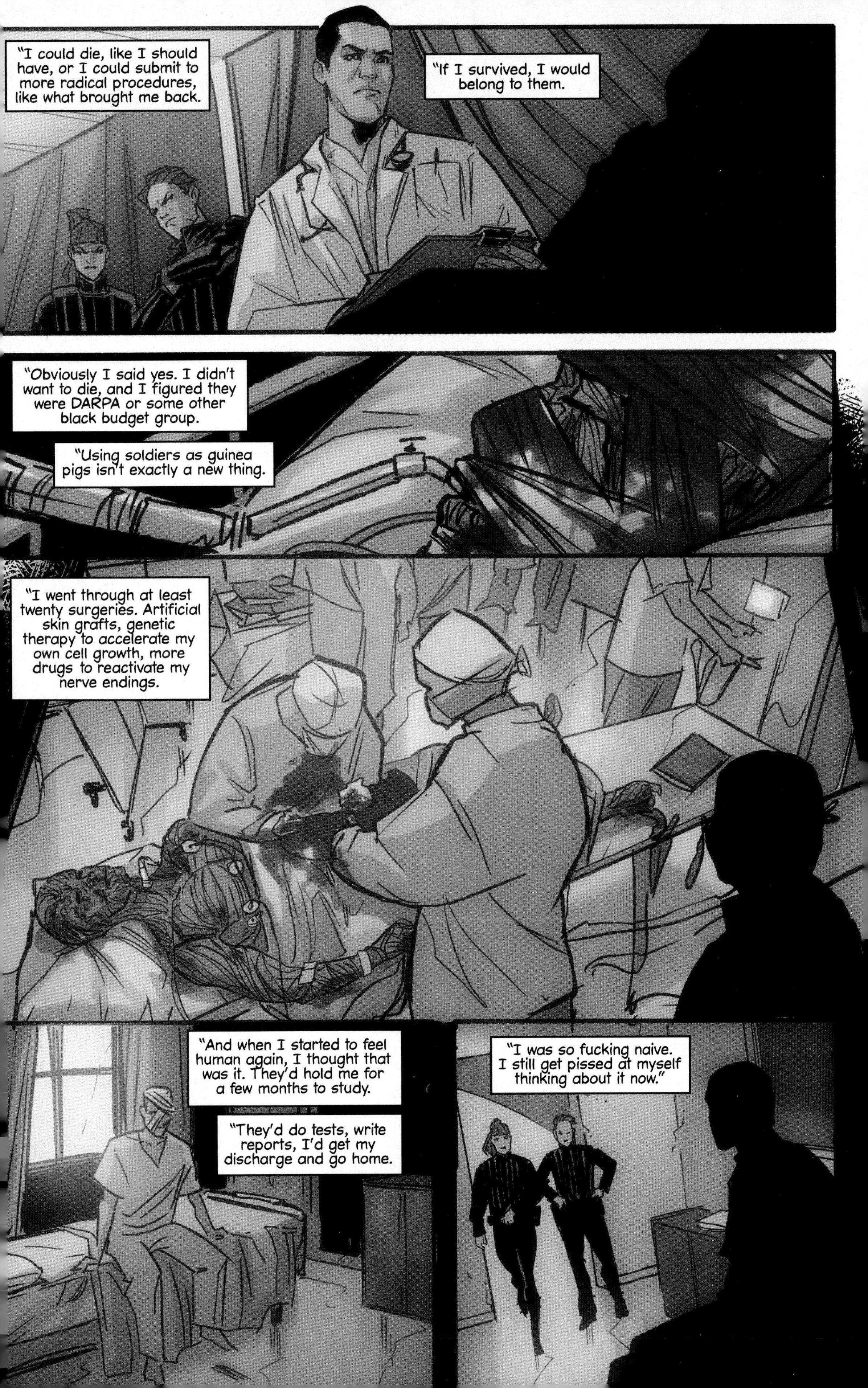
"I could die, like I should have, or I could submit to more radical procedures, like what brought me back.
"If I survived, I would belong to them.
"Obviously I said yes. I didn't want to die, and I figured they were DARPA or some other black budget group.
"Using soldiers as guinea pigs isn't exactly a new thing.
"I went through at least twenty surgeries. Artificial skin grafts, genetic therapy to accelerate my own cell growth, more drugs to reactivate my nerve endings.
"And when I started to feel human again, I thought that was it. They'd hold me for a few months to study.
"They'd do tests, write reports, I'd get my discharge and go home.
"I was so fucking naive. I still get pissed at myself thinking about it now."

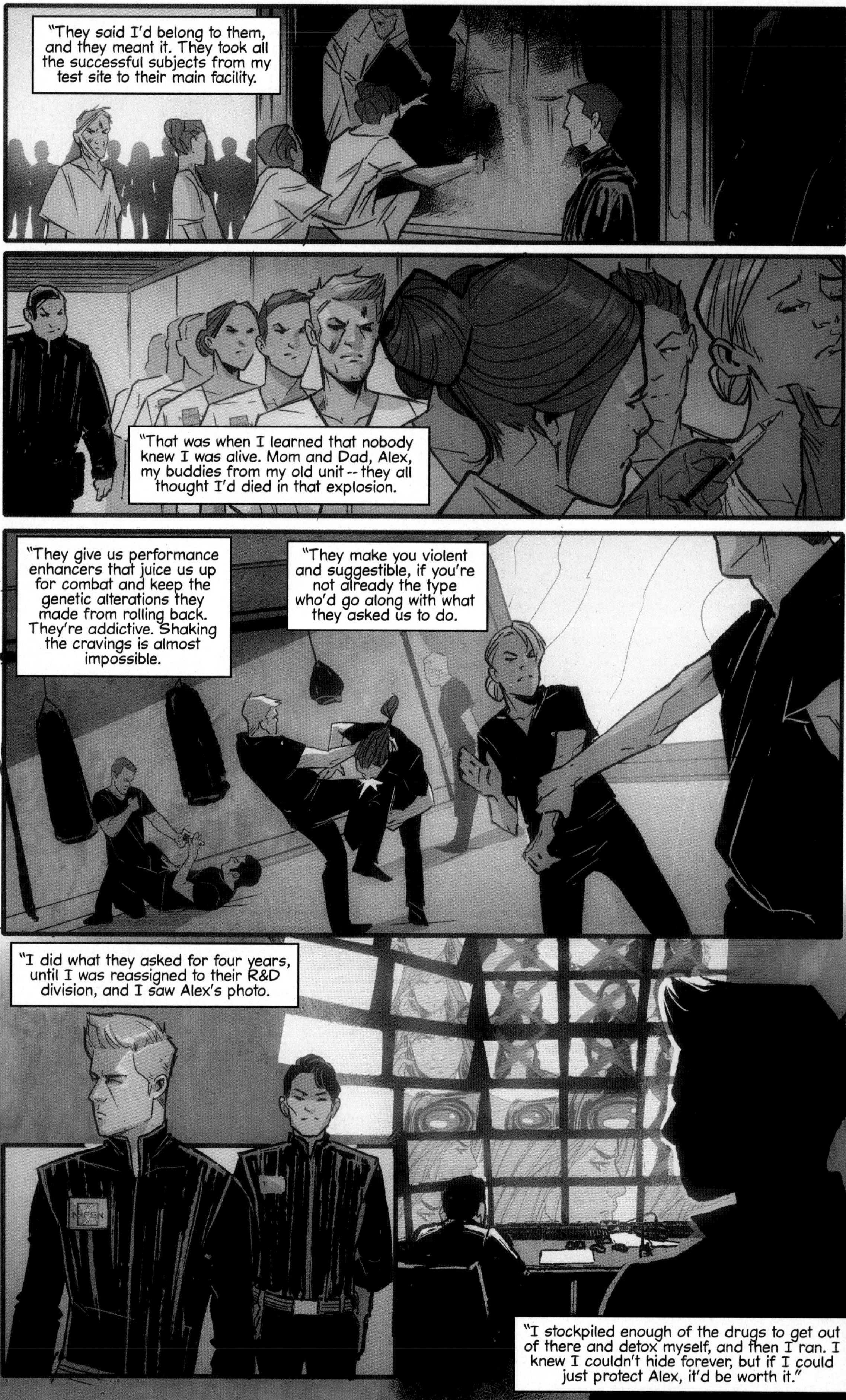
"They said I'd belong to them, and they meant it. They took all the successful subjects from my test site to their main facility.
"That was when I learned that nobody knew I was alive. Mom and Dad, Alex, my buddies from my old unit -- they all thought I'd died in that explosion.
"They give us performance enhancers that juice us up for combat and keep the genetic alterations they made from rolling back. They're addictive. Shaking the cravings is almost impossible.
"They make you violent and suggestible, if you're not already the type who'd go along with what they asked us to do.
"I did what they asked for four years, until I was reassigned to their R&D division, and I saw Alex's photo.
"I stockpiled enough of the drugs to get out of there and detox myself, and then I ran. I knew I couldn't hide forever, but if I could just protect Alex, it'd be worth it."

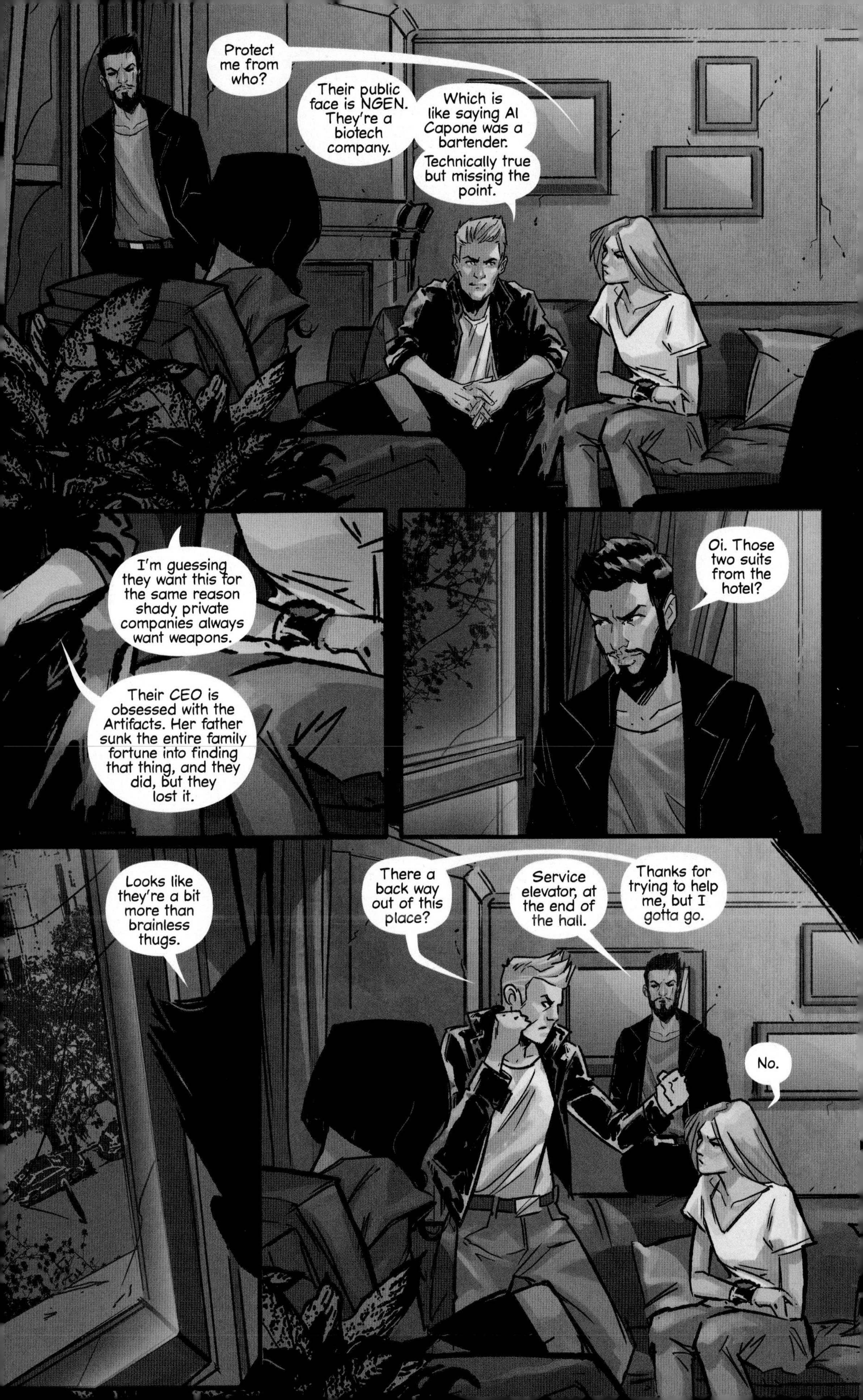
Protect me from who?
Their public face is NGEN. They're a biotech company.
Which is like saying Al Capone was a bartender.
Technically true but missing the point.
I'm guessing they want this for the same reason shady private companies always want weapons.
Their CEO is obsessed with the Artifacts. Her father sunk the entire family fortune into finding that thing, and they did, but they lost it.
Oi. Those two suits from the hotel?
Looks like they're a bit more than brainless thugs.
There a back way out of this place?
Service elevator, at the end of the hall.
Thanks for trying to help me, but I gotta go.
No.

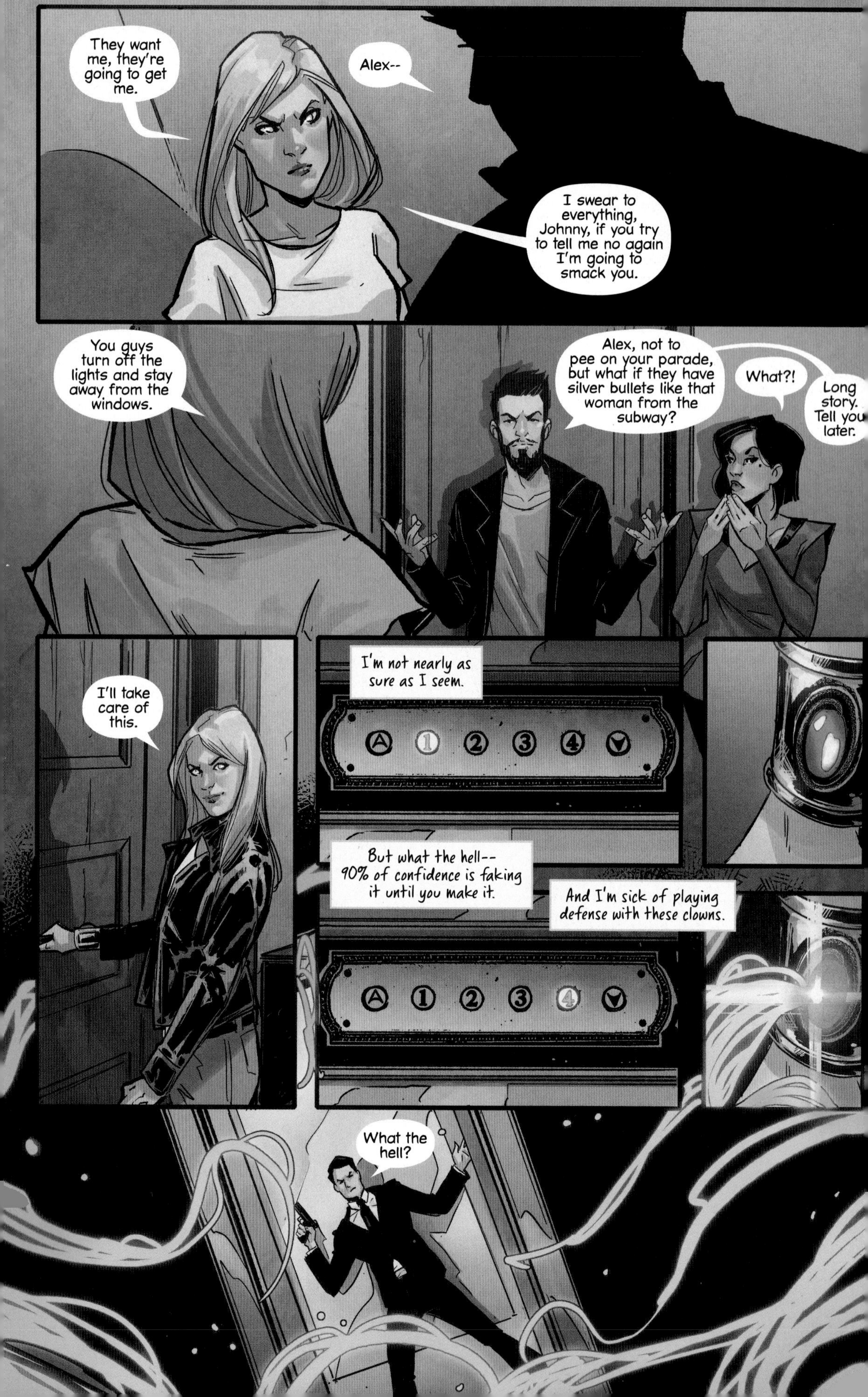
They want me, they're going to get me.
Alex--
I swear to everything, Johnny, if you try to tell me no again I'm going to smack you.
You guys turn off the lights and stay away from the windows.
Alex, not to pee on your parade, but what if they have silver bullets like that woman from the subway?
What?!
Long story. Tell you later.
I'll take care of this.
I'm not nearly as sure as I seem.
A 1 2 3 4
But what the hell-- 90% of confidence is faking it until you make it.
And I'm sick of playing defense with these clowns.
A 1 2 3 4
What the hell?

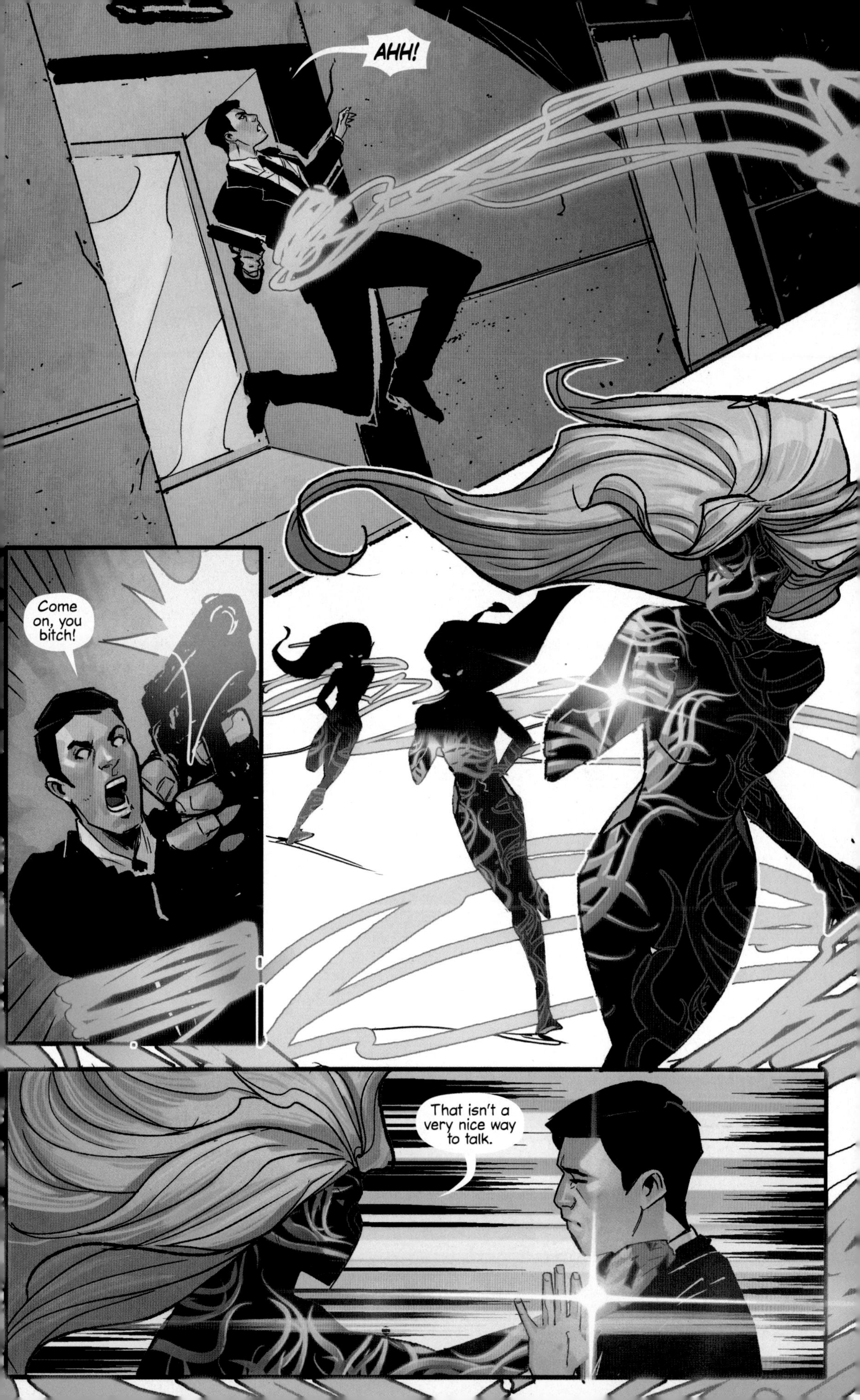
AHH!
Come on, you bitch!
That isn't a very nice way to talk.

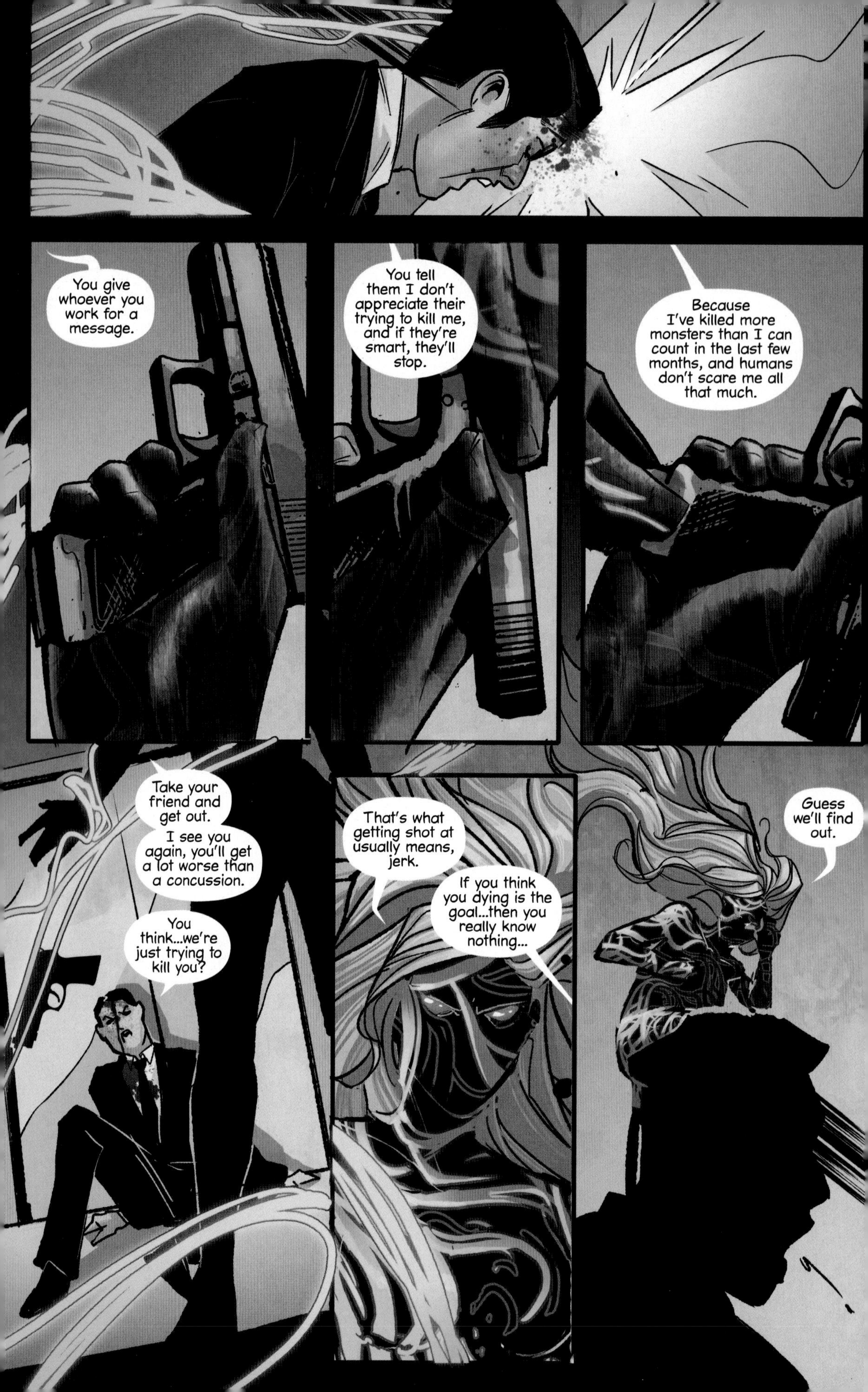
You give whoever you work for a message.
You tell them I don't appreciate their trying to kill me, and if they're smart, they'll stop.
Because I've killed more monsters than I can count in the last few months, and humans don't scare me all that much.
Take your friend and get out.
I see you again, you'll get a lot worse than a concussion.
You think...we're just trying to kill you?
That's what getting shot at usually means, jerk.
If you think you dying is the goal...then you really know nothing...
Guess we'll find out.

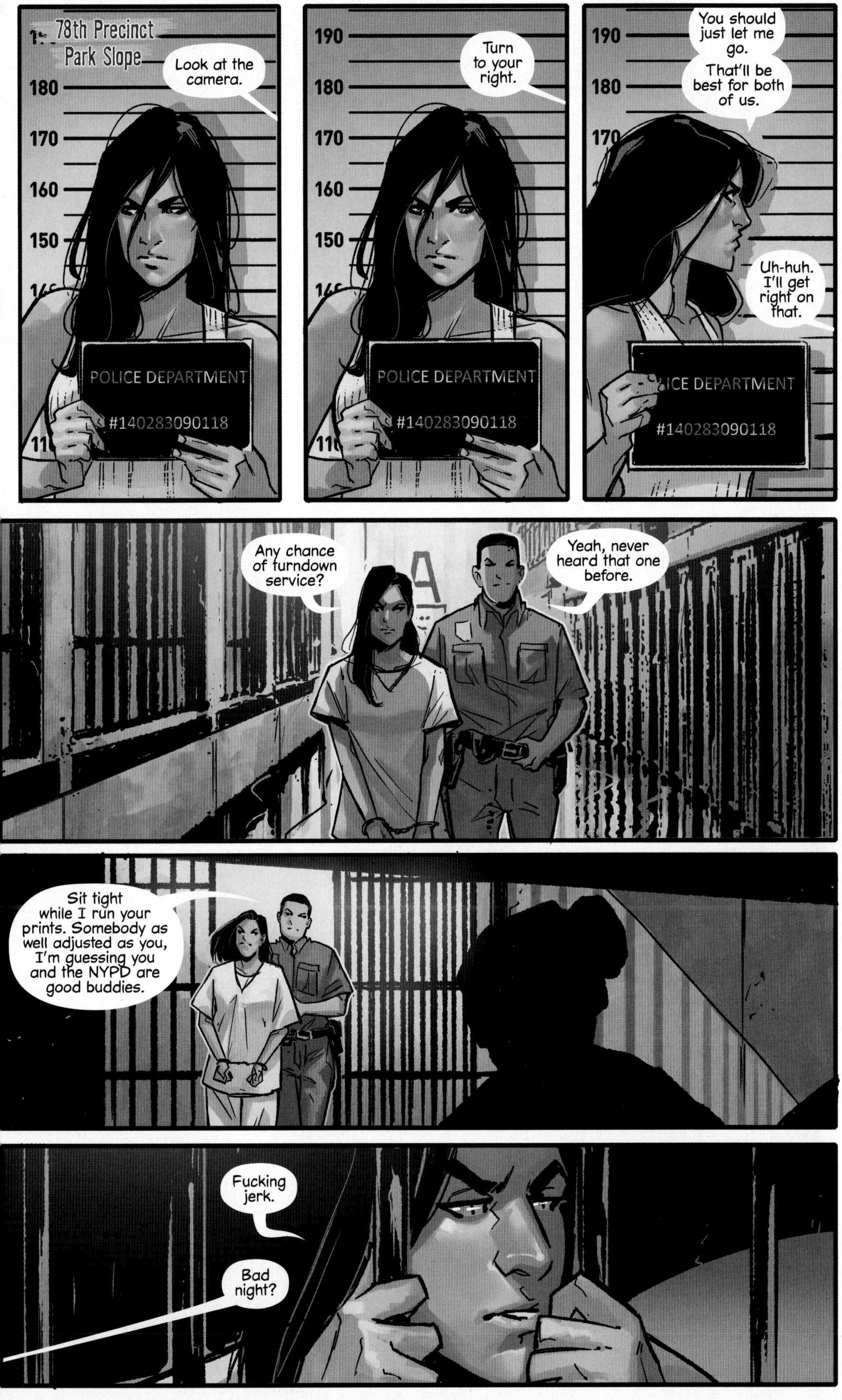
78th Precinct
Park Slope
Look at the camera.
POLICE DEPARTMENT
#140283090118
Turn to your right.
POLICE DEPARTMENT
#140283090118
You should just let me go.
That'll be best for both of us.
Uh-huh. I'll get right on that.
#140283090118
Any chance of turndown service?
Yeah, never heard that one before.
Sit tight while I run your prints. Somebody as well adjusted as you, I'm guessing you and the NYPD are good buddies.
Fucking jerk.
Bad night?

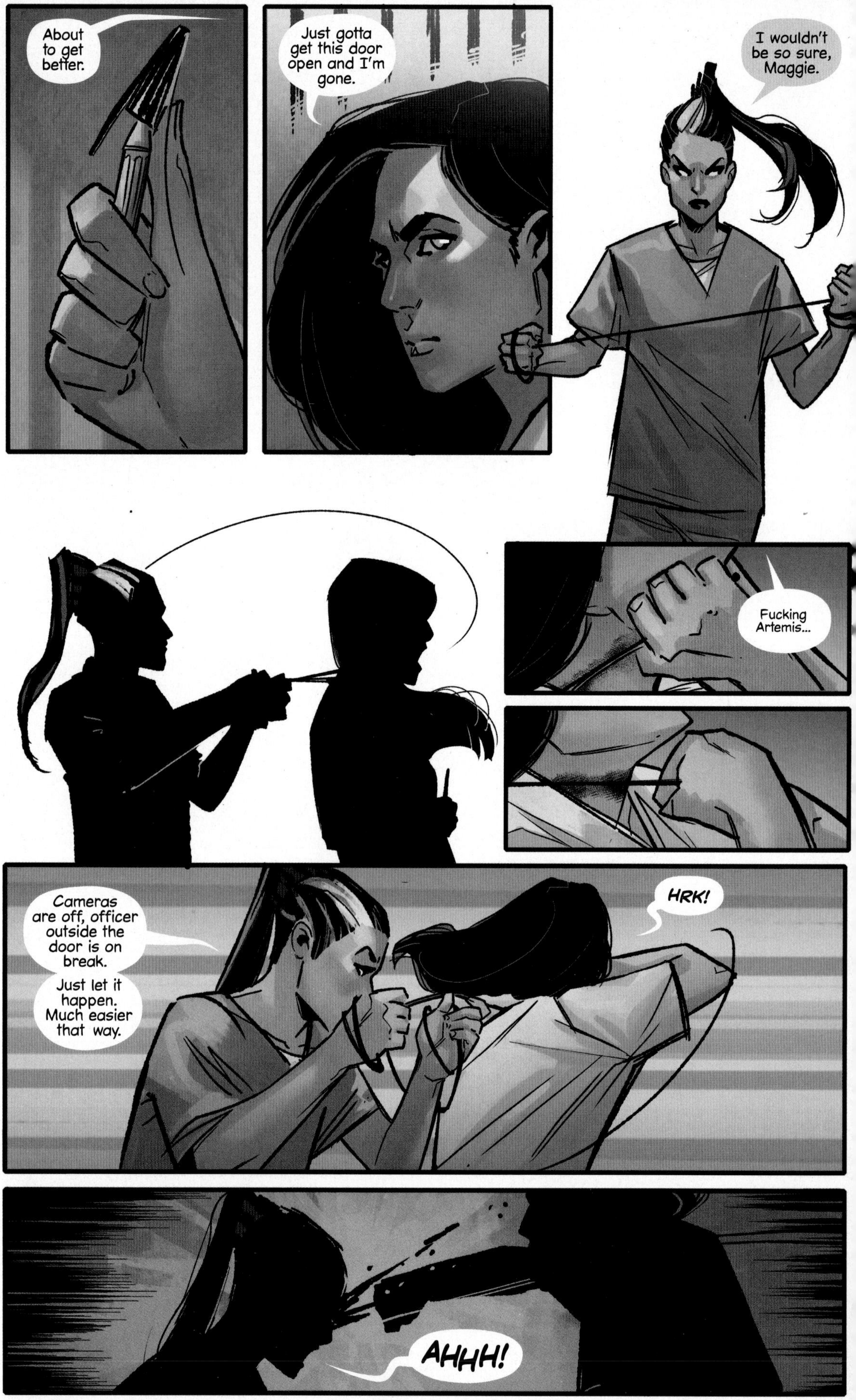
About to get better.
Just gotta get this door open and I'm gone.
I wouldn't be so sure, Maggie.
Fucking Artemis...
Cameras are off, officer outside the door is on break.
Just let it happen. Much easier that way.
HRK!
AHHH!

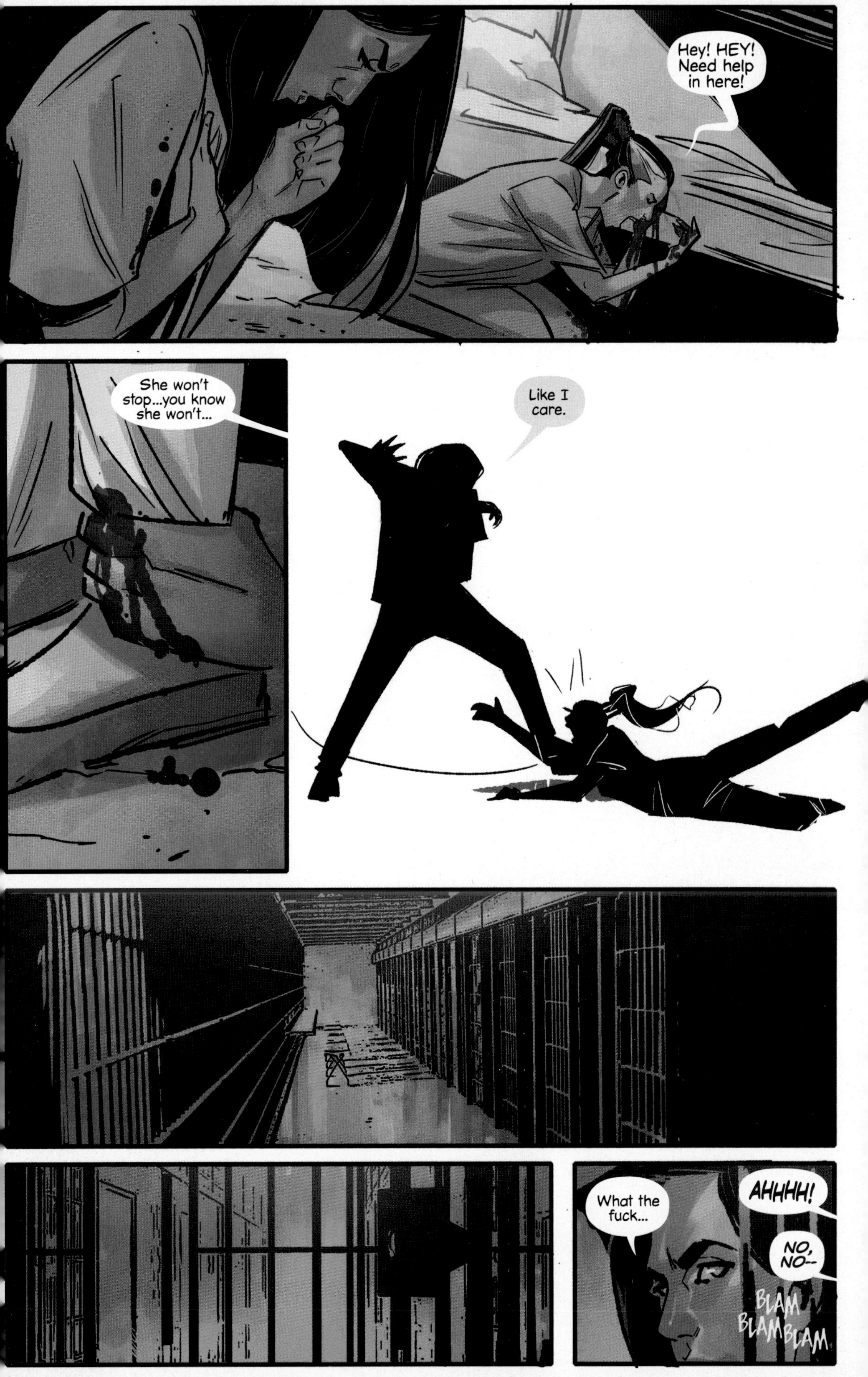
Hey! HEY! Need help in here!
She won't stop...you know she won't...
Like I care.
What the fuck...
AHHHH!
NO, NO--
BLAM BLAM BLAM

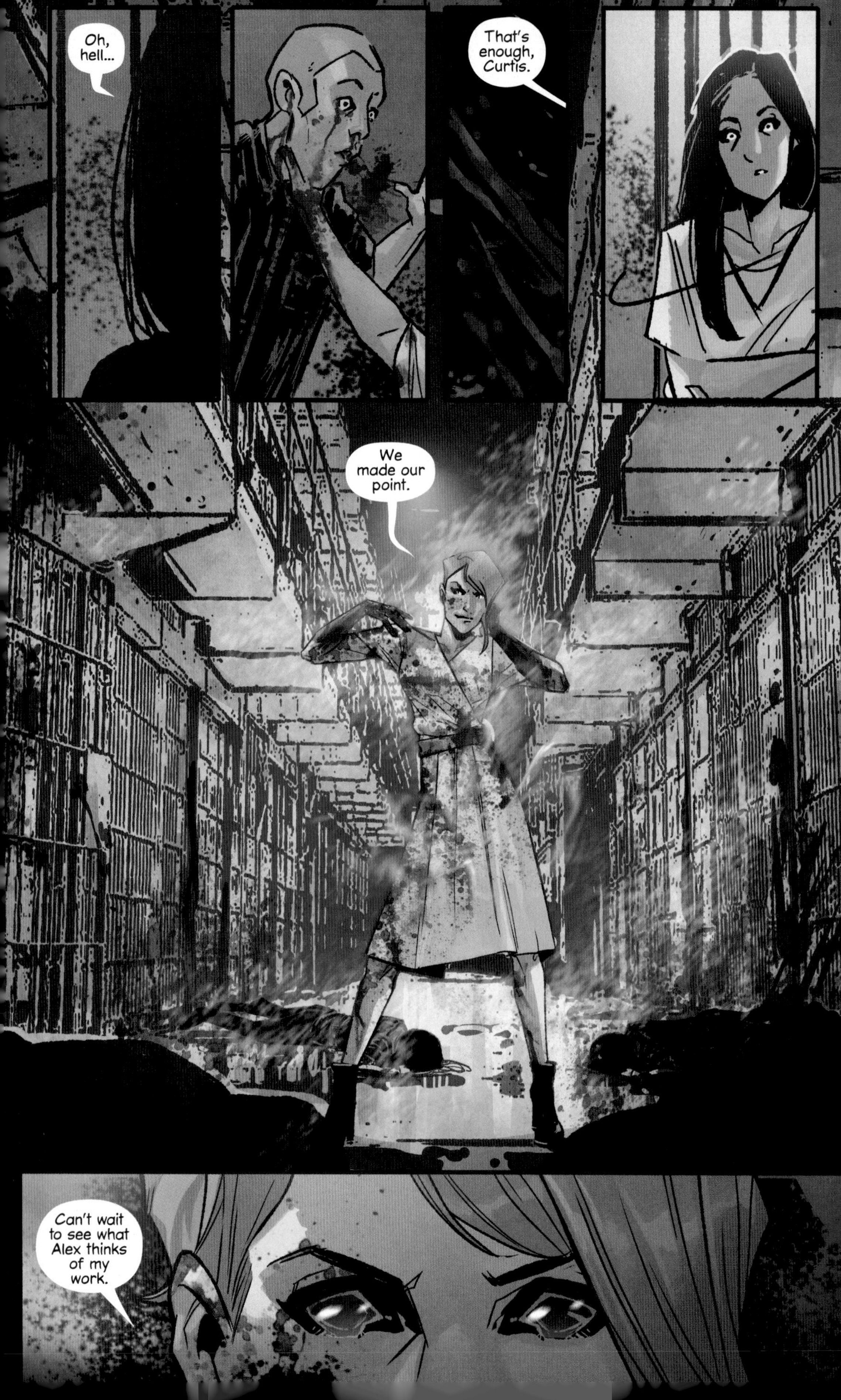
Oh, hell...
That's enough, Curtis.
We made our point.
Can't wait to see what Alex thinks of my work.

CHAPTER NINE

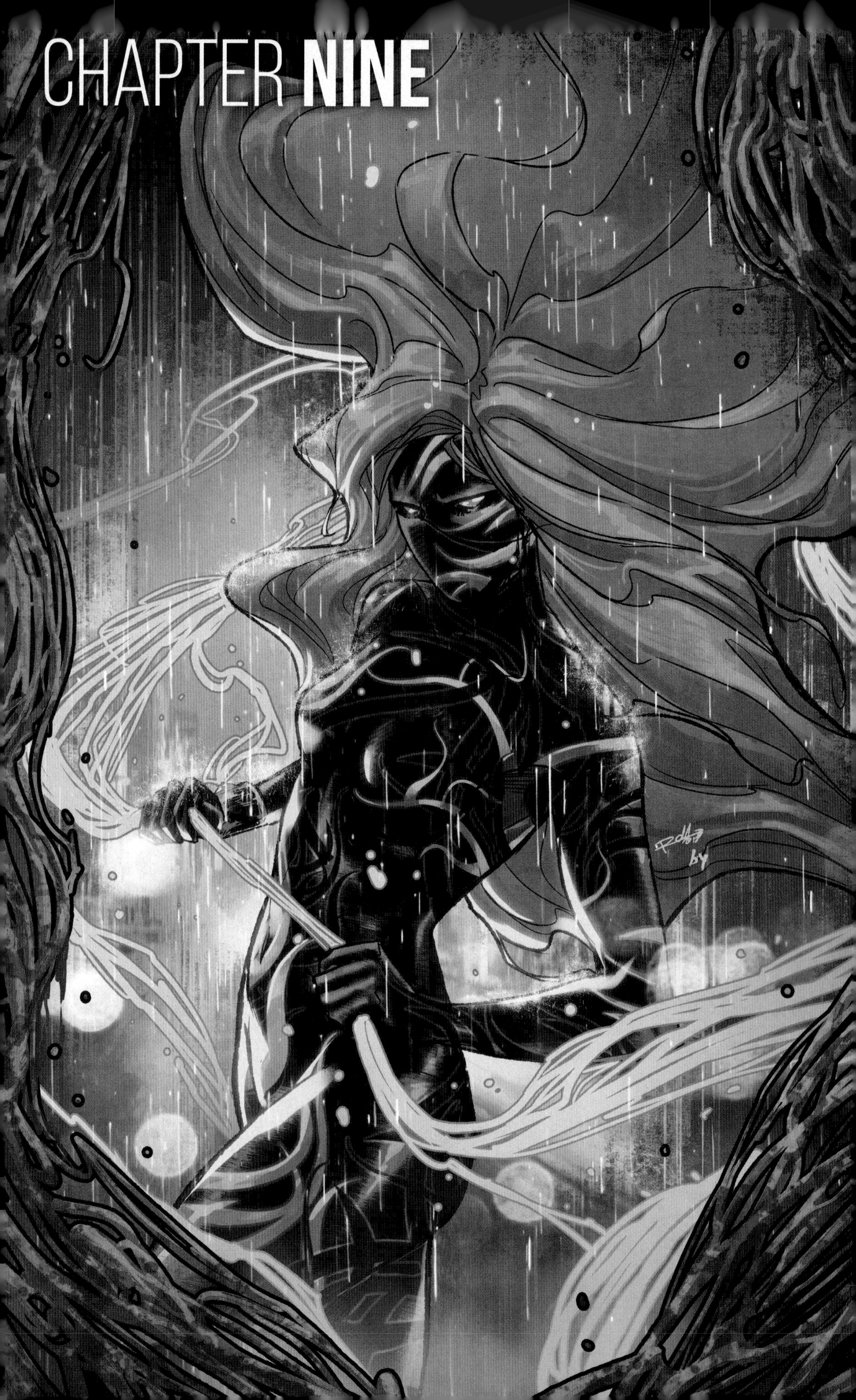

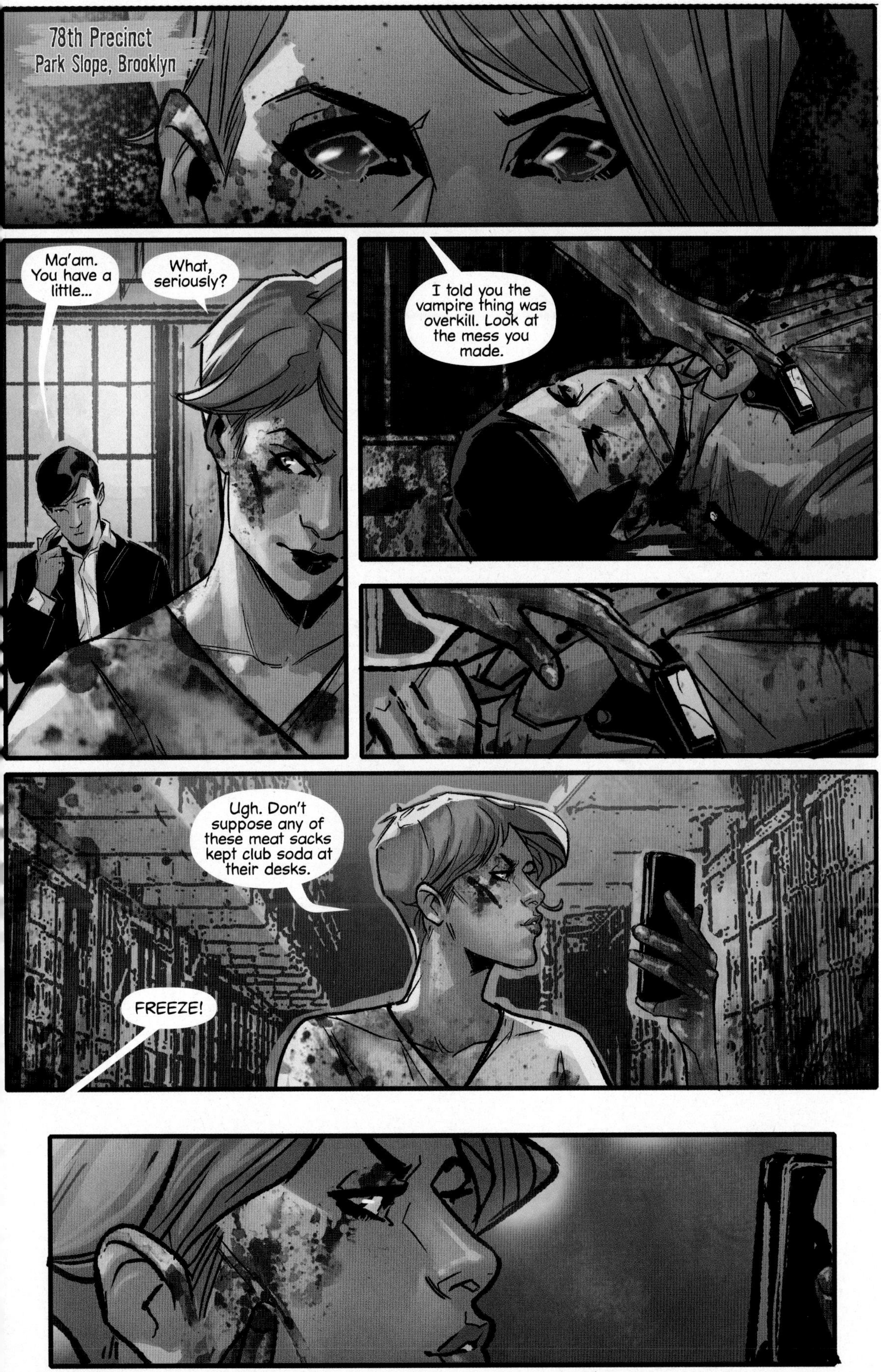
78th Precinct
Park Slope, Brooklyn
Ma'am. You have a little...
What, seriously?
I told you the vampire thing was overkill. Look at the mess you made.
Ugh. Don't suppose any of these meat sacks kept club soda at their desks.
FREEZE!

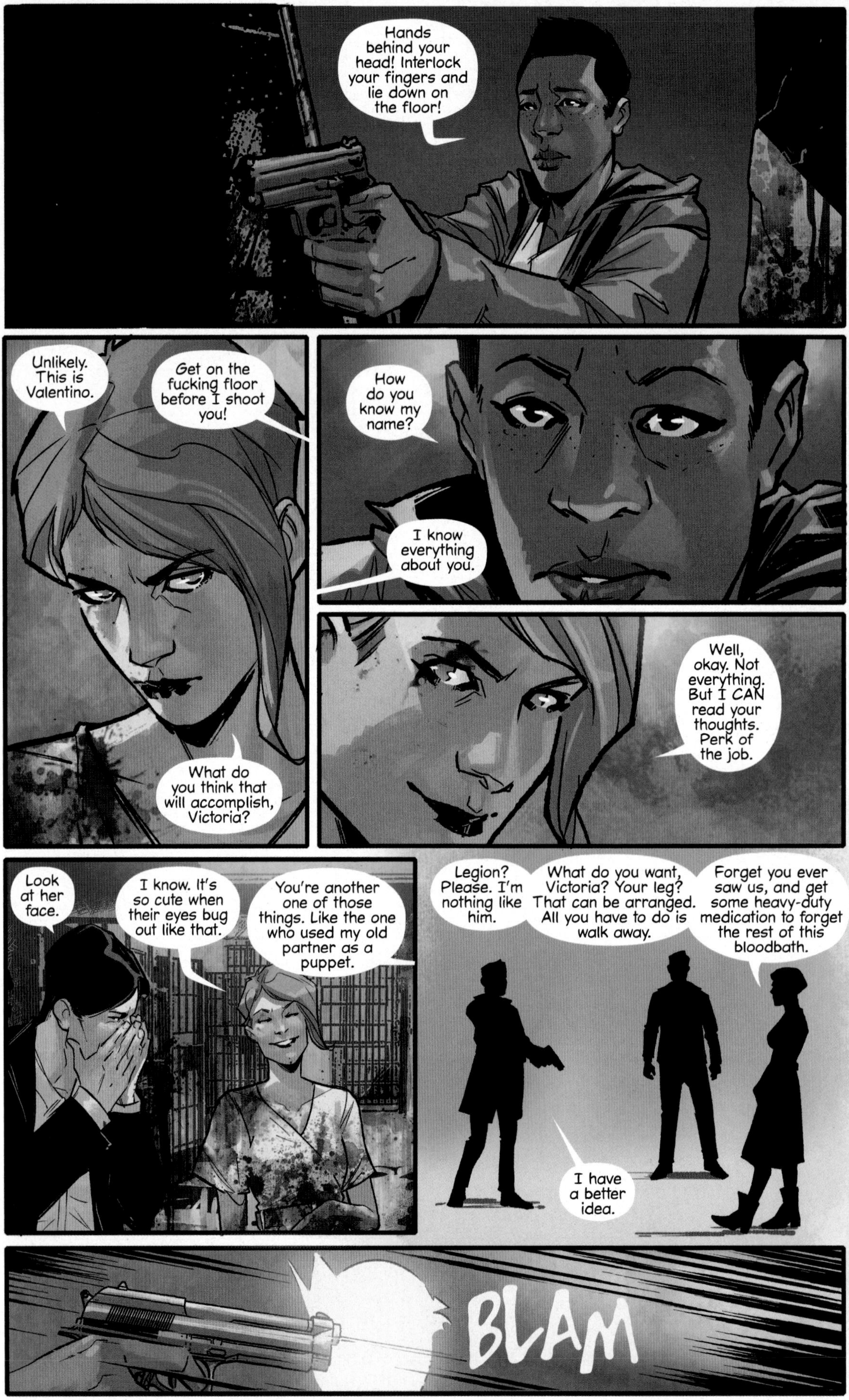
Hands behind your head! Interlock your fingers and lie down on the floor!
Unlikely. This is Valentino.
Get on the fucking floor before I shoot you!
How do you know my name?
I know everything about you.
What do you think that will accomplish, Victoria?
Well, okay. Not everything. But I CAN read your thoughts. Perk of the job.
Look at her face.
I know. It's so cute when their eyes bug out like that.
You're another one of those things. Like the one who used my old partner as a puppet.
Legion? Please. I'm nothing like him.
What do you want, Victoria? Your leg? That can be arranged. All you have to do is walk away.
Forget you ever saw us, and get some heavy-duty medication to forget the rest of this bloodbath.
I have a better idea.
BLAM

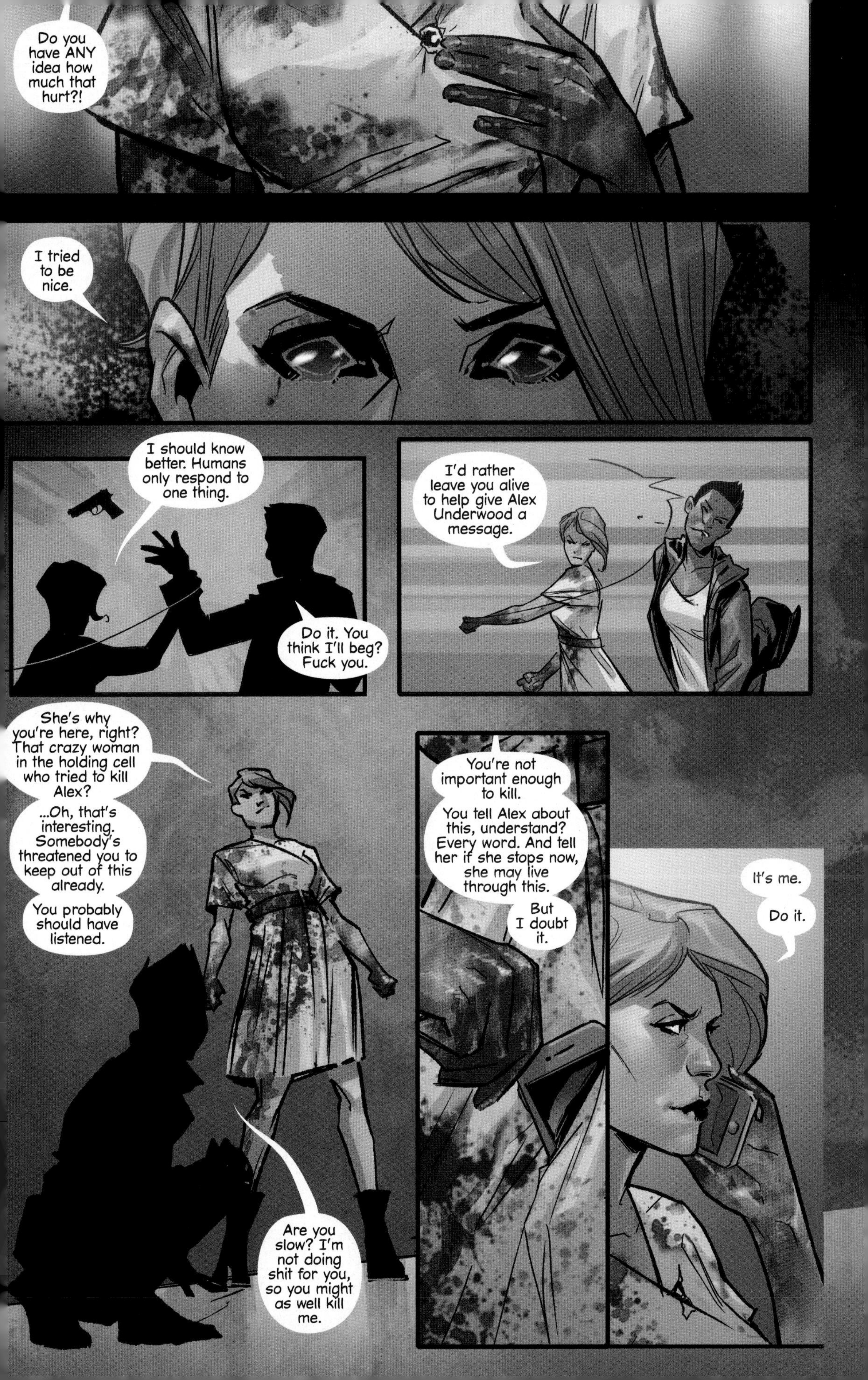
Do you have ANY idea how much that hurt?!
I tried to be nice.
I should know better. Humans only respond to one thing.
Do it. You think I'll beg? Fuck you.
I'd rather leave you alive to help give Alex Underwood a message.
She's why you're here, right? That crazy woman in the holding cell who tried to kill Alex?
...Oh, that's interesting. Somebody's threatened you to keep out of this already.
You probably should have listened.
Are you slow? I'm not doing shit for you, so you might as well kill me.
You're not important enough to kill.
You tell Alex about this, understand? Every word. And tell her if she stops now, she may live through this.
But I doubt it.
It's me.
Do it.

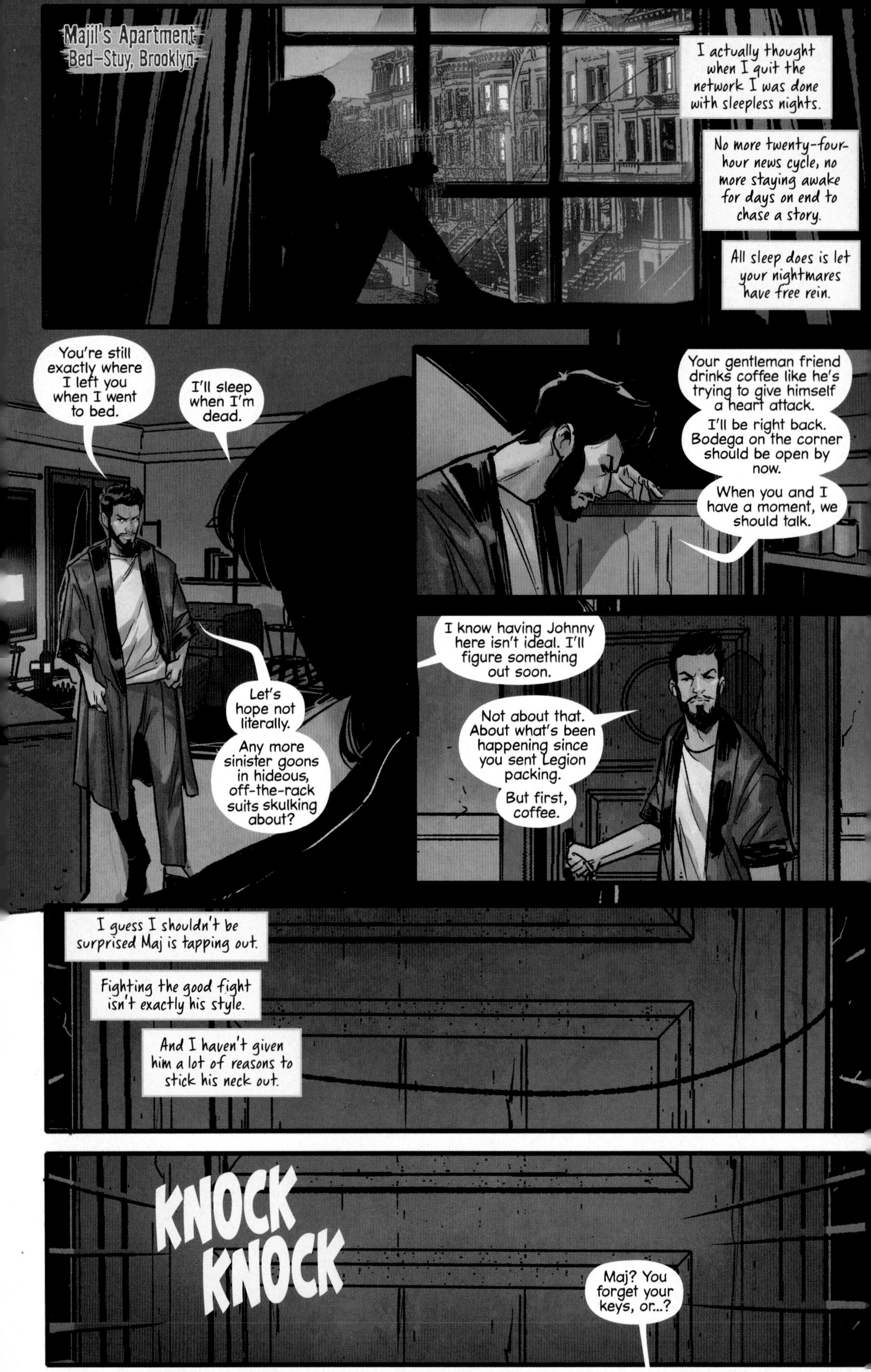
Majil's Apartment
Bed-Stuy, Brooklyn
I actually thought when I quit the network I was done with sleepless nights.
No more twenty-four-hour news cycle, no more staying awake for days on end to chase a story.
All sleep does is let your nightmares have free rein.
You're still exactly where I left you when I went to bed.
I'll sleep when I'm dead.
Let's hope not literally.
Any more sinister goons in hideous, off-the-rack suits skulking about?
Your gentleman friend drinks coffee like he's trying to give himself a heart attack.
I'll be right back. Bodega on the corner should be open by now.
When you and I have a moment, we should talk.
I know having Johnny here isn't ideal. I'll figure something out soon.
Not about that. About what's been happening since you sent Legion packing.
But first, coffee.
I guess I shouldn't be surprised Maj is tapping out.
Fighting the good fight isn't exactly his style.
And I haven't given him a lot of reasons to stick his neck out.
KNOCK KNOCK
Maj? You forget your keys, or...?

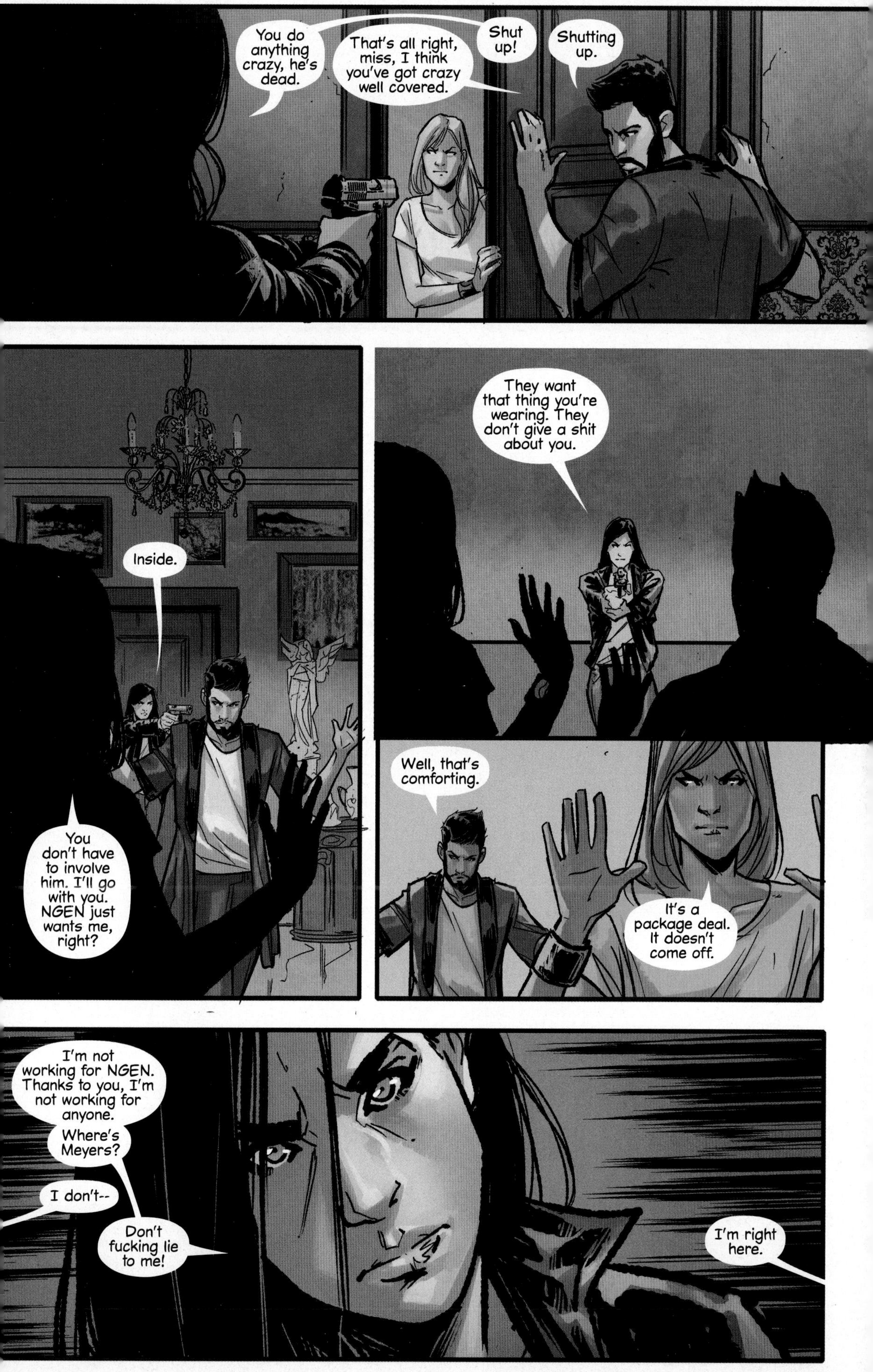
You do anything crazy, he's dead.
That's all right, miss, I think you've got crazy well covered.
Shut up!
Shutting up.
Inside.
You don't have to involve him. I'll go with you. NGEN just wants me, right?
They want that thing you're wearing. They don't give a shit about you.
Well, that's comforting.
It's a package deal. It doesn't come off.
I'm not working for NGEN. Thanks to you, I'm not working for anyone.
Where's Meyers?
I don't--
Don't fucking lie to me!
I'm right here.

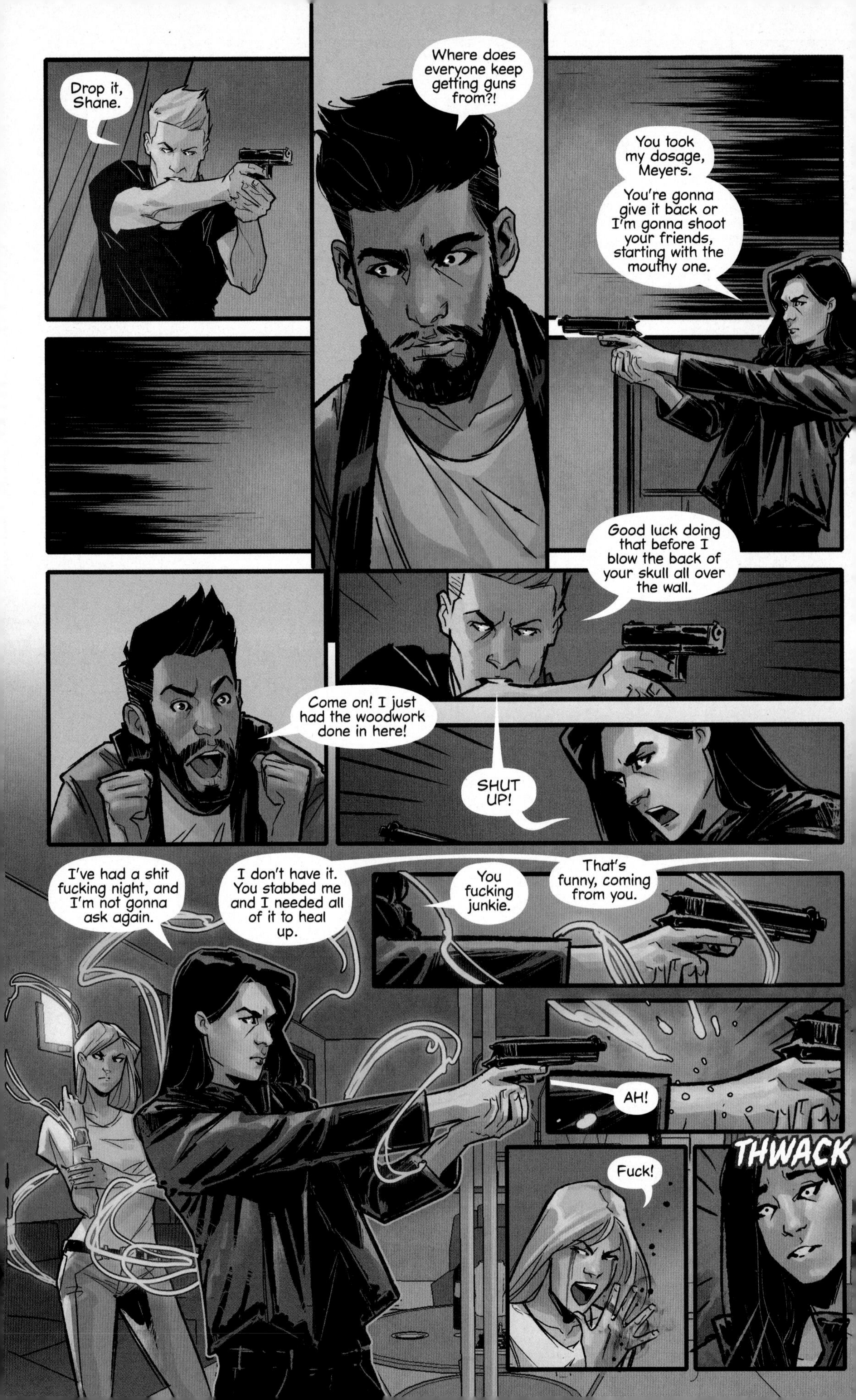

Drop it, Shane.
Where does everyone keep getting guns from?!
You took my dosage, Meyers.
You're gonna give it back or I'm gonna shoot your friends, starting with the mouthy one.
Good luck doing that before I blow the back of your skull all over the wall.
Come on! I just had the woodwork done in here!
SHUT UP!
I've had a shit fucking night, and I'm not gonna ask again.
I don't have it. You stabbed me and I needed all of it to heal up.
You fucking junkie.
That's funny, coming from you.
AH!
Fuck!
THWACK

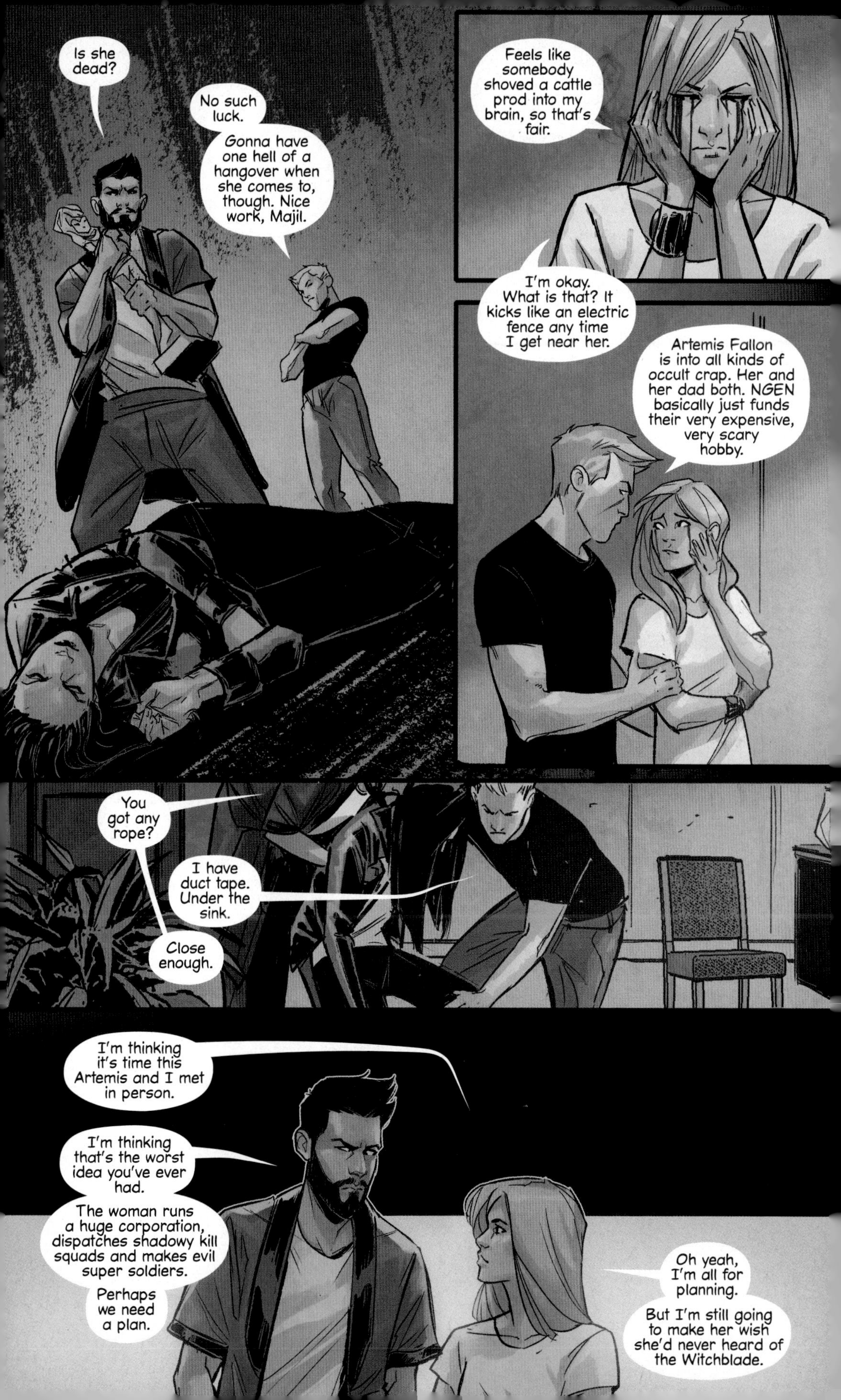
Is she dead?
No such luck.
Gonna have one hell of a hangover when she comes to, though. Nice work, Majil.
Feels like somebody shoved a cattle prod into my brain, so that's fair.
I'm okay. What is that? It kicks like an electric fence any time I get near her.
Artemis Fallon is into all kinds of occult crap. Her and her dad both. NGEN basically just funds their very expensive, very scary hobby.
You got any rope?
I have duct tape. Under the sink.
Close enough.
I'm thinking it's time this Artemis and I met in person.
I'm thinking that's the worst idea you've ever had.
The woman runs a huge corporation, dispatches shadowy kill squads and makes evil super soldiers.
Perhaps we need a plan.
Oh yeah, I'm all for planning.
But I'm still going to make her wish she'd never heard of the Witchblade.

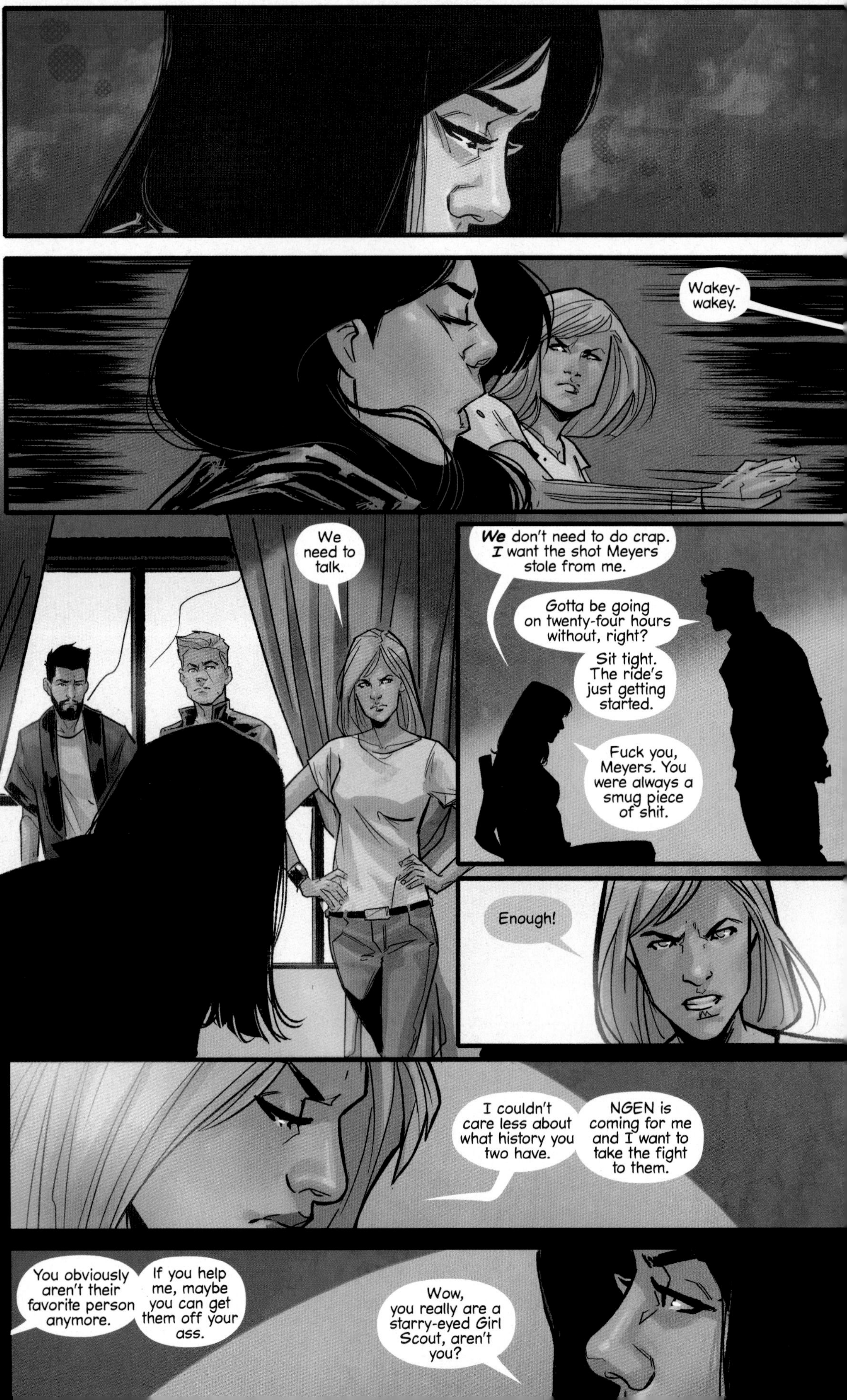

Wakey-wakey.
We need to talk.
We don't need to do crap. *I* want the shot Meyers stole from me.
Gotta be going on twenty-four hours without, right?
Sit tight. The ride's just getting started.
Fuck you, Meyers. You were always a smug piece of shit.
Enough!
I couldn't care less about what history you two have.
NGEN is coming for me and I want to take the fight to them.
You obviously aren't their favorite person anymore.
If you help me, maybe you can get them off your ass.
Wow, you really are a starry-eyed Girl Scout, aren't you?

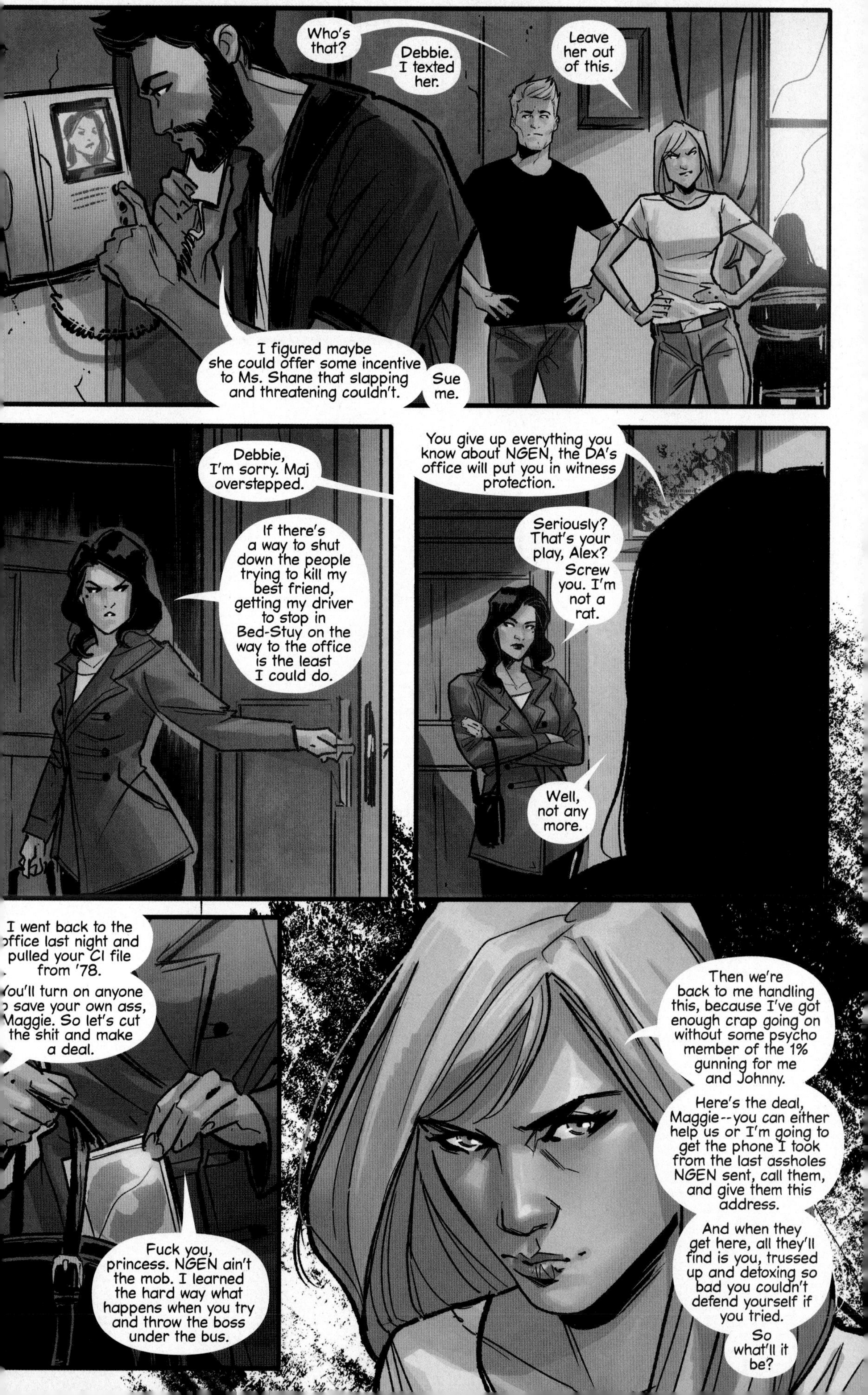
Who's that?
Debbie. I texted her.
Leave her out of this.
I figured maybe she could offer some incentive to Ms. Shane that slapping and threatening couldn't.
Sue me.
Debbie, I'm sorry. Maj overstepped.
If there's a way to shut down the people trying to kill my best friend, getting my driver to stop in Bed-Stuy on the way to the office is the least I could do.
You give up everything you know about NGEN, the DA's office will put you in witness protection.
Seriously? That's your play, Alex?
Screw you. I'm not a rat.
Well, not any more.
I went back to the office last night and pulled your CI file from '78.
You'll turn on anyone to save your own ass, Maggie. So let's cut the shit and make a deal.
Fuck you, princess. NGEN ain't the mob. I learned the hard way what happens when you try and throw the boss under the bus.
Then we're back to me handling this, because I've got enough crap going on without some psycho member of the 1% gunning for me and Johnny.
Here's the deal, Maggie--you can either help us or I'm going to get the phone I took from the last assholes NGEN sent, call them, and give them this address.
And when they get here, all they'll find is you, trussed up and detoxing so bad you couldn't defend yourself if you tried.
So what'll it be?

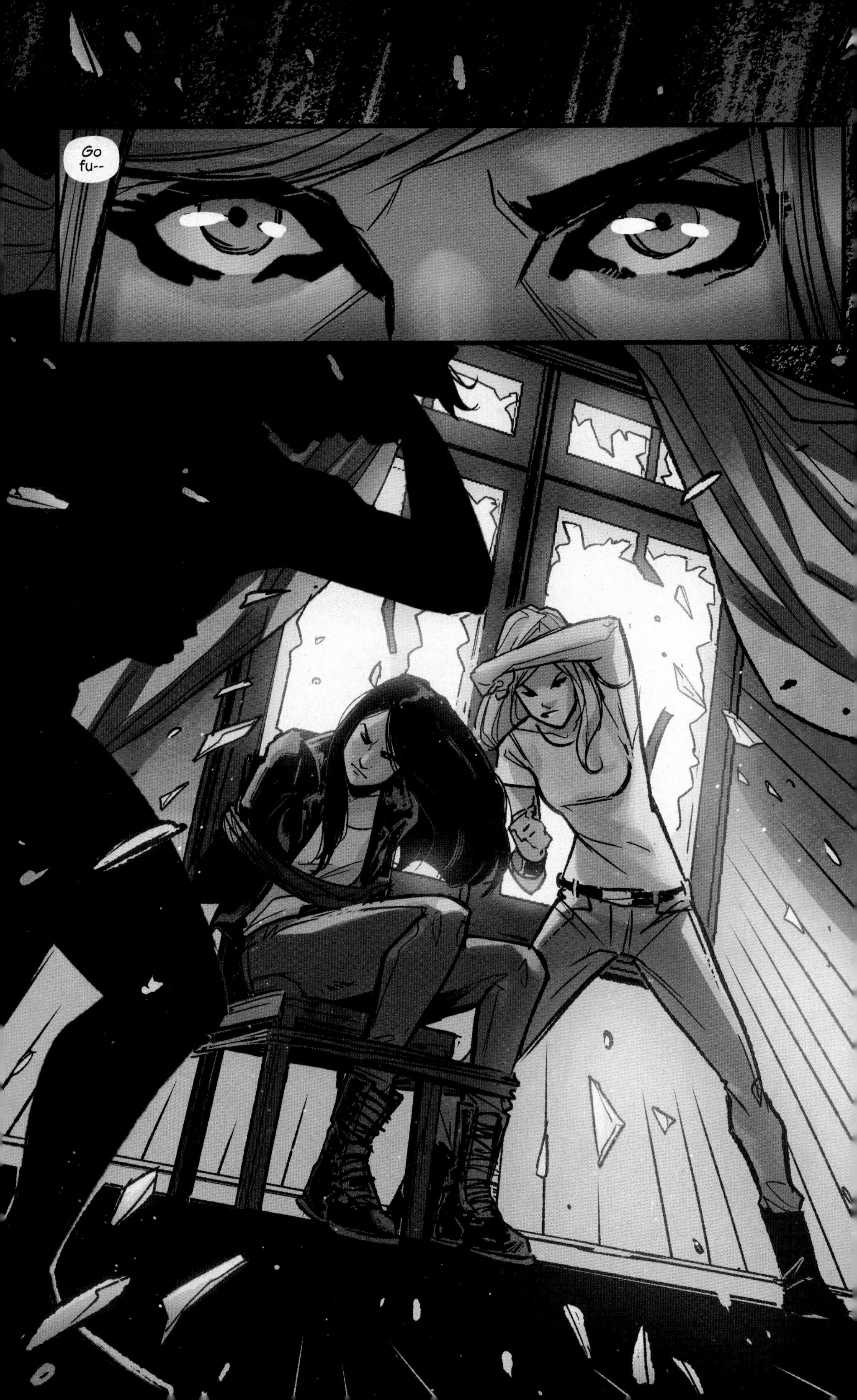
Go fu--

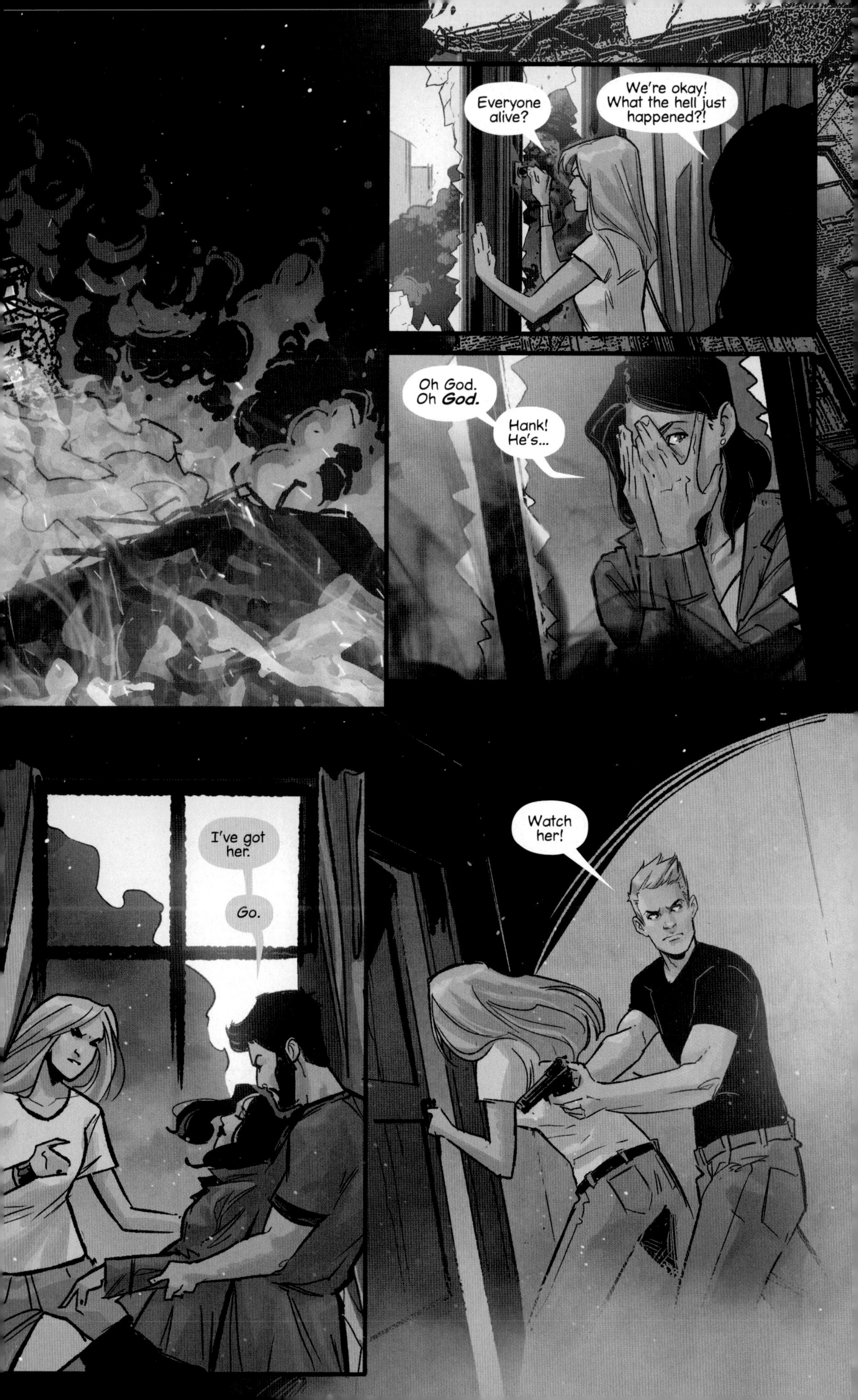
Everyone alive?
We're okay! What the hell just happened?!
Oh God. Oh **God.**
Hank! He's...
I've got her.
Go.
Watch her!

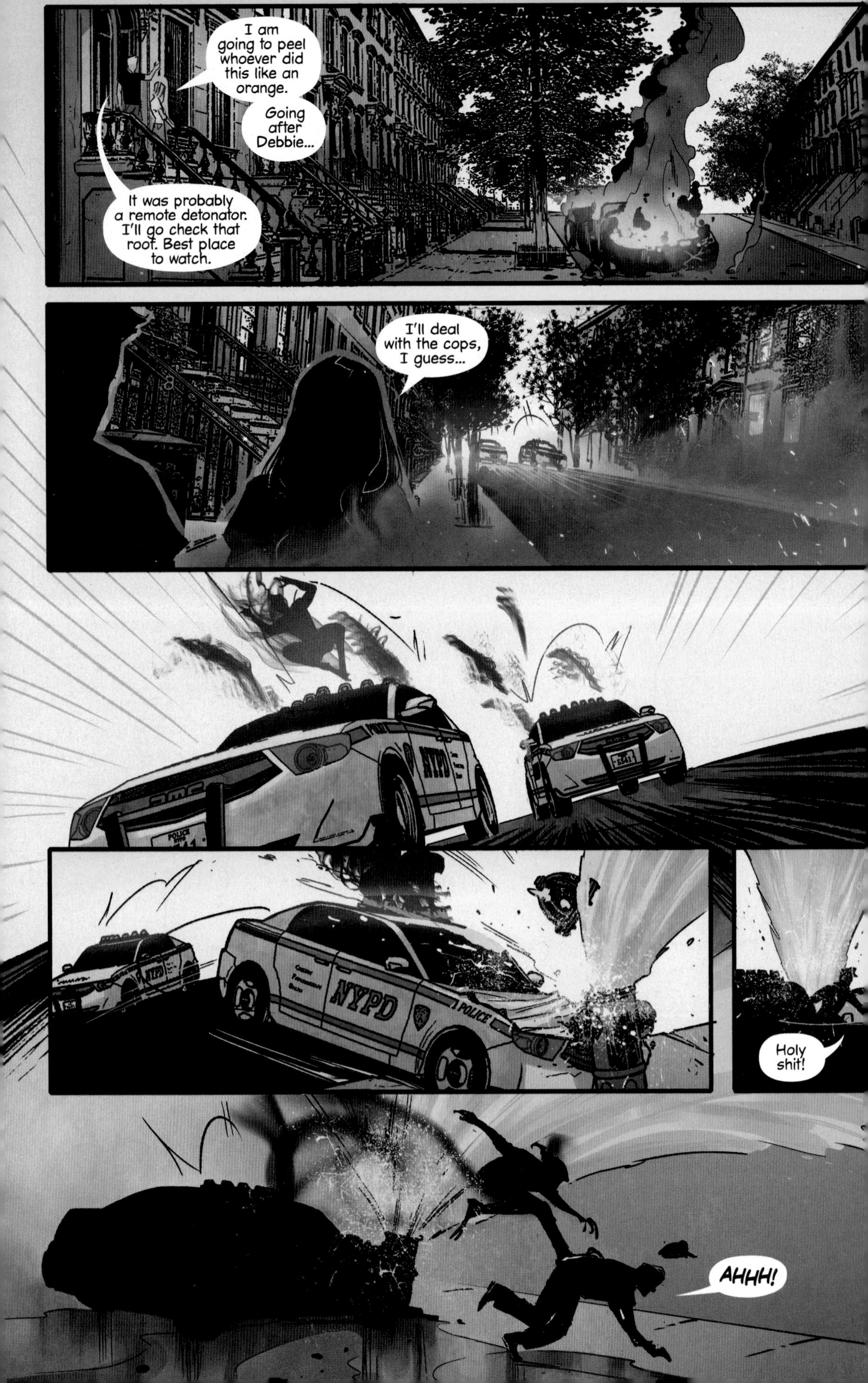
I am going to peel whoever did this like an orange.
Going after Debbie...
It was probably a remote detonator. I'll go check that roof. Best place to watch.
I'll deal with the cops, I guess...
NYPD
NYPD
Holy shit!
AHHH!

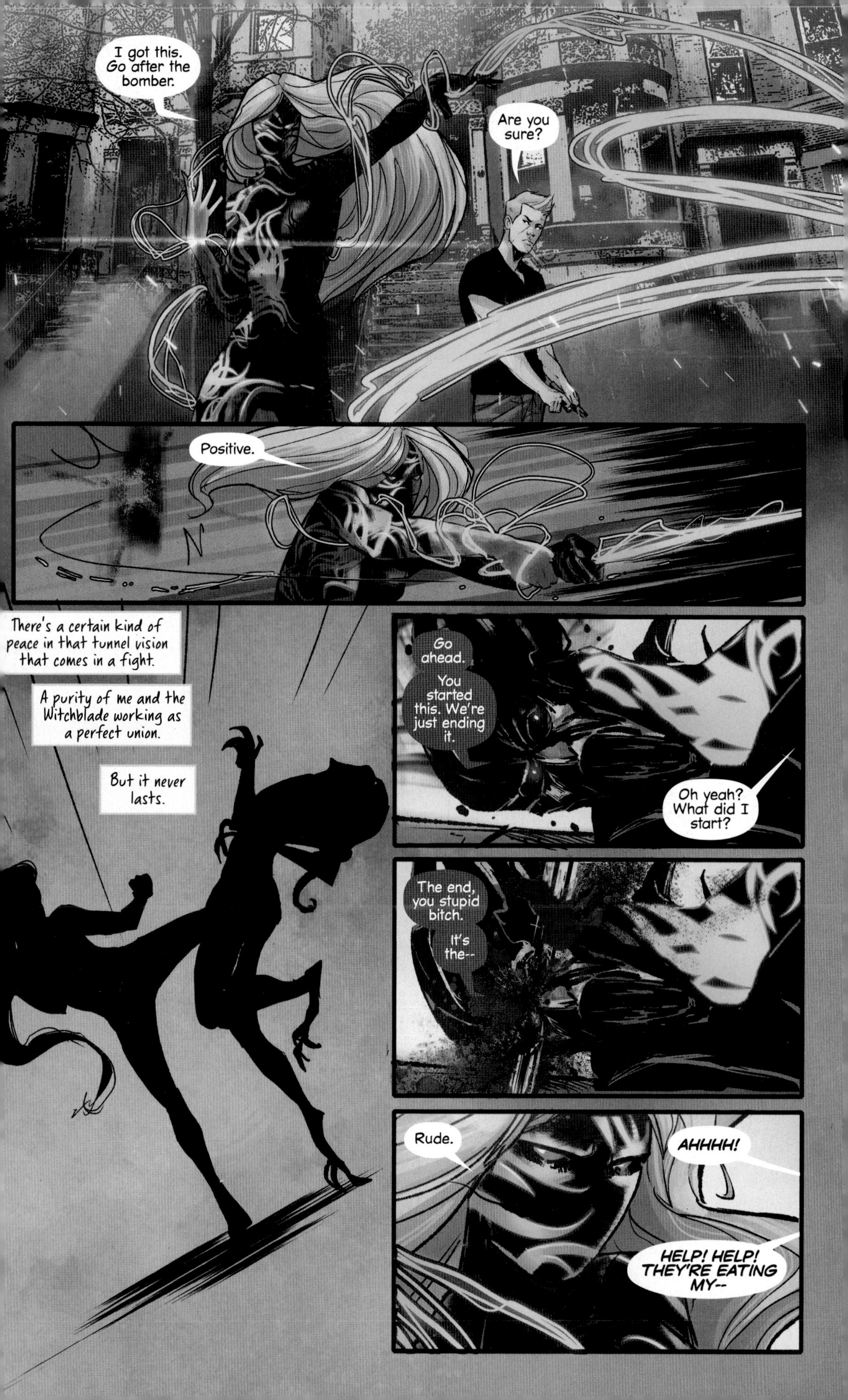
I got this. Go after the bomber.
Are you sure?
Positive.
There's a certain kind of peace in that tunnel vision that comes in a fight.
A purity of me and the Witchblade working as a perfect union.
But it never lasts.
Go ahead.
You started this. We're just ending it.
Oh yeah? What did I start?
The end, you stupid bitch.
It's the--
Rude.
AHHHH!
HELP! HELP! THEY'RE EATING MY--

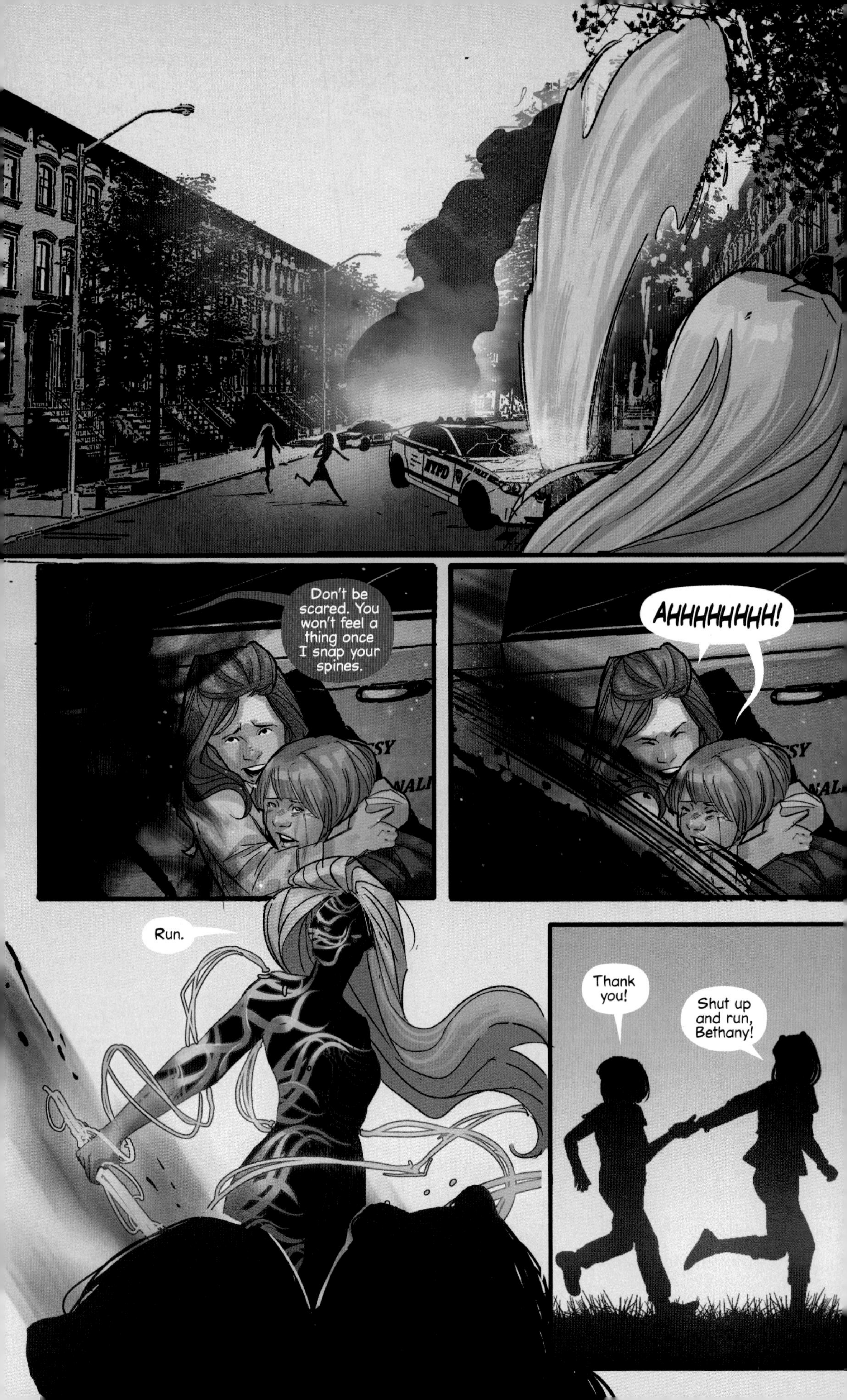
NYPD
Don't be scared. You won't feel a thing once I snap your spines.
AHHHHHHHH!
Run.
Thank you!
Shut up and run, Bethany!

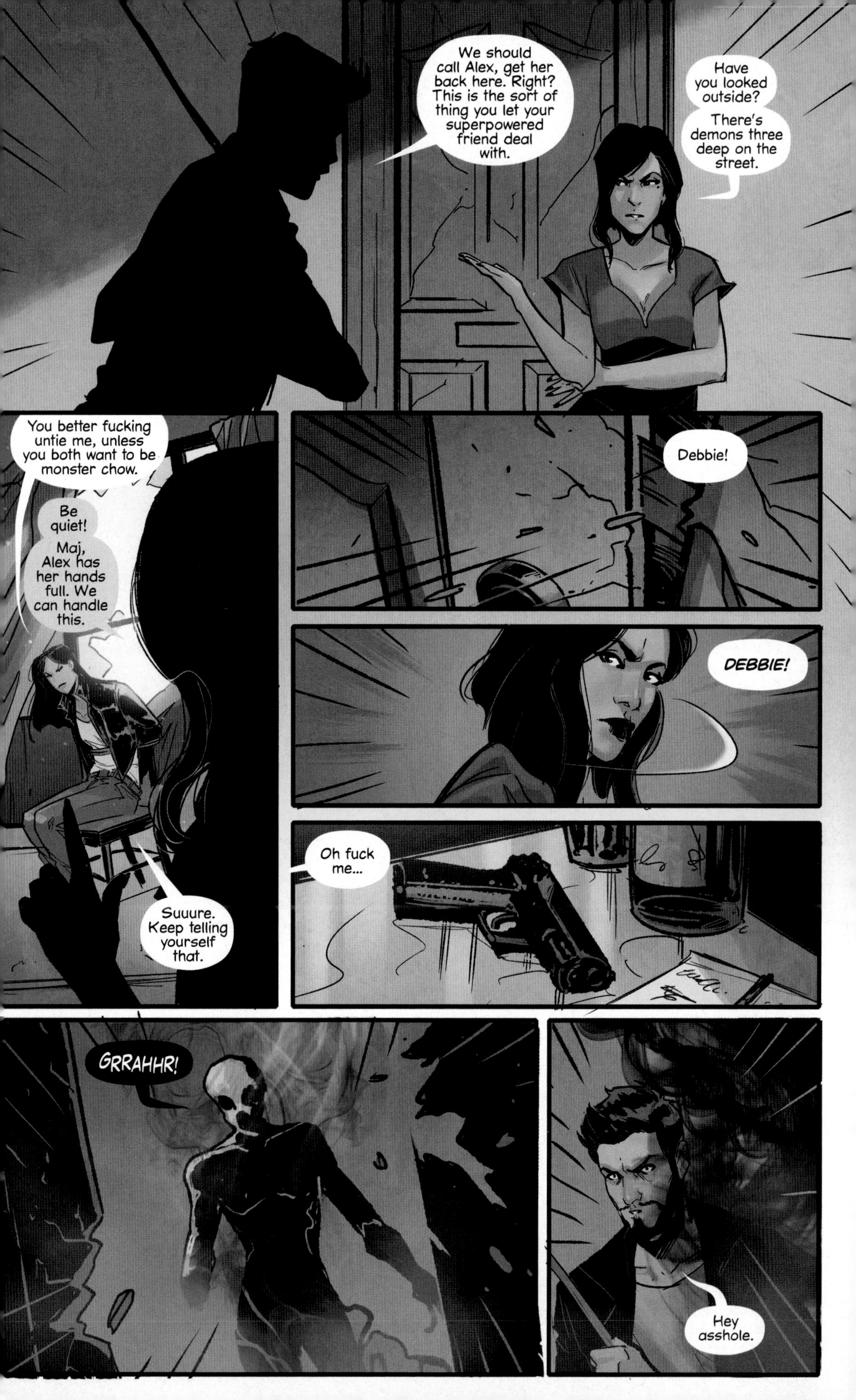
We should call Alex, get her back here. Right? This is the sort of thing you let your superpowered friend deal with.
Have you looked outside?
There's demons three deep on the street.
You better fucking untie me, unless you both want to be monster chow.
Be quiet!
Maj, Alex has her hands full. We can handle this.
Suuure. Keep telling yourself that.
Debbie!
DEBBIE!
Oh fuck me...
GRRAHHR!
Hey asshole.

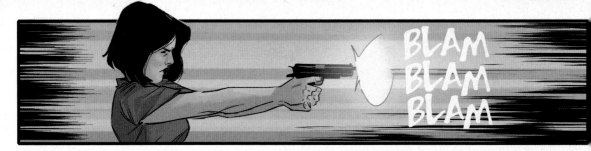

BLAM
BLAM
BLAM

Are you okay?!

Apart from demon brains on my favorite pajamas...yeah.
Never better.

What the hell?

It looks like Fallujah out there. If she can fight, I'm not leaving her taped to a chair.

...Fine. But I don't like it.

Feeling's mutual, Apu.

Oh, charmingly dated racism. I'm enjoying your company more by the second.

Yes! Knew I still had it.
Police scanner.

Jesus, that smells awful. Even for a dead body.

I hope Alex is all right.

I hope she doesn't do anything dumb protecting Johnny.

You don't like him either, I take it.

I don't like liars. I see way too many of them as it is.

Huh. You two aren't as dumb as you look.

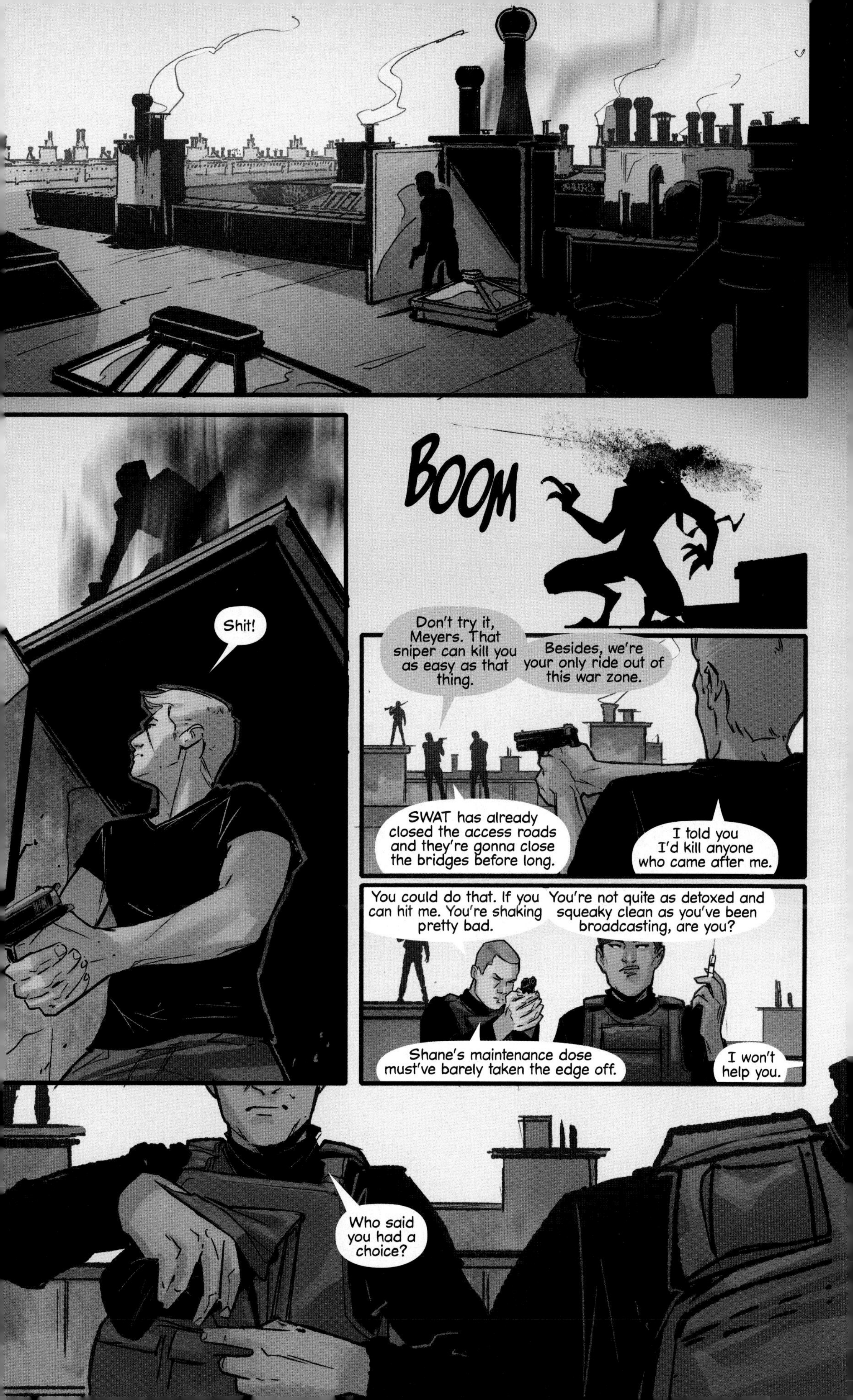

BOOM
Shit!
Don't try it, Meyers. That sniper can kill you as easy as that thing.
Besides, we're your only ride out of this war zone.
SWAT has already closed the access roads and they're gonna close the bridges before long.
I told you I'd kill anyone who came after me.
You could do that. If you can hit me. You're shaking pretty bad.
You're not quite as detoxed and squeaky clean as you've been broadcasting, are you?
Shane's maintenance dose must've barely taken the edge off.
I won't help you.
Who said you had a choice?

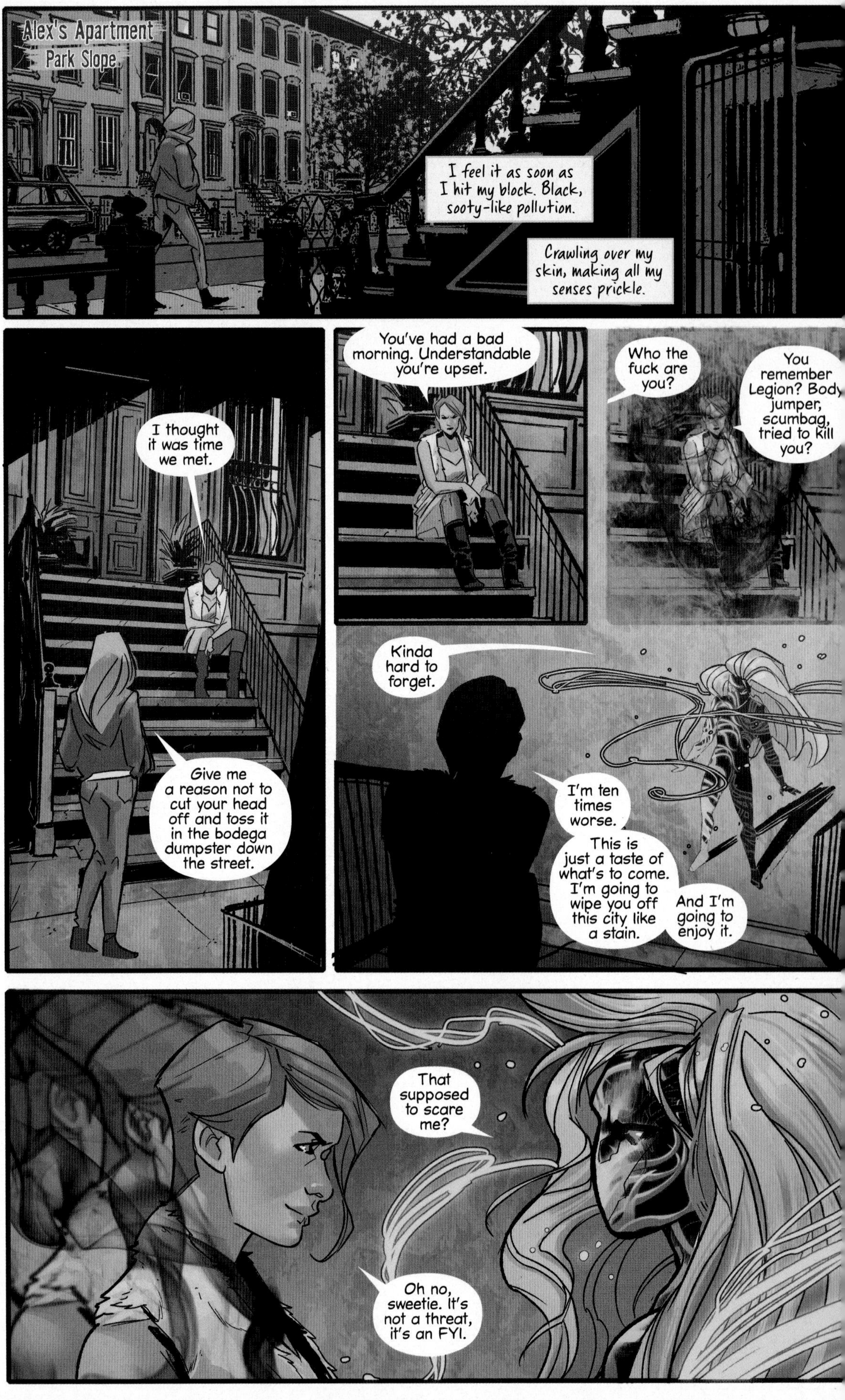

Alex's Apartment
Park Slope
I feel it as soon as I hit my block. Black, sooty-like pollution.
Crawling over my skin, making all my senses prickle.
I thought it was time we met.
Give me a reason not to cut your head off and toss it in the bodega dumpster down the street.
You've had a bad morning. Understandable you're upset.
Who the fuck are you?
You remember Legion? Body jumper, scumbag, tried to kill you?
Kinda hard to forget.
I'm ten times worse.
This is just a taste of what's to come. I'm going to wipe you off this city like a stain.
And I'm going to enjoy it.
That supposed to scare me?
Oh no, sweetie. It's not a threat, it's an FYI.

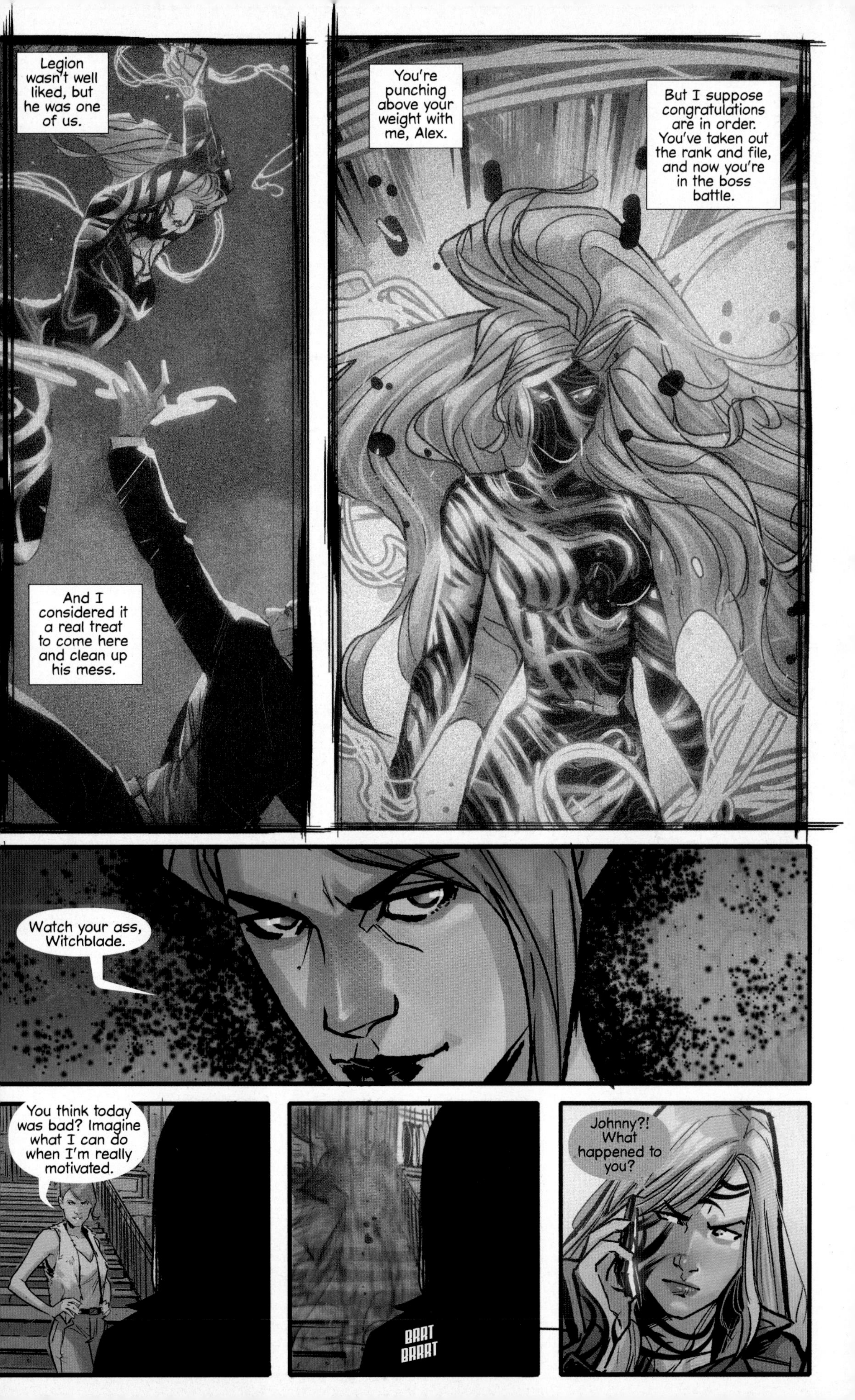
Legion wasn't well liked, but he was one of us.
And I considered it a real treat to come here and clean up his mess.
You're punching above your weight with me, Alex.
But I suppose congratulations are in order. You've taken out the rank and file, and now you're in the boss battle.
Watch your ass, Witchblade.
You think today was bad? Imagine what I can do when I'm really motivated.
BRRT BRRRT
Johnny?! What happened to you?

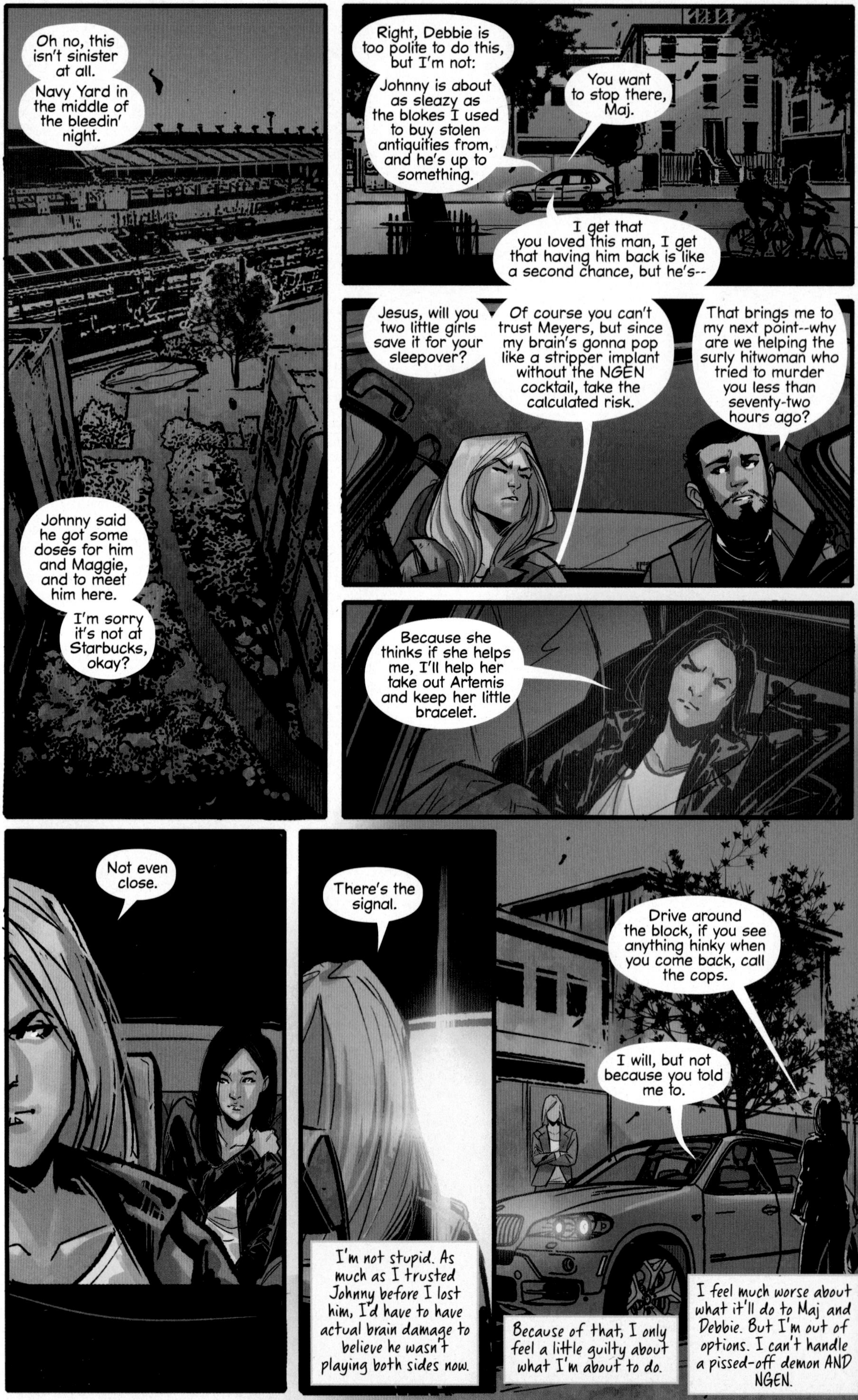

Oh no, this isn't sinister at all.
Navy Yard in the middle of the bleedin' night.
Right, Debbie is too polite to do this, but I'm not:
Johnny is about as sleazy as the blokes I used to buy stolen antiquities from, and he's up to something.
You want to stop there, Maj.
I get that you loved this man, I get that having him back is like a second chance, but he's--
Jesus, will you two little girls save it for your sleepover?
Of course you can't trust Meyers, but since my brain's gonna pop like a stripper implant without the NGEN cocktail, take the calculated risk.
That brings me to my next point--why are we helping the surly hitwoman who tried to murder you less than seventy-two hours ago?
Johnny said he got some doses for him and Maggie, and to meet him here.
I'm sorry it's not at Starbucks, okay?
Because she thinks if she helps me, I'll help her take out Artemis and keep her little bracelet.
Not even close.
There's the signal.
I'm not stupid. As much as I trusted Johnny before I lost him, I'd have to have actual brain damage to believe he wasn't playing both sides now.
Drive around the block, if you see anything hinky when you come back, call the cops.
I will, but not because you told me to.
Because of that, I only feel a little guilty about what I'm about to do.
I feel much worse about what it'll do to Maj and Debbie. But I'm out of options. I can't handle a pissed-off demon AND NGEN.

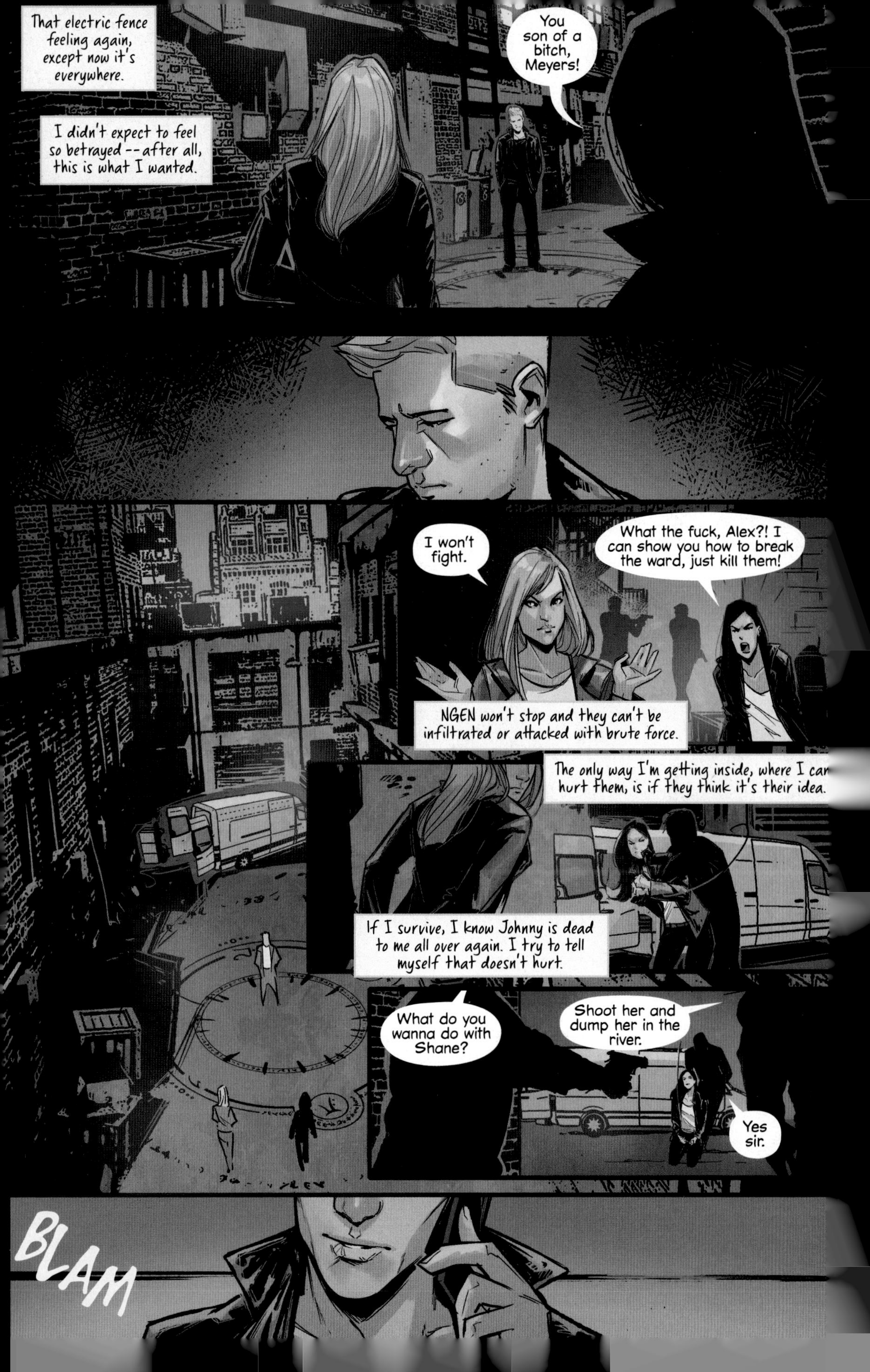
That electric fence feeling again, except now it's everywhere.
I didn't expect to feel so betrayed -- after all, this is what I wanted.
You son of a bitch, Meyers!
I won't fight.
What the fuck, Alex?! I can show you how to break the ward, just kill them!
NGEN won't stop and they can't be infiltrated or attacked with brute force.
The only way I'm getting inside, where I can hurt them, is if they think it's their idea.
If I survive, I know Johnny is dead to me all over again. I try to tell myself that doesn't hurt.
What do you wanna do with Shane?
Shoot her and dump her in the river.
Yes sir.
BLAM

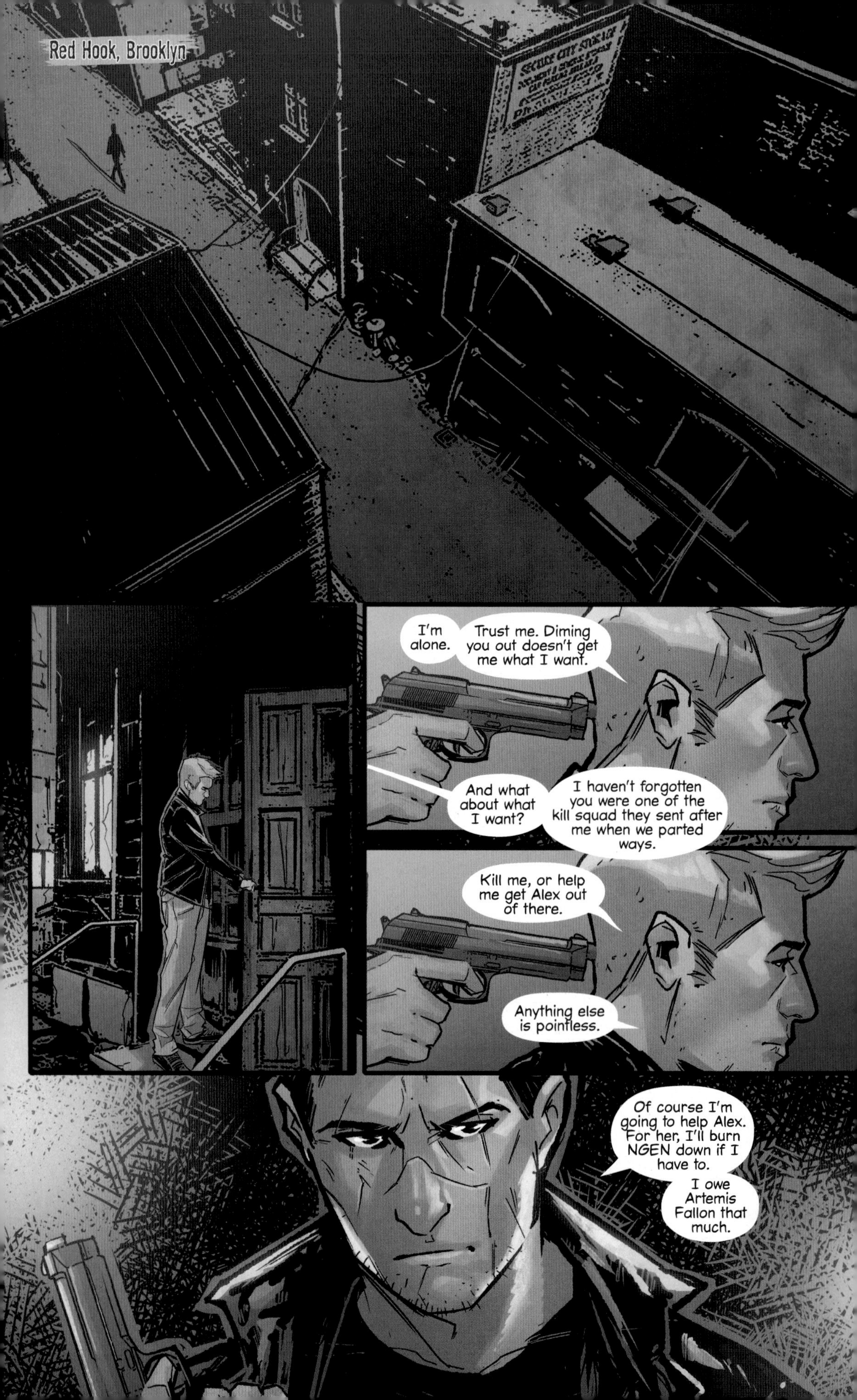
Red Hook, Brooklyn
I'm alone.
Trust me. Diming you out doesn't get me what I want.
And what about what I want?
I haven't forgotten you were one of the kill squad they sent after me when we parted ways.
Kill me, or help me get Alex out of there.
Anything else is pointless.
Of course I'm going to help Alex. For her, I'll burn NGEN down if I have to.
I owe Artemis Fallon that much.

CHAPTER TEN

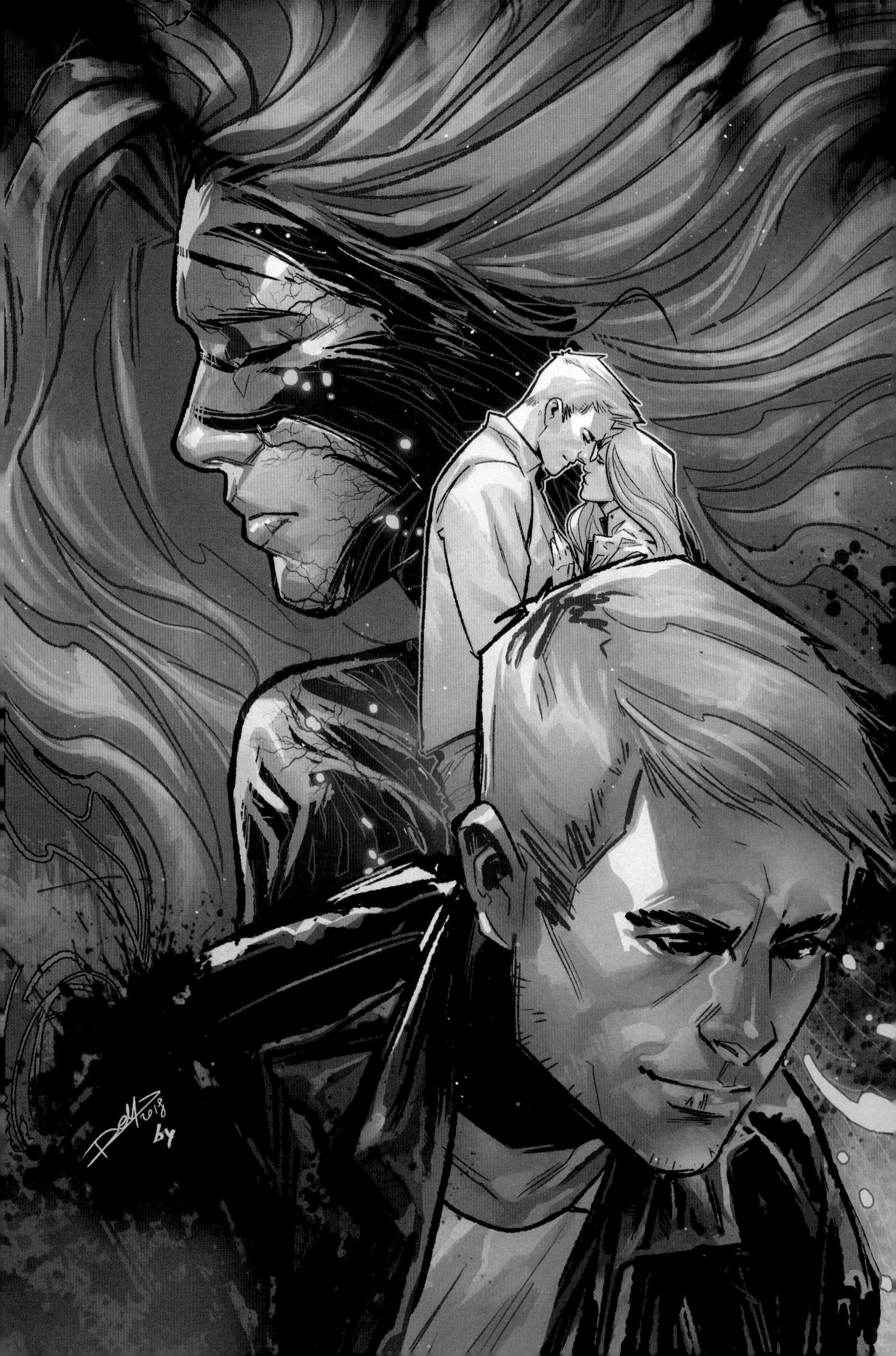

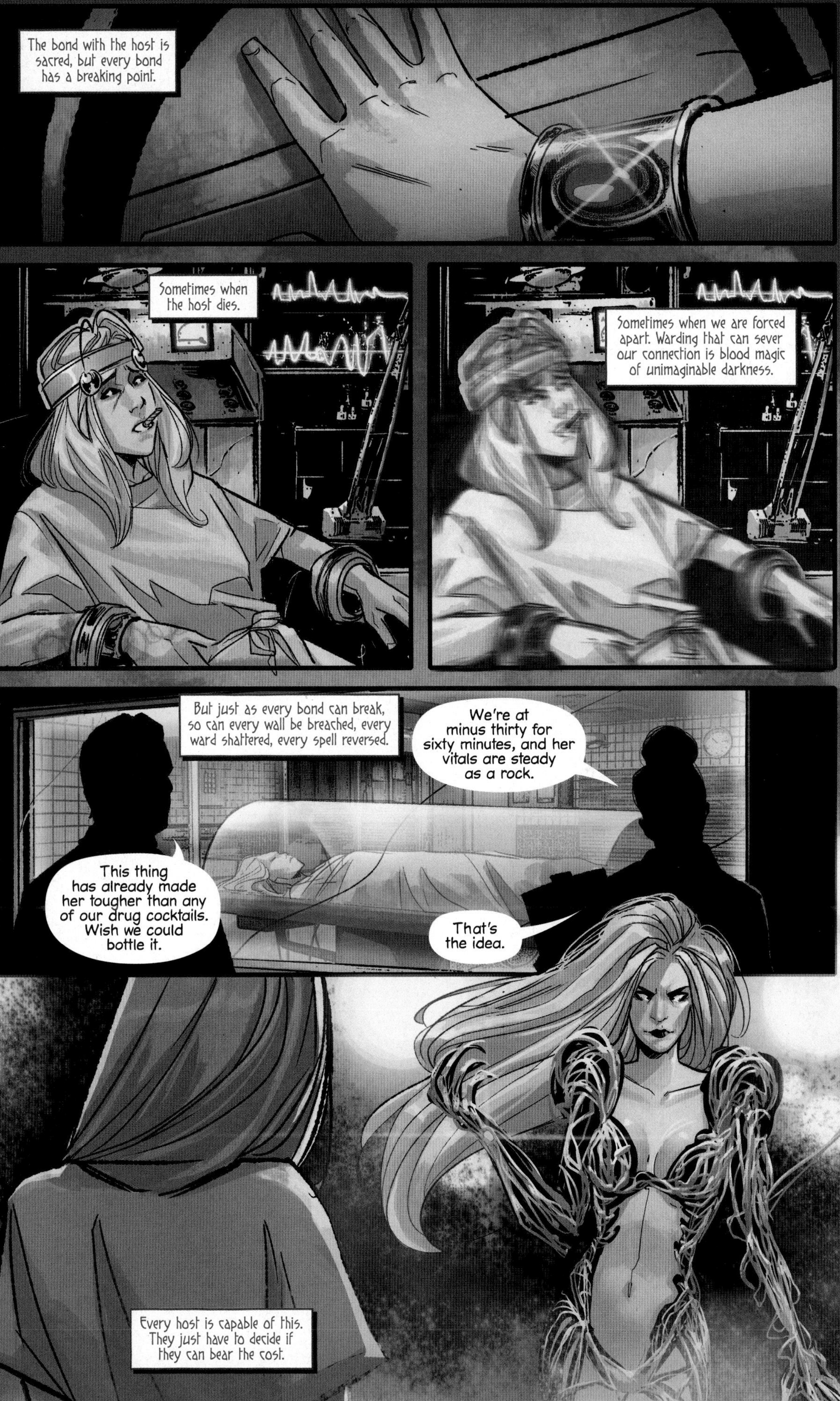
The bond with the host is sacred, but every bond has a breaking point.
Sometimes when the host dies.
Sometimes when we are forced apart. Warding that can sever our connection is blood magic of unimaginable darkness.
But just as every bond can break, so can every wall be breached, every ward shattered, every spell reversed.
We're at minus thirty for sixty minutes, and her vitals are steady as a rock.
This thing has already made her tougher than any of our drug cocktails. Wish we could bottle it.
That's the idea.
Every host is capable of this. They just have to decide if they can bear the cost.

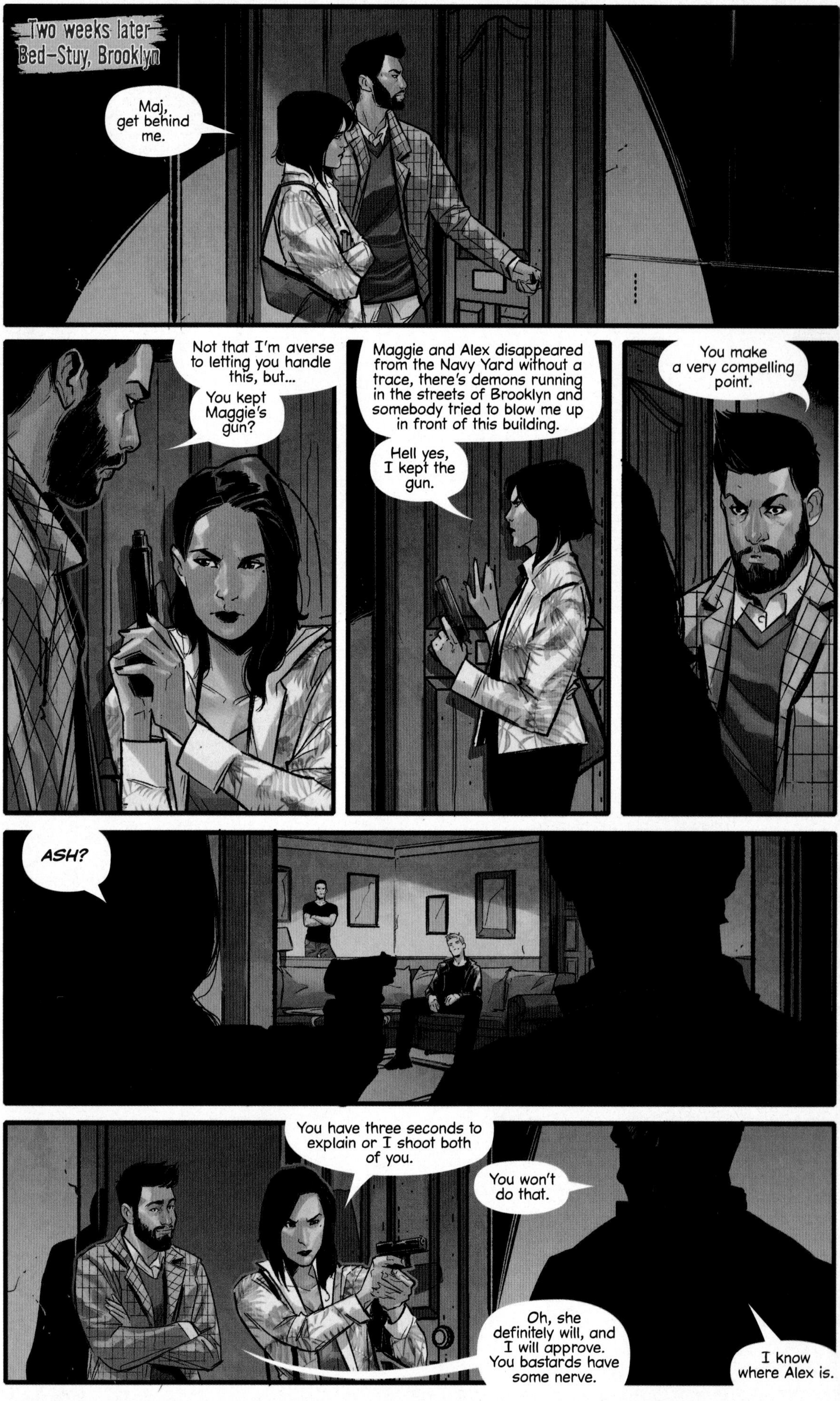
Two weeks later
Bed-Stuy, Brooklyn
Maj, get behind me.
Not that I'm averse to letting you handle this, but...
You kept Maggie's gun?
Maggie and Alex disappeared from the Navy Yard without a trace, there's demons running in the streets of Brooklyn and somebody tried to blow me up in front of this building.
Hell yes, I kept the gun.
You make a very compelling point.
ASH?
You have three seconds to explain or I shoot both of you.
You won't do that.
Oh, she definitely will, and I will approve. You bastards have some nerve.
I know where Alex is.

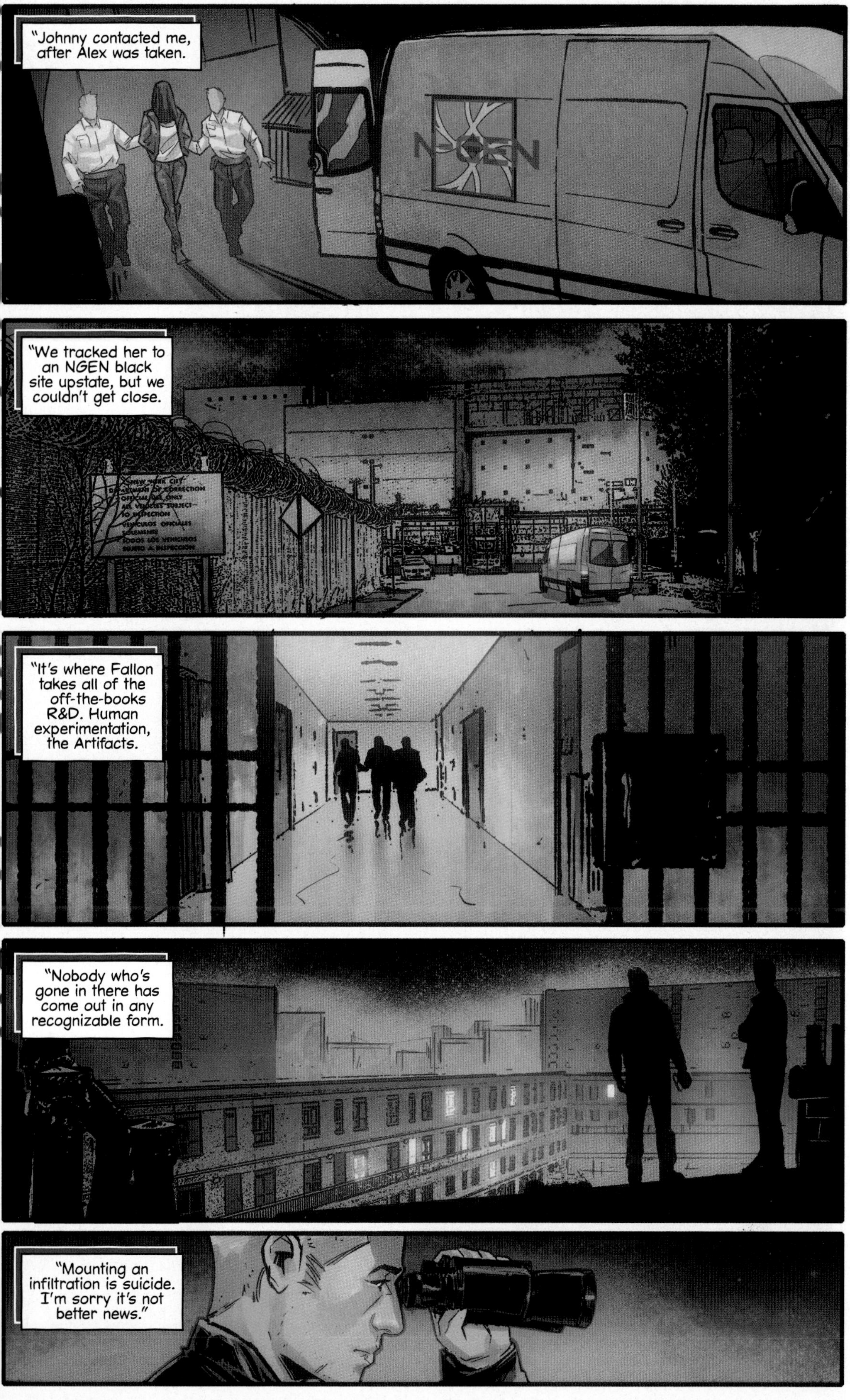
"Johnny contacted me, after Alex was taken.
"We tracked her to an NGEN black site upstate, but we couldn't get close.
"It's where Fallon takes all of the off-the-books R&D. Human experimentation, the Artifacts.
"Nobody who's gone in there has come out in any recognizable form.
"Mounting an infiltration is suicide. I'm sorry it's not better news."

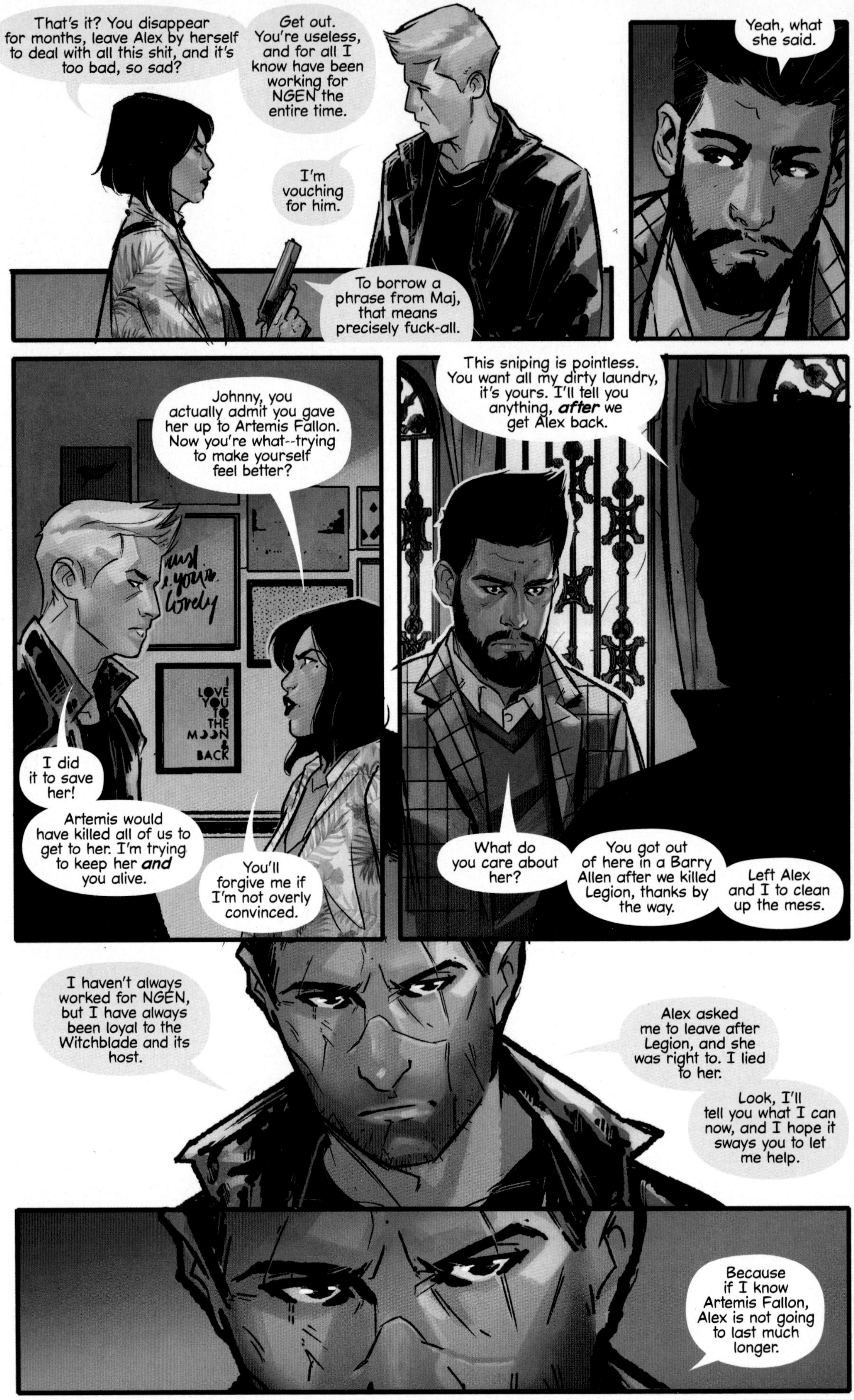
That's it? You disappear for months, leave Alex by herself to deal with all this shit, and it's too bad, so sad?
Get out. You're useless, and for all I know have been working for NGEN the entire time.
I'm vouching for him.
To borrow a phrase from Maj, that means precisely fuck-all.
Yeah, what she said.
Johnny, you actually admit you gave her up to Artemis Fallon. Now you're what--trying to make yourself feel better?
I did it to save her!
Artemis would have killed all of us to get to her. I'm trying to keep her *and* you alive.
You'll forgive me if I'm not overly convinced.
This sniping is pointless. You want all my dirty laundry, it's yours. I'll tell you anything, ***after*** we get Alex back.
What do you care about her?
You got out of here in a Barry Allen after we killed Legion, thanks by the way.
Left Alex and I to clean up the mess.
I haven't always worked for NGEN, but I have always been loyal to the Witchblade and its host.
Alex asked me to leave after Legion, and she was right to. I lied to her.
Look, I'll tell you what I can now, and I hope it sways you to let me help.
Because if I know Artemis Fallon, Alex is not going to last much longer.

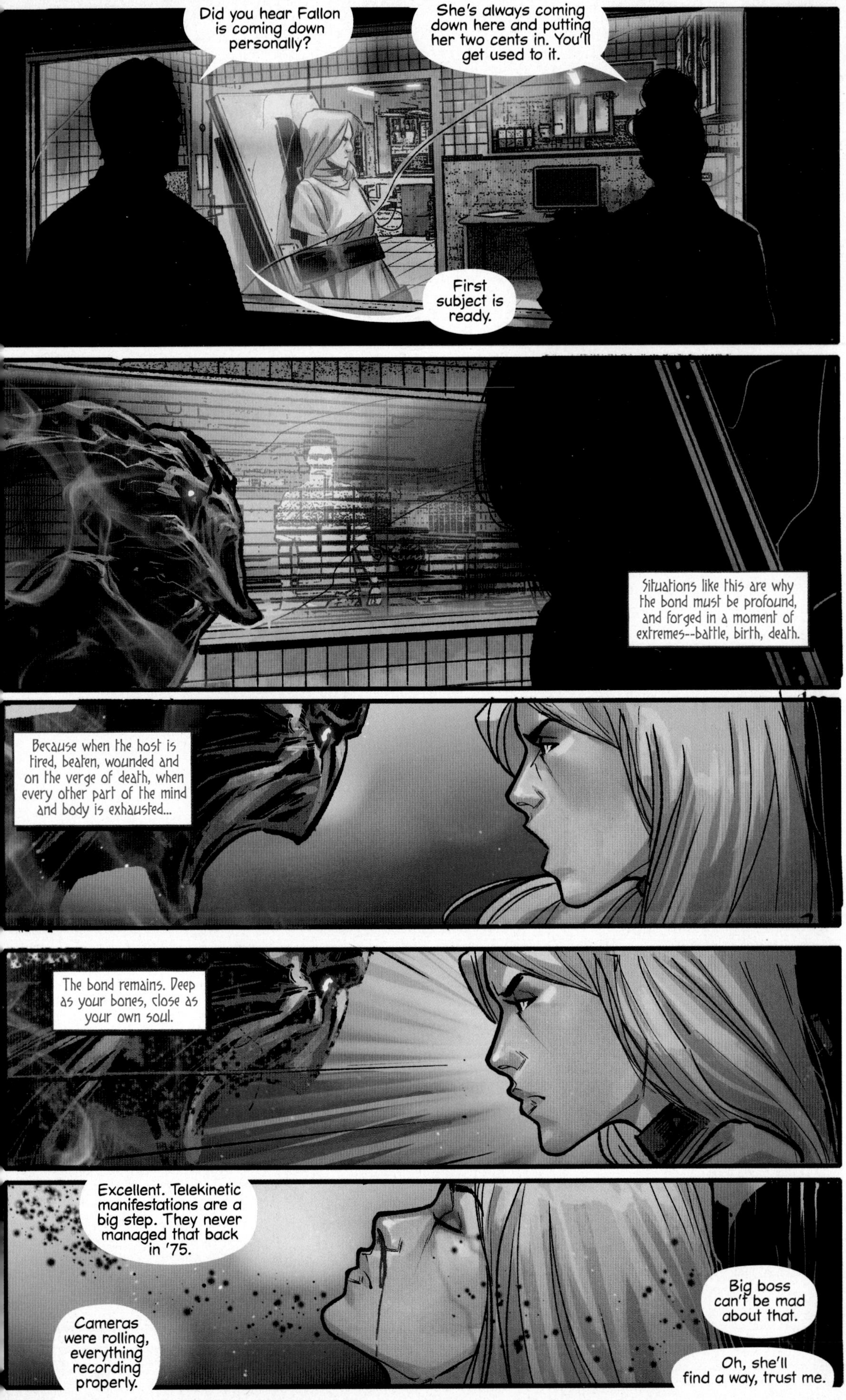
Did you hear Fallon is coming down personally?
She's always coming down here and putting her two cents in. You'll get used to it.
First subject is ready.
Situations like this are why the bond must be profound, and forged in a moment of extremes--battle, birth, death.
Because when the host is tired, beaten, wounded and on the verge of death, when every other part of the mind and body is exhausted...
The bond remains. Deep as your bones, close as your own soul.
Excellent. Telekinetic manifestations are a big step. They never managed that back in '75.
Cameras were rolling, everything recording properly.
Big boss can't be mad about that.
Oh, she'll find a way, trust me.

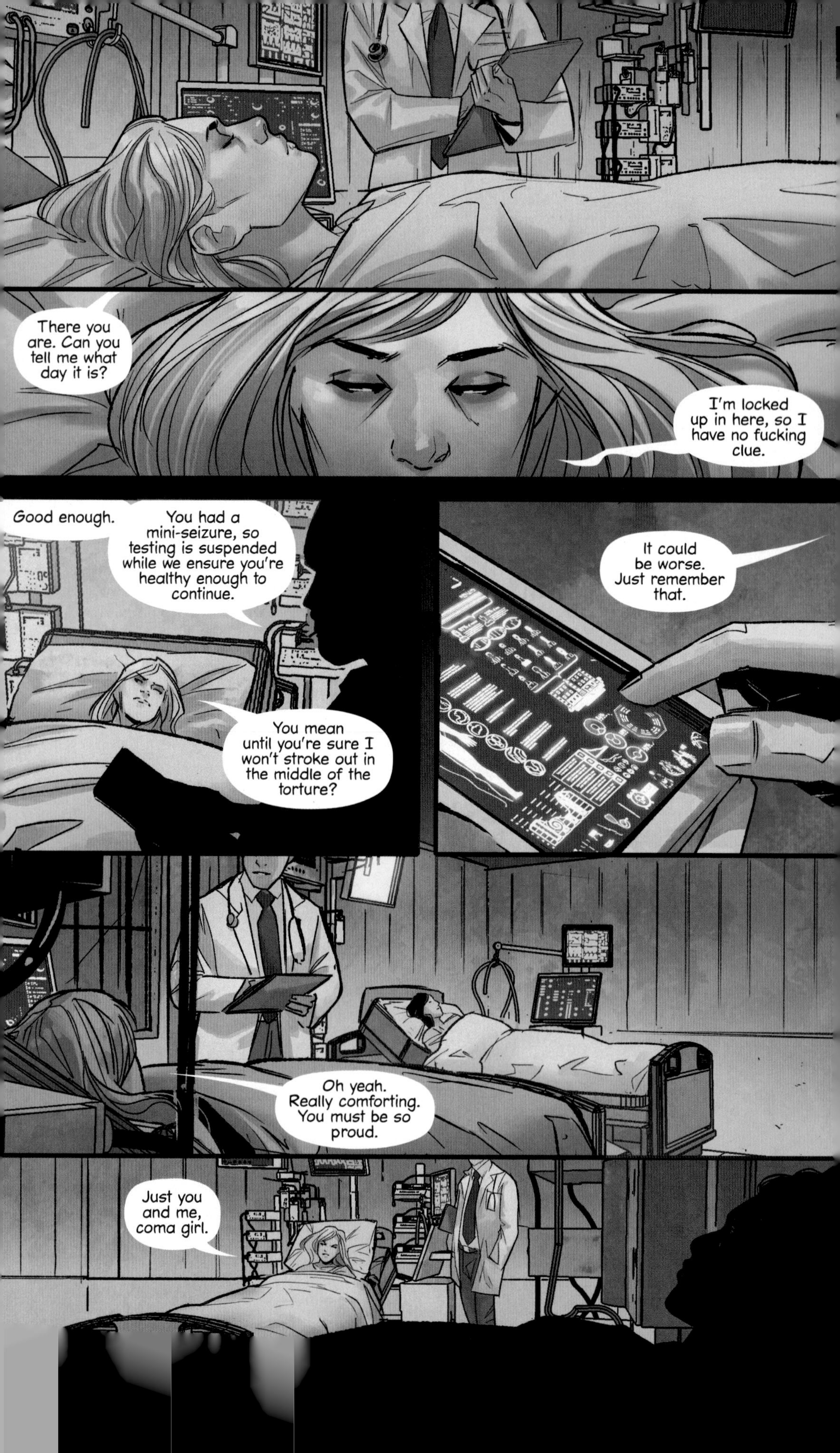
There you are. Can you tell me what day it is?
I'm locked up in here, so I have no fucking clue.
Good enough.
You had a mini-seizure, so testing is suspended while we ensure you're healthy enough to continue.
You mean until you're sure I won't stroke out in the middle of the torture?
It could be worse. Just remember that.
Oh yeah. Really comforting. You must be so proud.
Just you and me, coma girl.

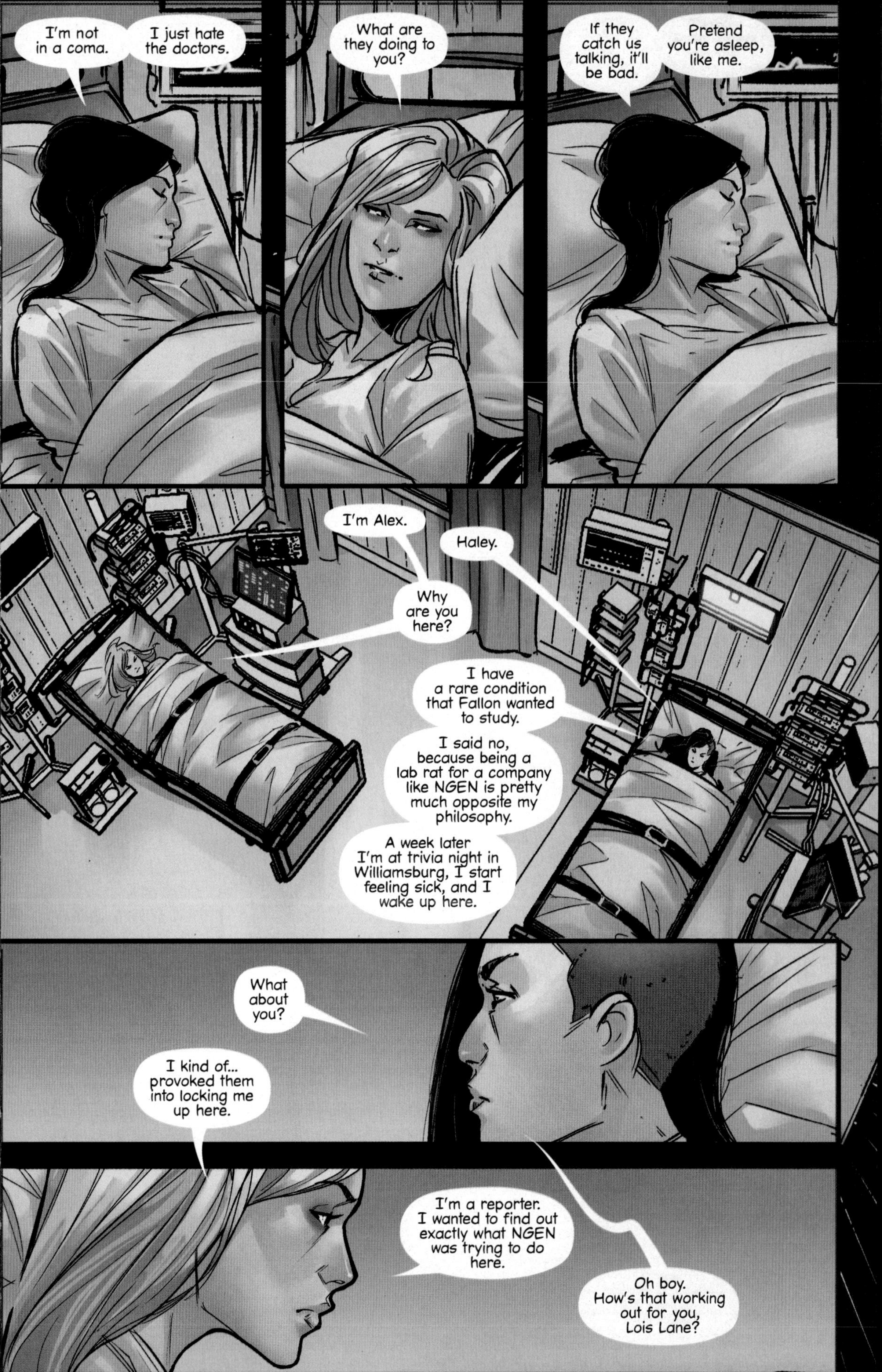
I'm not in a coma.
I just hate the doctors.
What are they doing to you?
If they catch us talking, it'll be bad.
Pretend you're asleep, like me.
I'm Alex.
Haley.
Why are you here?
I have a rare condition that Fallon wanted to study.
I said no, because being a lab rat for a company like NGEN is pretty much opposite my philosophy.
A week later I'm at trivia night in Williamsburg, I start feeling sick, and I wake up here.
What about you?
I kind of... provoked them into locking me up here.
I'm a reporter. I wanted to find out exactly what NGEN was trying to do here.
Oh boy. How's that working out for you, Lois Lane?

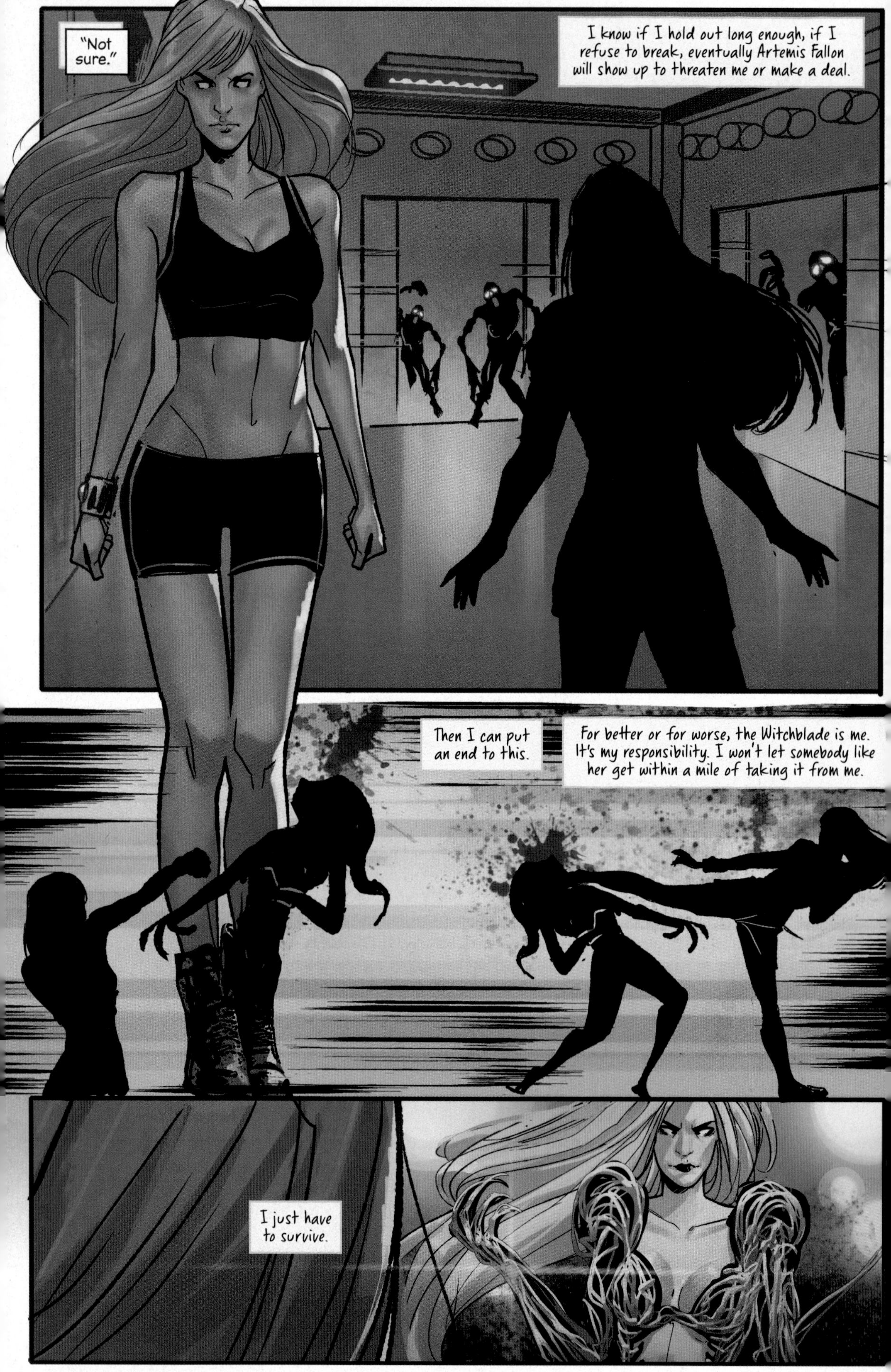
"Not sure."
I know if I hold out long enough, if I refuse to break, eventually Artemis Fallon will show up to threaten me or make a deal.
Then I can put an end to this.
For better or for worse, the Witchblade is me. It's my responsibility. I won't let somebody like her get within a mile of taking it from me.
I just have to survive.

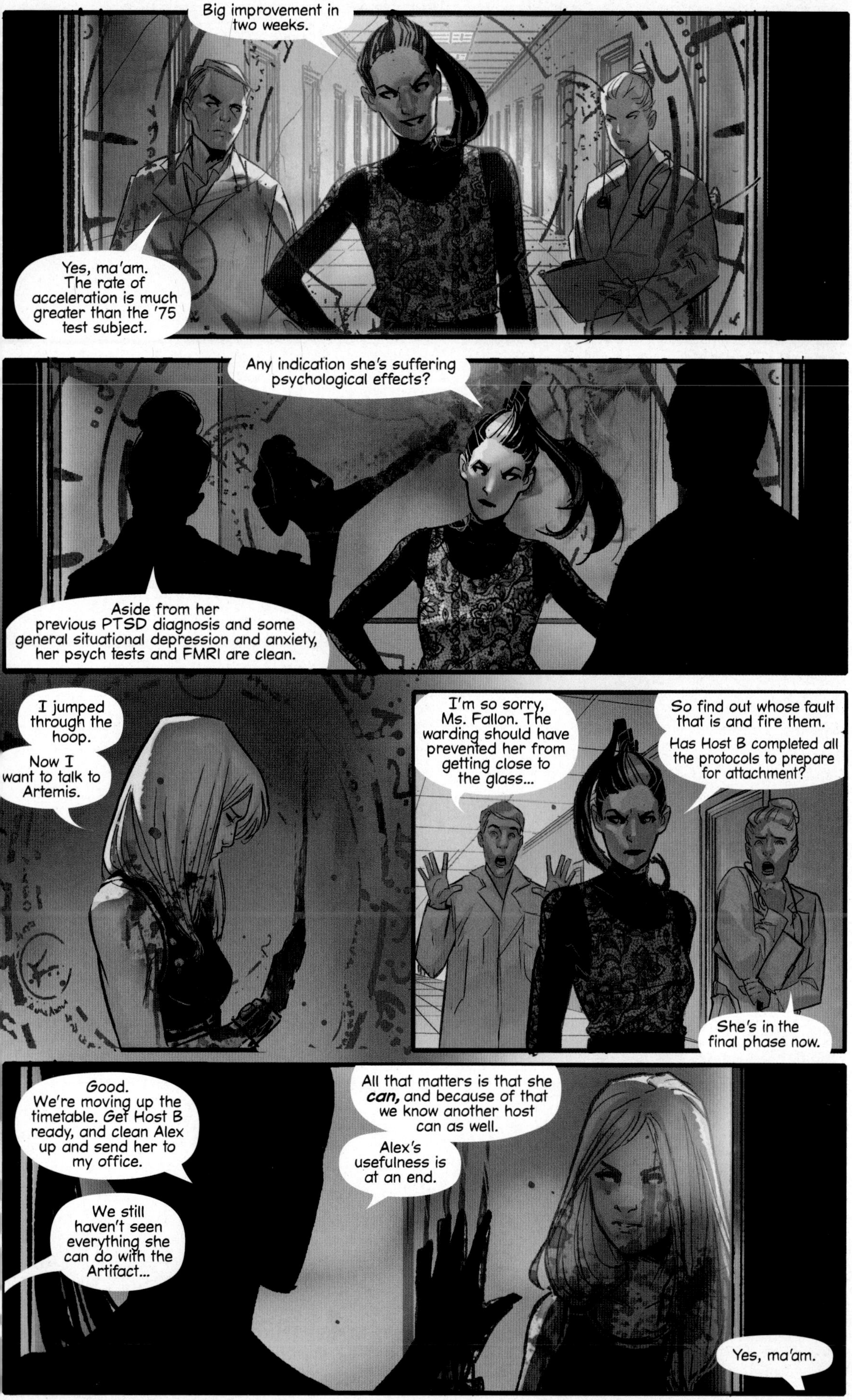
Big improvement in two weeks.
Yes, ma'am. The rate of acceleration is much greater than the '75 test subject.
Any indication she's suffering psychological effects?
Aside from her previous PTSD diagnosis and some general situational depression and anxiety, her psych tests and FMRI are clean.
I jumped through the hoop.
Now I want to talk to Artemis.
I'm so sorry, Ms. Fallon. The warding should have prevented her from getting close to the glass...
So find out whose fault that is and fire them.
Has Host B completed all the protocols to prepare for attachment?
She's in the final phase now.
Good. We're moving up the timetable. Get Host B ready, and clean Alex up and send her to my office.
We still haven't seen everything she can do with the Artifact...
All that matters is that she *can,* and because of that we know another host can as well.
Alex's usefulness is at an end.
Yes, ma'am.

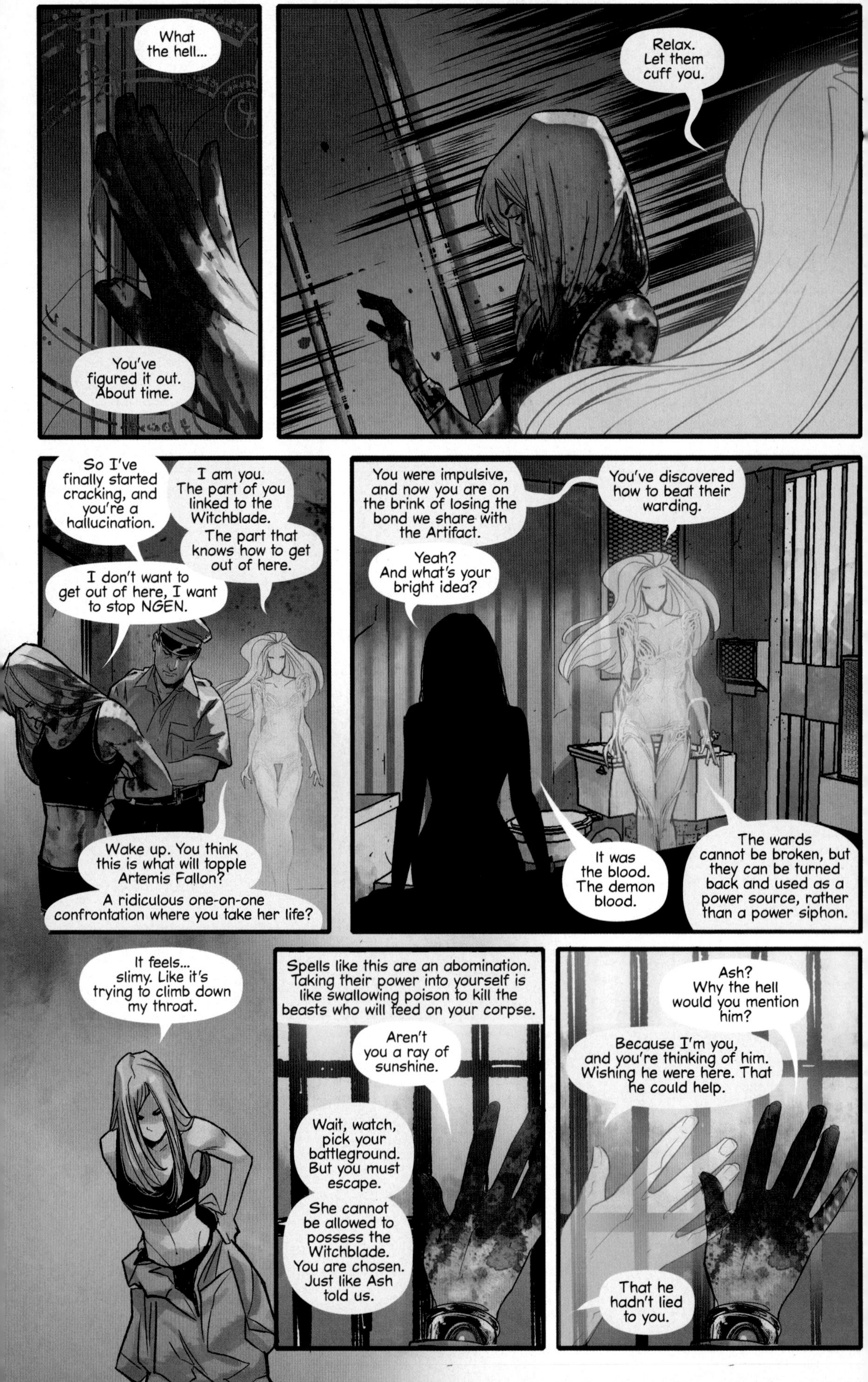
What the hell...
You've figured it out. About time.
Relax. Let them cuff you.
So I've finally started cracking, and you're a hallucination.
I am you. The part of you linked to the Witchblade.
The part that knows how to get out of here.
I don't want to get out of here, I want to stop NGEN.
Wake up. You think this is what will topple Artemis Fallon?
A ridiculous one-on-one confrontation where you take her life?
You were impulsive, and now you are on the brink of losing the bond we share with the Artifact.
You've discovered how to beat their warding.
Yeah? And what's your bright idea?
It was the blood. The demon blood.
The wards cannot be broken, but they can be turned back and used as a power source, rather than a power siphon.
It feels... slimy. Like it's trying to climb down my throat.
Spells like this are an abomination. Taking their power into yourself is like swallowing poison to kill the beasts who will feed on your corpse.
Aren't you a ray of sunshine.
Wait, watch, pick your battleground. But you must escape.
She cannot be allowed to possess the Witchblade. You are chosen. Just like Ash told us.
Ash? Why the hell would you mention him?
Because I'm you, and you're thinking of him. Wishing he were here. That he could help.
That he hadn't lied to you.

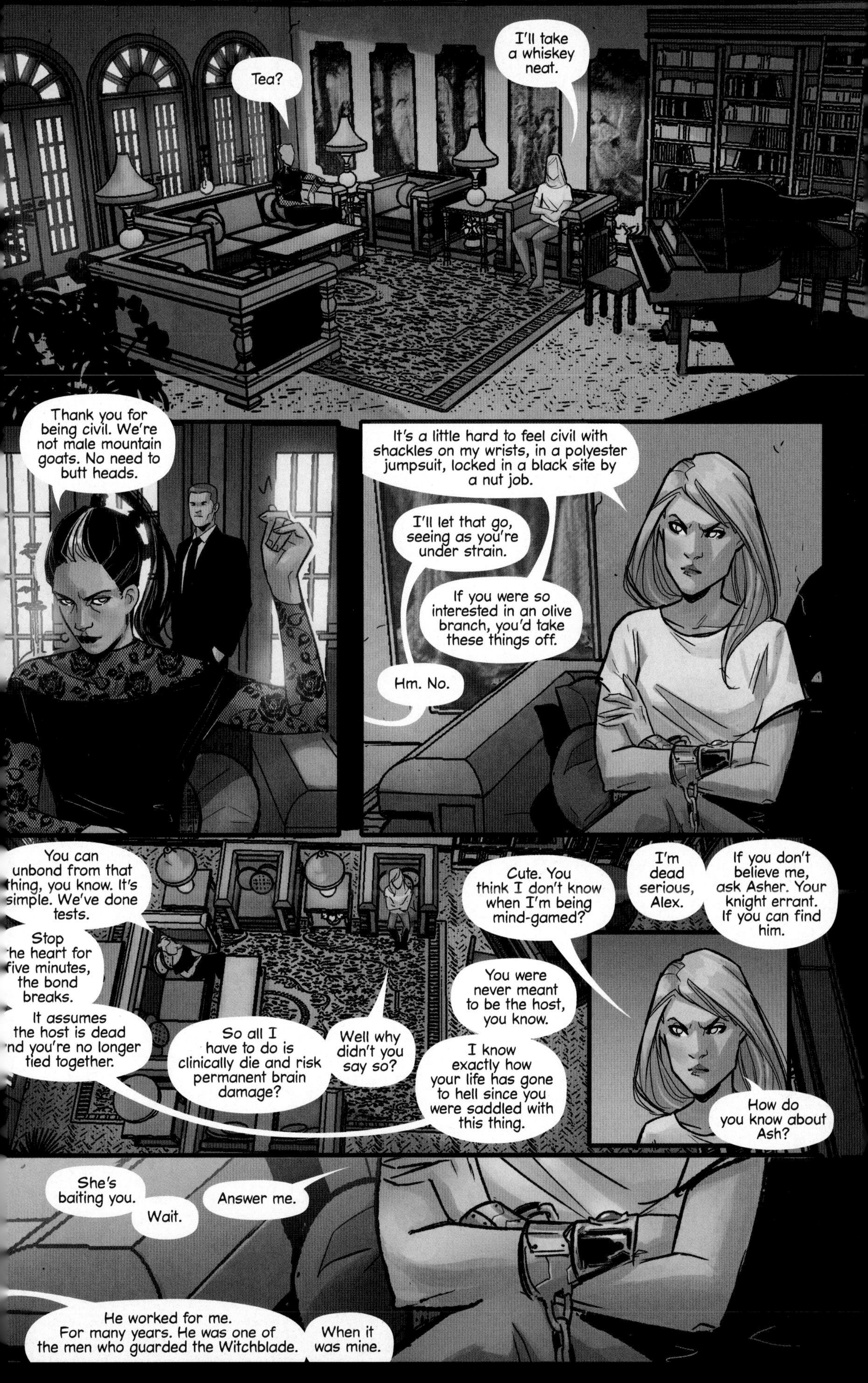
Tea?
I'll take a whiskey neat.
Thank you for being civil. We're not male mountain goats. No need to butt heads.
It's a little hard to feel civil with shackles on my wrists, in a polyester jumpsuit, locked in a black site by a nut job.
I'll let that go, seeing as you're under strain.
If you were so interested in an olive branch, you'd take these things off.
Hm. No.
You can unbond from that thing, you know. It's simple. We've done tests.
Stop he heart for five minutes, the bond breaks.
It assumes the host is dead nd you're no longer tied together.
So all I have to do is clinically die and risk permanent brain damage?
Well why didn't you say so?
Cute. You think I don't know when I'm being mind-gamed?
I'm dead serious, Alex.
If you don't believe me, ask Asher. Your knight errant. If you can find him.
You were never meant to be the host, you know.
I know exactly how your life has gone to hell since you were saddled with this thing.
How do you know about Ash?
She's baiting you.
Wait.
Answer me.
He worked for me. For many years. He was one of the men who guarded the Witchblade.
When it was mine.

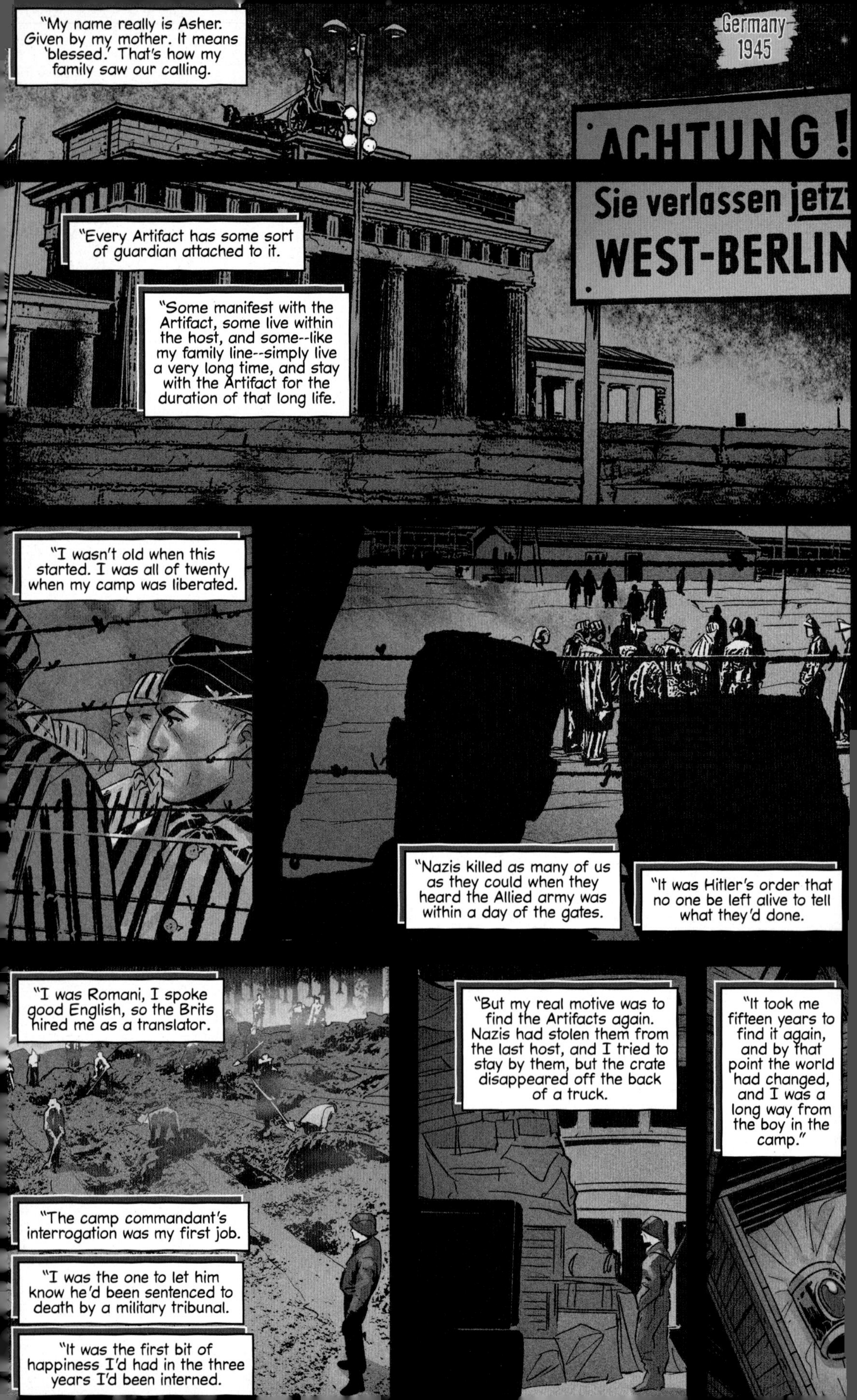
"My name really is Asher. Given by my mother. It means 'blessed.' That's how my family saw our calling.
Germany 1945
ACHTUNG!
Sie verlassen jetzt
WEST-BERLIN
"Every Artifact has some sort of guardian attached to it.
"Some manifest with the Artifact, some live within the host, and some--like my family line--simply live a very long time, and stay with the Artifact for the duration of that long life.
"I wasn't old when this started. I was all of twenty when my camp was liberated.
"Nazis killed as many of us as they could when they heard the Allied army was within a day of the gates.
"It was Hitler's order that no one be left alive to tell what they'd done.
"I was Romani, I spoke good English, so the Brits hired me as a translator.
"The camp commandant's interrogation was my first job.
"I was the one to let him know he'd been sentenced to death by a military tribunal.
"It was the first bit of happiness I'd had in the three years I'd been interned.
"But my real motive was to find the Artifacts again. Nazis had stolen them from the last host, and I tried to stay by them, but the crate disappeared off the back of a truck.
"It took me fifteen years to find it again, and by that point the world had changed, and I was a long way from the boy in the camp."

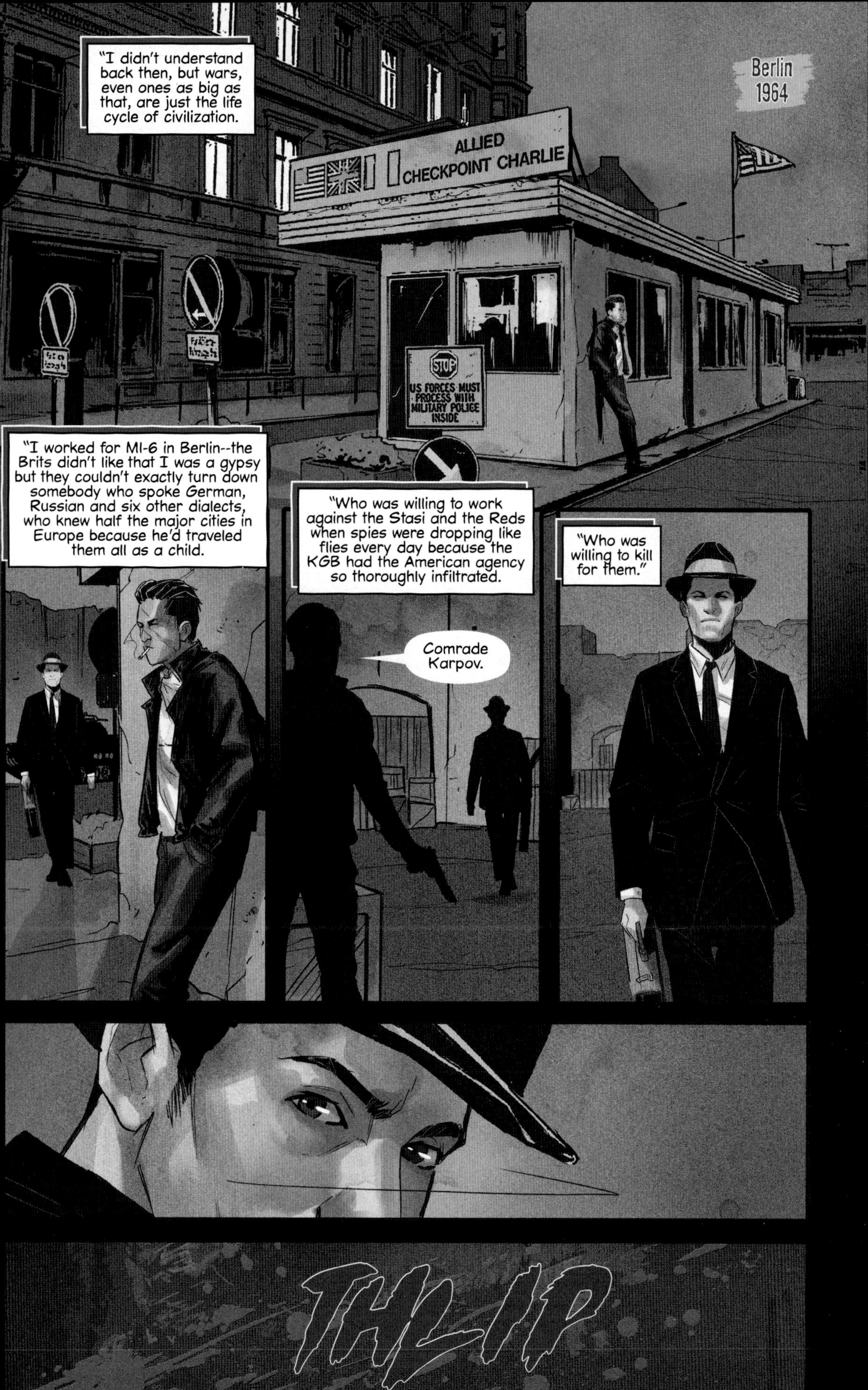
"I didn't understand back then, but wars, even ones as big as that, are just the life cycle of civilization.
Berlin 1964
ALLIED CHECKPOINT CHARLIE
STOP
US FORCES MUST PROCESS WITH MILITARY POLICE INSIDE
"I worked for MI-6 in Berlin--the Brits didn't like that I was a gypsy but they couldn't exactly turn down somebody who spoke German, Russian and six other dialects, who knew half the major cities in Europe because he'd traveled them all as a child.
"Who was willing to work against the Stasi and the Reds when spies were dropping like flies every day because the KGB had the American agency so thoroughly infiltrated.
Comrade Karpov.
"Who was willing to kill for them."
THLIP

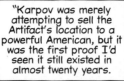

"Karpov was merely attempting to sell the Artifact's location to a powerful American, but it was the first proof I'd seen it still existed in almost twenty years.

"I came to realize that enemies and allies really mean nothing. Nobody with designs on power should have the Witchblade.

"I saw how pointless it was to try and stay on a side, and instead merely tried to stay with the Artifact, as I was meant to.

"I went where the Witchblade went, and when Fallon got his hands on it, I went to work for him. An ex-spy with my pedigree was an irresistible temptation for a man like him."

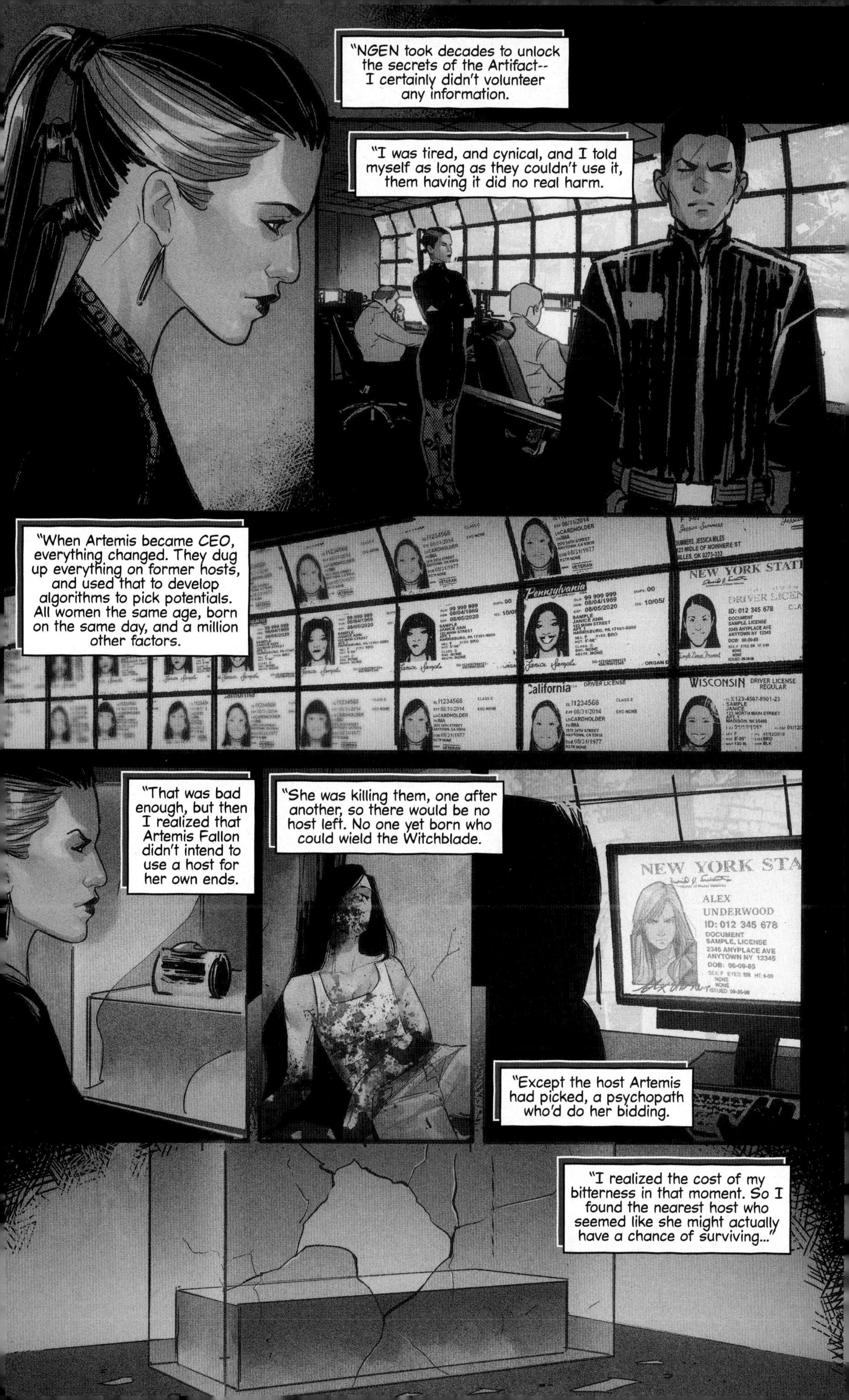
"NGEN took decades to unlock the secrets of the Artifact-- I certainly didn't volunteer any information.
"I was tired, and cynical, and I told myself as long as they couldn't use it, them having it did no real harm.
"When Artemis became CEO, everything changed. They dug up everything on former hosts, and used that to develop algorithms to pick potentials. All women the same age, born on the same day, and a million other factors.
Pennsylvania
California
WISCONSIN DRIVER LICENSE REGULAR
"That was bad enough, but then I realized that Artemis Fallon didn't intend to use a host for her own ends.
"She was killing them, one after another, so there would be no host left. No one yet born who could wield the Witchblade.
NEW YORK STA
ALEX
UNDERWOOD
ID: 012 345 678
DOCUMENT
SAMPLE, LICENSE
2345 ANYPLACE AVE
ANYTOWN NY 12345
DOB: 06-09-85
"Except the host Artemis had picked, a psychopath who'd do her bidding.
"I realized the cost of my bitterness in that moment. So I found the nearest host who seemed like she might actually have a chance of surviving..."

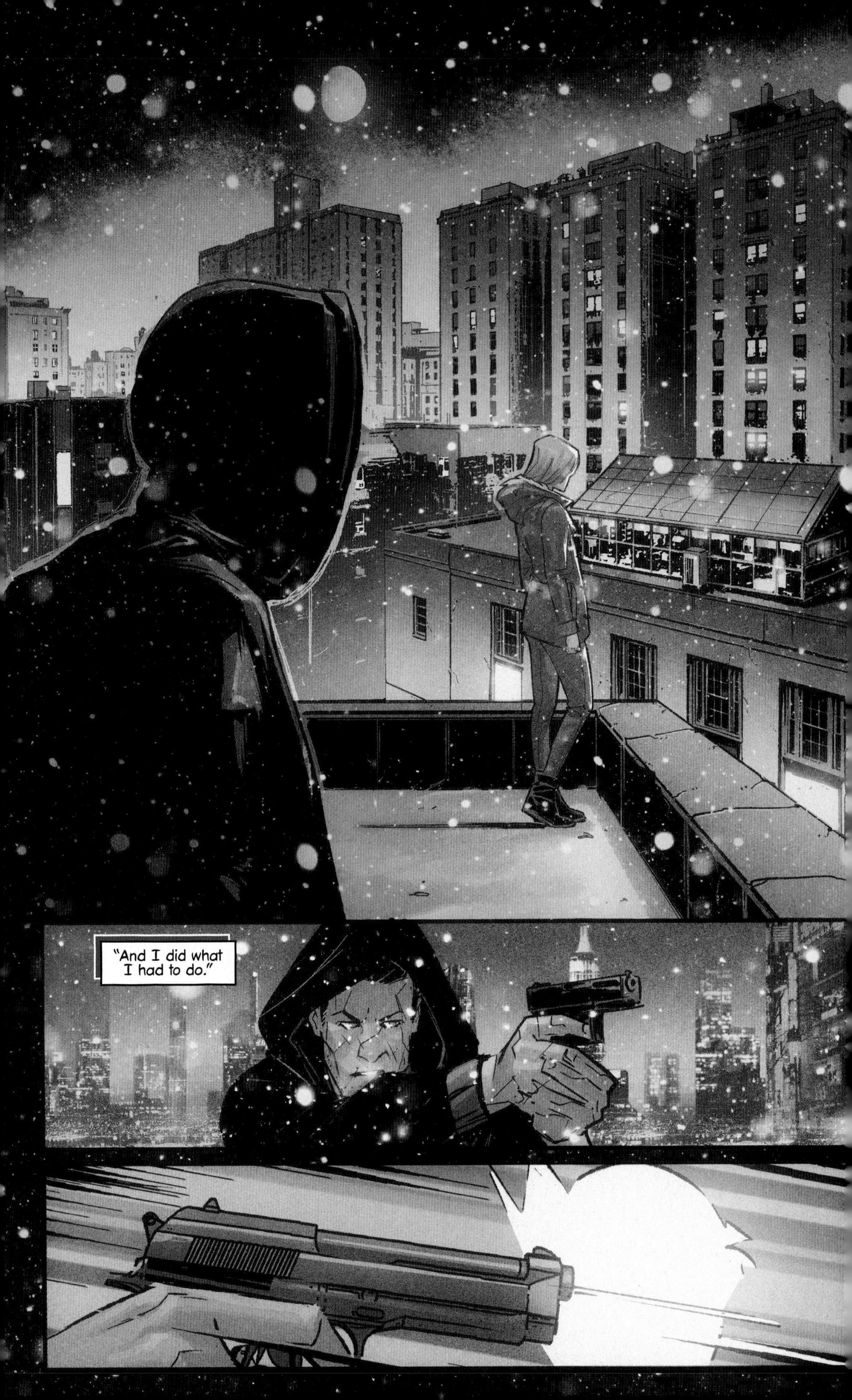
"And I did what I had to do."

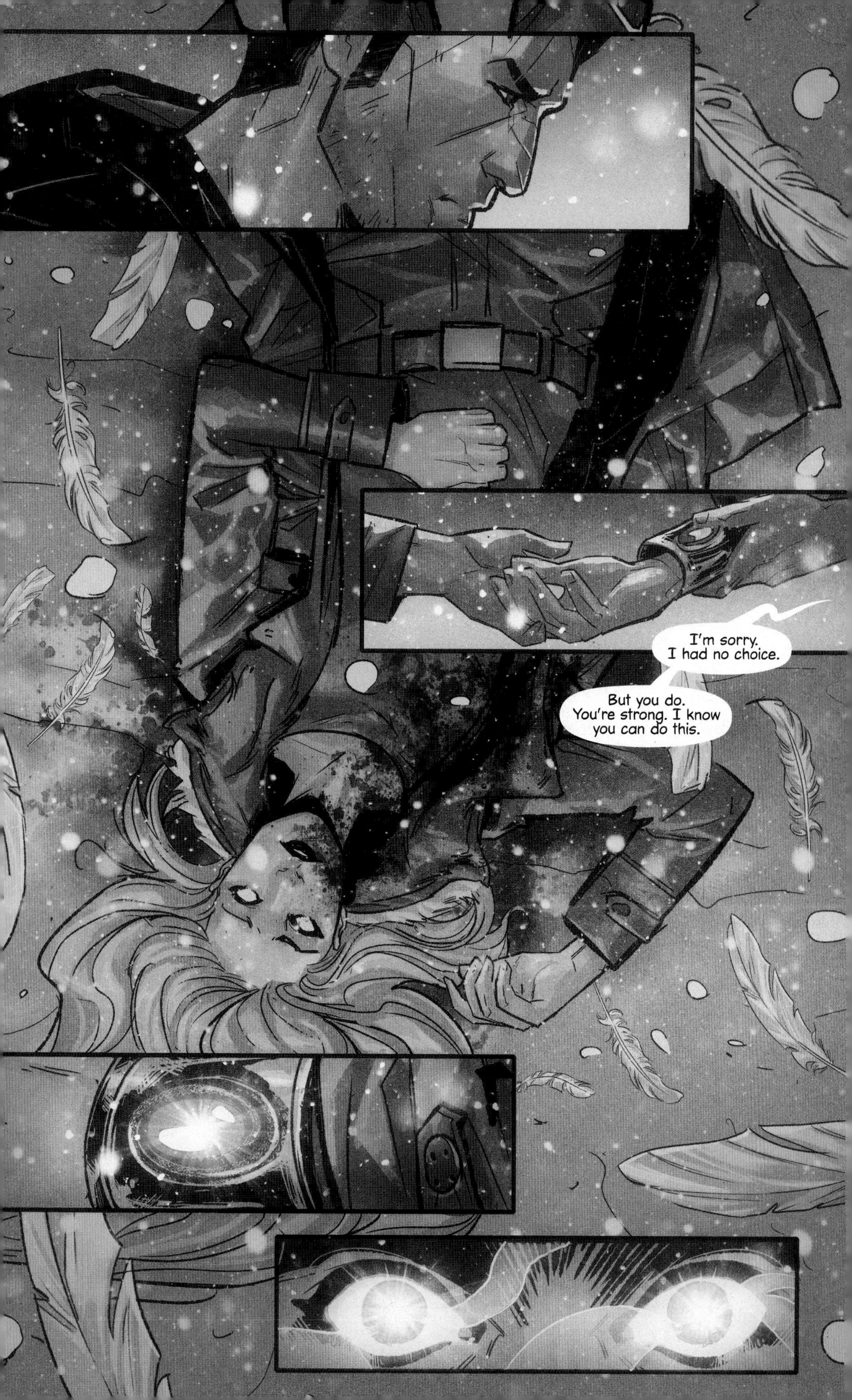
I'm sorry. I had no choice.
But you do. You're strong. I know you can do this.

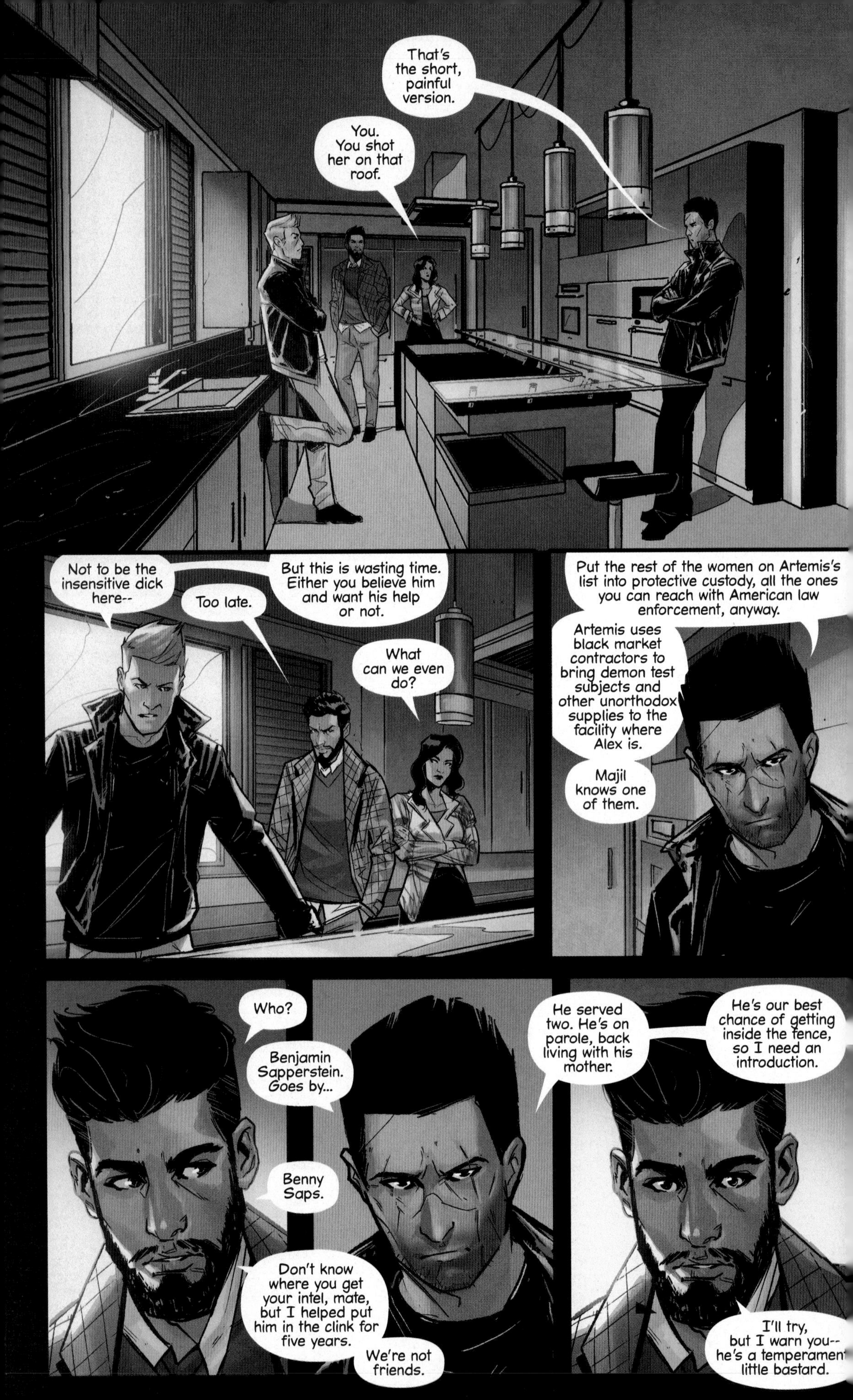

You. You shot her on that roof.
That's the short, painful version.
Not to be the insensitive dick here--
Too late.
But this is wasting time. Either you believe him and want his help or not.
What can we even do?
Put the rest of the women on Artemis's list into protective custody, all the ones you can reach with American law enforcement, anyway.
Artemis uses black market contractors to bring demon test subjects and other unorthodox supplies to the facility where Alex is.
Majil knows one of them.
Who?
Benjamin Sapperstein. Goes by...
Benny Saps.
Don't know where you get your intel, mate, but I helped put him in the clink for five years.
We're not friends.
He served two. He's on parole, back living with his mother.
He's our best chance of getting inside the fence, so I need an introduction.
I'll try, but I warn you-- he's a temperamen little bastard.

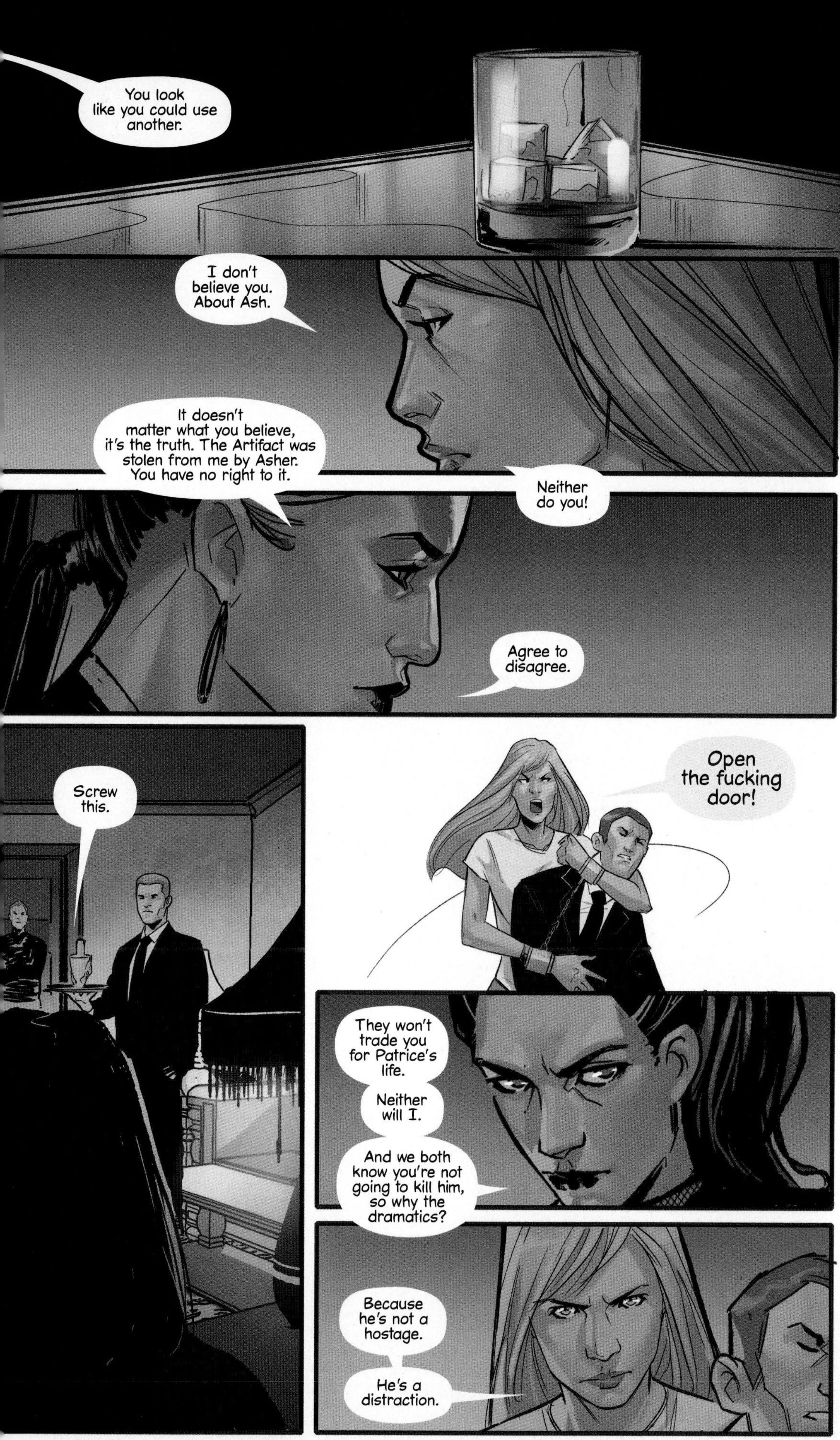
You look like you could use another.
I don't believe you. About Ash.
It doesn't matter what you believe, it's the truth. The Artifact was stolen from me by Asher. You have no right to it.
Neither do you!
Agree to disagree.
Screw this.
Open the fucking door!
They won't trade you for Patrice's life.
Neither will I.
And we both know you're not going to kill him, so why the dramatics?
Because he's not a hostage.
He's a distraction.

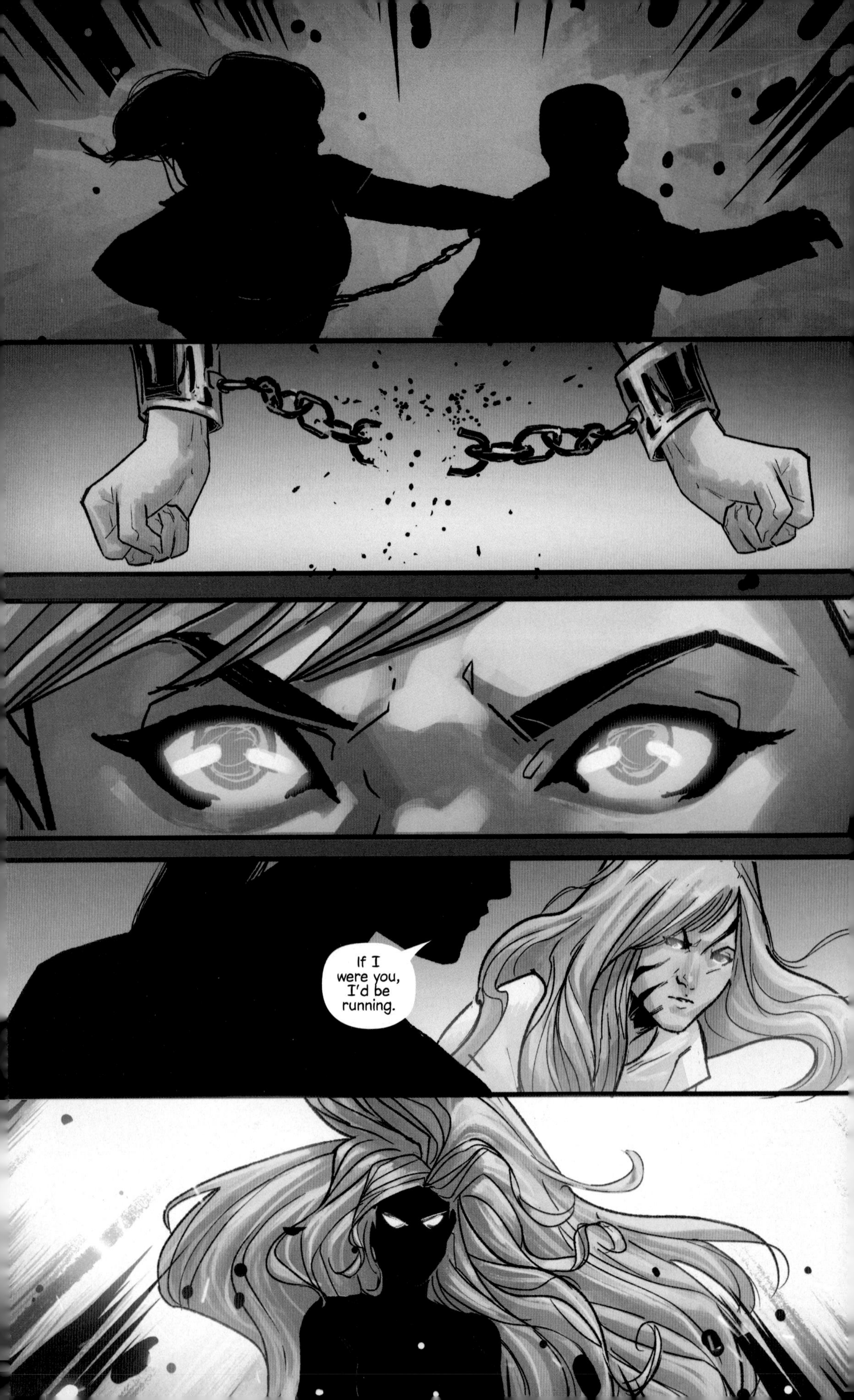
If I were you, I'd be running.

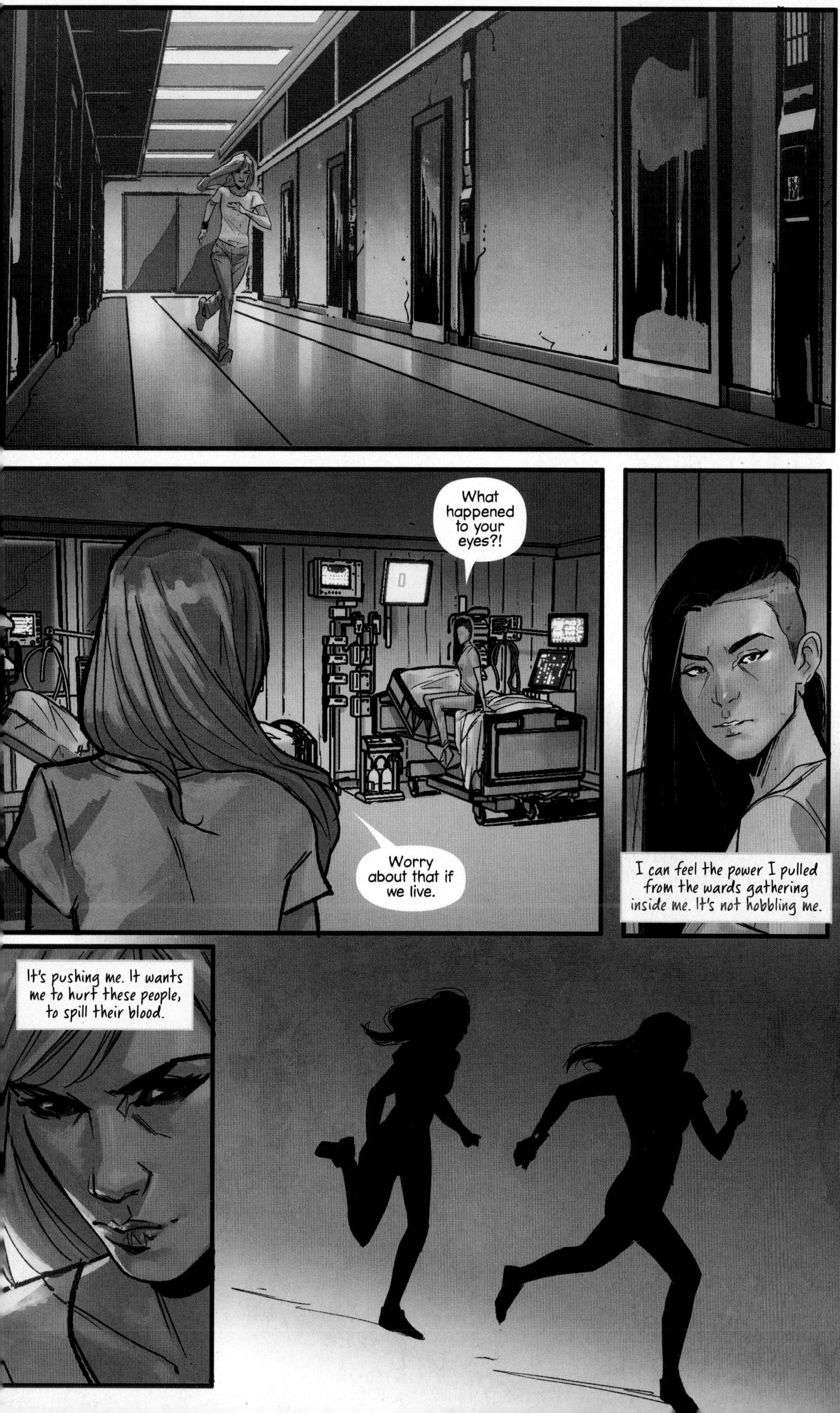
What happened to your eyes?!
Worry about that if we live.
I can feel the power I pulled from the wards gathering inside me. It's not hobbling me.
It's pushing me. It wants me to hurt these people, to spill their blood.

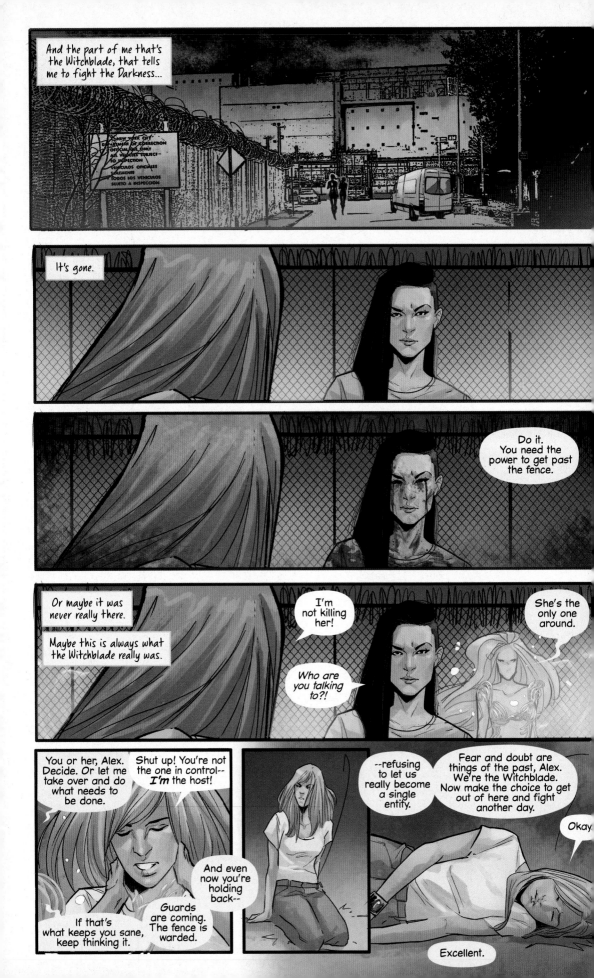

And the part of me that's the Witchblade, that tells me to fight the Darkness...

It's gone.

Do it. You need the power to get past the fence.

Or maybe it was never really there.

Maybe this is always what the Witchblade really was.

I'm not killing her!

She's the only one around.

Who are you talking to?!

You or her, Alex. Decide. Or let me take over and do what needs to be done.

Shut up! You're not the one in control--*I'm* the host!

--refusing to let us really become a single entity.

Fear and doubt are things of the past, Alex. We're the Witchblade. Now make the choice to get out of here and fight another day.

Okay.

And even now you're holding back--

If that's what keeps you sane, keep thinking it.

Guards are coming. The fence is warded.

Excellent.

CHAPTER ELEVEN

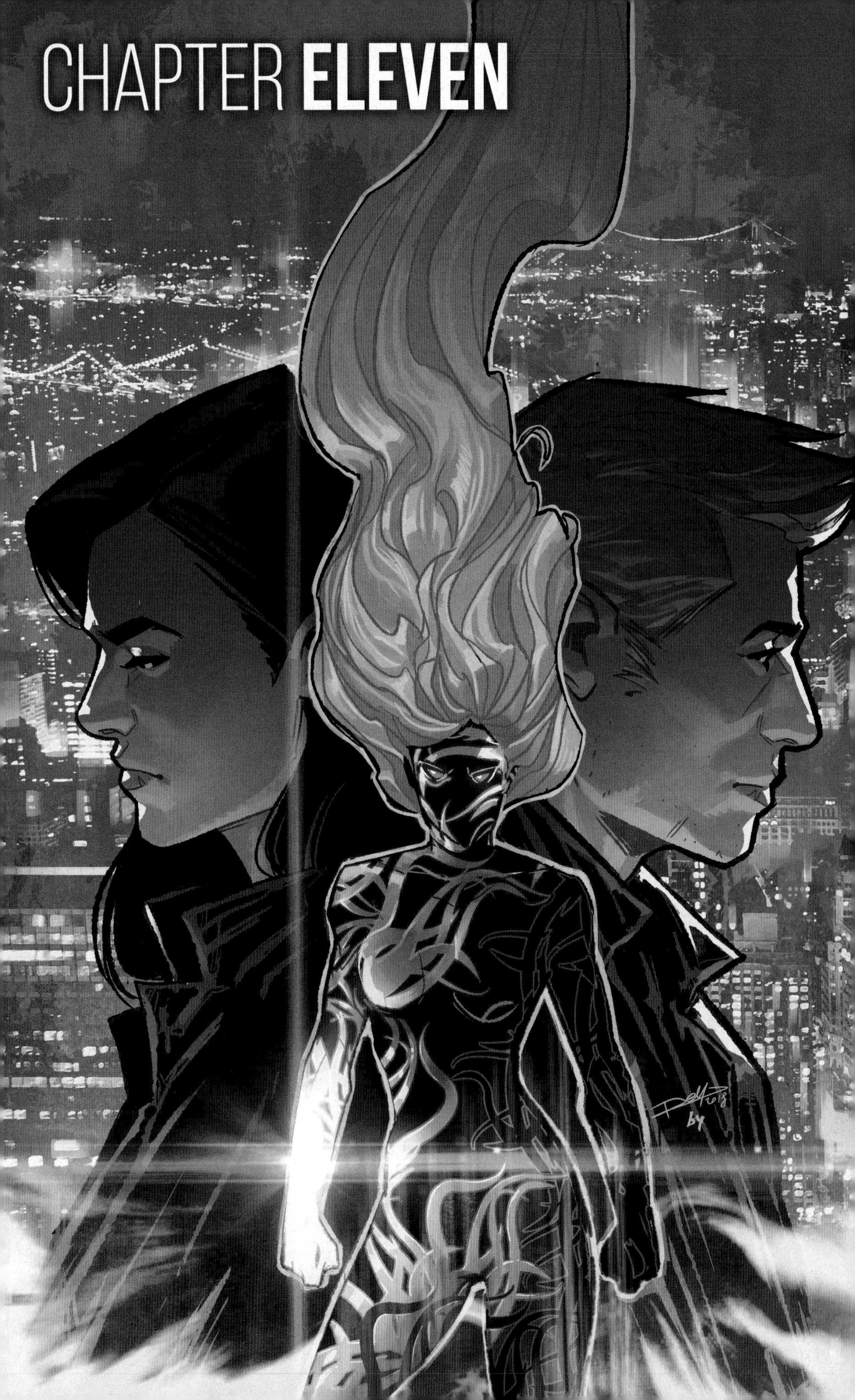

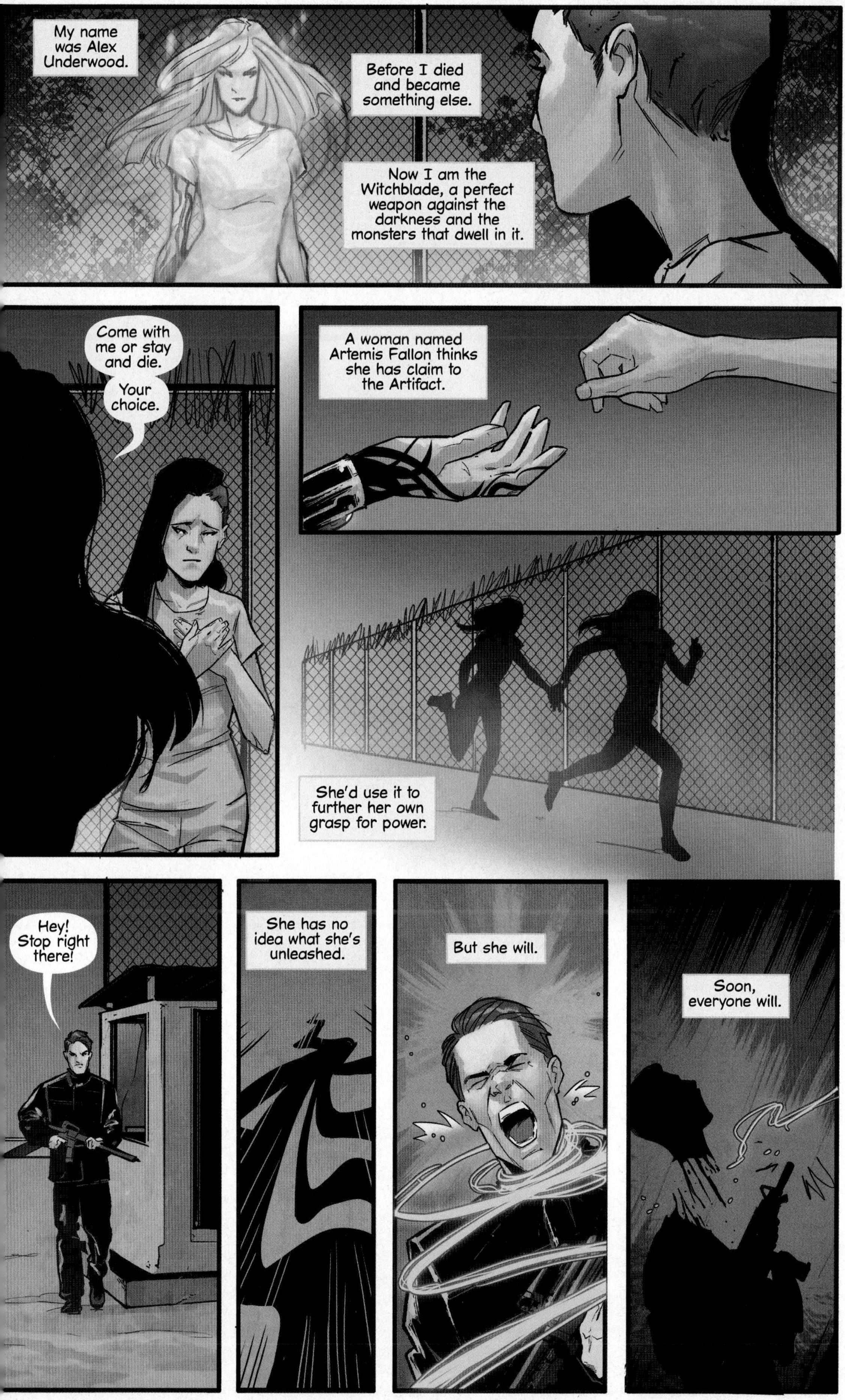
My name was Alex Underwood.
Before I died and became something else.
Now I am the Witchblade, a perfect weapon against the darkness and the monsters that dwell in it.
Come with me or stay and die.
Your choice.
A woman named Artemis Fallon thinks she has claim to the Artifact.
She'd use it to further her own grasp for power.
Hey! Stop right there!
She has no idea what she's unleashed.
But she will.
Soon, everyone will.

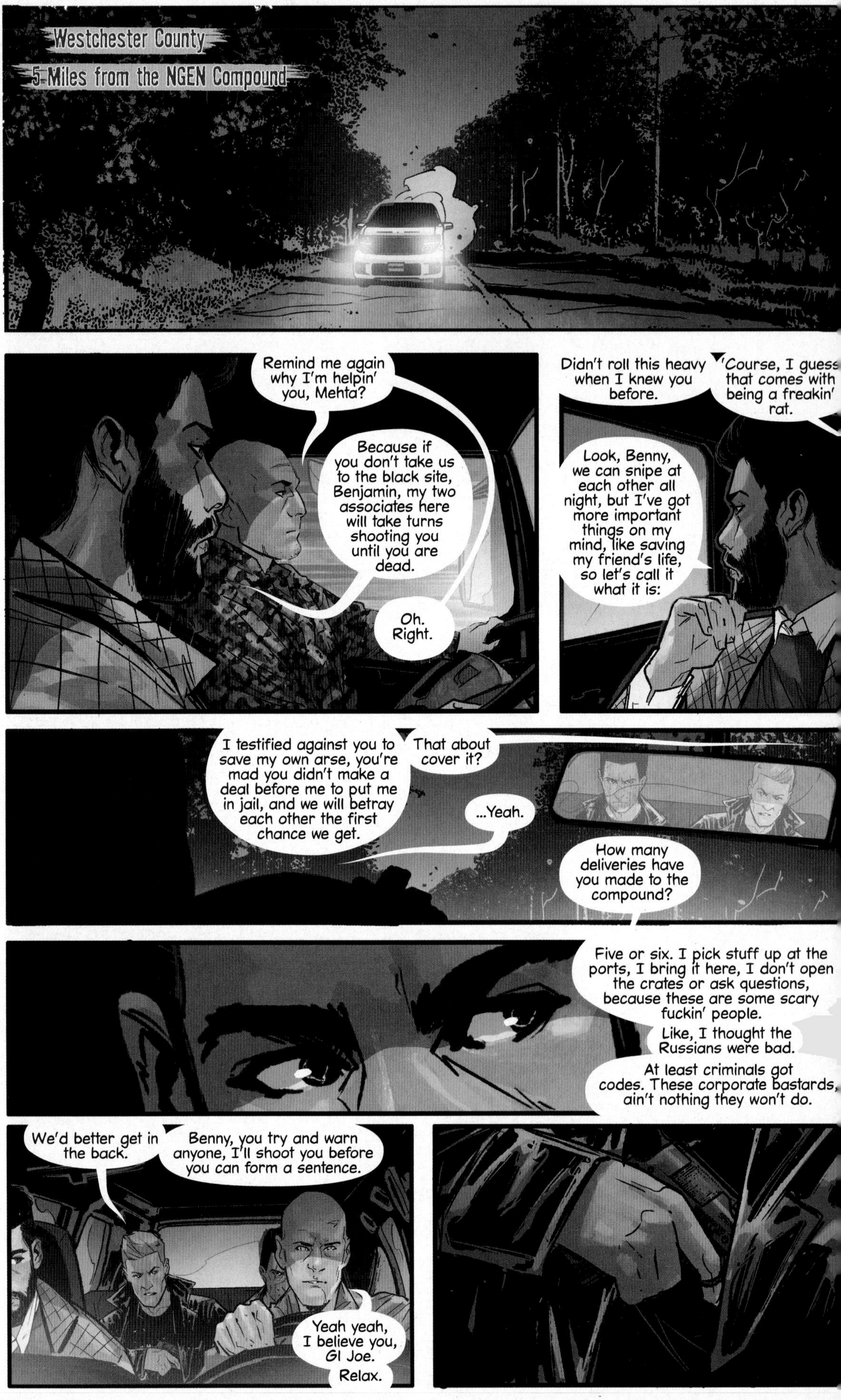
Westchester County
5 Miles from the NGEN Compound
Remind me again why I'm helpin' you, Mehta?
Because if you don't take us to the black site, Benjamin, my two associates here will take turns shooting you until you are dead.
Oh. Right.
Didn't roll this heavy when I knew you before.
'Course, I guess that comes with being a freakin' rat.
Look, Benny, we can snipe at each other all night, but I've got more important things on my mind, like saving my friend's life, so let's call it what it is:
I testified against you to save my own arse, you're mad you didn't make a deal before me to put me in jail, and we will betray each other the first chance we get.
That about cover it?
...Yeah.
How many deliveries have you made to the compound?
Five or six. I pick stuff up at the ports, I bring it here, I don't open the crates or ask questions, because these are some scary fuckin' people.
Like, I thought the Russians were bad.
At least criminals got codes. These corporate bastards, ain't nothing they won't do.
We'd better get in the back.
Benny, you try and warn anyone, I'll shoot you before you can form a sentence.
Yeah yeah, I believe you, GI Joe.
Relax.

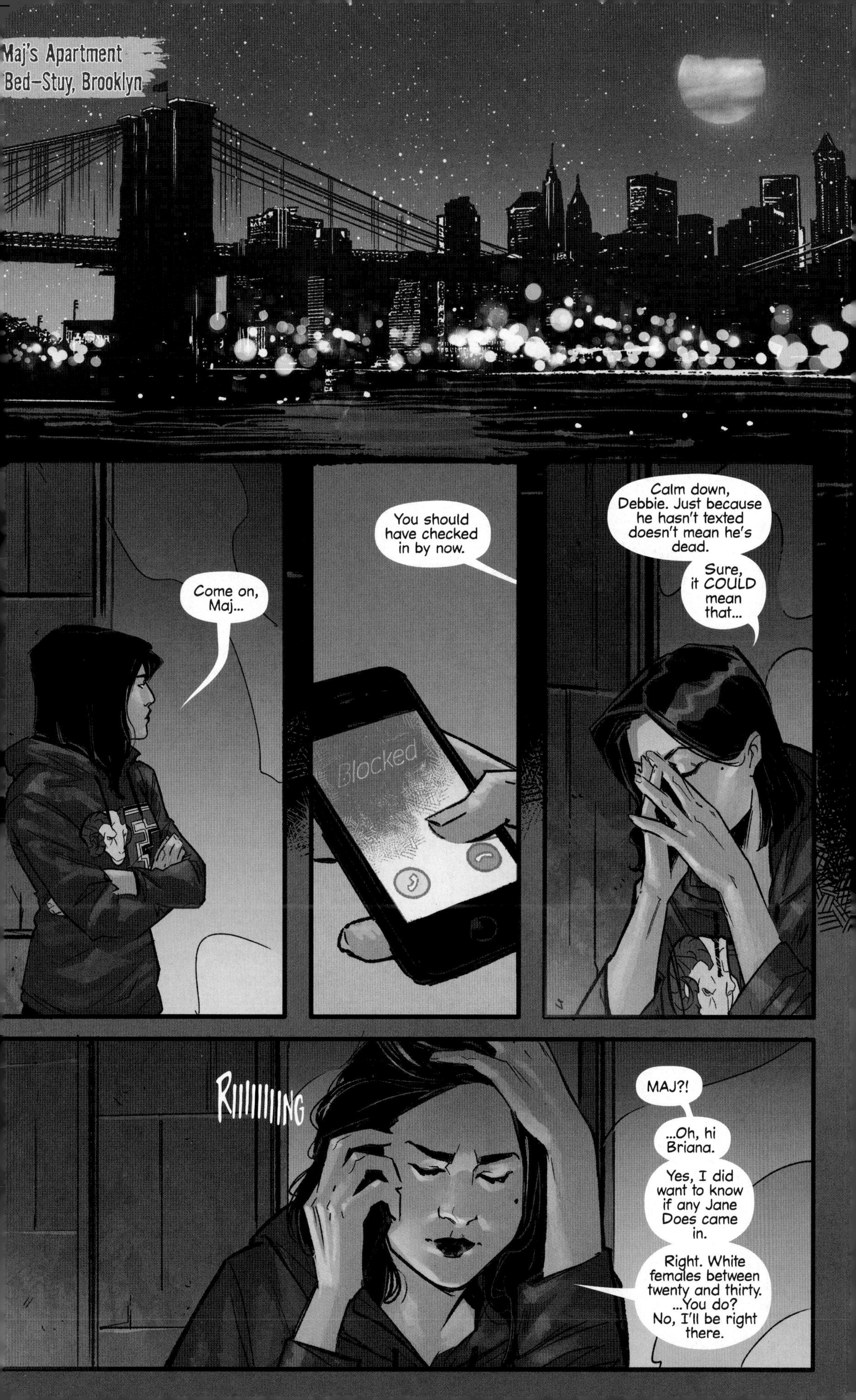
Maj's Apartment
Bed-Stuy, Brooklyn
Come on, Maj...
You should have checked in by now.
Blocked
Calm down, Debbie. Just because he hasn't texted doesn't mean he's dead.
Sure, it COULD mean that...
RIIIIIIING
MAJ?!
...Oh, hi Briana.
Yes, I did want to know if any Jane Does came in.
Right. White females between twenty and thirty. ...You do? No, I'll be right there.

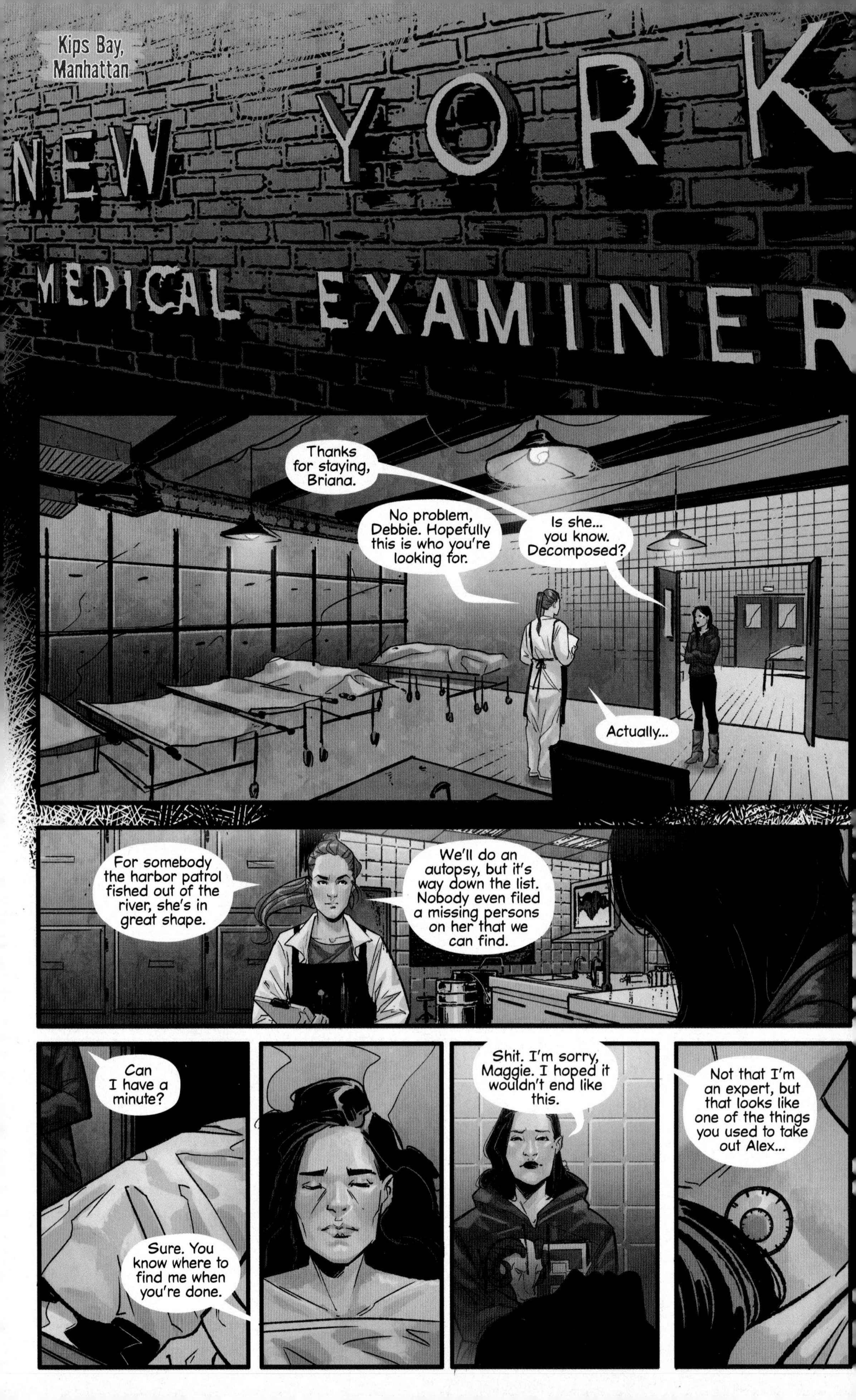
Kips Bay, Manhattan
NEW YORK
MEDICAL EXAMINER
Thanks for staying, Briana.
No problem, Debbie. Hopefully this is who you're looking for.
Is she... you know. Decomposed?
Actually...
For somebody the harbor patrol fished out of the river, she's in great shape.
We'll do an autopsy, but it's way down the list. Nobody even filed a missing persons on her that we can find.
Can I have a minute?
Sure. You know where to find me when you're done.
Shit. I'm sorry, Maggie. I hoped it wouldn't end like this.
Not that I'm an expert, but that looks like one of the things you used to take out Alex...

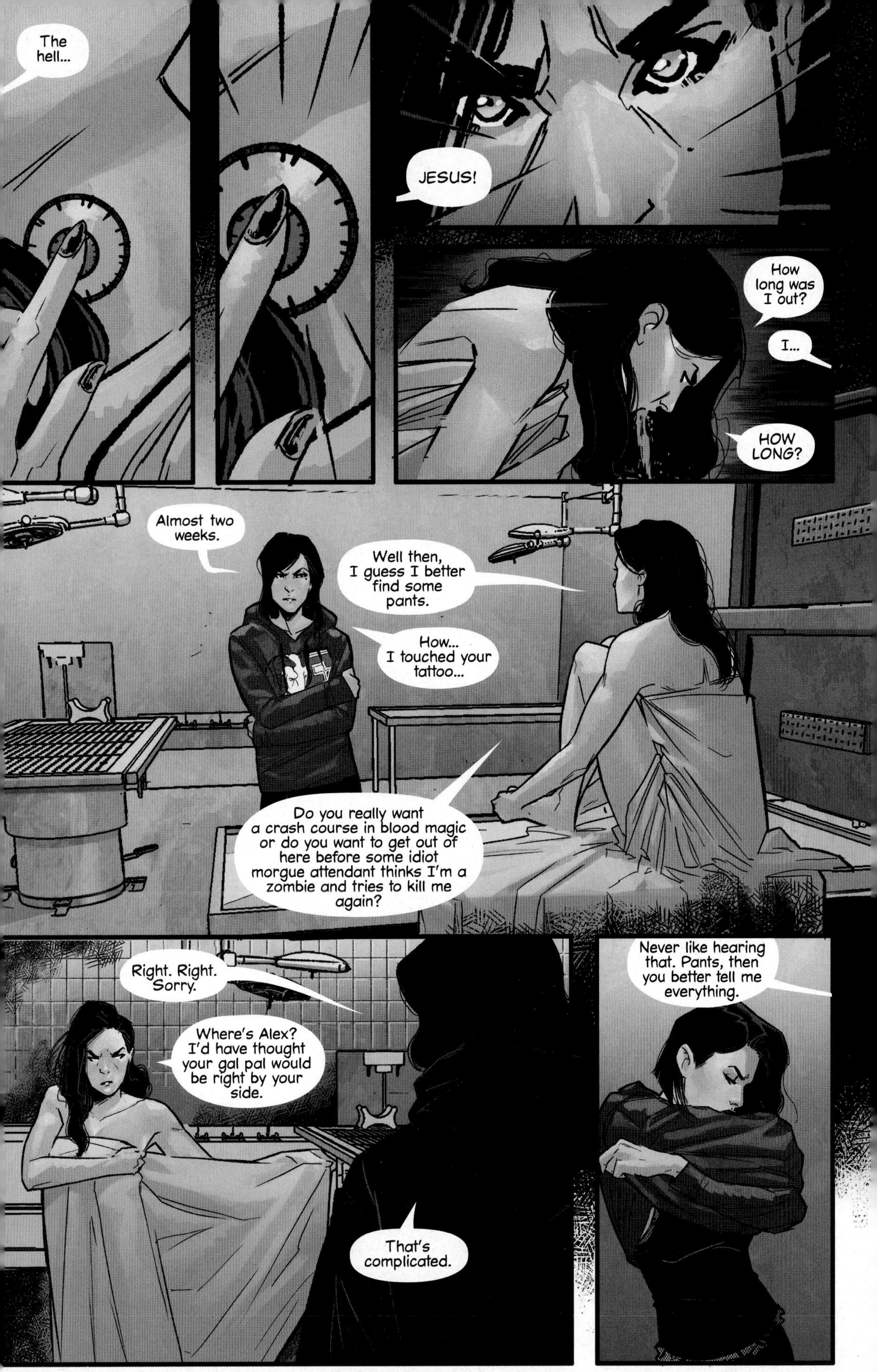
The hell...
JESUS!
How long was I out?
I...
HOW LONG?
Almost two weeks.
Well then, I guess I better find some pants.
How... I touched your tattoo...
Do you really want a crash course in blood magic or do you want to get out of here before some idiot morgue attendant thinks I'm a zombie and tries to kill me again?
Right. Right. Sorry.
Where's Alex? I'd have thought your gal pal would be right by your side.
That's complicated.
Never like hearing that. Pants, then you better tell me everything.

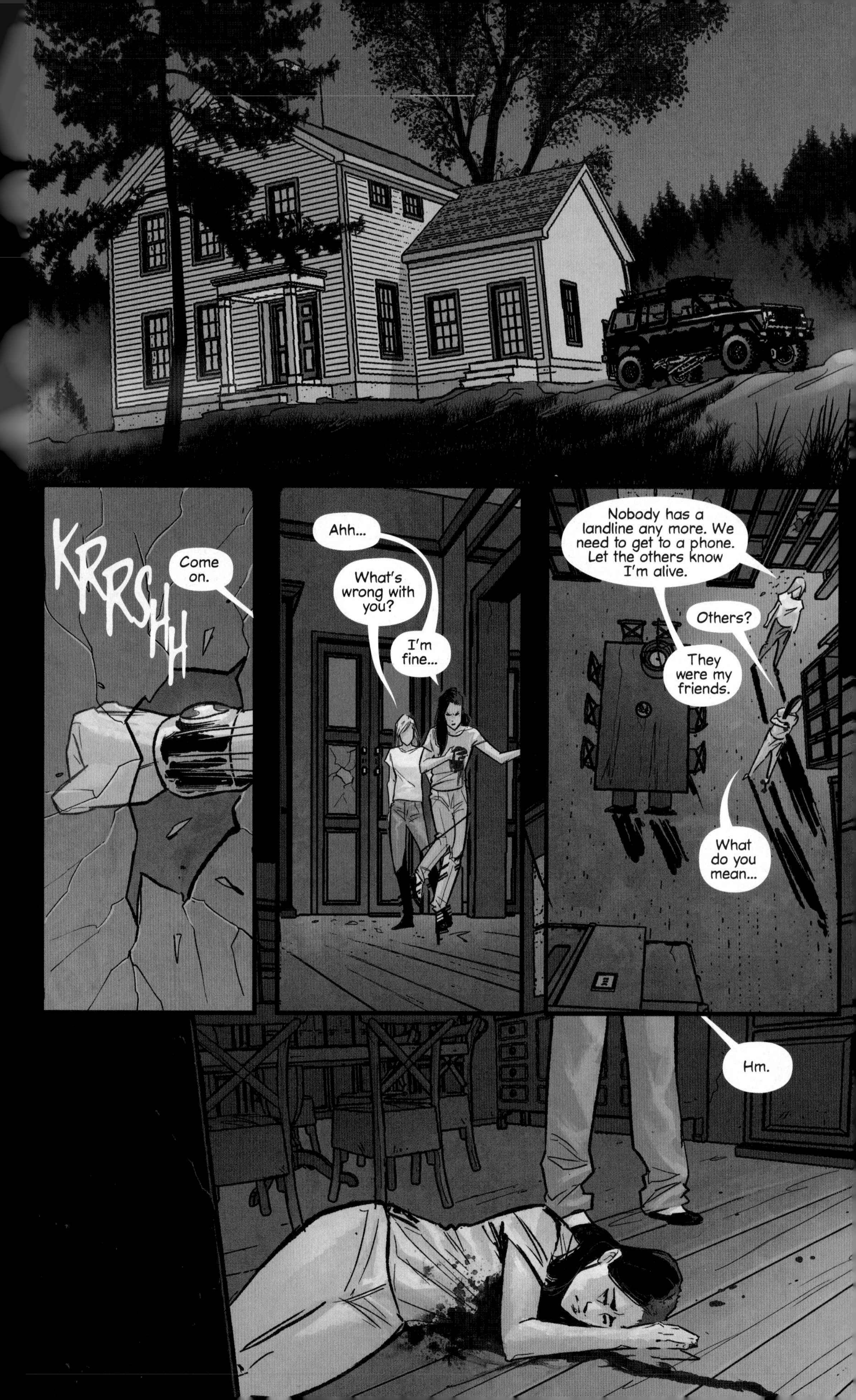
KRRSHH
Come on.
Ahh...
What's wrong with you?
I'm fine...
Nobody has a landline any more. We need to get to a phone. Let the others know I'm alive.
Others?
They were my friends.
What do you mean...
Hm.

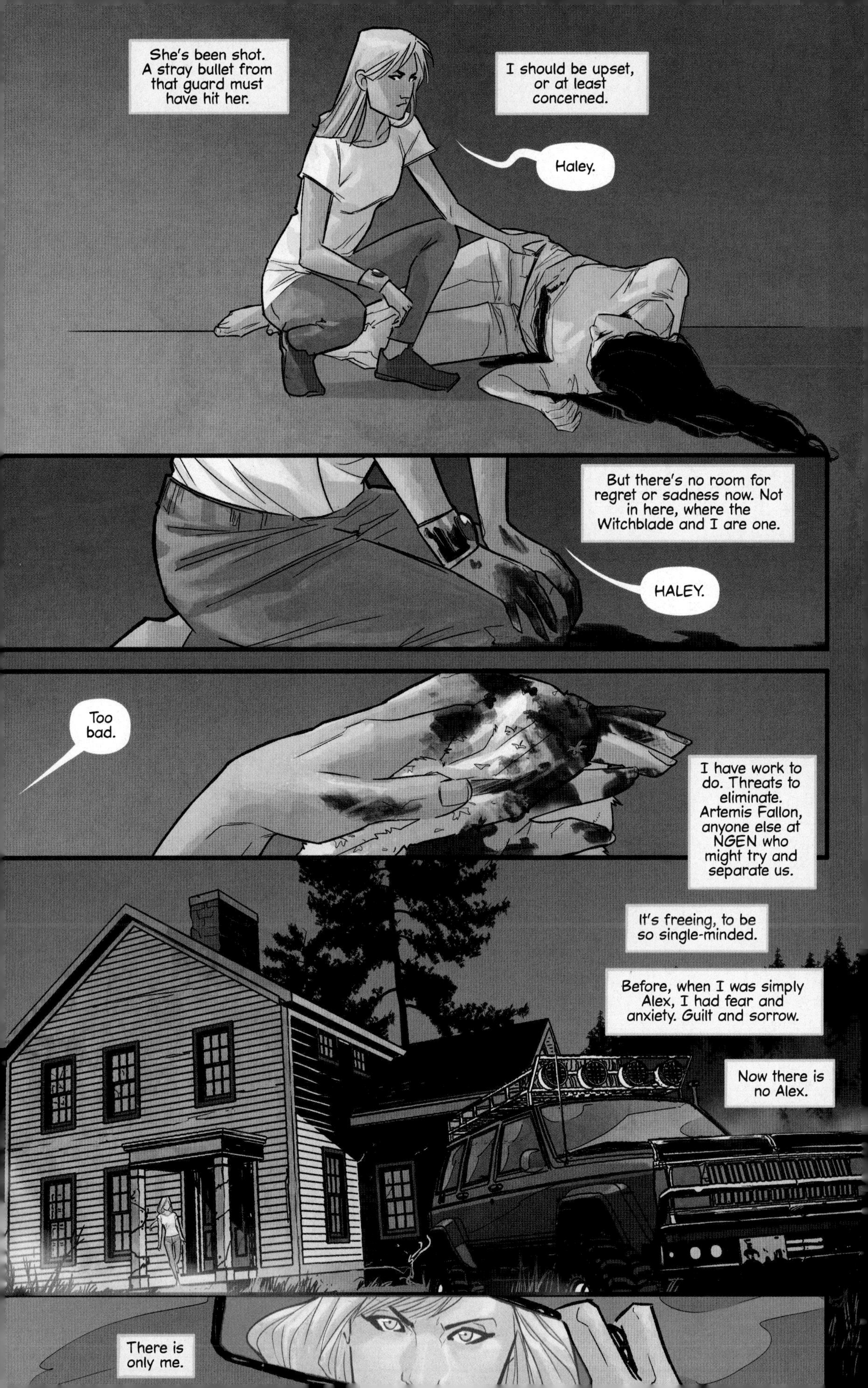
She's been shot. A stray bullet from that guard must have hit her.
I should be upset, or at least concerned.
Haley.
But there's no room for regret or sadness now. Not in here, where the Witchblade and I are one.
HALEY.
Too bad.
I have work to do. Threats to eliminate. Artemis Fallon, anyone else at NGEN who might try and separate us.
It's freeing, to be so single-minded.
Before, when I was simply Alex, I had fear and anxiety. Guilt and sorrow.
Now there is no Alex.
There is only me.

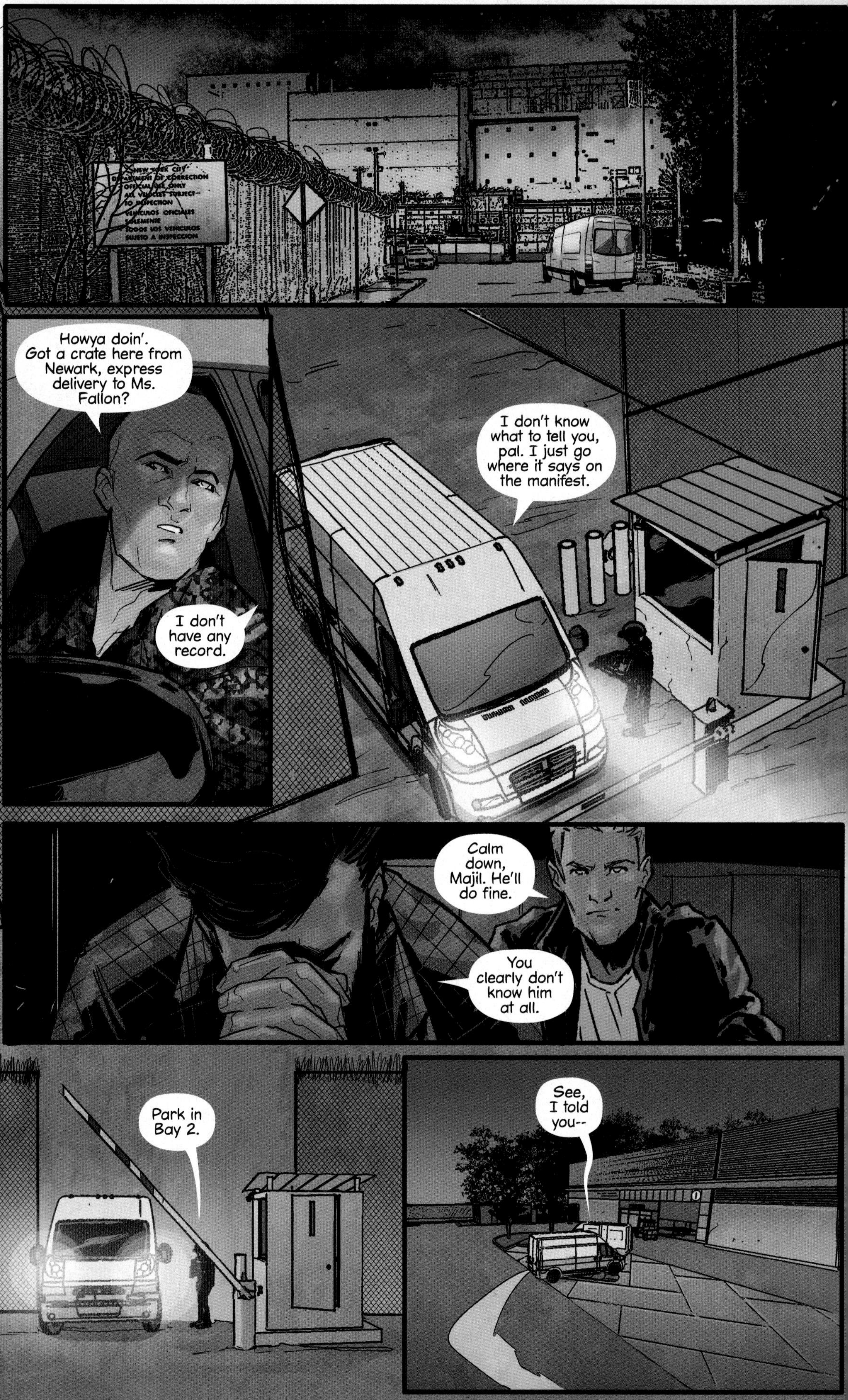
NEW YORK CITY DEPARTMENT OF CORRECTION OFFICIAL USE ONLY ALL VEHICLES SUBJECT TO INSPECTION VEHICULOS OFICIALES SOLAMENTE TODOS LOS VEHICULOS SUJETO A INSPECCION
Howya doin'. Got a crate here from Newark, express delivery to Ms. Fallon?
I don't have any record.
I don't know what to tell you, pal. I just go where it says on the manifest.
Calm down, Majil. He'll do fine.
You clearly don't know him at all.
Park in Bay 2.
See, I told you--

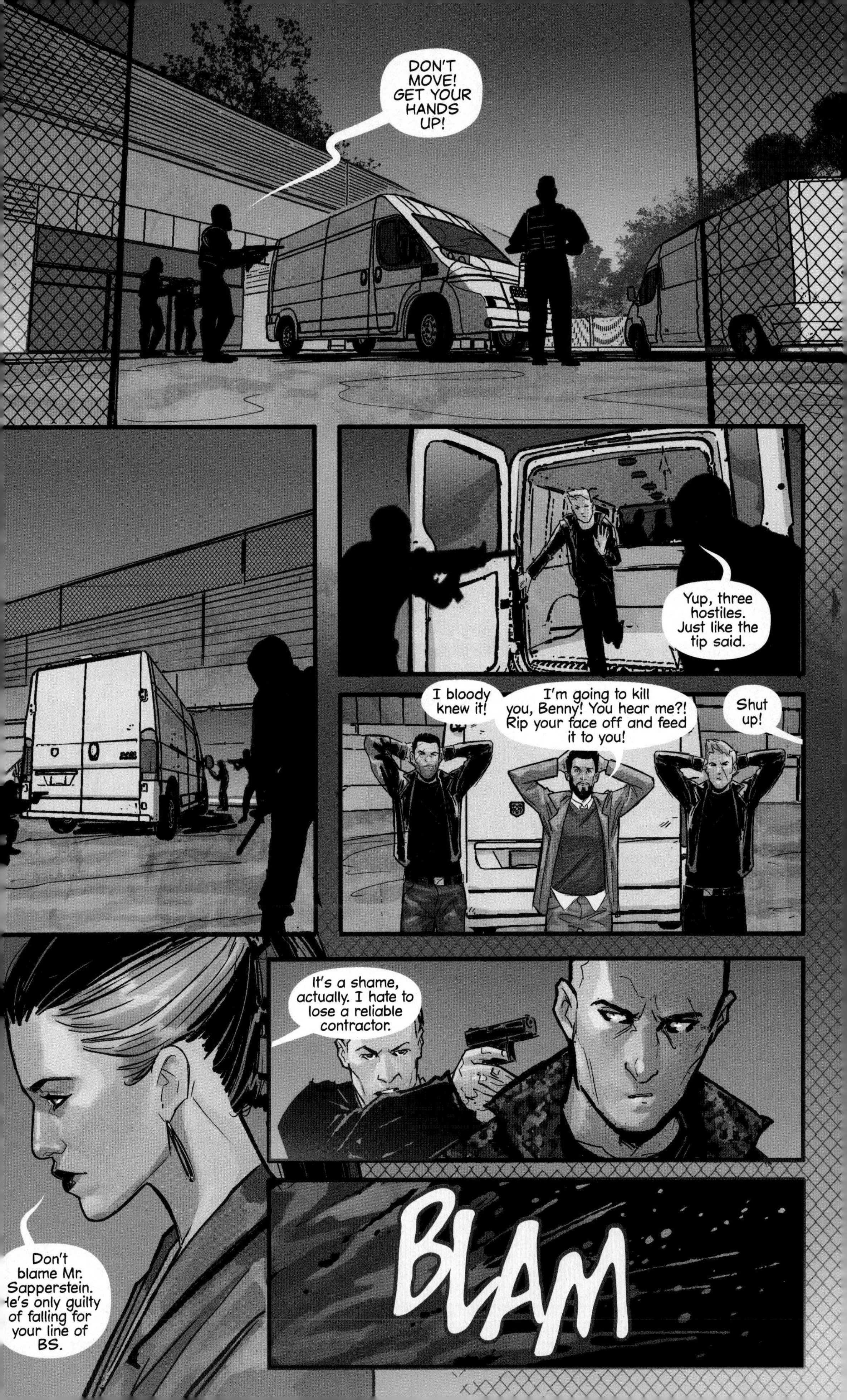
DON'T MOVE! GET YOUR HANDS UP!
Yup, three hostiles. Just like the tip said.
I bloody knew it!
I'm going to kill you, Benny! You hear me?! Rip your face off and feed it to you!
Shut up!
It's a shame, actually. I hate to lose a reliable contractor.
Don't blame Mr. Sapperstein. He's only guilty of falling for your line of BS.
BLAM

Fuck!

Calm down, Mr. Mehta. I'm not going to kill any of you. Not yet.

You and Mr. Meyers are actually one of the few things that can bring Alex back here.

Back? She escaped already? I told you that this Guantanamo crap wouldn't hold her.

Yes, yes, we all know how much you love being right, John. Sweaty, dark circles, and you've lost weight. I bet you're aching for a shot right now.

Go to Hell.

Says the junkie who sold out his first love to me.

So this is your plan? Hold us hostage and wait for Alex to come back and save us?

You three were foolish enough to think she needed a rescue, why shouldn't she be just as foolish?

I can't wait to watch her rip the flesh from your bones, Artemis. Take Mr. Meyers and his friend to a holding cell. Make sure they're treated well. Asher and I have a few things to get straight between us once and for all.

You don't scare me.

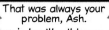

The Witchblade is only as good as the woman wearing it, and Alex has way too many feelings to handle it properly. You chose very poorly, Asher.

That was always your problem, Ash. Fear is healthy. It keeps you from walking into the jaws of a snake. You don't feel fear, it swallows you. Still, you'll be useful. We already adapted whatever's keeping you young to make a round of soldiers in my father's day. Imagine what I can learn from you when there's no incentive to keep you alive.

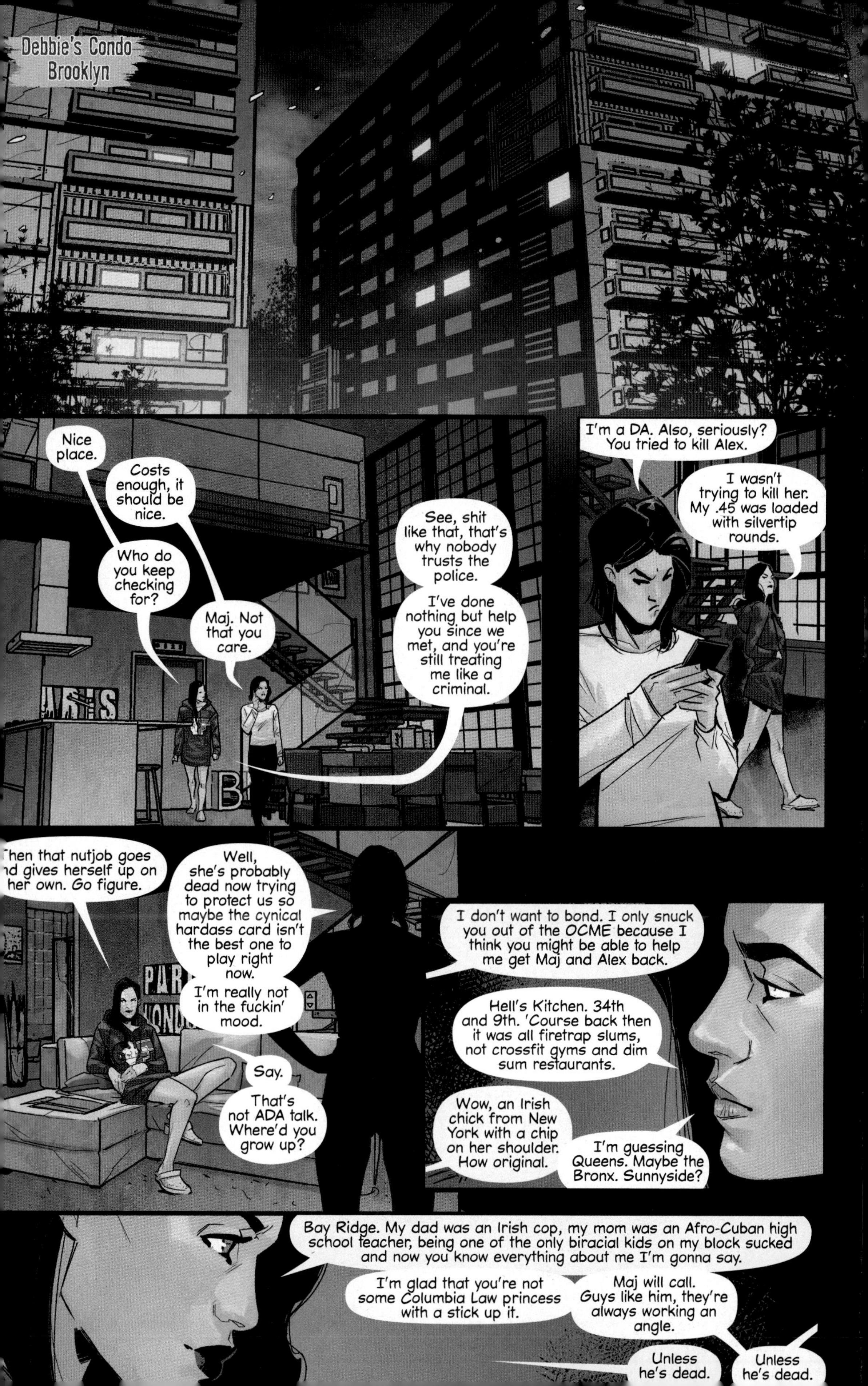
Debbie's Condo
Brooklyn
Nice place.
Costs enough, it should be nice.
Who do you keep checking for?
Maj. Not that you care.
See, shit like that, that's why nobody trusts the police.
I've done nothing but help you since we met, and you're still treating me like a criminal.
I'm a DA. Also, seriously? You tried to kill Alex.
I wasn't trying to kill her. My .45 was loaded with silvertip rounds.
Then that nutjob goes and gives herself up on her own. Go figure.
Well, she's probably dead now trying to protect us so maybe the cynical hardass card isn't the best one to play right now.
I'm really not in the fuckin' mood.
Say.
That's not ADA talk. Where'd you grow up?
I don't want to bond. I only snuck you out of the OCME because I think you might be able to help me get Maj and Alex back.
Hell's Kitchen. 34th and 9th. 'Course back then it was all firetrap slums, not crossfit gyms and dim sum restaurants.
Wow, an Irish chick from New York with a chip on her shoulder. How original.
I'm guessing Queens. Maybe the Bronx. Sunnyside?
Bay Ridge. My dad was an Irish cop, my mom was an Afro-Cuban high school teacher, being one of the only biracial kids on my block sucked and now you know everything about me I'm gonna say.
I'm glad that you're not some Columbia Law princess with a stick up it.
Maj will call. Guys like him, they're always working an angle.
Unless he's dead.
Unless he's dead.

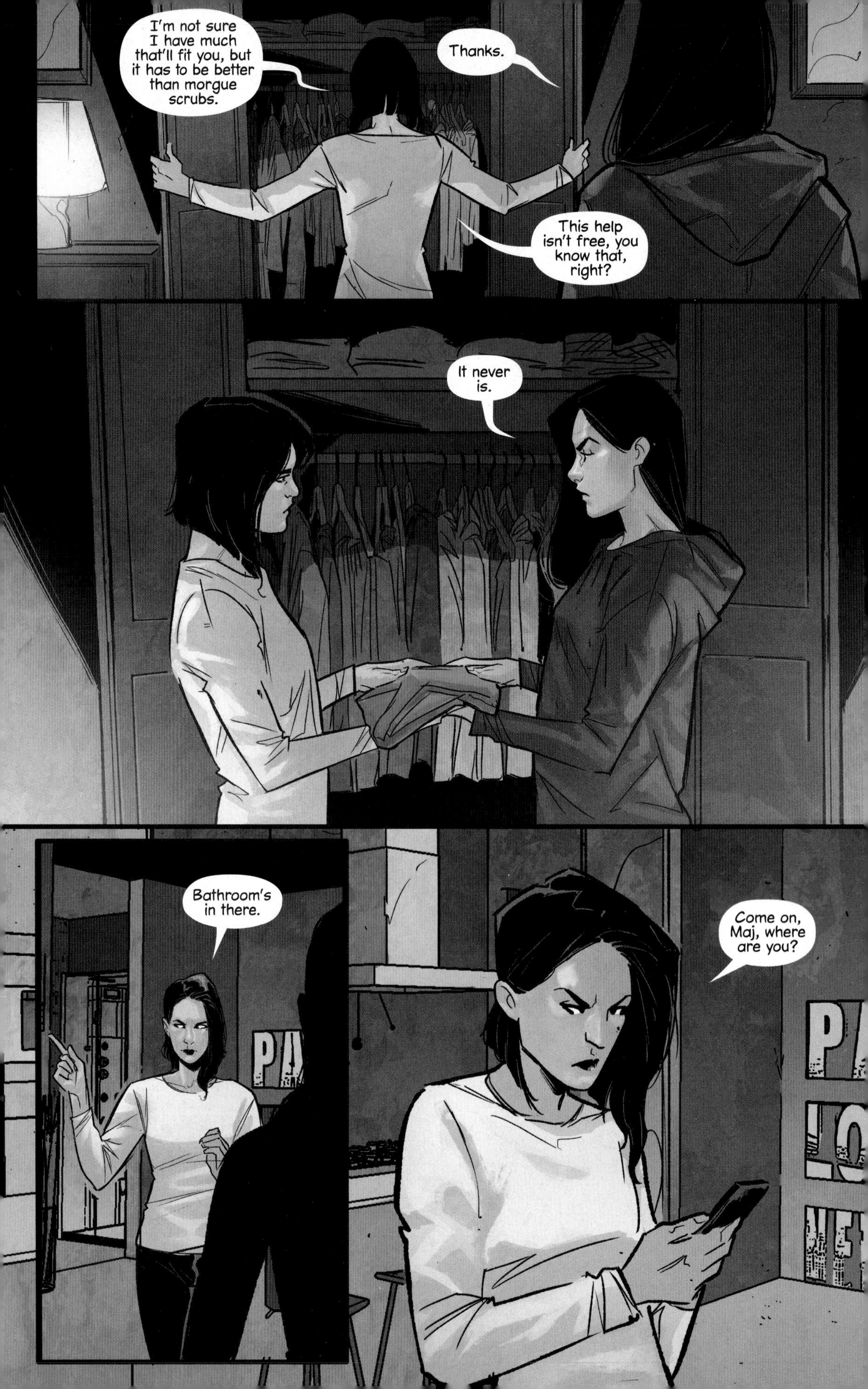
I'm not sure I have much that'll fit you, but it has to be better than morgue scrubs.
Thanks.
This help isn't free, you know that, right?
It never is.
Bathroom's in there.
Come on, Maj, where are you?

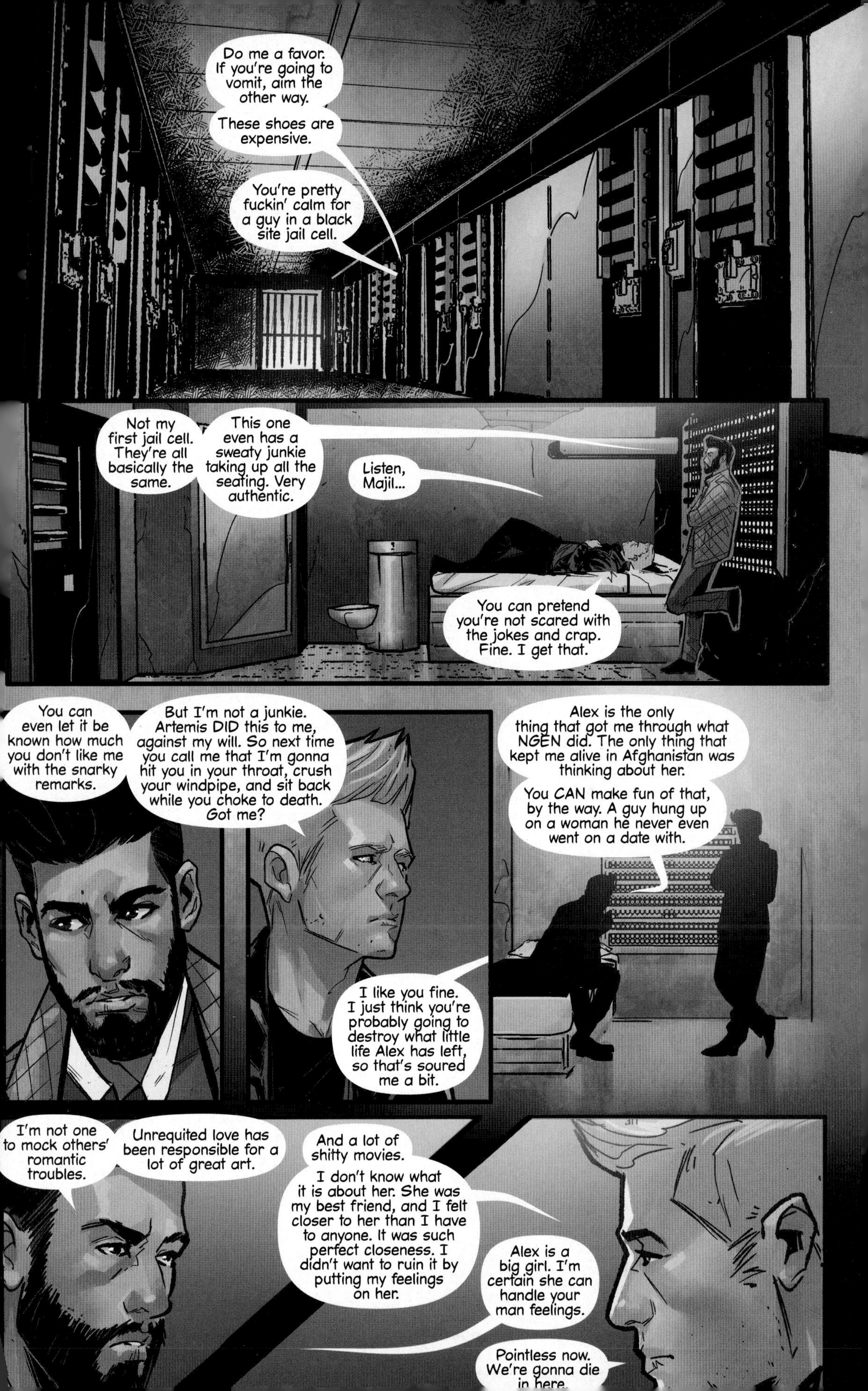
Do me a favor. If you're going to vomit, aim the other way.
These shoes are expensive.
You're pretty fuckin' calm for a guy in a black site jail cell.
Not my first jail cell. They're all basically the same.
This one even has a sweaty junkie taking up all the seating. Very authentic.
Listen, Majil...
You can pretend you're not scared with the jokes and crap. Fine. I get that.
You can even let it be known how much you don't like me with the snarky remarks.
But I'm not a junkie. Artemis DID this to me, against my will. So next time you call me that I'm gonna hit you in your throat, crush your windpipe, and sit back while you choke to death. Got me?
I like you fine. I just think you're probably going to destroy what little life Alex has left, so that's soured me a bit.
Alex is the only thing that got me through what NGEN did. The only thing that kept me alive in Afghanistan was thinking about her.
You CAN make fun of that, by the way. A guy hung up on a woman he never even went on a date with.
I'm not one to mock others' romantic troubles.
Unrequited love has been responsible for a lot of great art.
And a lot of shitty movies.
I don't know what it is about her. She was my best friend, and I felt closer to her than I have to anyone. It was such perfect closeness. I didn't want to ruin it by putting my feelings on her.
Alex is a big girl. I'm certain she can handle your man feelings.
Pointless now. We're gonna die in here.

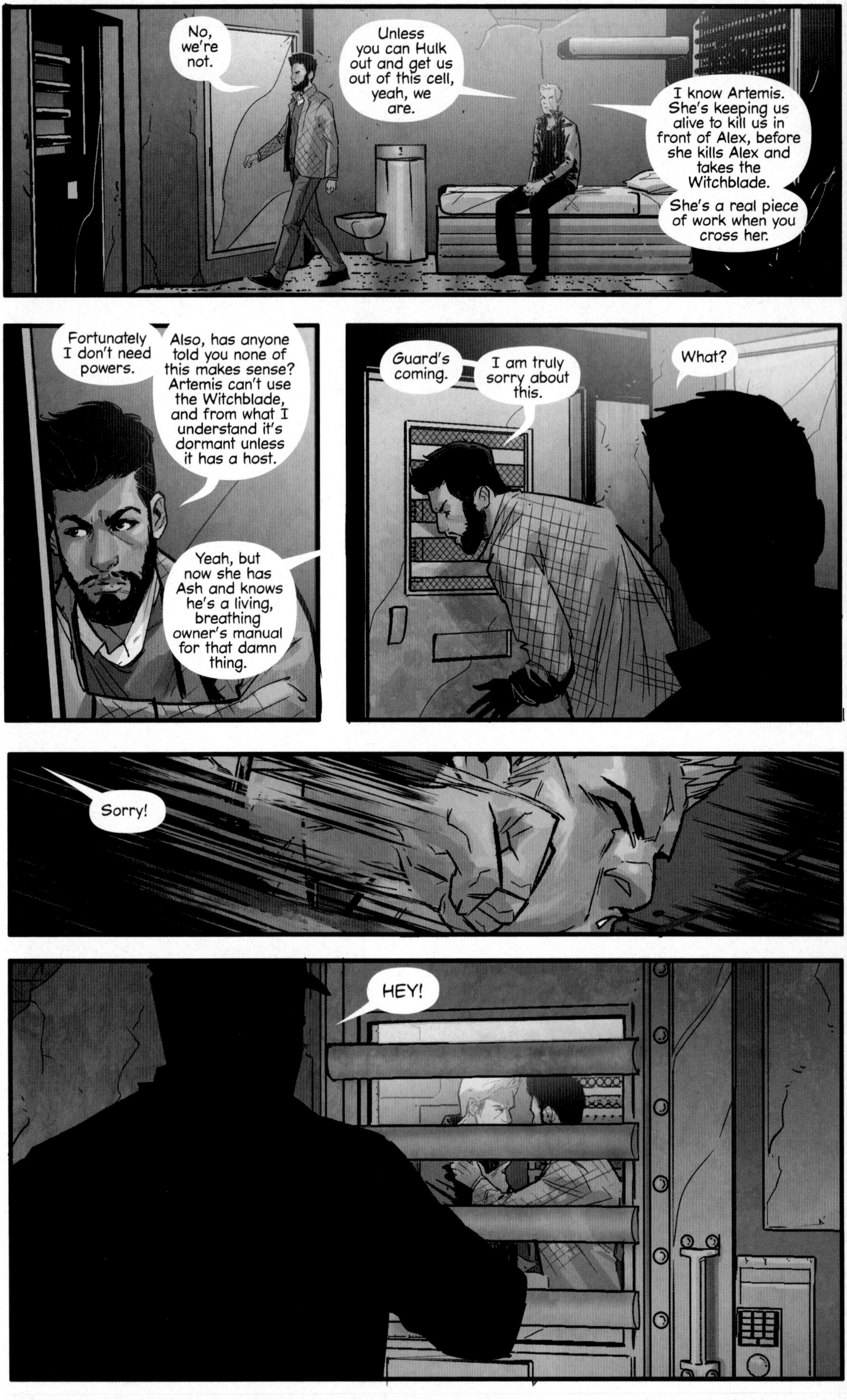
No, we're not.
Unless you can Hulk out and get us out of this cell, yeah, we are.
I know Artemis. She's keeping us alive to kill us in front of Alex, before she kills Alex and takes the Witchblade.
She's a real piece of work when you cross her.
Fortunately I don't need powers.
Also, has anyone told you none of this makes sense? Artemis can't use the Witchblade, and from what I understand it's dormant unless it has a host.
Yeah, but now she has Ash and knows he's a living, breathing owner's manual for that damn thing.
Guard's coming.
I am truly sorry about this.
What?
Sorry!
HEY!

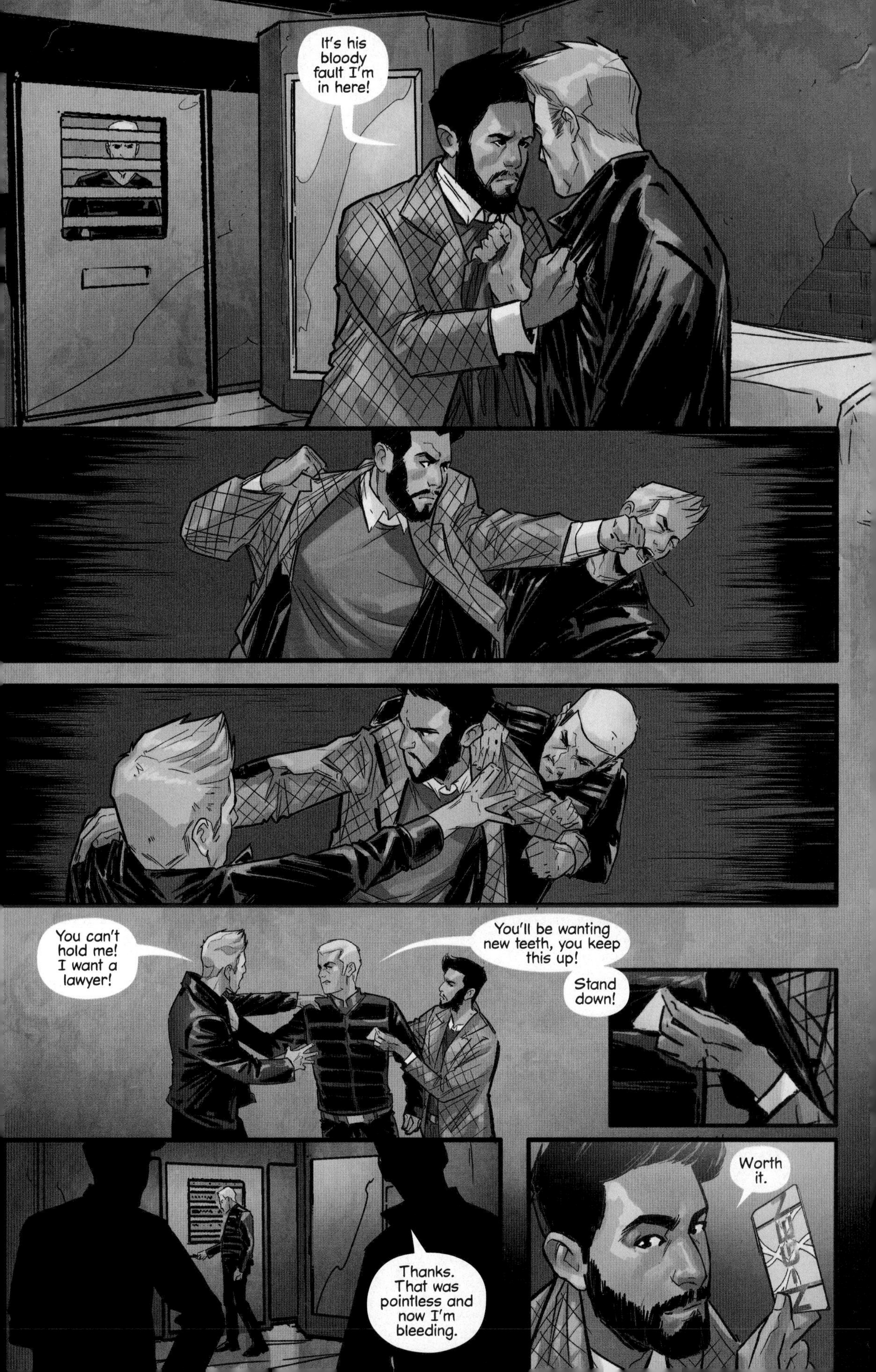
It's his bloody fault I'm in here!
You can't hold me! I want a lawyer!
You'll be wanting new teeth, you keep this up!
Stand down!
Thanks. That was pointless and now I'm bleeding.
Worth it.

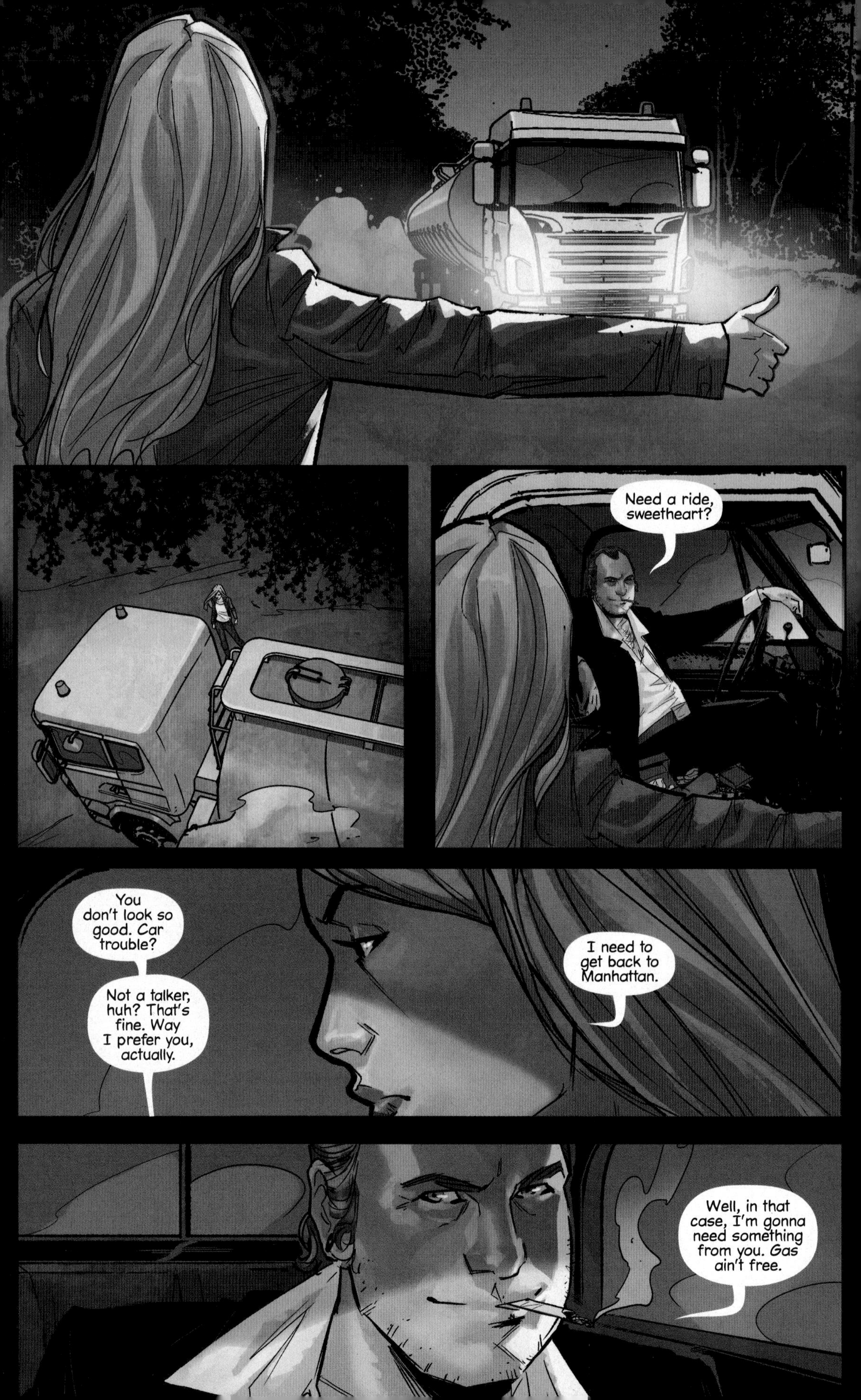
Need a ride, sweetheart?
You don't look so good. Car trouble?
Not a talker, huh? That's fine. Way I prefer you, actually.
I need to get back to Manhattan.
Well, in that case, I'm gonna need something from you. Gas ain't free.

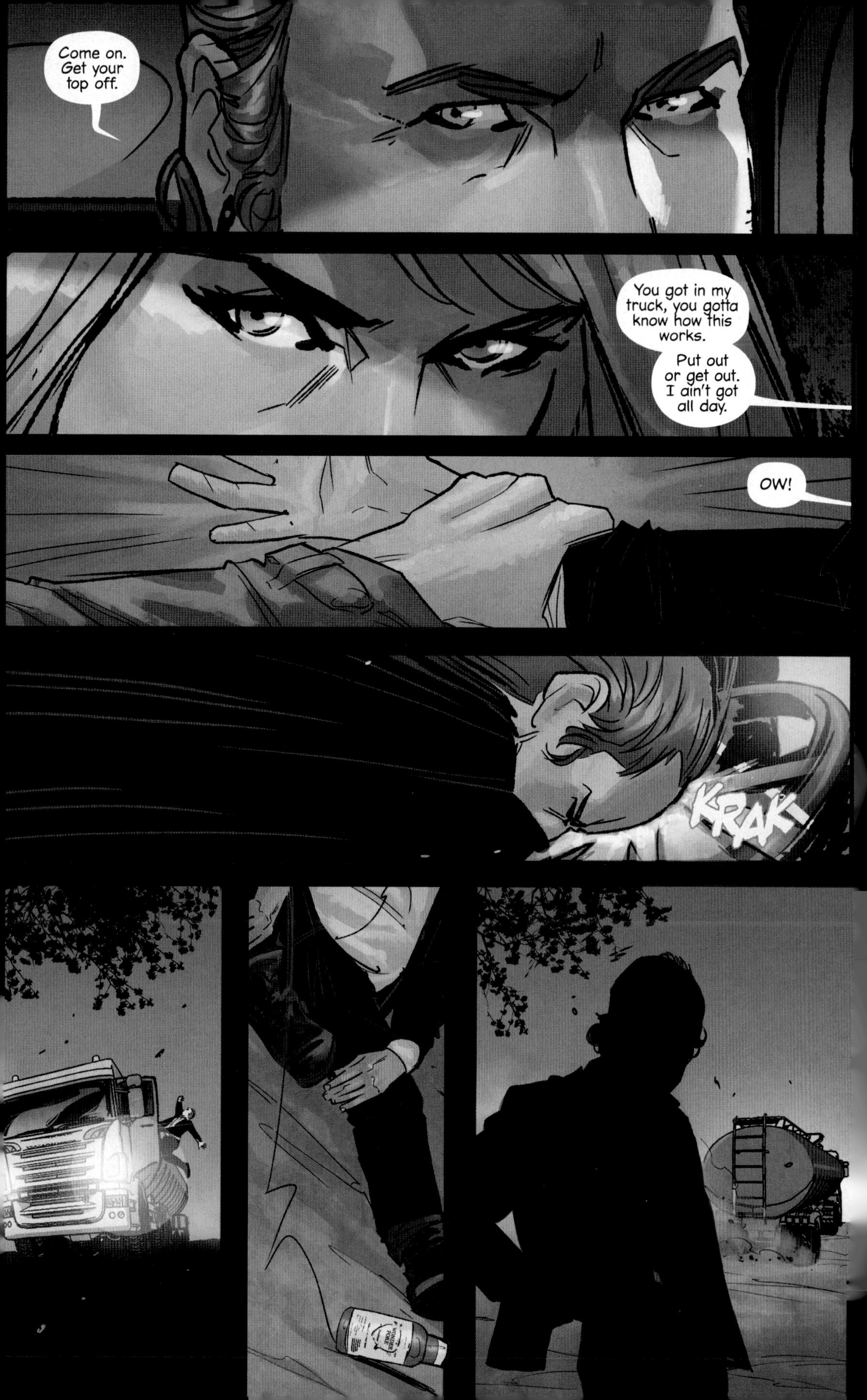
Come on. Get your top off.
You got in my truck, you gotta know how this works.
Put out or get out. I ain't got all day.
OW!
KRAK!

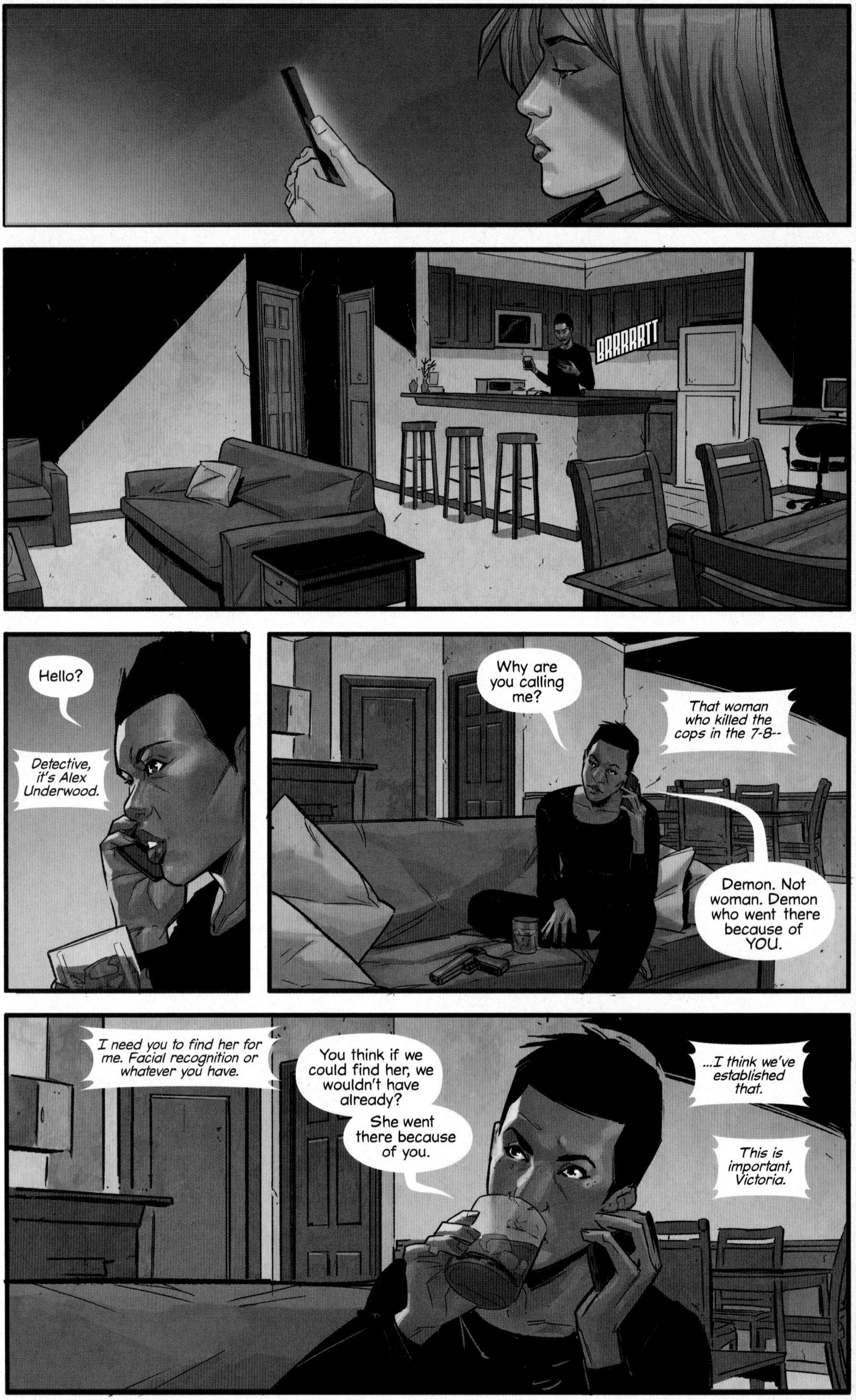
BRRRRRTT
Hello?
Detective, it's Alex Underwood.
Why are you calling me?
That woman who killed the cops in the 7-8--
Demon. Not woman. Demon who went there because of YOU.
I need you to find her for me. Facial recognition or whatever you have.
You think if we could find her, we wouldn't have already?
She went there because of you.
...I think we've established that.
This is important, Victoria.

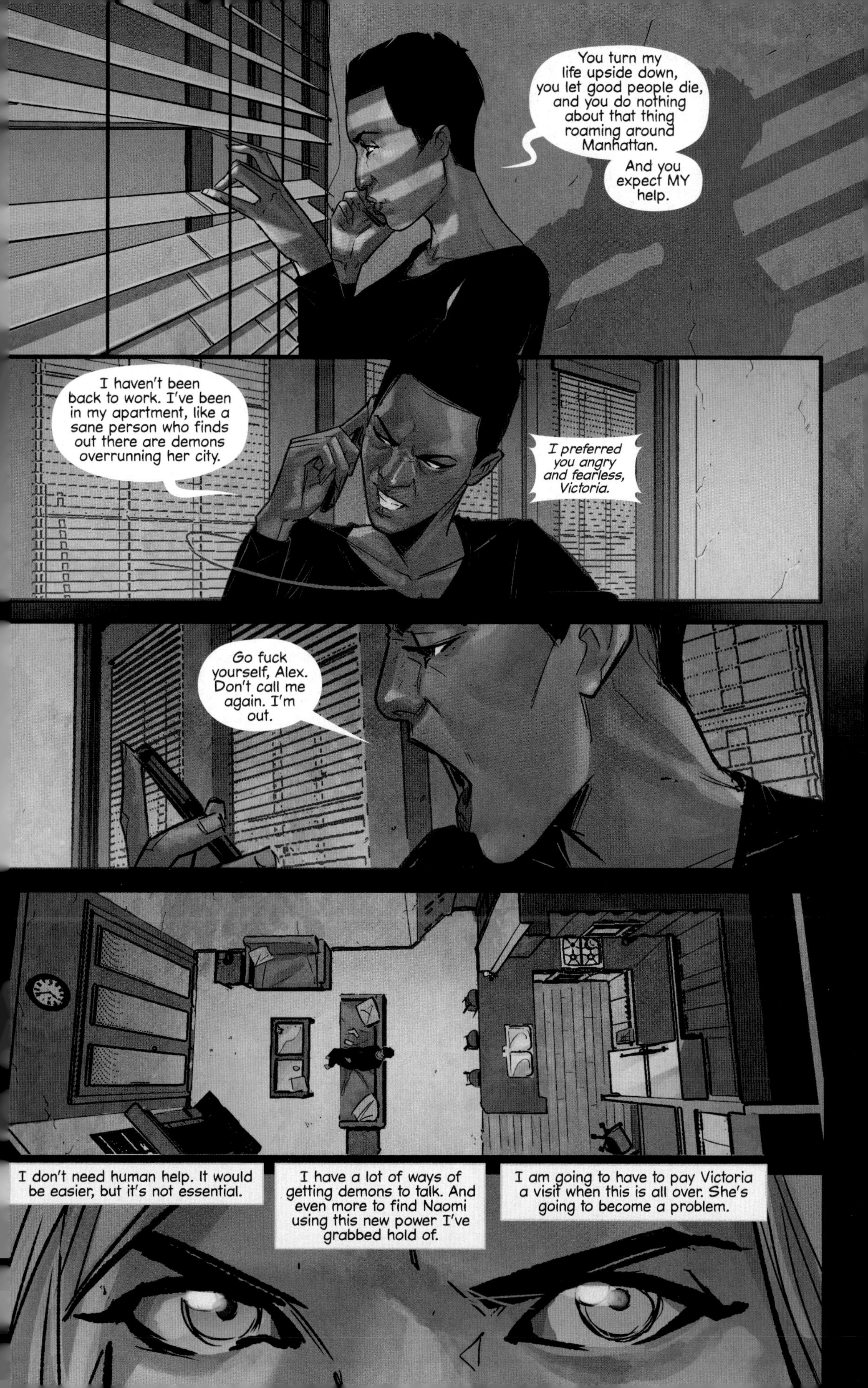
You turn my life upside down, you let good people die, and you do nothing about that thing roaming around Manhattan.
And you expect MY help.
I haven't been back to work. I've been in my apartment, like a sane person who finds out there are demons overrunning her city.
I preferred you angry and fearless, Victoria.
Go fuck yourself, Alex. Don't call me again. I'm out.
I don't need human help. It would be easier, but it's not essential.
I have a lot of ways of getting demons to talk. And even more to find Naomi using this new power I've grabbed hold of.
I am going to have to pay Victoria a visit when this is all over. She's going to become a problem.

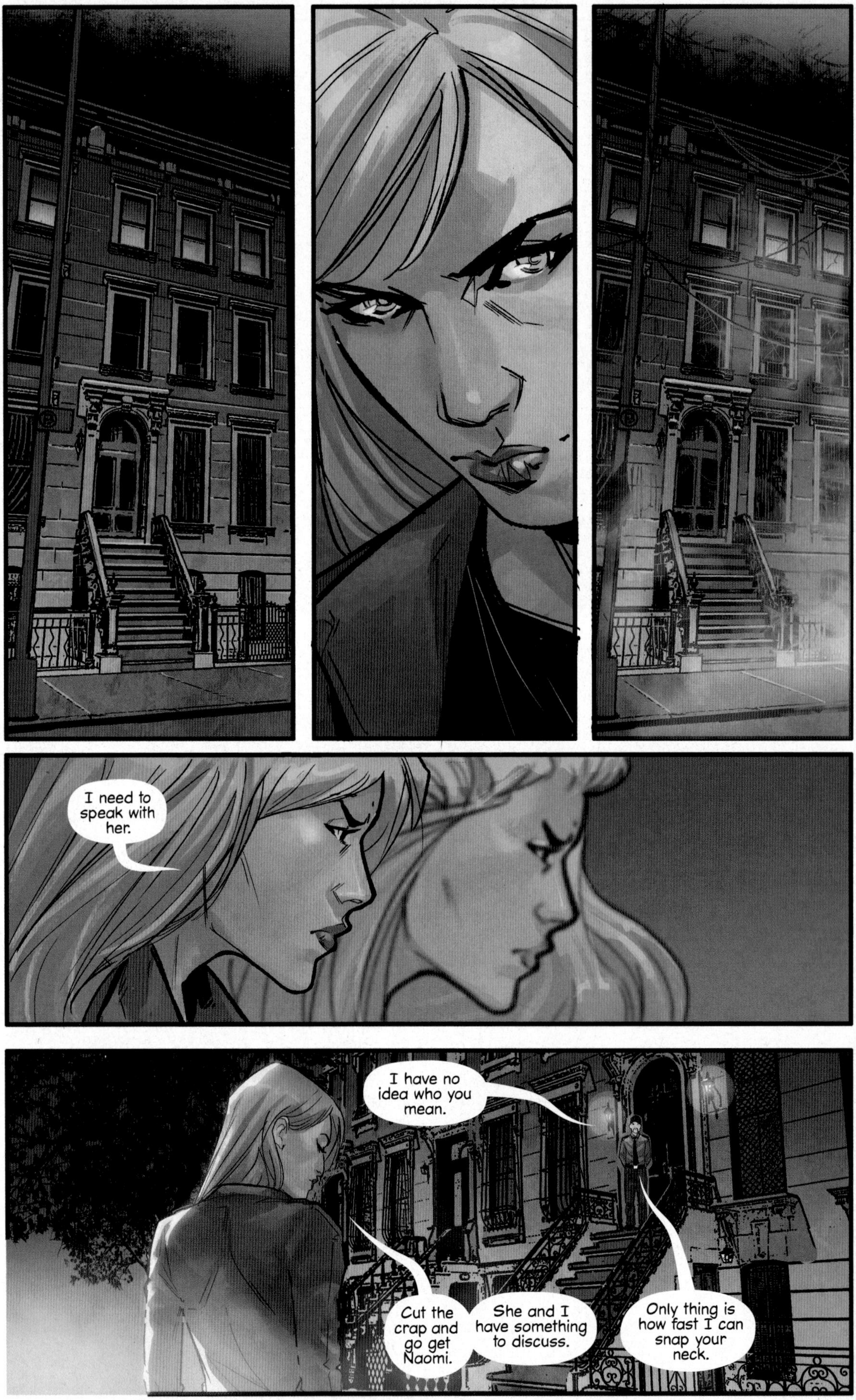
I need to speak with her.
I have no idea who you mean.
Cut the crap and go get Naomi.
She and I have something to discuss.
Only thing is how fast I can snap your neck.

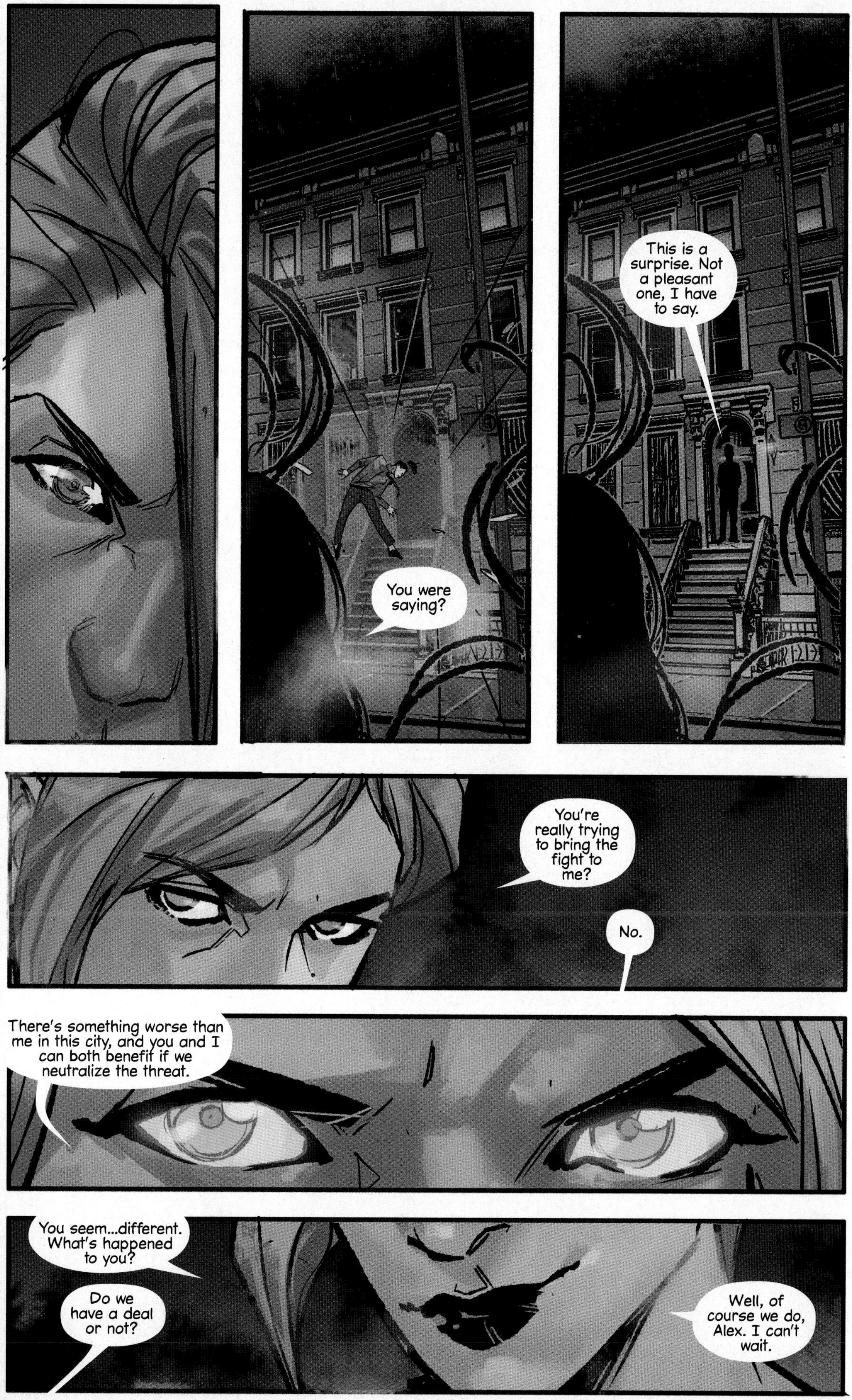
You were saying?
This is a surprise. Not a pleasant one, I have to say.
You're really trying to bring the fight to me?
No.
There's something worse than me in this city, and you and I can both benefit if we neutralize the threat.
You seem...different. What's happened to you?
Do we have a deal or not?
Well, of course we do, Alex. I can't wait.

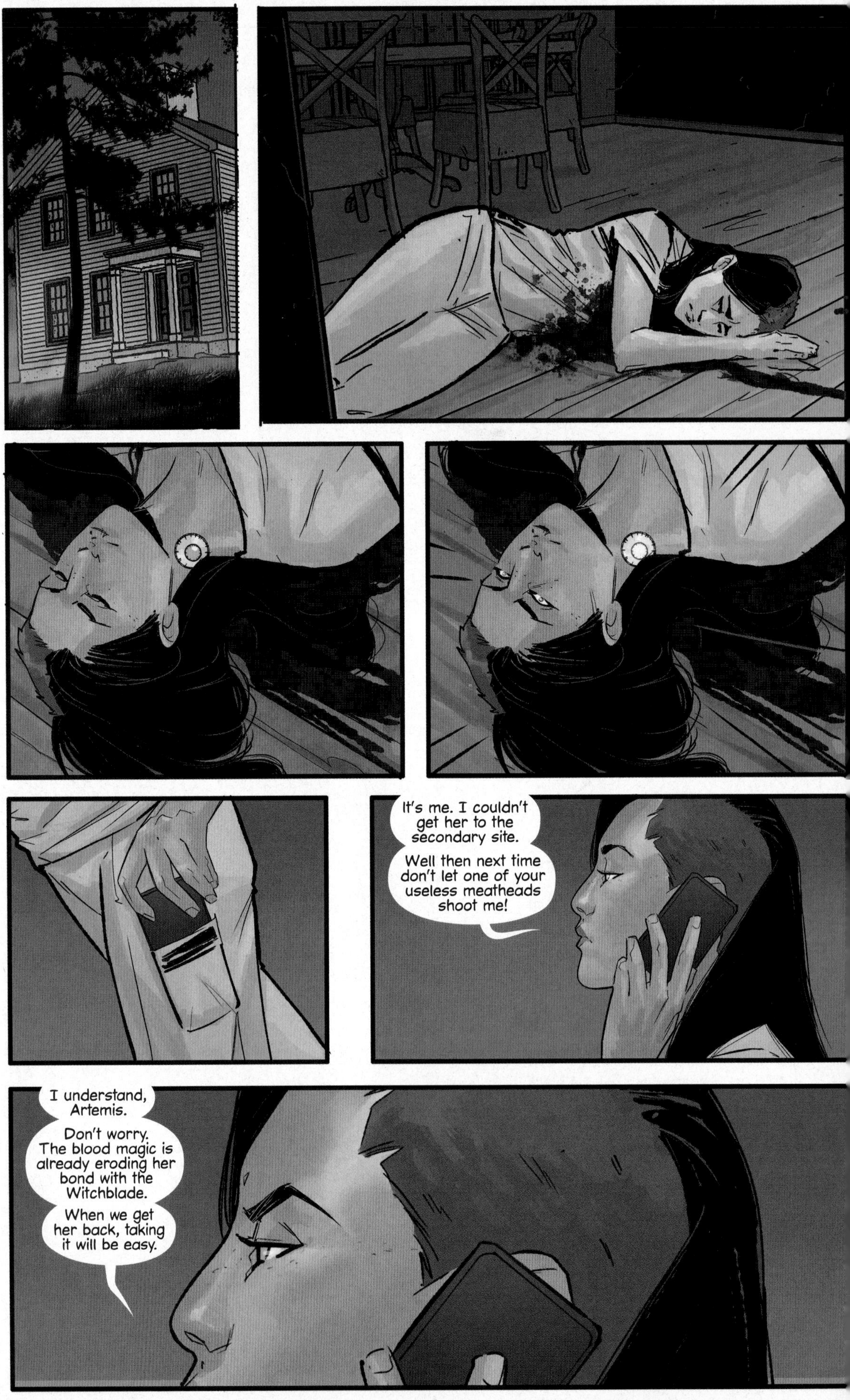
It's me. I couldn't get her to the secondary site.
Well then next time don't let one of your useless meatheads shoot me!
I understand, Artemis.
Don't worry. The blood magic is already eroding her bond with the Witchblade.
When we get her back, taking it will be easy.

CHAPTER **TWELVE**

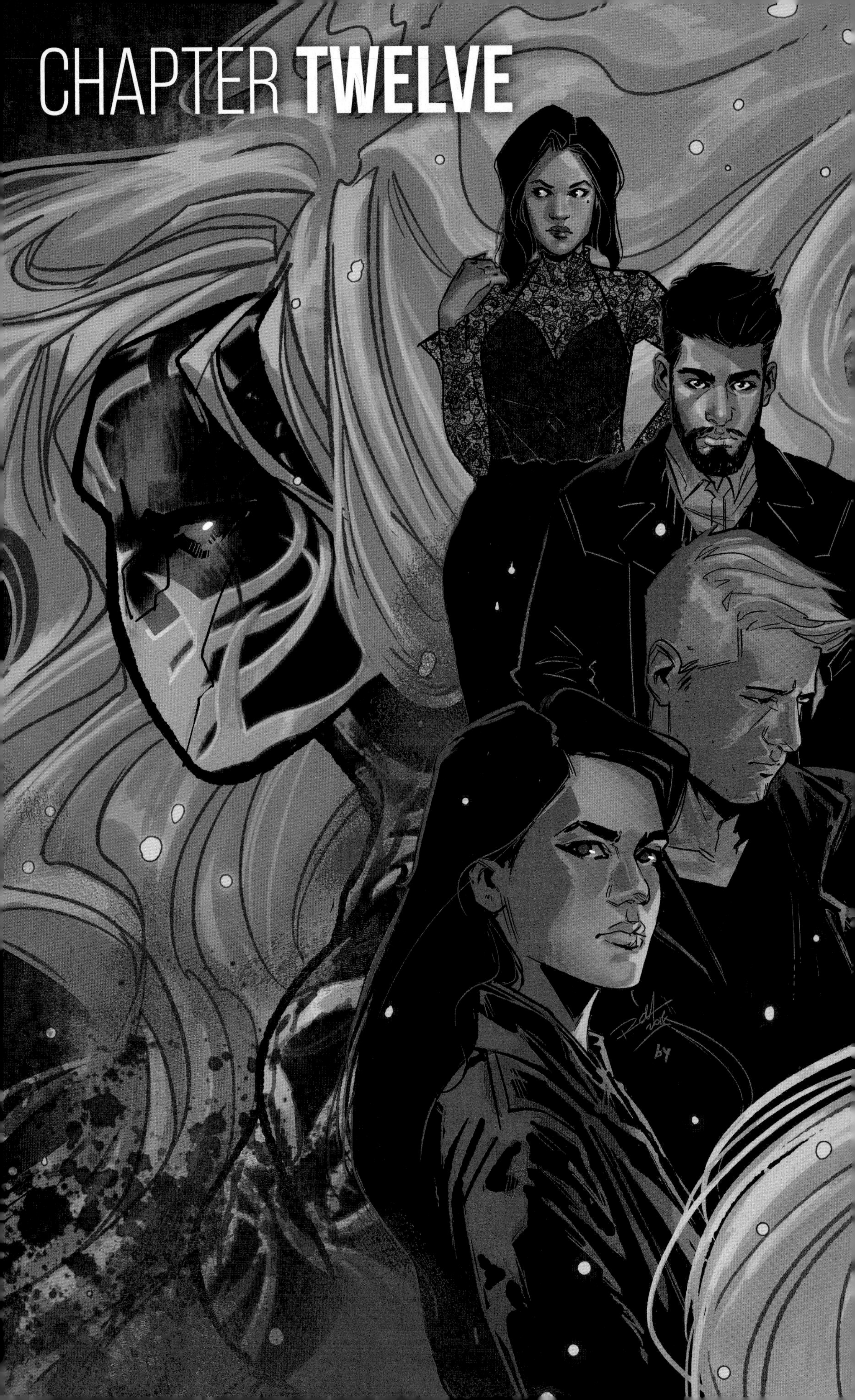

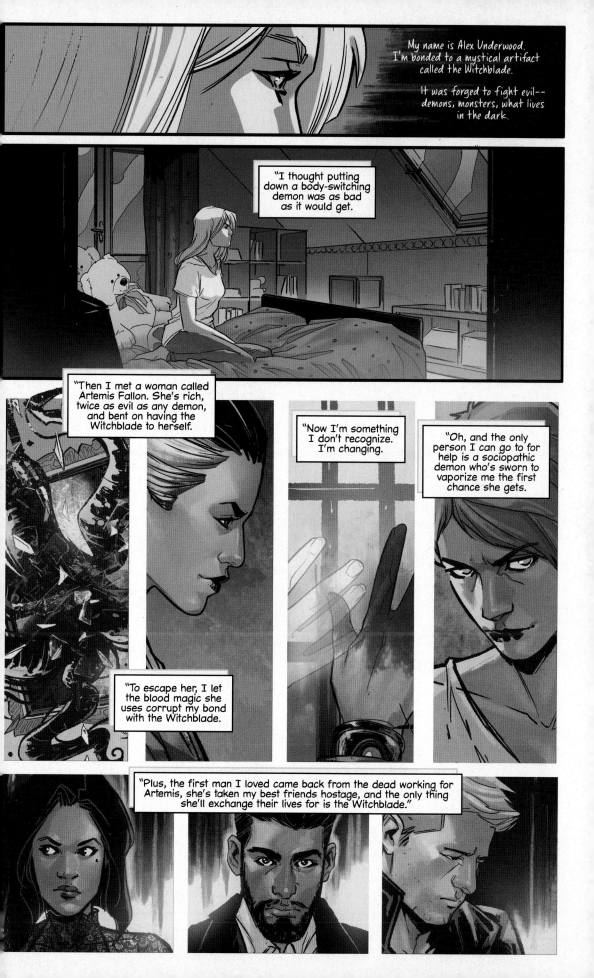

My name is Alex Underwood. I'm bonded to a mystical artifact called the Witchblade.

It was forged to fight evil-- demons, monsters, what lives in the dark.

"I thought putting down a body-switching demon was as bad as it would get.

"Then I met a woman called Artemis Fallon. She's rich, twice as evil as any demon, and bent on having the Witchblade to herself.

"Now I'm something I don't recognize. I'm changing.

"Oh, and the only person I can go to for help is a sociopathic demon who's sworn to vaporize me the first chance she gets.

"To escape her, I let the blood magic she uses corrupt my bond with the Witchblade.

"Plus, the first man I loved came back from the dead working for Artemis, she's taken my best friends hostage, and the only thing she'll exchange their lives for is the Witchblade."

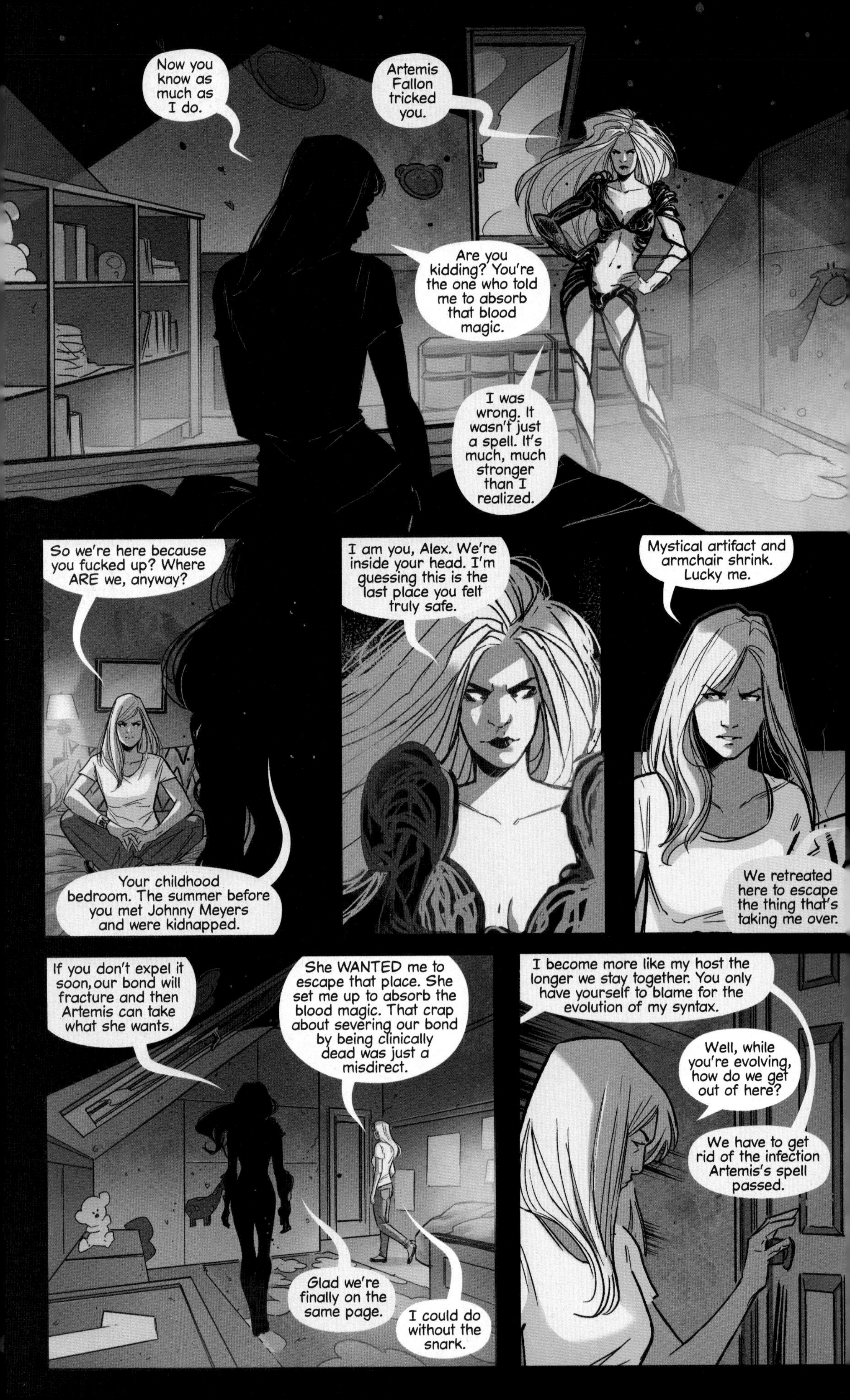
Now you know as much as I do.
Artemis Fallon tricked you.
Are you kidding? You're the one who told me to absorb that blood magic.
I was wrong. It wasn't just a spell. It's much, much stronger than I realized.
So we're here because you fucked up? Where ARE we, anyway?
Your childhood bedroom. The summer before you met Johnny Meyers and were kidnapped.
I am you, Alex. We're inside your head. I'm guessing this is the last place you felt truly safe.
Mystical artifact and armchair shrink. Lucky me.
We retreated here to escape the thing that's taking me over.
If you don't expel it soon, our bond will fracture and then Artemis can take what she wants.
She WANTED me to escape that place. She set me up to absorb the blood magic. That crap about severing our bond by being clinically dead was just a misdirect.
Glad we're finally on the same page.
I could do without the snark.
I become more like my host the longer we stay together. You only have yourself to blame for the evolution of my syntax.
Well, while you're evolving, how do we get out of here?
We have to get rid of the infection Artemis's spell passed.

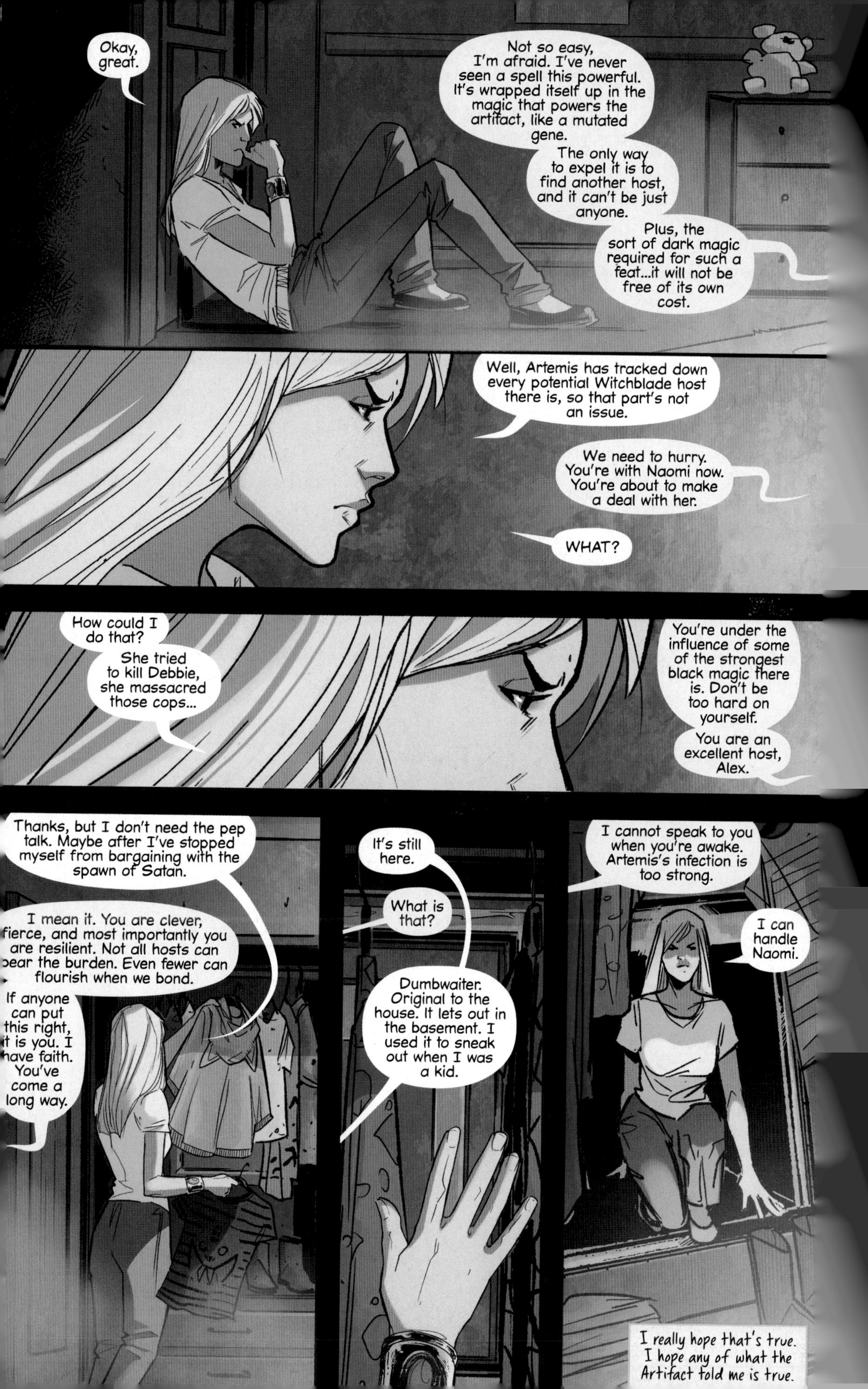

Okay, great.
Not so easy, I'm afraid. I've never seen a spell this powerful. It's wrapped itself up in the magic that powers the artifact, like a mutated gene.
The only way to expel it is to find another host, and it can't be just anyone.
Plus, the sort of dark magic required for such a feat...it will not be free of its own cost.
Well, Artemis has tracked down every potential Witchblade host there is, so that part's not an issue.
We need to hurry. You're with Naomi now. You're about to make a deal with her.
WHAT?
How could I do that?
She tried to kill Debbie, she massacred those cops...
You're under the influence of some of the strongest black magic there is. Don't be too hard on yourself.
You are an excellent host, Alex.
Thanks, but I don't need the pep talk. Maybe after I've stopped myself from bargaining with the spawn of Satan.
I mean it. You are clever, fierce, and most importantly you are resilient. Not all hosts can bear the burden. Even fewer can flourish when we bond.
If anyone can put this right, it is you. I have faith. You've come a long way.
It's still here.
What is that?
Dumbwaiter. Original to the house. It lets out in the basement. I used it to sneak out when I was a kid.
I cannot speak to you when you're awake. Artemis's infection is too strong.
I can handle Naomi.
I really hope that's true. I hope any of what the Artifact told me is true.

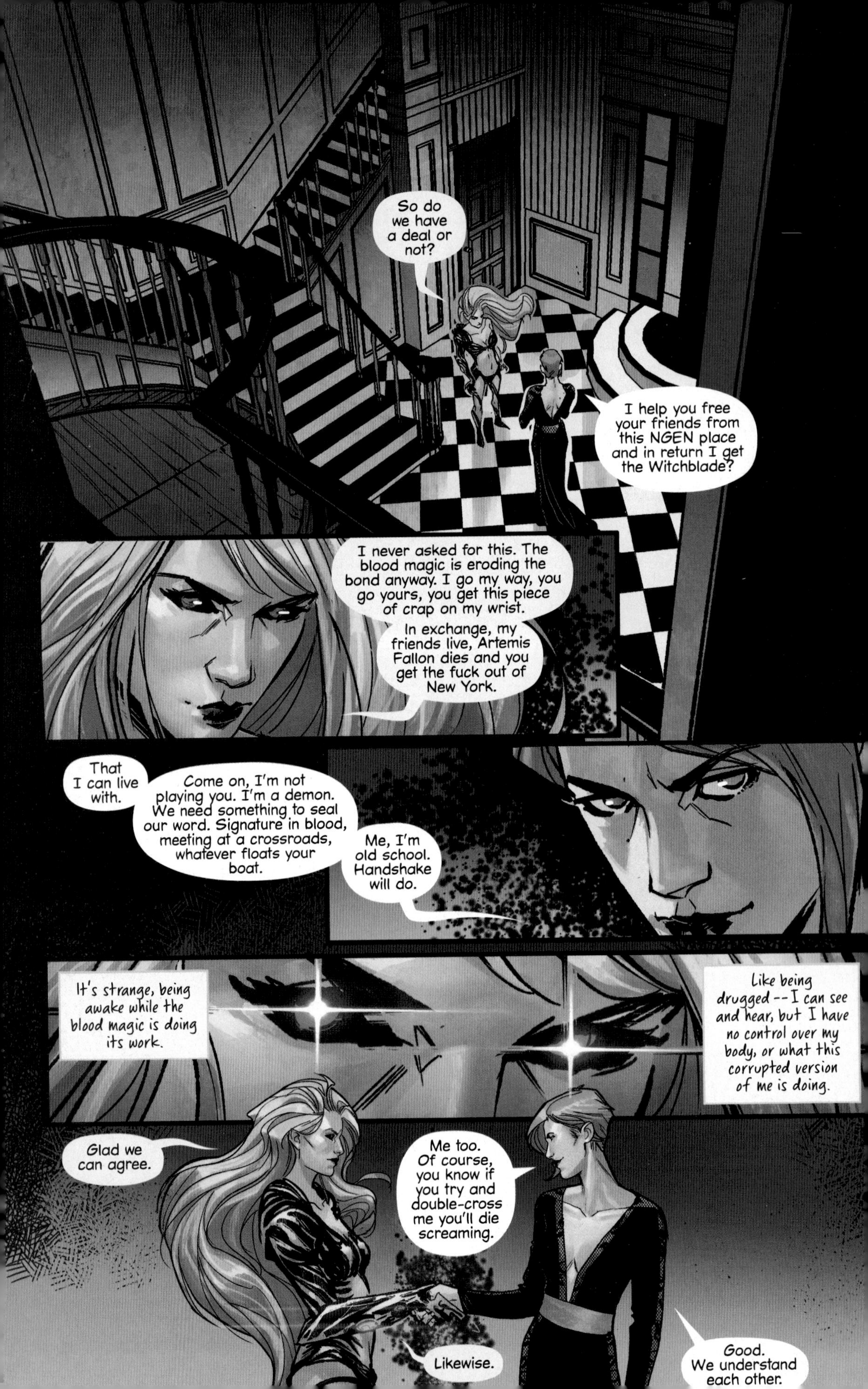
So do we have a deal or not?
I help you free your friends from this NGEN place and in return I get the Witchblade?
I never asked for this. The blood magic is eroding the bond anyway. I go my way, you go yours, you get this piece of crap on my wrist.
In exchange, my friends live, Artemis Fallon dies and you get the fuck out of New York.
That I can live with.
Come on, I'm not playing you. I'm a demon. We need something to seal our word. Signature in blood, meeting at a crossroads, whatever floats your boat.
Me, I'm old school. Handshake will do.
It's strange, being awake while the blood magic is doing its work.
Like being drugged -- I can see and hear, but I have no control over my body, or what this corrupted version of me is doing.
Glad we can agree.
Me too. Of course, you know if you try and double-cross me you'll die screaming.
Likewise.
Good. We understand each other.

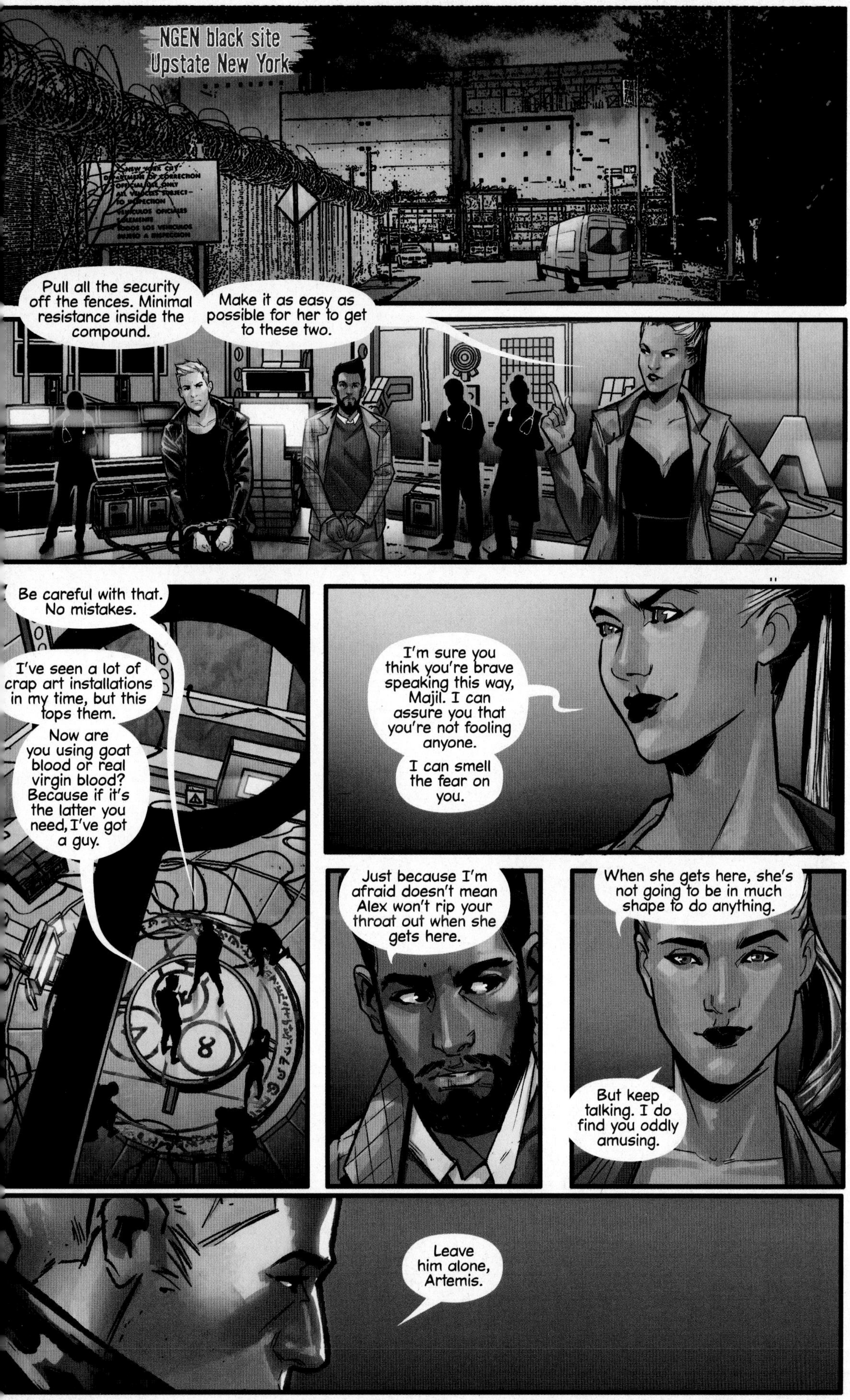

NGEN black site
Upstate New York
Pull all the security off the fences. Minimal resistance inside the compound.
Make it as easy as possible for her to get to these two.
Be careful with that. No mistakes.
I've seen a lot of crap art installations in my time, but this tops them.
Now are you using goat blood or real virgin blood? Because if it's the latter you need, I've got a guy.
I'm sure you think you're brave speaking this way, Majil. I can assure you that you're not fooling anyone.
I can smell the fear on you.
Just because I'm afraid doesn't mean Alex won't rip your throat out when she gets here.
When she gets here, she's not going to be in much shape to do anything.
But keep talking. I do find you oddly amusing.
Leave him alone, Artemis.

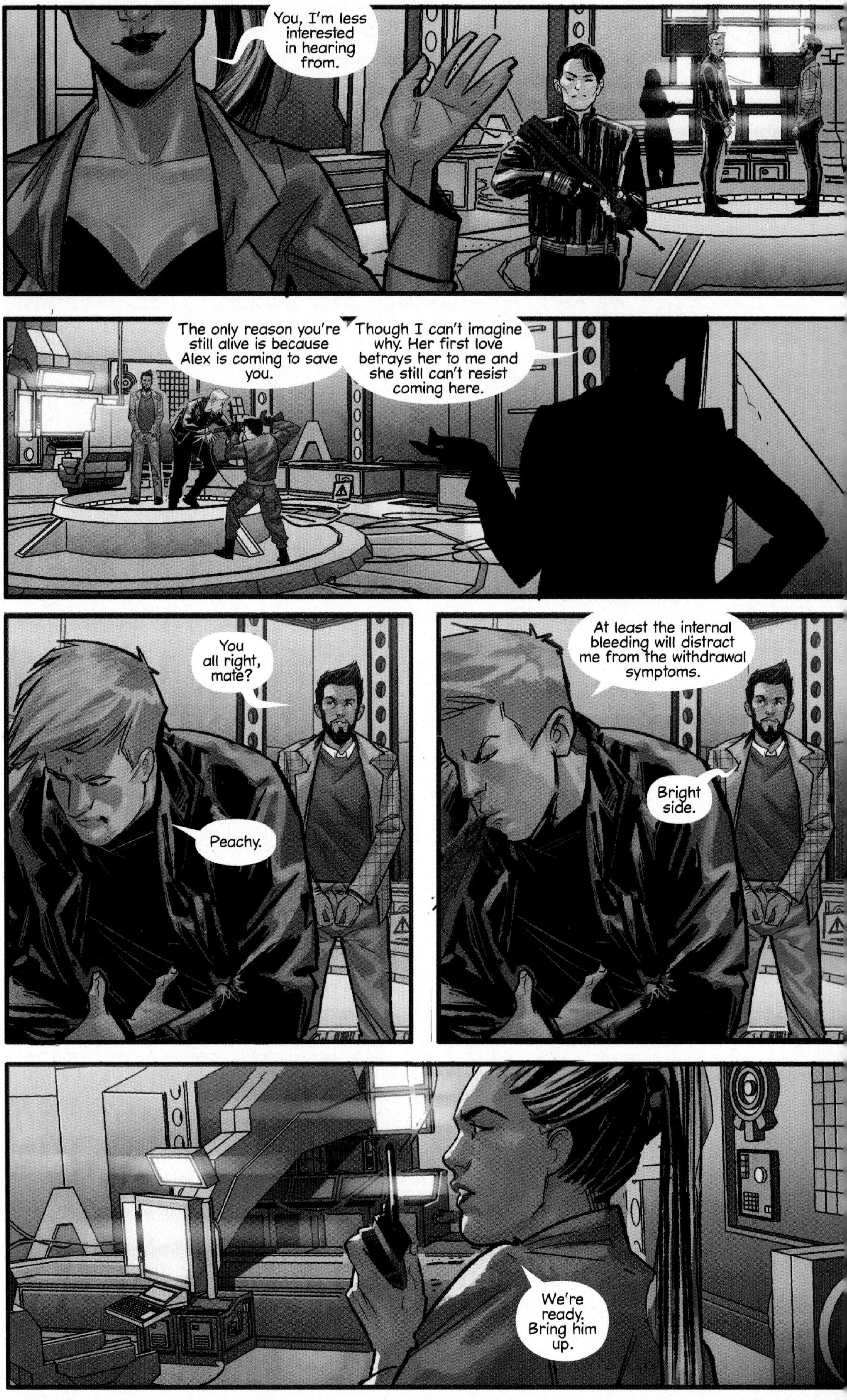
You, I'm less interested in hearing from.
The only reason you're still alive is because Alex is coming to save you.
Though I can't imagine why. Her first love betrays her to me and she still can't resist coming here.
You all right, mate?
Peachy.
At least the internal bleeding will distract me from the withdrawal symptoms.
Bright side.
We're ready. Bring him up.

We had to dose him again. He was starting to act up.

Asher. I need you to hear me. You will tell me if this sigil is correct, and you will not lie.

If you do, the pain will begin all over again.

Bloody hell.

This is only a taste of what she can do. Bet Ash regrets that whole "can't die" thing right about now.

All I need is a few seconds to slip these cuffs. I have the keycard. I can make a run for it.

Simmer down, Jason Bourne. They'll shoot you before you get ten feet.

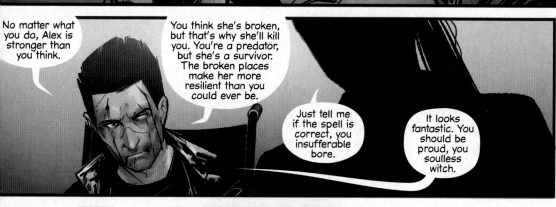

No matter what you do, Alex is stronger than you think.

You think she's broken, but that's why she'll kill you. You're a predator, but she's a survivor. The broken places make her more resilient than you could ever be.

Just tell me if the spell is correct, you insufferable bore.

It looks fantastic. You should be proud, you soulless witch.

All right, if you're the expert, what do we do?

Wait for Artemis to be distracted. And when you see Alex again on the other side of this, please tell her how sorry I am. For all of it.

Tell her yourself.

We both know I'm not getting out of this in one piece.

It's all right! Backup generators will come on.

This is a good sign.

It means she's here.

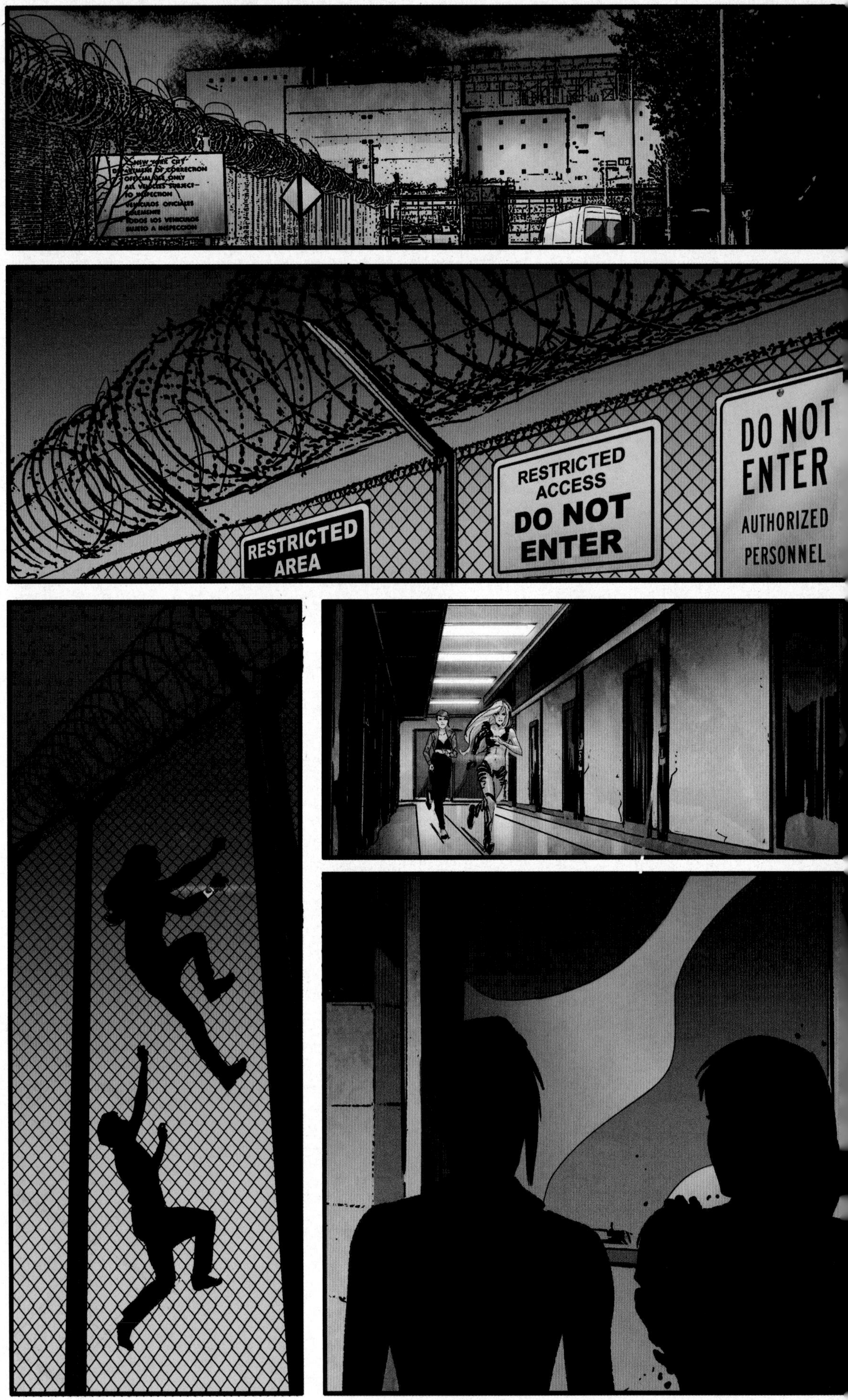

RESTRICTED AREA
RESTRICTED ACCESS DO NOT ENTER
DO NOT ENTER AUTHORIZED PERSONNEL

Credit where it's due, they rolled out the red carpet.

I haven't had that much fun since my visit to the 78th Precinct.

Shut up.

There's heavy warding on the door, so after you.

You better be more useful once we're in there. Otherwise the deal is off.

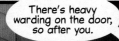

I'm going to put this bad attitude down to the blood spell currently tearing your mind and soul apart.

Otherwise I might be sort of offended.

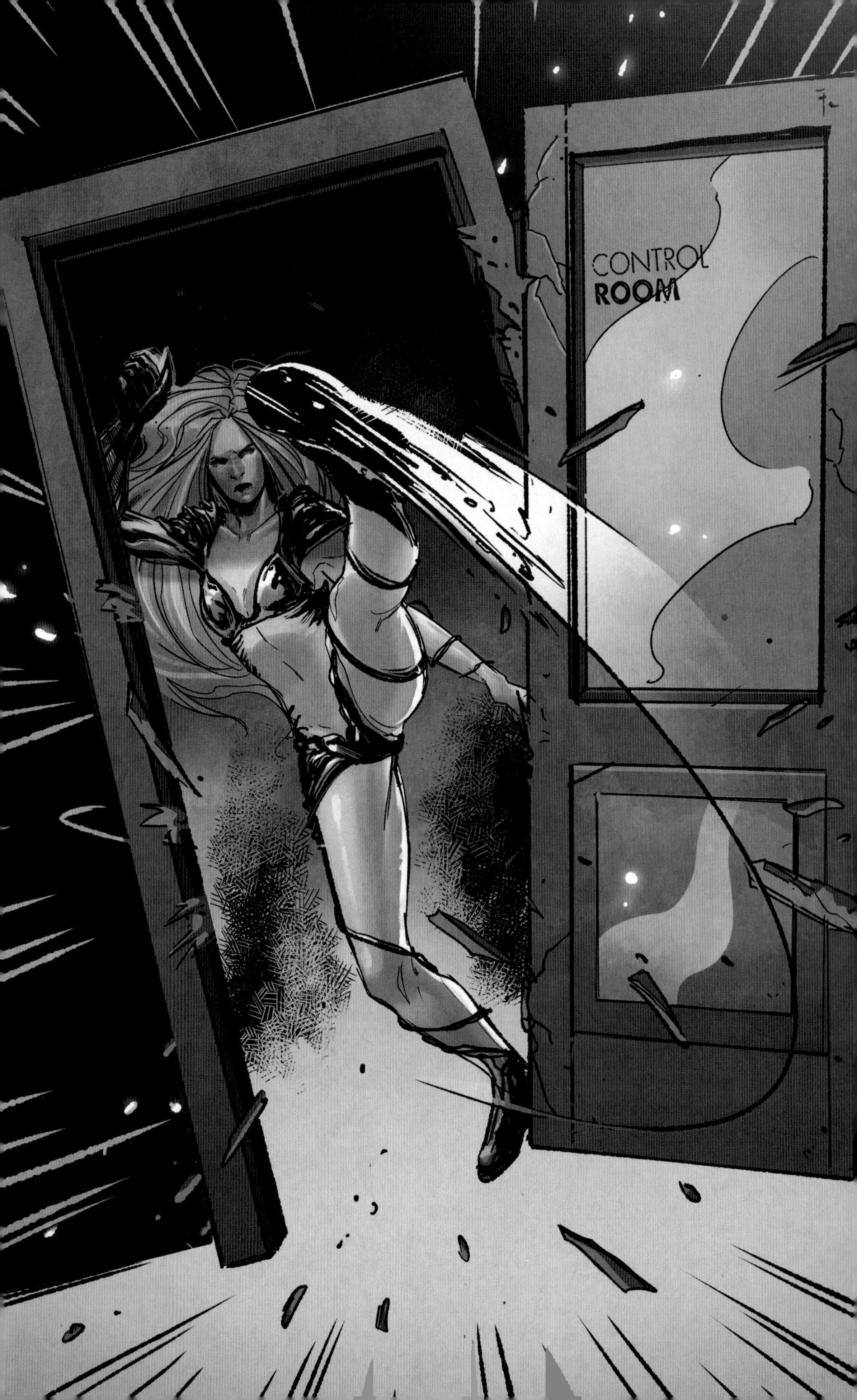
CONTROL
ROOM

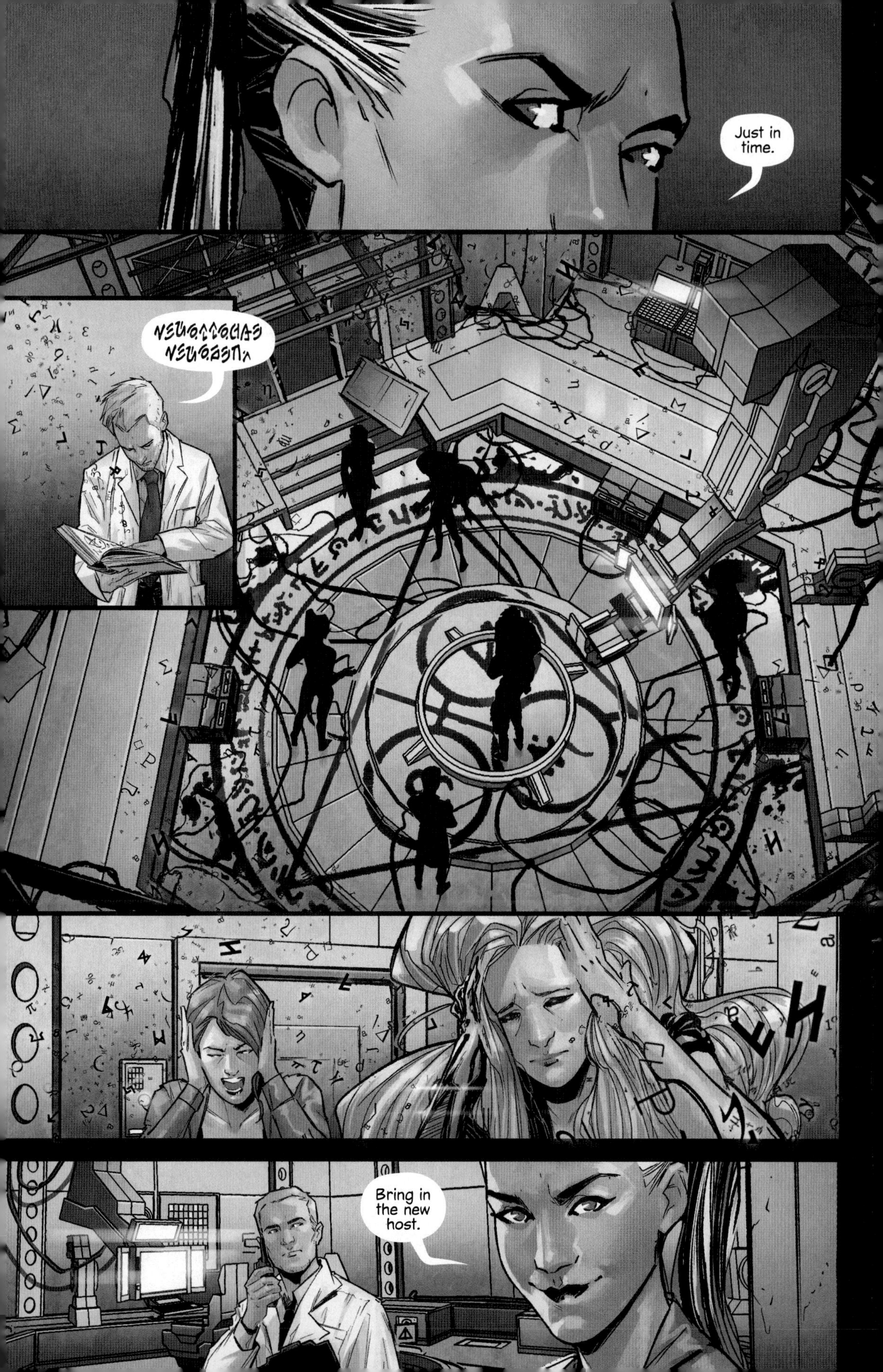
Just in time.
Bring in the new host.

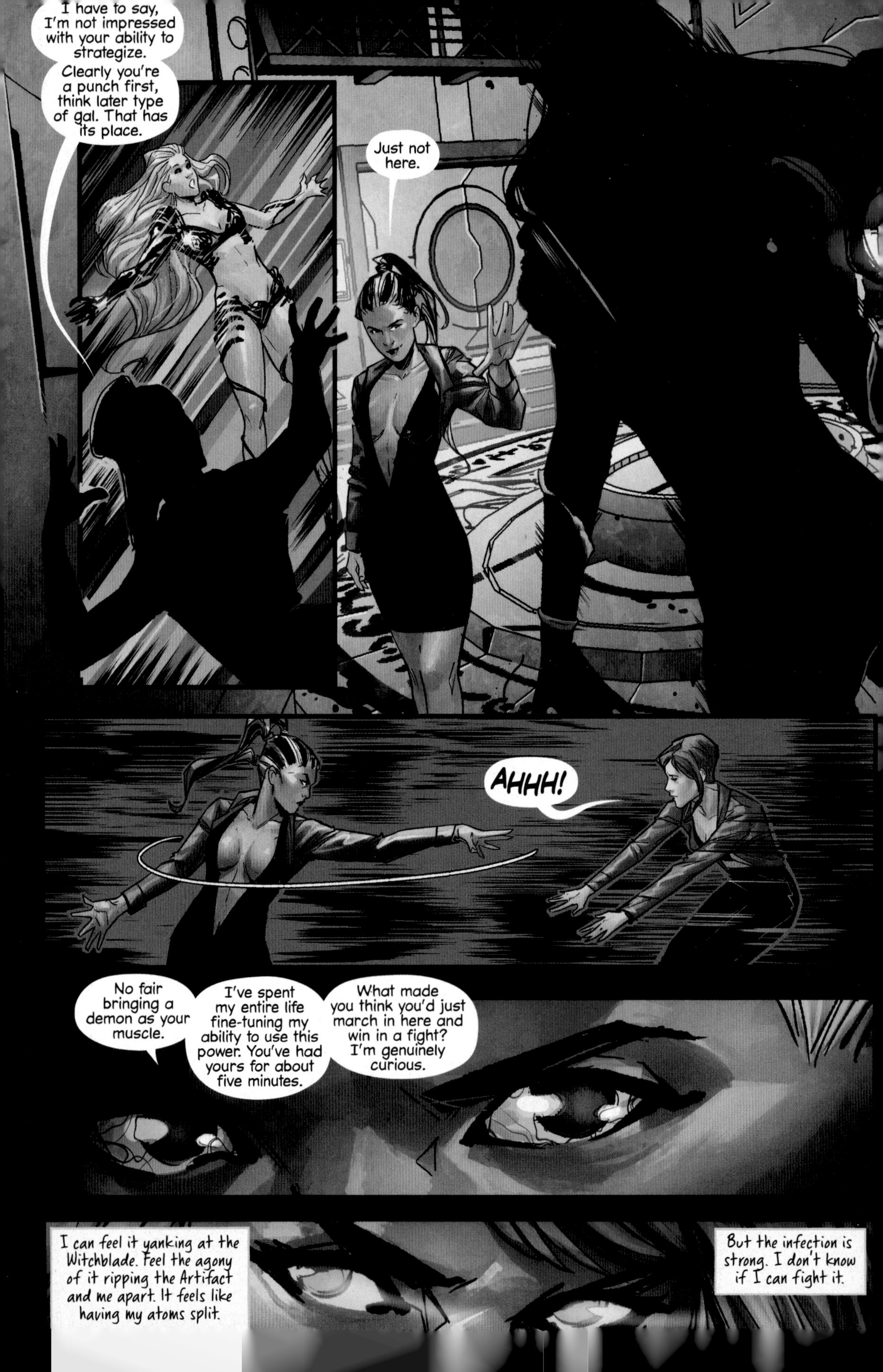
I have to say, I'm not impressed with your ability to strategize.
Clearly you're a punch first, think later type of gal. That has its place.
Just not here.
AHHH!
No fair bringing a demon as your muscle.
I've spent my entire life fine-tuning my ability to use this power. You've had yours for about five minutes.
What made you think you'd just march in here and win in a fight? I'm genuinely curious.
I can feel it yanking at the Witchblade. Feel the agony of it ripping the Artifact and me apart. It feels like having my atoms split.
But the infection is strong. I don't know if I can fight it.

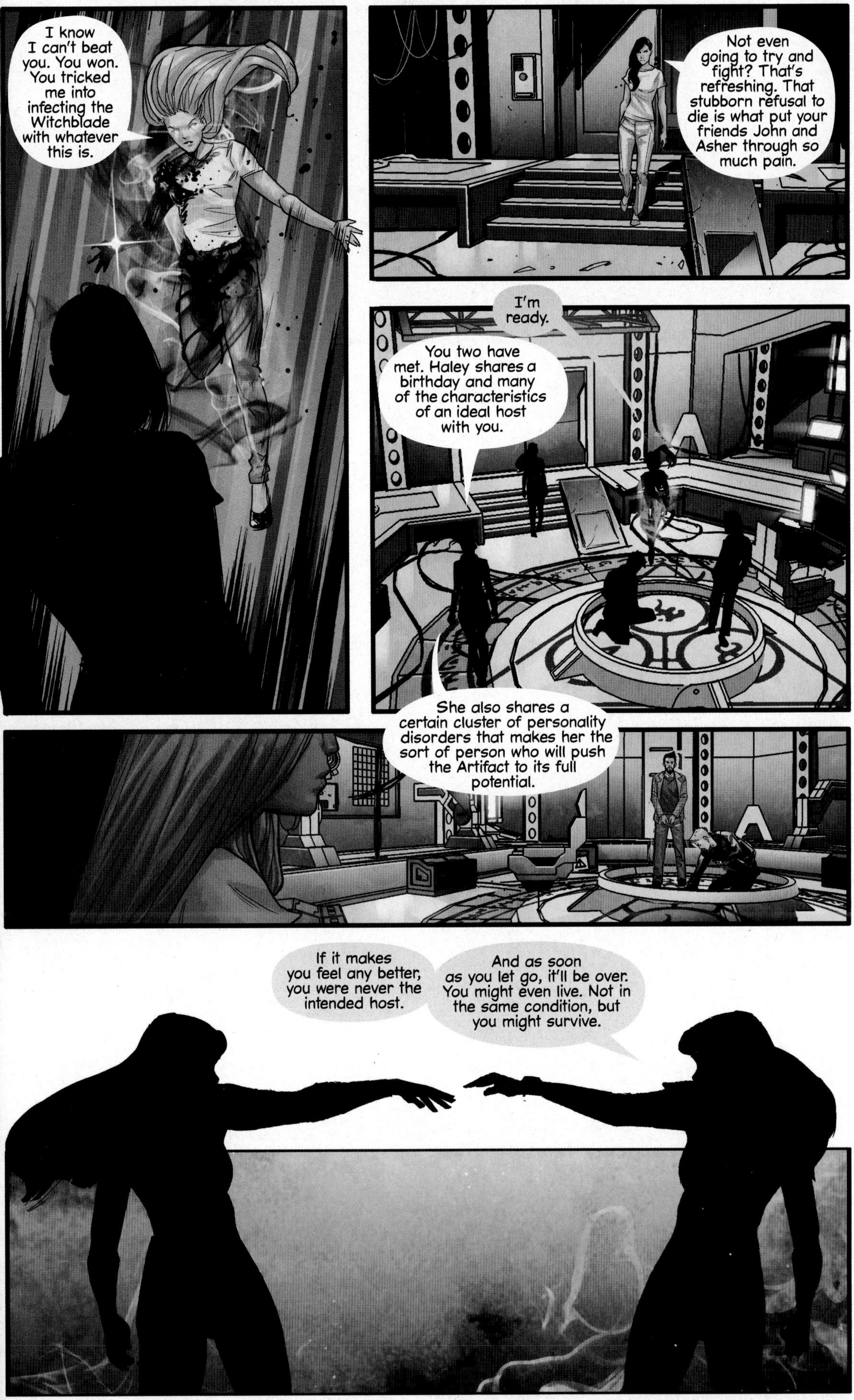

I know I can't beat you. You won. You tricked me into infecting the Witchblade with whatever this is.
Not even going to try and fight? That's refreshing. That stubborn refusal to die is what put your friends John and Asher through so much pain.
I'm ready.
You two have met. Haley shares a birthday and many of the characteristics of an ideal host with you.
She also shares a certain cluster of personality disorders that makes her the sort of person who will push the Artifact to its full potential.
If it makes you feel any better, you were never the intended host.
And as soon as you let go, it'll be over. You might even live. Not in the same condition, but you might survive.

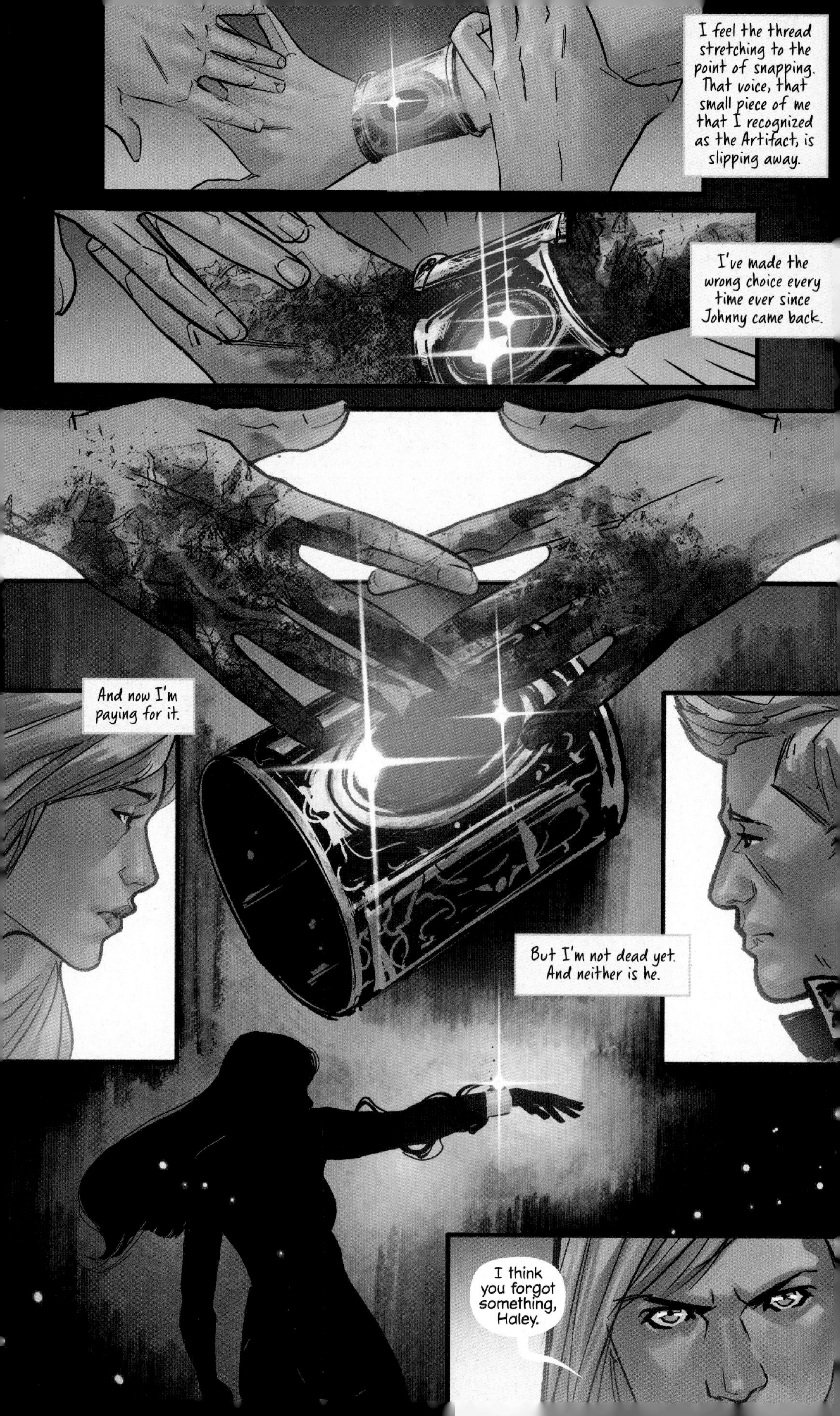
I feel the thread stretching to the point of snapping. That voice, that small piece of me that I recognized as the Artifact, is slipping away.
I've made the wrong choice every time ever since Johnny came back.
And now I'm paying for it.
But I'm not dead yet. And neither is he.
I think you forgot something, Haley.

I can feel the channel opened by her touch, like a cyclone sucking everything but the black magic out of me.

I can feel that magic eating through me like acid in my blood. Heart racing, vision blurring, pain like I've never felt as every cell in my body gets infected and dies.

I'm not the intended host.

But neither are you.

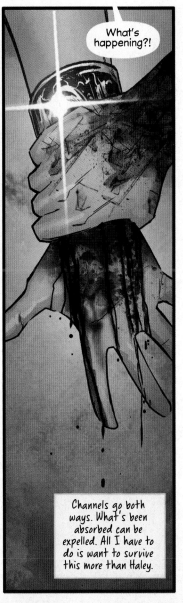

What's happening?!

Channels go both ways. What's been absorbed can be expelled. All I have to do is want to survive this more than Haley.

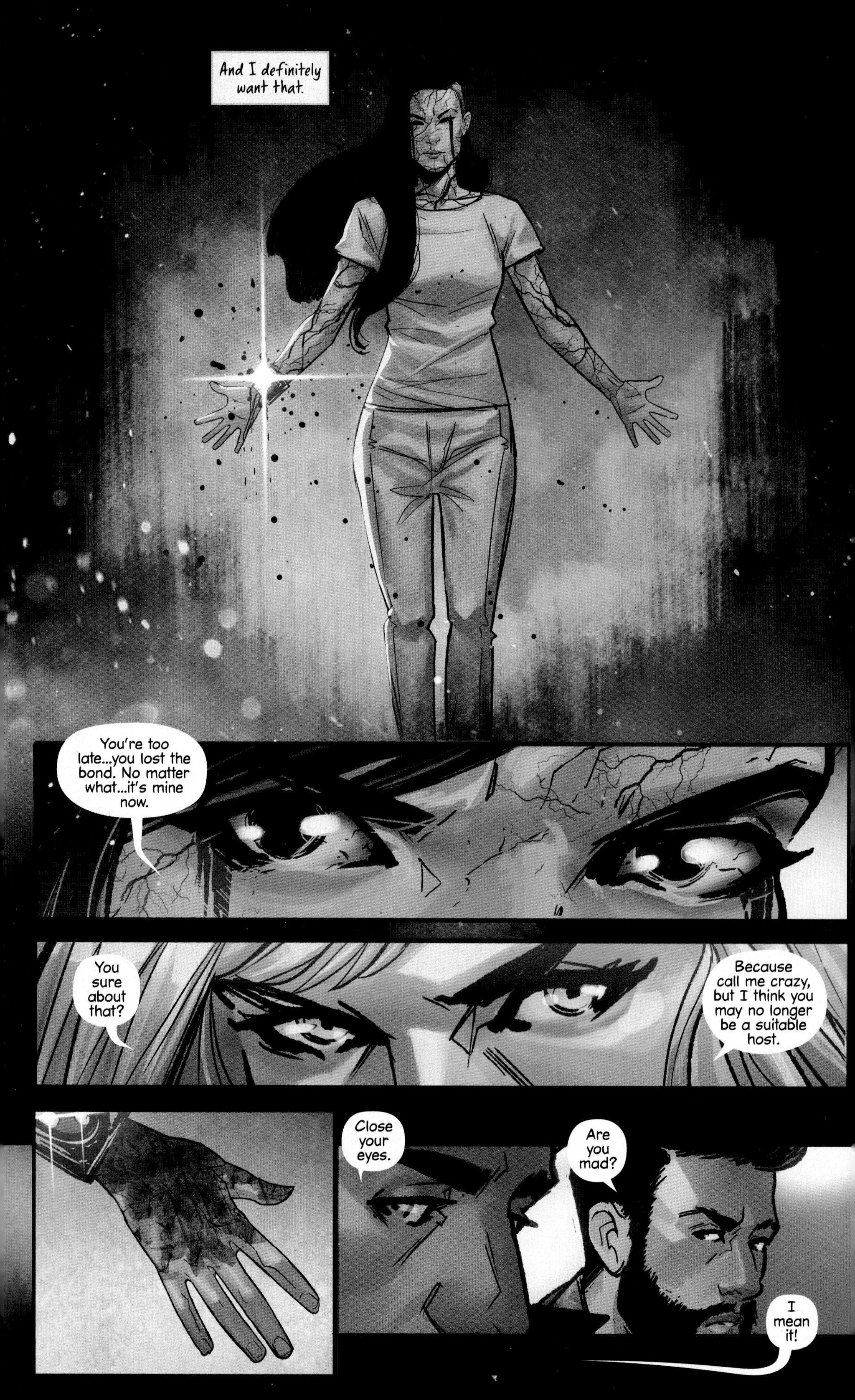
And I definitely want that.
You're too late...you lost the bond. No matter what...it's mine now.
You sure about that?
Because call me crazy, but I think you may no longer be a suitable host.
Close your eyes.
Are you mad?
I mean it!

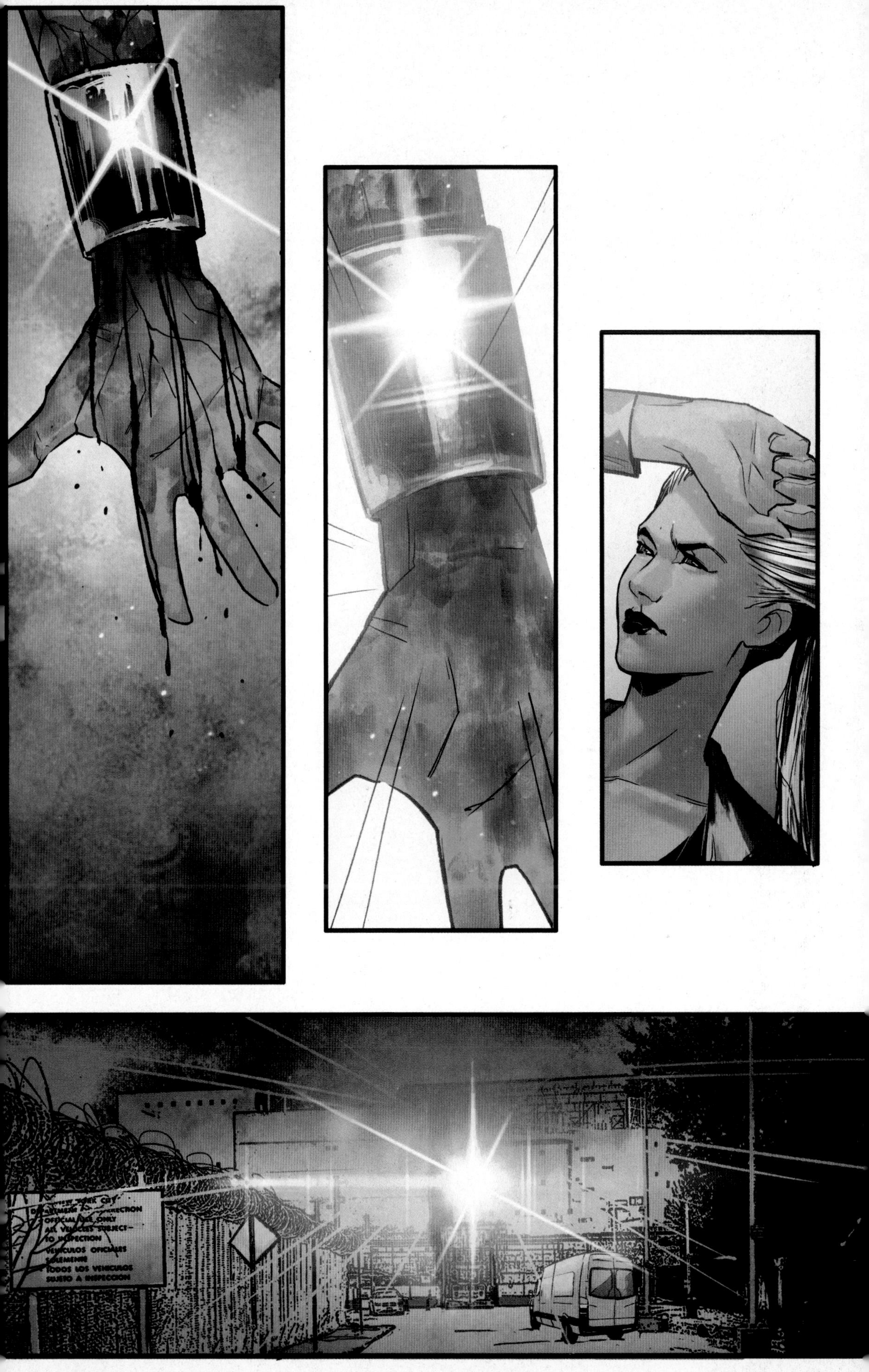
OFFICIAL USE ONLY
VEHICULOS OFICIALES
TODOS LOS VEHICULOS
SUJETO A INSPECCION

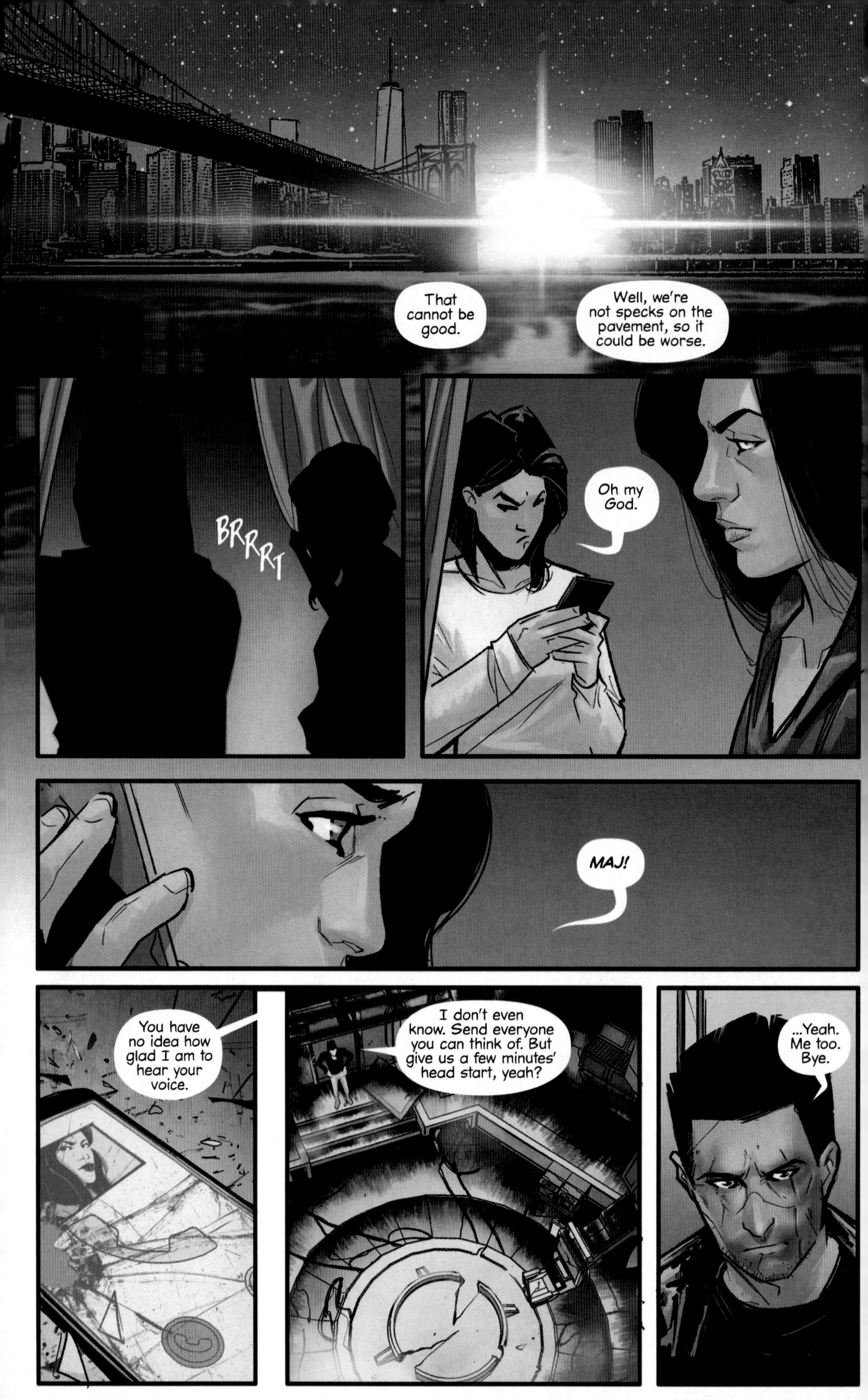

That cannot be good.
Well, we're not specks on the pavement, so it could be worse.
BRRRT
Oh my God.
MAJ!
You have no idea how glad I am to hear your voice.
I don't even know. Send everyone you can think of. But give us a few minutes' head start, yeah?
...Yeah. Me too. Bye.

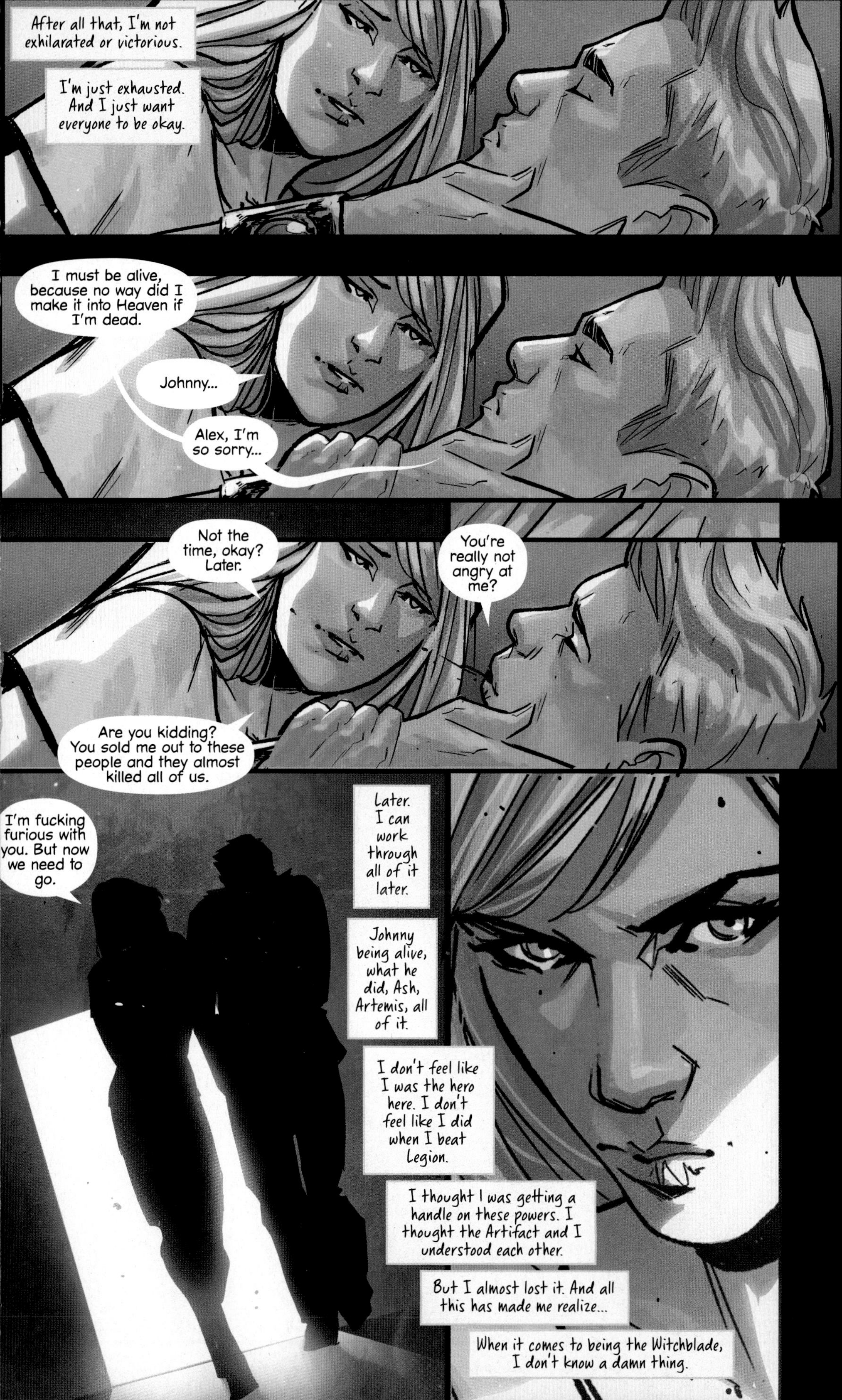
After all that, I'm not exhilarated or victorious.
I'm just exhausted. And I just want everyone to be okay.
I must be alive, because no way did I make it into Heaven if I'm dead.
Johnny...
Alex, I'm so sorry...
Not the time, okay? Later.
You're really not angry at me?
Are you kidding? You sold me out to these people and they almost killed all of us.
I'm fucking furious with you. But now we need to go.
Later. I can work through all of it later.
Johnny being alive, what he did, Ash, Artemis, all of it.
I don't feel like I was the hero here. I don't feel like I did when I beat Legion.
I thought I was getting a handle on these powers. I thought the Artifact and I understood each other.
But I almost lost it. And all this has made me realize...
When it comes to being the Witchblade, I don't know a damn thing.

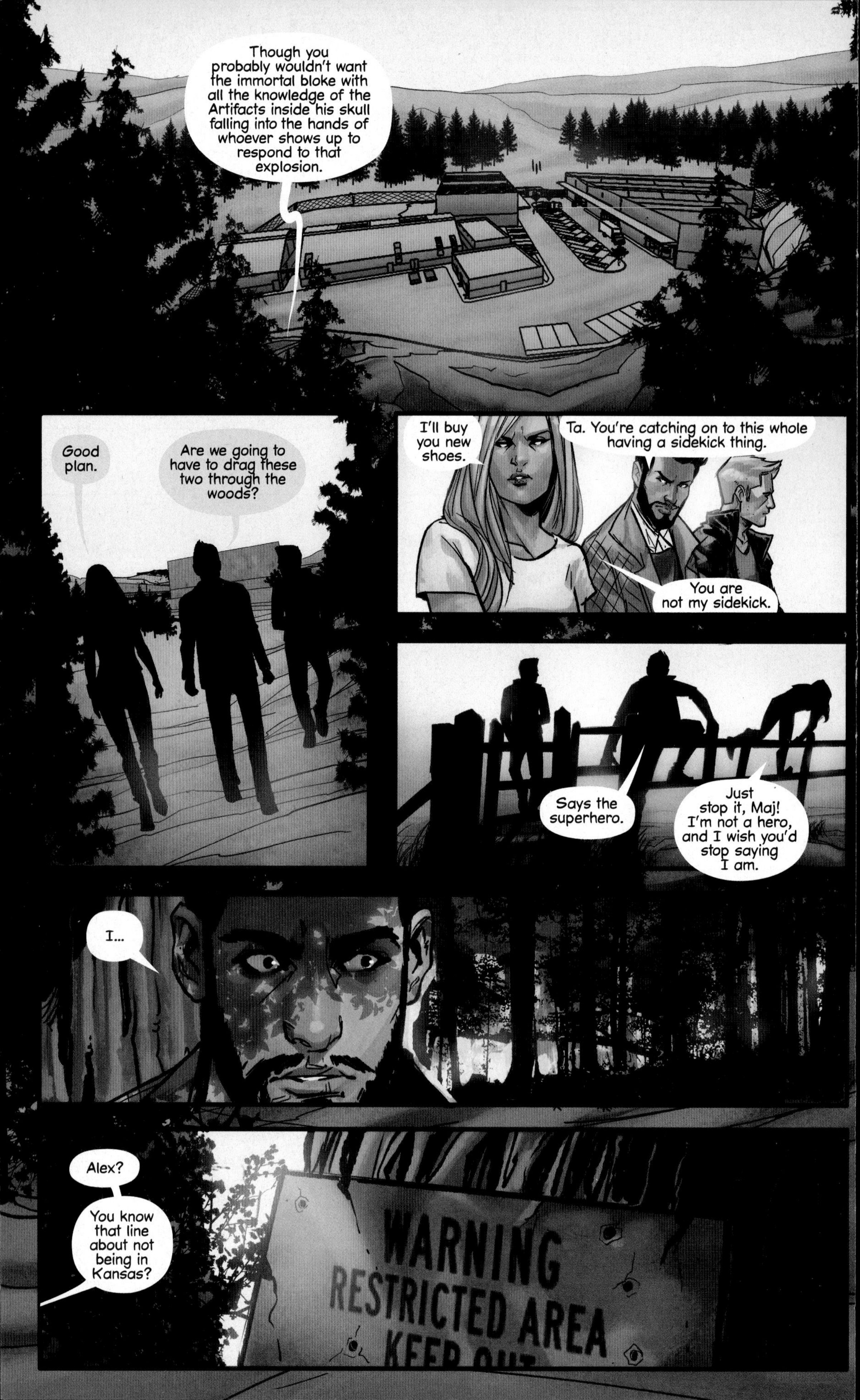

Though you probably wouldn't want the immortal bloke with all the knowledge of the Artifacts inside his skull falling into the hands of whoever shows up to respond to that explosion.
Good plan.
Are we going to have to drag these two through the woods?
I'll buy you new shoes.
Ta. You're catching on to this whole having a sidekick thing.
You are not my sidekick.
Says the superhero.
Just stop it, Maj! I'm not a hero, and I wish you'd stop saying I am.
I...
Alex?
You know that line about not being in Kansas?
WARNING
RESTRICTED AREA

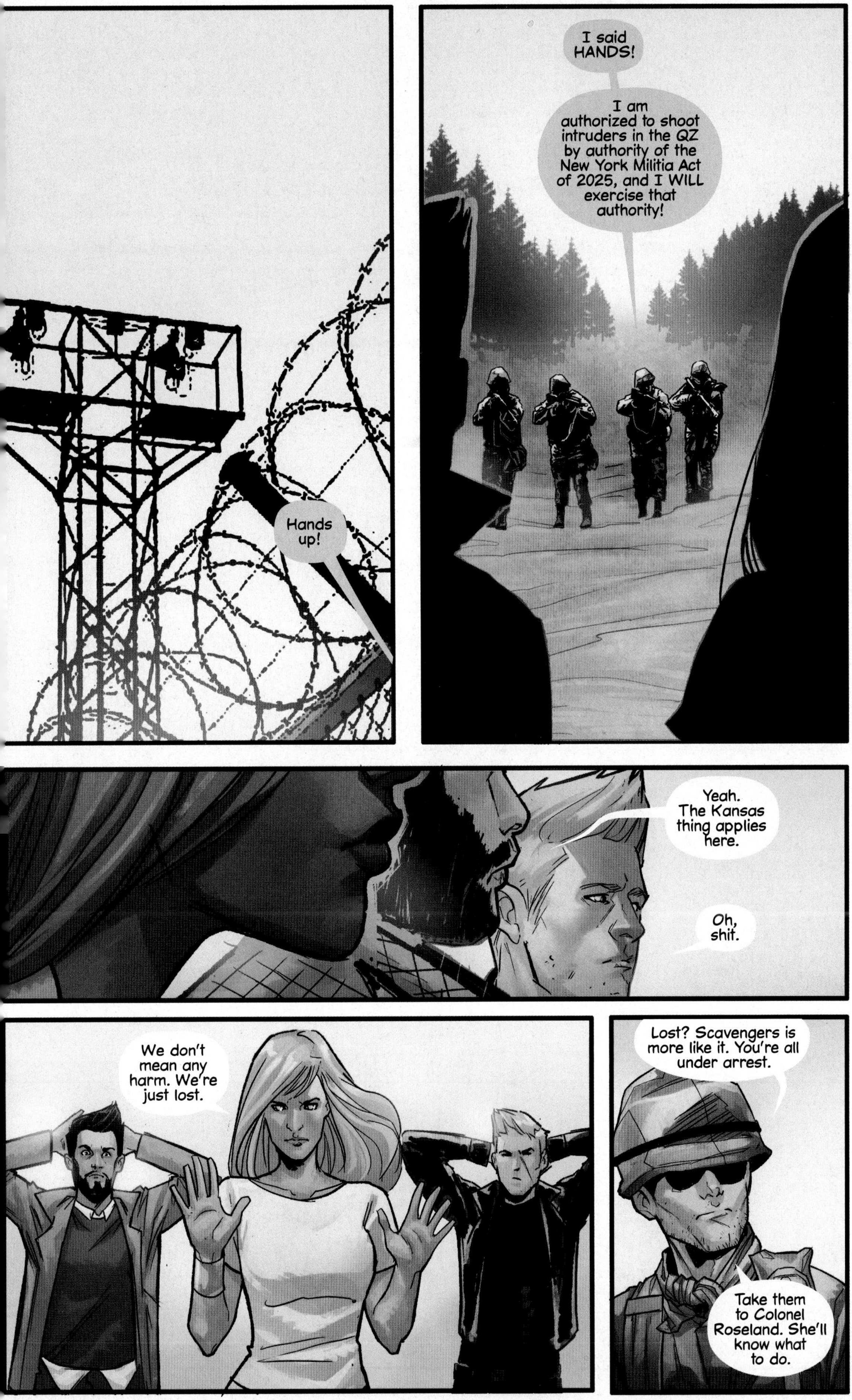
Hands up!
I said HANDS!
I am authorized to shoot intruders in the QZ by authority of the New York Militia Act of 2025, and I WILL exercise that authority!
Yeah. The Kansas thing applies here.
Oh, shit.
We don't mean any harm. We're just lost.
Lost? Scavengers is more like it. You're all under arrest.
Take them to Colonel Roseland. She'll know what to do.

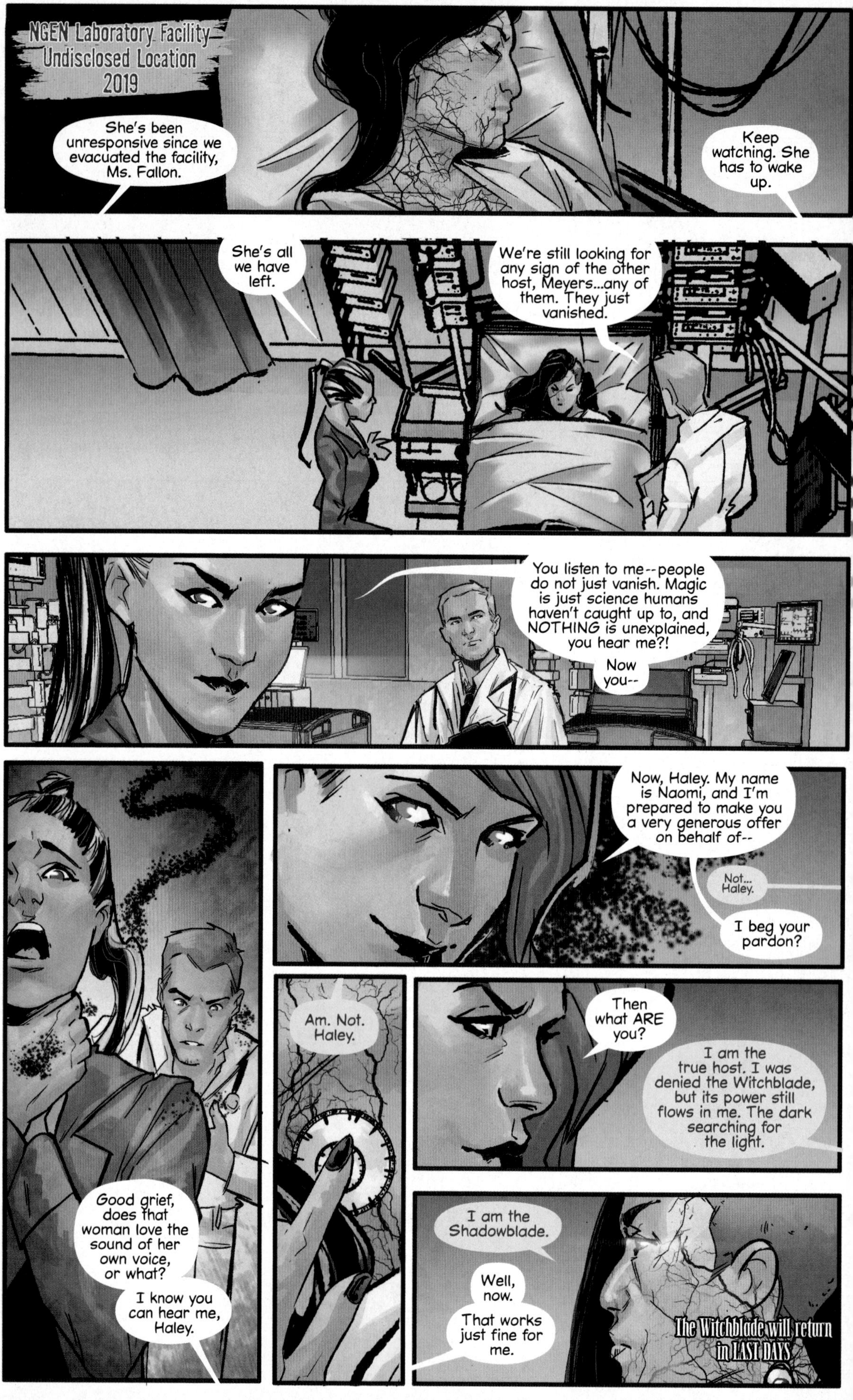

NGEN Laboratory Facility
Undisclosed Location
2019
She's been unresponsive since we evacuated the facility, Ms. Fallon.
Keep watching. She has to wake up.
She's all we have left.
We're still looking for any sign of the other host, Meyers...any of them. They just vanished.
You listen to me--people do not just vanish. Magic is just science humans haven't caught up to, and NOTHING is unexplained, you hear me?!
Now you--
Good grief, does that woman love the sound of her own voice, or what?
I know you can hear me, Haley.
Now, Haley. My name is Naomi, and I'm prepared to make you a very generous offer on behalf of--
Not... Haley.
I beg your pardon?
Am. Not. Haley.
Then what ARE you?
I am the true host. I was denied the Witchblade, but its power still flows in me. The dark searching for the light.
I am the Shadowblade.
Well, now.
That works just fine for me.
The Witchblade will return in LAST DAYS

COVER GALLERY

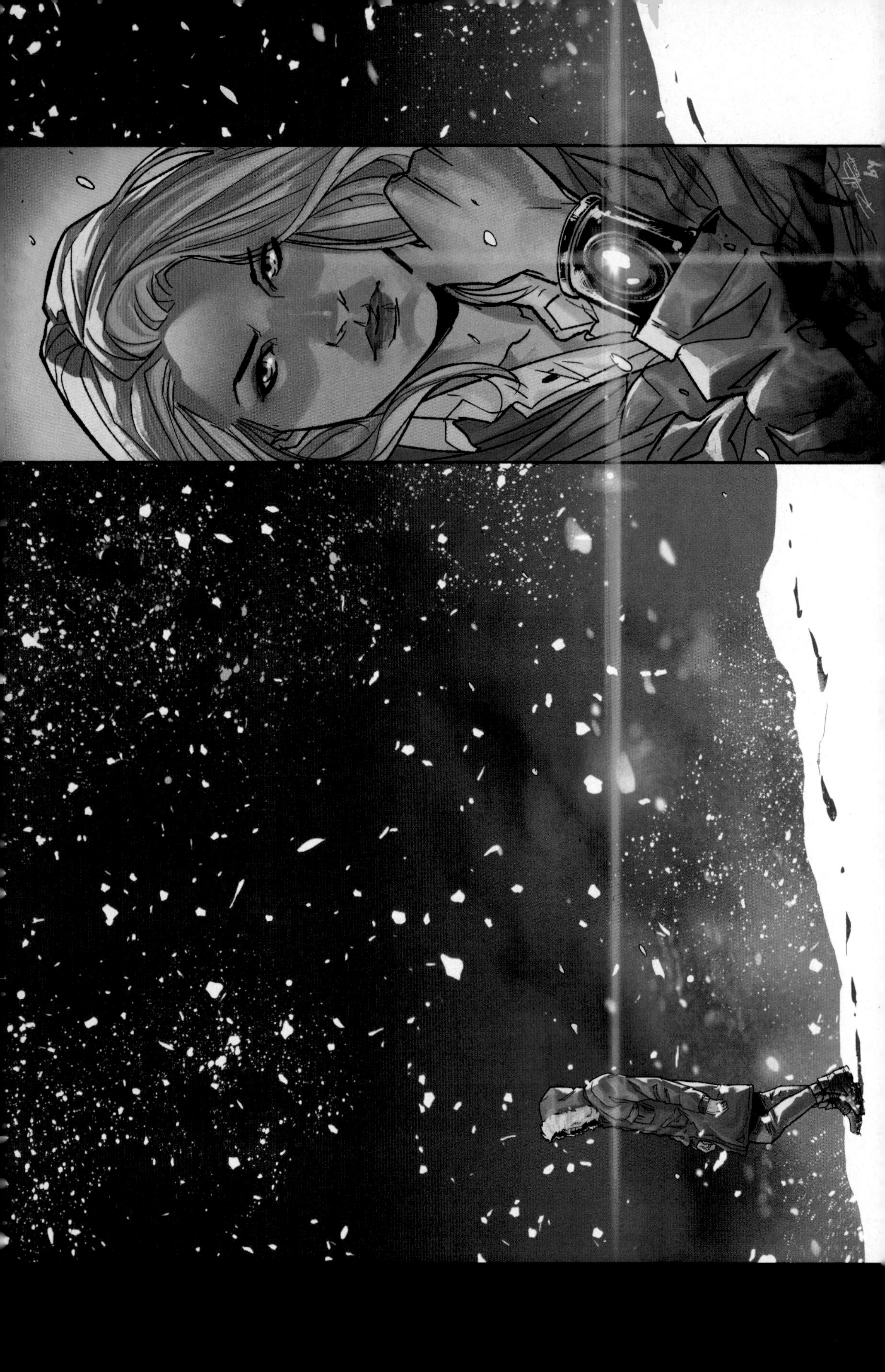

ISSUE 7 **COVER** — ROBERTA **INGRANATA** BRYAN **VALENZA**

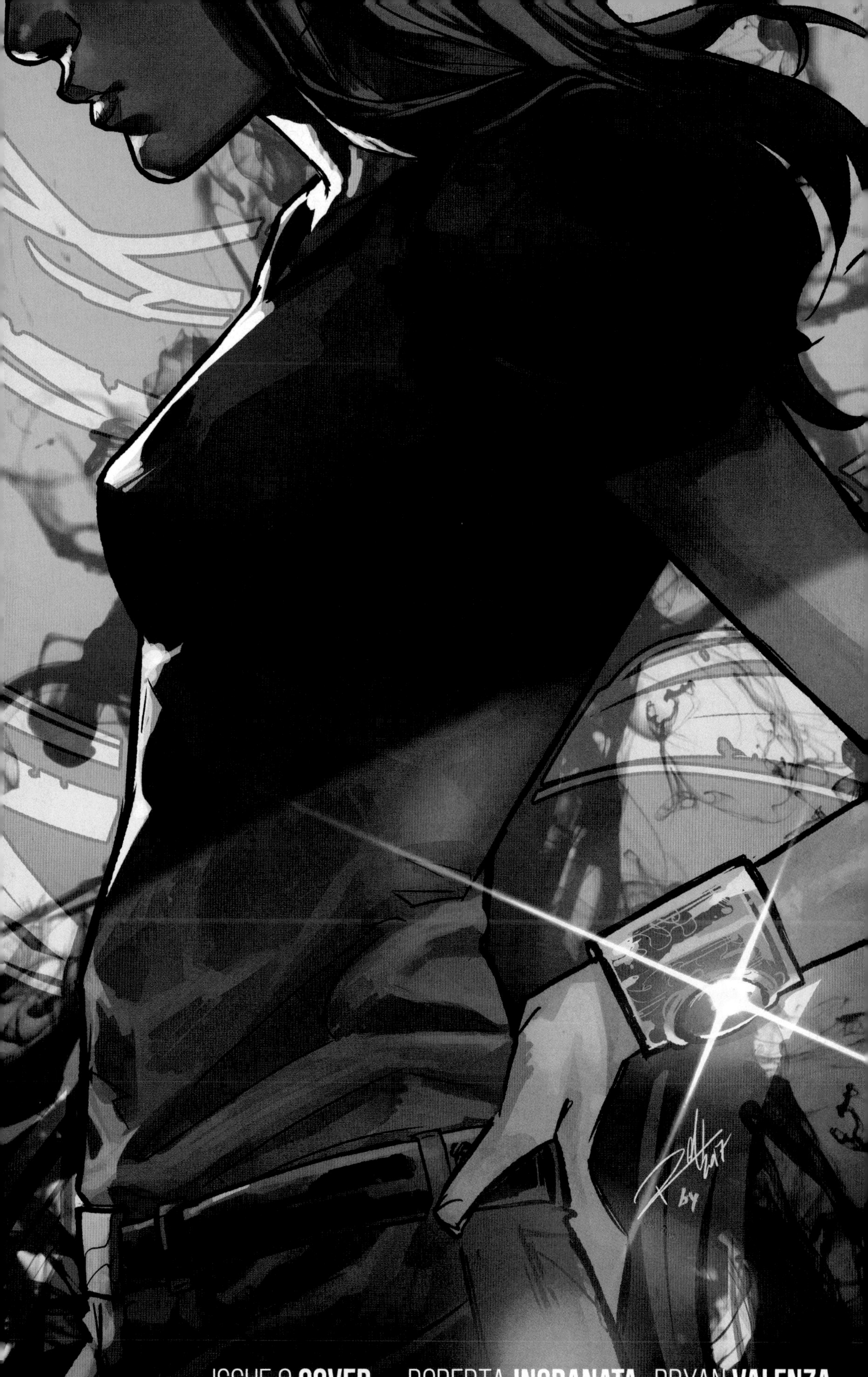

ISSUE 8 **COVER** — ROBERTA **INGRANATA** BRYAN **VALENZA**

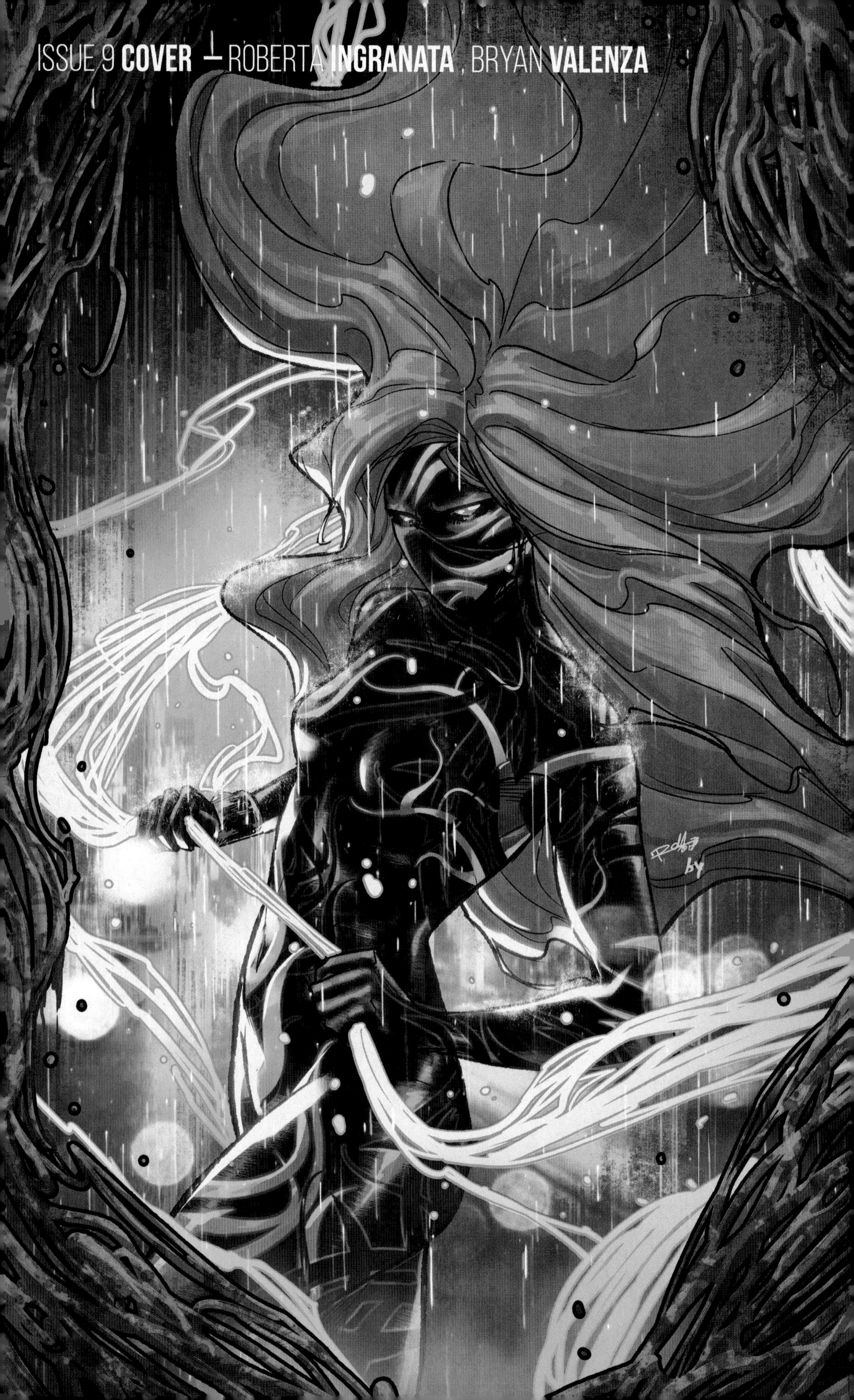

ISSUE 9 **COVER** — ROBERTA **INGRANATA**, BRYAN **VALENZA**

ISSUE 10 **COVER** — ROBERTA **INGRANATA** , BRYAN **VALENZA**

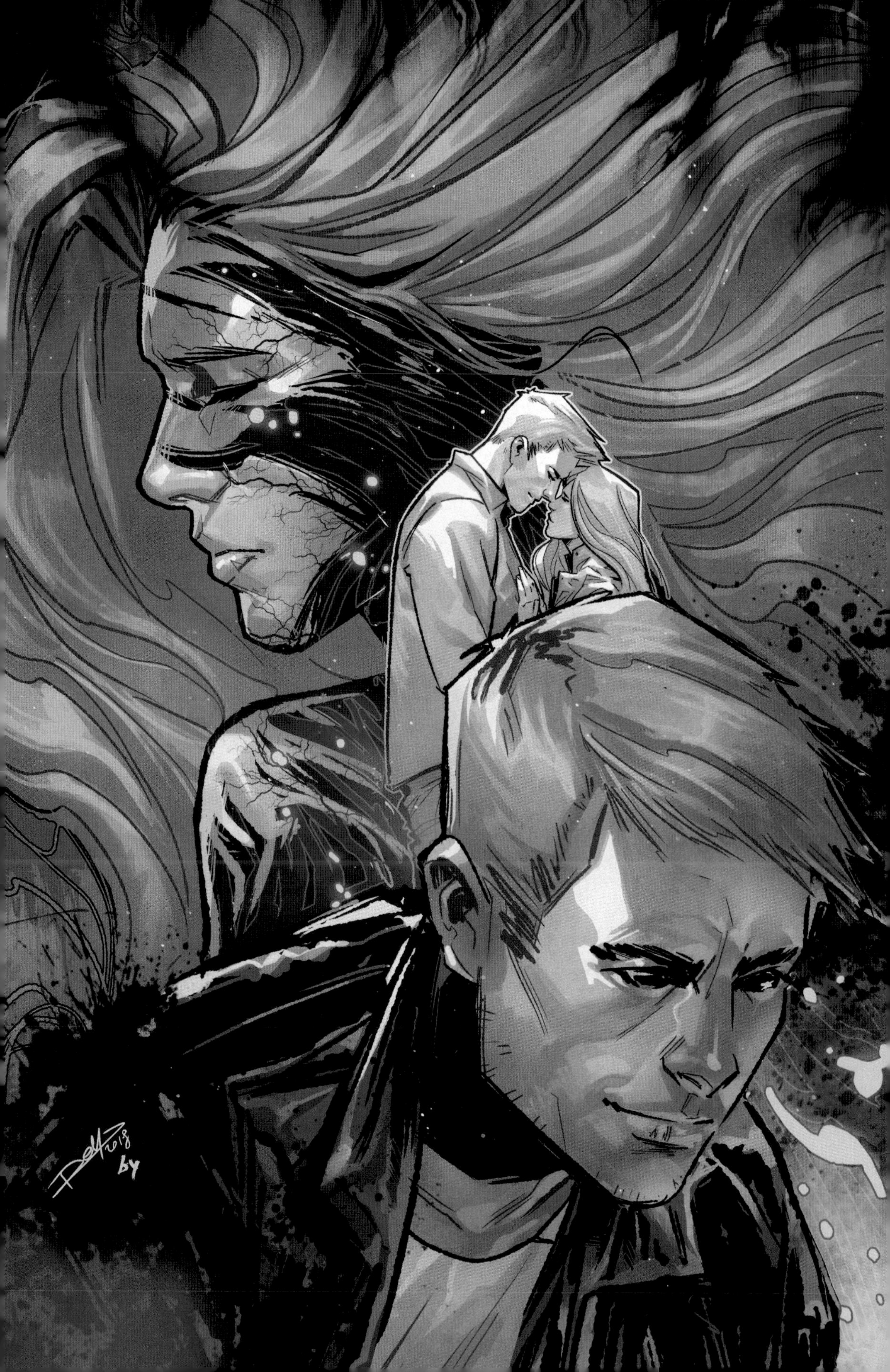

ISSUE 11 **COVER** — ROBERTA **INGRANATA**, BRYAN **VALENZA**

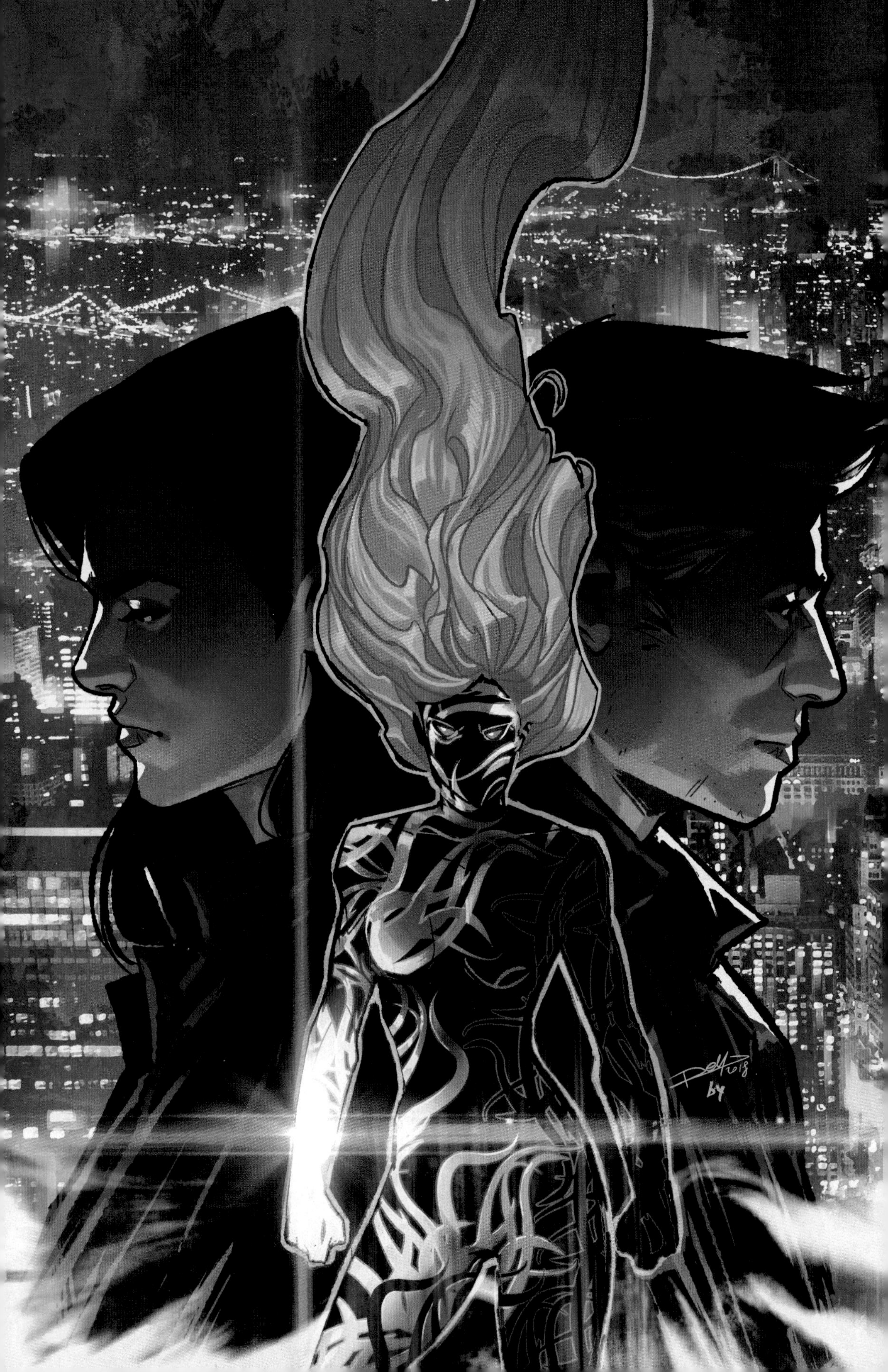

ISSUE 12 **COVER A** — ROBERTA **INGRANATA**, BRYAN **VALENZA**

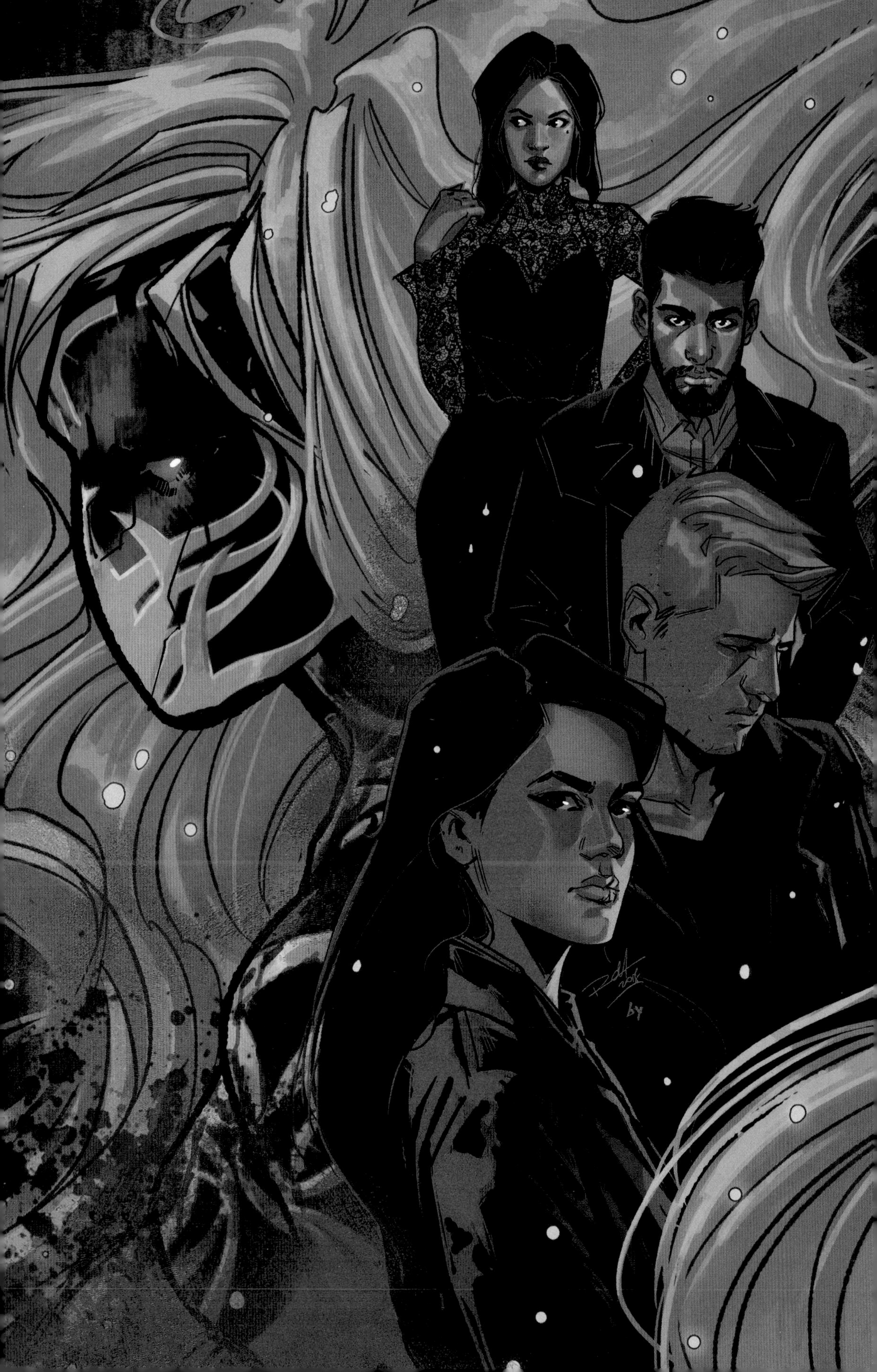

ISSUE 12 **COVER B** — FARAH **NURMALIZA**

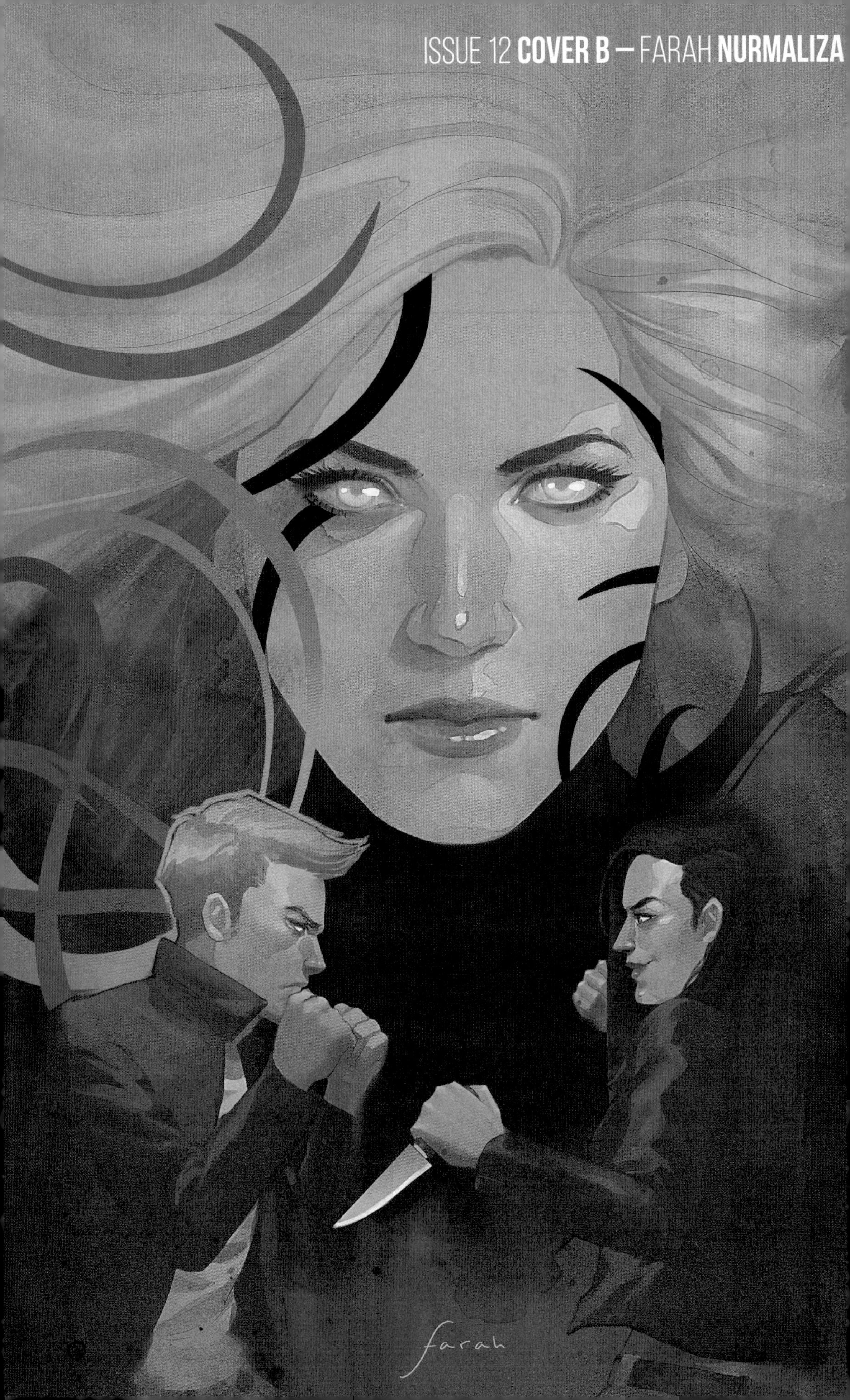
farah

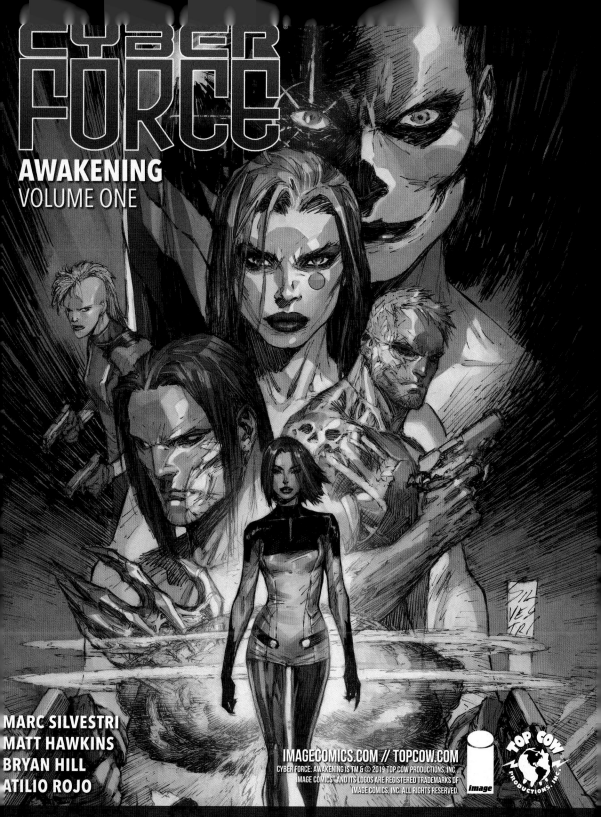

CYBER FORCE
AWAKENING
VOLUME ONE

MARC SILVESTRI
MATT HAWKINS
BRYAN HILL
ATILIO ROJO

"Everything from the fast-paced, thematic plot to the balanced characterization made this story feel very satisfying."
—**COMICSVERSE**

"The revival of CYBER FORCE is more than just timely, it is an engaging narrative that is executed beautifully."
—**COMIC WATCH**

"CYBER FORCE is back and more exciting and relevant than ever."
—**SPARTANTOWN**

"CYBER FORCE is fun, interesting, and continues to add layers to its story as characters are slowly being intertwined."
—**GEEKS WORLD WIDE**

AVAILABLE NOW IN TRADE PAPERBACK

DAN WICKLINE   PHILLIP SEVY

THE FREEZE

VOLUME ONE

"THE FREEZE promises a horrifying new apocalypse you do not want to give the cold shoulder."
—AiPT!

"In a world where dozens of new titles debut every week, FREEZE manages to feature one of the most original plots you find on the shelves."
—COMICBOOK.COM

"THE FREEZE is a terrific high concept that has quickly become full of possibilities."
—HORROR TALK

AVAILABLE MAY 2019

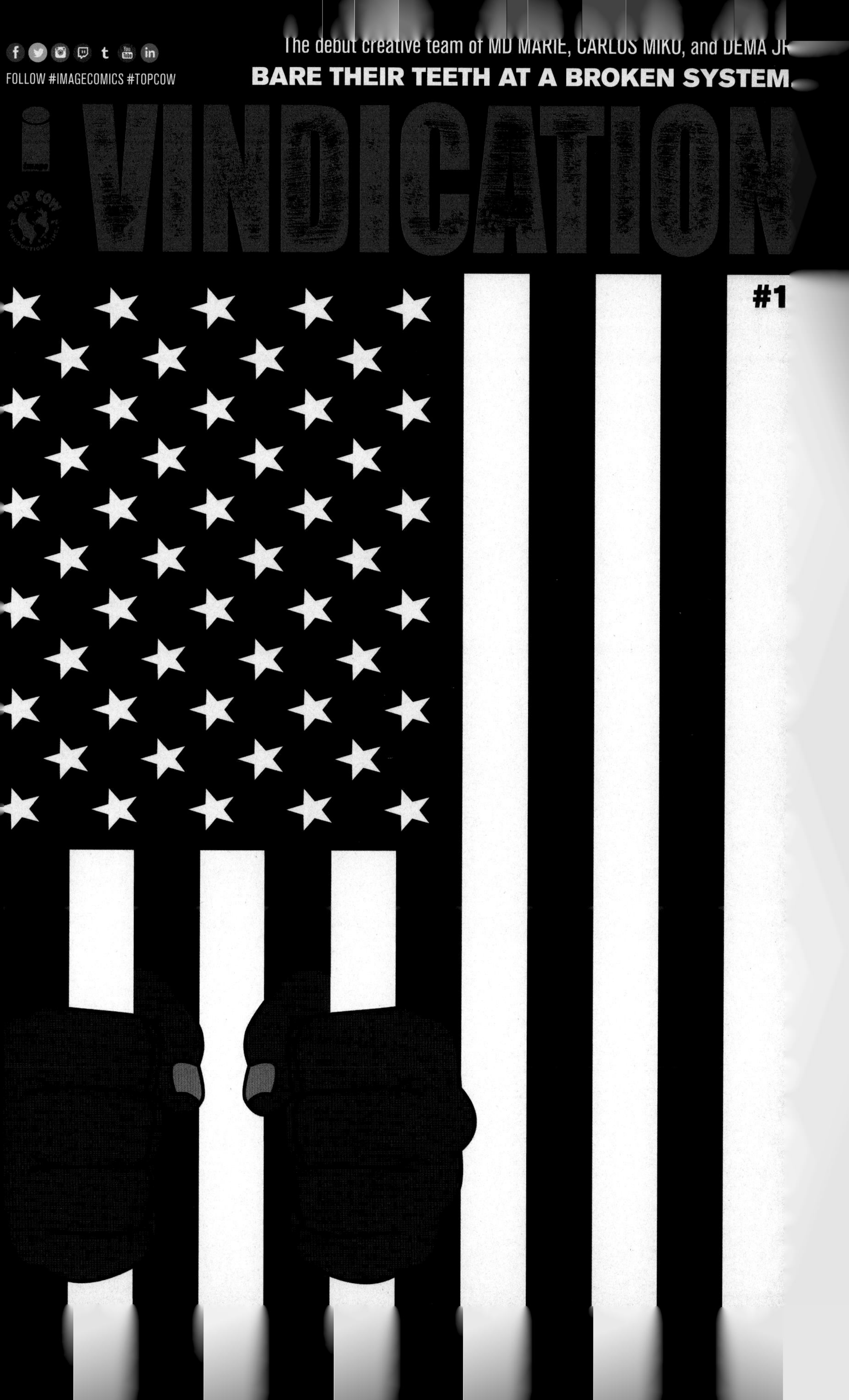

FOLLOW #IMAGECOMICS #TOPCOW
The debut creative team of MD MARIE, CARLOS MIKO, and DEMA J
BARE THEIR TEETH AT A BROKEN SYSTEM.
VINDICATION
#1

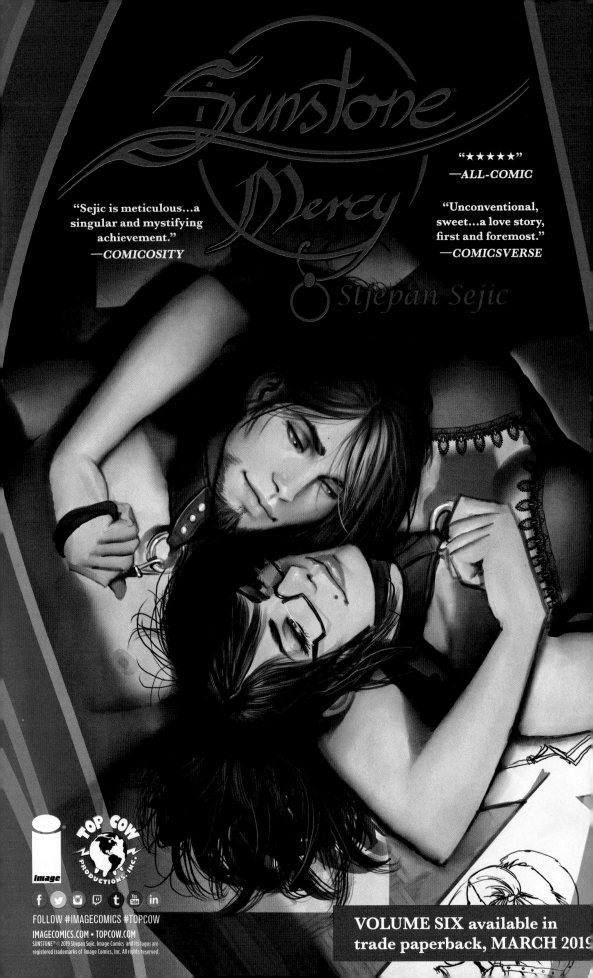

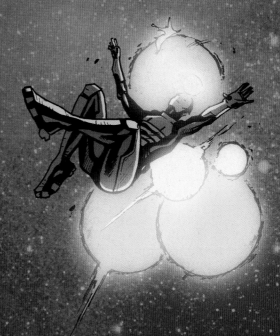

The Top Cow essentials checklist:

For more ISBN and ordering information on our latest collections go to:
www.topcow.com
Ask your retailer about our catalogue of collected editions,
digests, and hard covers or check the listings at:
Barnes and Noble, Amazon.com,
and other fine retailers.

To find your nearest comic shop go to:
www.comicshoplocator.com